Firefly Island

Firefly Island

A NOVEL BY

Daniel Arenson

This novel is a work of fiction. Names, characters, places and incidents are either the product of the author's imagination, or, if real, used fictitiously.

ISBN: 978-0-9866028-3-2
Second Edition
First Printing: August 2007

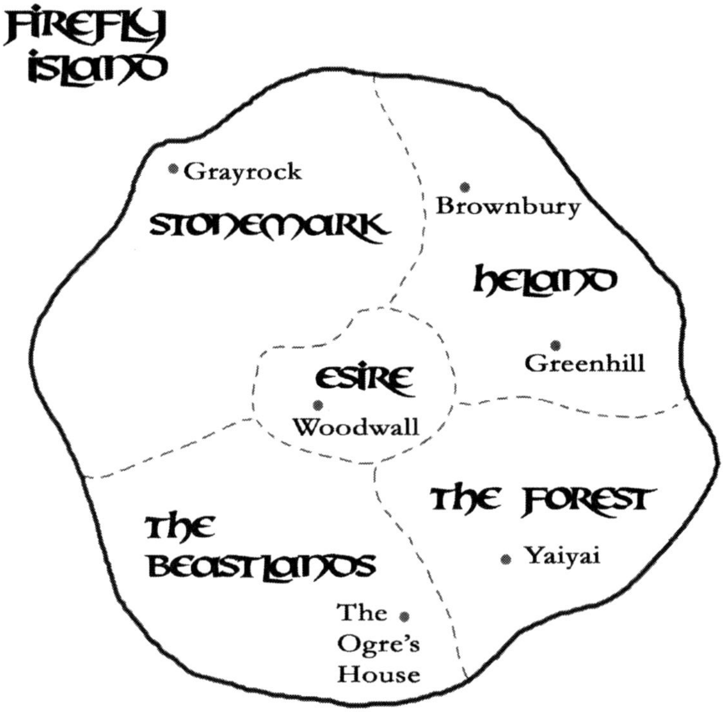

FIREFLY ISLAND
Grayrock
STONEMARK
Brownbury
HELAND
Greenhill
ESIRE
Woodwall
THE FOREST
Yaiyai
THE BEASTLANDS
The Ogre's House

Prologue
Two Promises

The little girl huddled in the corner, weeping silently. Her hair covered her face, strewn with straw. Lice crawled in her kerchief. Her stockings were torn, and her toes peeked out of holes in her shoes, blue with cold. She was hugging a doll—a frayed, tattered thing that only her love made more than rags. Her teardrops soaked the toy as she rocked it, and her lips mumbled into its ears. "It'll be all right, Stuffings, don't be scared. I won't let the monster hurt you...."

Joren, her older brother, sat watching her helplessly. He was only eleven years old, and already his heart ached. Like many boys his age, he had heard poems about wounded hearts and thought those only words. Yet now his heart actually hurt, a physical pain in his chest, as if all his tears had gathered there and lay swollen, pulsing. Hesitantly he reached forward and touched his sister's hair.

"Aeolia," he said.

She drew away, huddling deeper into the corner under the slanting roofbeams. She began to tremble, which made the straw on the floor crackle. The walls also shivered, jostled by the wind. The roof also shed tears, leaking raindrops through its thatch. The entire attic was weeping, Joren thought. All but him. He could not weep, though he wanted to, also.

"Aeoly," he tried again, softer this time, using her favorite diminutive. "I brought you something. A gift."

She said nothing, but her mumbling stopped. It was nighttime, and only a small lantern lit the attic. Shadows cloaked the girl. Joren could see only the whites of her eyes, glistening in the lamplight, watching him, peeking from her sodden hair.

"Here," he said, handing her a cloth bundle. He held it extended for a long time, while she only watched him. Then, finally, the straw crackled closer, and the girl's hand protruded from the shadows. She snatched the bundle and retreated back into the corner. Joren could see her moving, unfolding the cloth. The tangy, earthy smell of goat cheese filled the attic, mingling with the smells of mold and wet wood.

"I got it from Old Monny, down at Chalk Corner," Joren said, trying to hide that aching heart. "So you and Stuffings will have something to eat on the way."

Still she did not answer. The only sounds were the dripping raindrops, the rattling walls, and the crackling straw. Finally, when Joren was about to speak again, came a shaky whisper from the shadows.

"But I can't go now. It's raining."

That ache again, stronger. Gingerly, Joren crept into the corner, under the rafters and onto the straw pile. He knelt beside his sister. She cowered like a wounded animal, hugging her doll, shivering. Joren plucked the straw from her hair and parted the almond-brown strands, revealing her round, white face. Tears blurred her honey eyes and spiked her lashes. Her lips quivered. *So little,* Joren thought. She was so little. Better one child with food than two without, their father had said, but how could something so little possibly understand?

"Daddy says you must," he said.

"Stuffings is scared. She doesn't want the monster to take us." Tears rolled down her cheeks and fell into her lap. Joren felt her shivering beneath his palm.

"Then you must be brave," he said. "Let Stuffings see how brave you can be."

"She can't see, Joren, remember? You never brought me buttons for her eyes."

He smiled sadly. He had been saving copperdrops for buttons, but bought the cheese instead. Perhaps that had been wrong. The ache returned, sharp and twisting, erasing his smile. If it were only her being sold, he thought, only good-bye. But it was more. Joren would make her lose more than just freedom. He touched her cheek. Her tears wet his hand.

"Don't cry, Aeoly," he whispered. "You're six years old. You're a big girl now." He knew how she loved to hear that.

"Really?" she asked, raising her red-rimmed eyes with hope.

Joren nodded with all the solemnity of his older years. "You must be like King Sinther now—strong as stone."

A soft smile touched her lips. She loved to hear stories of the stone king, who felt no pain. "Strong as stone," she mumbled.

Joren forced himself to smile back. He had never done anything more difficult. "You're a big girl, and I want you to make a big girl's promise. Can you do that, Aeoly? Can you make me a promise?"

She gave a small shrug, with only one shoulder, like she always did. A "rug," he would call it, which always made her laugh. He wondered if he would ever see her do it again.

"What promise?" Her voice was small, trying not to tremble.

Joren took her hand, struggling to keep his face from showing his pain. But when he opened his mouth to speak, it was suddenly all too much. The words caught in his throat. He had to look away for fear he'd cry. How could he do this? To ask her to give up her talent, the only power she might have where she went....

But if anyone ever knew....

Joren managed to recompose his face. He held her little hand tight.

"Promise to keep your magic secret, Aeoly. Promise never to link again."

Her voice was confused. "But I like linking."

Her words tweaked Joren's heart, so hard he winced. If King Sinther ever discovered her magic, ever discovered that Aeolia, by linking, could hurt him past his impenetrable skin....

Sinther, his heart stony like his skin, would do anything to kill the one who could defeat him.

Joren shut his eyes. Tears swam behind his lids. His voice shook. "I know, Aeoly, I know, Dewdrop, I know.... But some people don't, Aeoly, some people would hurt you if they knew. You must keep it secret. Never link to anyone again. Never ever. Promise me, Aeoly."

She opened her mouth, but before words could leave her throat, a tinkling sound came from downstairs. Coins bouncing against a table. Aeolia huddled deeper into the corner, hugging her doll tight. Her fingers dug into the frayed cloth so hard her knuckles whitened. She was shivering again.

"I'll promise," she whispered. "But only if you promise something, too."

The stairs began to creak with a slow, heavy pace, heavier than a man's. The walls moaned and bent, and thatch fell from the roofbeams. The lantern swung on its chain, swirling shadows like bad dreams. Joren found himself clutching straw in his fists.

"What is it? What do you want me to promise?"

Aeolia flung herself forward, out of the shadows, and wrapped her arms around him. Her grip was so tight he could hardly breathe.

"That you'll save me, Joren!" she sobbed. "Promise you'll save me from the monster."

From the stairway came ragged wheezing, loud as bellows and coarse as sand. A stench like sweat and rot and bad breath filtered into the loft, so sickening it churned Joren's stomach. Aeolia's fingers dug into his back. She panted into his shirt.

"How can I save you?" he whispered. "I'm only a child."

"I'll wait till you're bigger!"

The footsteps paused outside. Joren could see, in the crack beneath the door, the shadows of huge feet. Keys rattled in the lock, struggling against the rust. An impossibly deep voice grumbled foreign, guttural curses.

"Aeoly, I won't come of age for ten years."

"I'll wait for you! Promise me, Joren, promise you'll do it!"

Lightning flashed, bright and blinding. Thunder shook the floor. The wind slammed open the window, and the lantern guttered out. Darkness and storm filled the room. The straw flurried. The thatch flew from the roofbeams. Rain and hail buffeted Joren's face, sharp and stinging. Wind flapped his shirt, bit his eyes, roared in his ears. He could hardly see or hear. He tried to rise, to go close the shutters, but Aeolia's hand held him fast. He turned his head and glimpsed her in the flickering lightning. Her skin was flushed, her hair billowed, her doll had been blown from her grasp. As the storm raged around her she sat unmoving, holding his arm, staring at him steadily even as the door creaked open.

Joren nodded, sorrow swelling in his throat.

"I promise, Aeoly. I promise."

Chapter One
The Beastlands, Ten Years Later

The well was deep and the bucket heavy. Aeolia grimaced as she heaved. The rope chafed her palms and her muscles ached. Her heels dug into the soil. The smell of moss filled her nostrils, and the dripping water laughed like pixies in her ears. When the bucket finally reached the top, she wrapped her arms around it. It was so wide her fingers did not meet. She pulled, tilting the wet wood, and spilled the water into the second bucket at her feet.

When her bucket was full, she straightened, knuckled her back and loosened her limbs. Splashing water had dampened her skirt, and she shivered. It was a cold morning, one for dozing by a fire or snuggling under down. For a moment Aeolia let her mind drift and remember mugs of hot milk, dog-eared picture books, clay tops, and a shabby rag doll. Those comforts were far away now, and her current companions were the broom and the duster, the shackles and the cane.

A sudden gust flurried dry leaves round her bare feet. Her hair blew over her eyes. She tucked the almond strands back into her kerchief and glanced at the sky. The clouds were as dark as the bruises on her back. It would soon rain. A skein of geese glided across the livid canopy, and Aeolia followed them with her eyes, fingering the tattoo on her hand. *Perhaps this year I will fly away too,* she thought. It was her tenth year from home. She was sixteen.

She gazed over the surrounding land, trying to imagine how it would feel seeing it for the last time. Hills rolled into the distance, patched with copses of birch and maple with leaves turning orange and gold. Boulders jutted like teeth from valleys of bindweed and thyme. Woodsmoke plumed in the distance, but the town that held its hearths was hidden in the folds of the land.

Aeolia sighed. The landscape had become as familiar as her own round face. She wondered if she would ever see a different horizon.

She turned away and lifted her bucket with a wince. The weight tugged at her arms, and the iron handle dug into her palms. Fetters jingling, she began hobbling up the cobbled path. With every step the bucket tilted, and water splashed to feed the weeds pushing from under the cobblestones. The old oak's branches creaked in the breeze. Dry leaves landed in Aeolia's hair or hit the ground to scuttle along like beetles. A raven fluttered off a swaying branch and perched on a cobwebbed plow. A lizard, startled by the bird, crossed the path and disappeared under a bramble.

The tall, brooding cottage sat at the end of the path like a neglected tombstone. Its unpainted walls were decaying, and its roof lacked half its tiles. The chimney looked ready to collapse. Beanstalks climbed the walls and ruptured the windows, like a great, green fist clutching the house. As the ogre aged and his sight dimmed he cared less about such matters, and railed about the broken shutters only if his joints ached that day. Secretly, Aeolia suspected he liked his house rotting and old, for he himself was so.

The front steps were as tall as Aeolia's knees. She sat down on the first, holding the bucket so it dangled between her legs. She pushed herself up step by step—the only way to climb in her shackles—and stood up on the porch. Spiders fled from her feet to disappear between the floor planks. Two crows fluttered off the old spinning wheel into the air. With a sigh of relief, Aeolia dropped her bucket beside the front door. After wiping her sore hands on her apron, she stood on tiptoe, reached overhead, and grabbed the doorknob. The door creaked open, and Aeolia dragged her bucket inside.

The living room smelled of decay—a faint, constant odor Aeolia attributed to the rotting wood. Objects crowded every corner: animal heads hung on the walls, rare stones perched on the mantel, a bearskin lay on the floor. Dried roses, a tobacco box, and a pipe sat on a cherry table. Beside the table stood an old sofa, fleece pushing out of tatters in its green upholstery. Everything in the room was twice too large for Aeolia. The tabletop reached her shoulder. The sofa towered over her head. She could have stood in the fireplace. She always felt dwarfed and insignificant beside this giant furniture, like a fluff of dust.

She could hear the ogre snoring upstairs, a sound like chains dragging over stone. Creaks accompanied the snores—the ogre's daughter pacing her room. A shiver ran down Aeolia's spine. The attic was a strange place. It always chilled her to think of it. She went upstairs only to change the linens and empty the chamber pots, and always worked quickly and rushed back down, glad to escape the soupy air and sickly ogress.

The house had a basement, too. Aeolia had never been in it, and the ogres never spoke of it, but she had seen the trapdoor hidden beneath the sofa. When she had once asked where the trapdoor led, the ogre caned her so hard he broke her arm. She never asked again, but once, when the ogre and his daughter slept, she had crawled under the sofa and tried the trapdoor. It had been locked, and so Aeolia was left to guess what lay below.

Embers still glowed in the hearth from last night. Aeolia stirred them with the poker. An earthenware mug hung over the embers from a wire, and she filled it from her bucket; the ogre liked hot water with his breakfast. For a moment she stood gazing into the fire, warming her hands and remembering their own small hearth in Stonemark where she and her brother would play. She thought how they would never be young again, and a lump filled her throat. But he would come this year, she told herself. He had promised.

She left the water to boil and dragged her shackles into the pantry. Shelves lined the small room, bulging with sacks and jars and bundles and kegs. Strings of garlic, ham sausages, and sheaves of oats hung from the roofbeams. Sundry smells of spices tickled the nose: paprika, cumin, curry, and sage. Aeolia took a plate from a cupboard and filled it with the ogre's favorite foods: a chunk of licorice, some figs stuffed with peanuts, a stick of rhubarb, and a clump of honeyed seaweed. She stepped back into the living room and placed the food and boiling water on the table.

It was not long before the snoring upstairs died. Aeolia heard the springs in his bed creak, a thump as his feet hit the floor, the dim trickle of him filling his chamber pot. Soon the stairs began to moan, his cane tapped, his breath wheezed loud and coarse. Aeolia clutched a handful of her skirt and took a step back as the sounds grew closer. The staircase first revealed large, bare feet and the hard, wooden butt of a cane. Then, as the ogre continued descending, came bandy legs, a potbelly, and finally a hunchback and a fleshy, yellow face.

Aeolia curtsied. "Good morning, Master."

The ogre bunched his tufted eyebrows and brushed past her wordlessly. Even with his stoop he stood twice her height, and his cane was wide as her arm. The floor creaked mournfully under his weight; he had fattened with age, and his woolen vest looked ready to pop its buttons. A stench like congealed blood clung to him, and his beard rustled with lice. He reached his chair, sat down with a groan, and laid his cane across his lap.

Aeolia frowned. Something was wrong with the ogre today. He did not run his finger along the armrest, checking for dust as always, only twiddled his thumbs and stared into his lap. He did not wolf down his food as was his wont, but seemed scarcely to notice the plate. Usually grumpy, this morning he seemed positively pensive.

"Is something wrong, Master?" Aeolia asked.

The ogre's beady, close-set eyes flicked up in surprise, as if he had just noticed Aeolia. He wiped his bulbous nose with his sleeve and spoke in his deep, guttural voice. "I am worried about my daughter."

"Is she melancholy again?"

The ogre nodded. "Worse than ever, yes indeed. She sleeps all day and night."

"I can hear her pacing upstairs, Master."

The ogre gripped his cane, and Aeolia winced, cursing herself for contradicting him. But the ogre soon loosened his grasp, his ire gone so quickly only Aeolia's pounding heart testified it had existed.

"Her eyes are open," the ogre said, "but they see only dreams. Her mouth speaks, but reports only the sight of her eyes."

"Truly, Master? I've not noticed."

The ogre scratched himself. "She appears lucid, yes indeed. But listen to her talk and it is all fantasy. She is delusional with glumness, I fear. You must remember never to believe her words. Whatever fiddlesticks she speaks, know it is her madness speaking."

"I will remember, Master."

The ogre grunted and lifted his plate. His red nose—large and round like a human head—twitched over the food. He thrust out his jaw and tilted the plate over his rotting fangs, letting the food slide into his mouth. He chewed the lot slowly, gazing into the fire as if lost in thought. Aeolia helped push back what food dripped down his chin.

After swallowing his breakfast he began sipping his water. Aeolia stepped into the pantry and packed him a fresh leg of goat for his lunch. She filled his wineskin with cider. When she returned to the living room the ogre had drained his mug, and she helped him rise from his chair. He limped toward the wall, where his coat and hat hung on pegs, and Aeolia climbed her ladder and helped him dress. She opened the door and bid him good-bye. The ogre grunted and limped outside, where the wind flapped his coat and drowned the tapping of his hard, hard cane.

Aeolia shut the door behind him. He would be gone shepherding all day, she knew, and meanwhile she had plenty to do: dust the house, tend to the ogress, change the linens, wash the dishes, wash the laundry, sweep the chimney, wax the floors, feed the livestock, milk the goat, collect the eggs, weed the vegetable patch, clean the sheep pen, chop firewood, butcher a pig, kindle a fire, cook dinner, and finally dust again. Dusting was the most important chore, for the ogre's nose was sensitive to dust, and one of his favorite sayings was: "The cane flies with the sneeze."

I wish I were like my King Sinther, Aeolia thought, *with skin made of stone, skin a cane cannot break.* Nobody could hurt the terrible Sinther, Aeolia knew. Not one person in the world.

Well, except that one person from the legends, Aeolia remembered. The tales whispered of one who could reach past Sinther's stone skin, could hurt the wicked king. *But then, surely those are only legends,* Aeolia thought. Surely if such a one truly lived, Sinther would have ordered him killed long ago.

"Enough fairytales for now!" Aeolia scolded herself. She was always telling herself stories when she should be working. With a sigh, she took her feather-duster from its shelf and ran it over the animal heads, the dry flowers, the decaying windowsills.

As usual, when she dusted beneath the sofa she wondered what lay below the trapdoor. She had imagined many possibilities: a chest of glinting golddrops, a deformed son fed secretly whenever she slept, a suit of armor and a rusty sword, the ghosts of the house's dead builders, a dusty grimoire with golden binding, a passageway that led to an underground land of fairies.... Aeolia delighted in imagining these wonderful or horrible secrets, and she often lay awake at night, inventing their stories.

She would also imagine her rescue. These dreams were not pleasurable but wistful, and they did not ease her loneliness but made it swell. And yet she thought of Joren every day, of the promises they had exchanged so long ago. She had kept hers, though she did not understand it, and prayed that this year, as Joren came of age, he would keep his. She shut her eyes as she dusted and tried to imagine how he would look now. Would his hair still be spiky, his gray eyes still brave? He would be handsome, she knew, and he would love her like only a brother loves his younger sister. They would live together, away from their callous father, and forget their past lives and simply be happy.

Aeolia sighed. Suddenly she felt a need to escape the cluttered living room, with its towering furniture and ever-present stench. She laid down the duster, lifted her wicker basket, and hobbled outside to collect the ogress's breakfast. She stood on the porch and breathed the crisp air, banishing her brother from her mind; his memory was so sweet it hurt, and she was better off without it. The clouds had darkened and it was drizzling. When Aeolia stepped off the porch her feet sank into the mud. The raindrops matted her hair down over her face, and the wind whipped at her skirt.

She walked toward the sheep pen, careful to avoid the fairy rings in the grass. Behind the pen, she followed the old picket fence, her feet pressing into the soft, wet clover that carpeted the ground. At the end of the yard, where the land swept down into a valley of mist, grew the enchanted cherry tree, its bark glistening with raindrops.

Aeolia loved this tree, a magical tree that bore fruit all year. It was her favorite place on the farm, the only place where she felt solace. She climbed onto a mossy rock, stood on tiptoe to reach the high branches, and began collecting cherries. She smiled as she picked, imagining the scent of rain, sedge, and cherries a perfume she wore, and when she shut her eyes she could almost imagine her woolen dress a gown.

A bell, ringing in the wind, disrupted her reverie. Aeolia turned her head and looked back at the cottage, and in the attic window she saw a shadow stir. She shivered, placed a last cherry in her basket, and hopped off the rock. Basket in hand, she squelched through the moss and mud back to the house. She wiped her feet on the doormat and stepped inside.

The bell rang loudly upstairs, a flat sound like wood on flesh. Aeolia bit her lip, approached the staircase but paused before climbing. She looked up into the shadows and shivered again. The attic always frightened her. The bell continued ringing, however, and so Aeolia swallowed, sat down, and began climbing. With every stair the air became sultrier, smelling of sweat and decay, so thick Aeolia felt it stroke her skin. She reached the top stair and stood up in the shadowy hallway. Burrows honeycombed the floor, and Aeolia heard beetles chirping inside. The bell's ringing came from behind a tall, peeling door. Aeolia turned the clammy knob, and the door slowly creaked open.

The room inside was dark and stuffy. Its hot air filled Aeolia's lungs like smoke. The window was ajar, casting dusty sheets of light, and Aeolia could see ants marching along the walls. The ogress lay in her bed like one of the shadows, her face cloaked in darkness. Her long feet, yellow toenails cracked, hung between the posts. She was so thin, her bones showed beneath the sheets, making her look like a shrouded skeleton.

Aeolia twisted her fingers behind her back and said, "Good morning, Mistress."

The ogress's frail hand passed through a shaft of light to place her bell on a nightstand.

"I shall have my cherries now," came a grainy whisper from the shadows. The ogress never spoke above a whisper.

"Of course, Mistress."

Aeolia shuffled toward the head of the bed. The ogress's eyes glinted in the shadows as they watched her. Her shriveled lips parted to reveal a gaping, toothless cavern. Aeolia took a cherry from her basket and placed it on her mistress's white tongue. The ogress chewed slowly with hard gums, then spat the pit into Aeolia's hand. The process repeated itself three more times, and then the ogress turned her head away.

"Is that all you want today?" Aeolia asked.

The ogress nodded. "Chewing tires me. Toss the rest out the window."

Aeolia bit her lip and gazed at the remaining cherries in the basket.

The ogress laughed—a hollow, sickly sound, more a cough than a laugh. "You want to eat them yourself, hmmm?"

Aeolia shrugged one shoulder. "No one will eat them outside."

"The worms and beetles will eat."

Aeolia lowered her head and nodded. She shuffled to the window and opened the shutters, thankful for the fresh air and light. For a moment she gazed longingly at the northern horizon, thinking of her brother. Then she tightened her lips and tossed the cherries. They hit the mud and sank. Aeolia turned from the window, her throat tight.

Her mistress was watching her, a wry smile on her lips. In the new light Aeolia now saw her yellow, papery skin, the sacks beneath her sunken eyes, the white wisps on her balding scalp.

"Was it cruel of me, girl, hmmm?" the ogress asked.

"It was cruel," Aeolia replied quietly.

"Do you imagine freedom any kinder?"

The question surprised Aeolia. One never talked of such matters. It was as taboo as mentioning the basement. She stood silently, lost for words.

"Don't be embarrassed," the ogress said. "My papa's cane beats only sheep now. He cannot hear you."

"If I were free I would have eaten the cherries."

"But cherries are not enough, are they? A woman needs more than cherries, does she not?" The ogress propped herself up on her elbows. Her eyes flared and blood rushed into her cheeks. "What about love, hmmm? You forgot about love, didn't you?"

Aeolia took a step back. She remembered the ogre's words about his daughter's madness, but decided it safest to play along.

"I have no love here," she said.

The ogress cackled. "Be glad! Love is cruel and whimsical. It calls you beautiful but laughs behind your back, taunts and leaves you with nothing but a ring and broken heart. Look at *you!* Look what your family did to you. They sold you for three golddrops!"

The ogress was mad, there was no doubt of that. Her words still hurt, however, and Aeolia could not let them stand.

"My father sold me," she said, not without anger. "My brother loves me still."

The ogress leaned forward, reached out, and grabbed Aeolia's shoulders. Aeolia squirmed but the ogress held her tight. Her bony fingers dug like claws. Her yellow face—long as a horse's—was thrust so close Aeolia could smell her breath, stench of morning mingled with the scent of cherries. She wanted to turn her head away, but something in her mistress's eyes held her, and she stared back.

"Are you certain?" the ogress whispered. "Are you certain he, too, would not betray you?"

Aeolia thought of her home, of her father who was so churlish, she often thought she must be a changeling. But her brother had always comforted her. Joren had always made her laugh, even when her father made her cry.

Aeolia nodded. "I am certain. Joren loves me. He would never betray me."

The ogress's eyes glinted a moment longer, and then they dimmed. Her grip relaxed and she fell back into her bed. She looked tired and spent, and her breath was shallow. She looked defeated. With a long sigh she pulled the covers to her neck, shut her eyes, and mumbled sleepy words.

"There is a Stoneson in town looking for you."

Aeolia's heart stopped in her breast. Her hands fell limp to her sides. Slow as sunrise, she uttered, "What did you say?"

The ogress began to snore. Heedlessly, Aeolia grabbed her shoulders and shook. "Mistress, please, don't sleep now!"

The ogress's head slumped sideways. She would not wake. The madness, Aeolia thought, it was only the madness speaking! And yet... he had promised, it might be true, he might be here, in town, but a day away, looking for her....

"Is my brother here?" she asked, shaking the ogress and shaking herself. "Have you talked to him? Oh, please wake up!"

She would not, and Aeolia wrung her hands, trembling. *Is my mistress only taunting me?* she wondered. *Is she simply speaking dreams?* This was the year of Joren's promise; surely the ogress couldn't know that. Perhaps she wasn't delusional. Perhaps the ogre had claimed so simply to discredit words he knew she'd speak. Joy bubbled in Aeolia's belly as she convinced herself that Joren was truly near.

A smile trembling on her lips, she shuffled out the room and downstairs.

She spent the day waiting.

For the next few hours, she worked at her chores in a daze. She kept thinking of Joren, imagining how she would hug him, planning their future. *Today might be my last day here,* she kept thinking. *I might never see the ogres again.*

By noon she began worrying. As she stood outside, brushing cinder out of her hair, she kept glancing at the hills, waiting for Joren to appear. He never did. Aeolia's excitement slowly curdled. She told herself she must be patient, that Joren was slow because he was thorough, that he would arrive in time. She gazed at the tattoo on her hand and told herself that soon it would be meaningless, that soon she'd be able to forget its words. Joren would not betray her like the ogress had said. He had promised and he would come.

But where was he?

Afternoon's shadows began unfurling, and still Joren did not appear. The butchered pig sat in a pot of paprika, bubbling in the hearth, filling the living room with the smell of spices and bones and blood. Aeolia nibbled her lip as she stirred the broth, and her fingers tapped against the ladle. Her worry gnawed on her like a dog on a bone. A thought sneaked into her mind that Joren might miss the lonesome farm, that he would never find her. The thought was too horrible to bear. She twisted her toes and continued waiting.

With twilight's frogs trilling outside, Aeolia decided she could wait no longer. Though she trembled at the thought, she knew what she must do. She would do the impossible, what she had never dared. She would leave the cottage. She would go to town. If Joren would not come, she would seek him herself.

But how could she? The ogre shepherded outside, blocking her way, and his dogs were trained to scent strangers in the hills. Even if Aeolia did slip past him, he would discover her escape when he returned, and Aeolia could not expect to outrun his dogs, not while hobbled. If she went to town, she knew, it had to be with the ogre's permission.

She forced herself to wait till he returned. It was not long. The sun had hardly touched the horizon when she heard the tapping of his cane outside, the baaing of sheep as he goaded them into their pen. Aeolia quickly filled his bowl—big as a watermelon half—with the goulash and set it on the table. She lit the candles in their iron sconces. Knowing her face must be spelling guilt, she covered it with her hair. She heard the cane tap up the stairs and onto the porch, and she opened the door.

"Good evening, Master."

The ogre grunted and limped inside, bringing the smells of sheep and grass and sweat. Aeolia climbed her ladder and helped him remove his coat and hat. The ogre limped toward his sofa and sat down heavily, sniffing his food and salivating into his beard. He licked his chops and brought the bowl to his lips. As he chewed, bones crunched and juice trickled down his chin. Aeolia watched him eat, twisting her fingers behind her back, till he lowered the empty bowl with a satisfied belch.

"Now," he said, as she knew he would, "fetch me my jug of wine to wash this fine food down, yes indeed."

Aeolia nodded and stepped into the pantry. A hanging lantern lit the cluttered room. With every gale outside, the shutters rattled, the lantern swung, and shadows danced like demons. From one shelf Aeolia fetched the clay jug that held the ogre's weekly supply of crabapple wine. It was half-full and heavy. Aeolia carried it with both arms back into the living room.

"Ah, excellent!" The ogre rubbed his hands together. "Bring it here."

"Yes, Master."

Aeolia took a step forward, her knees shaking. She took another step, swallowed hard. With the third step, heart in mouth, she feigned to stumble. She tossed the jug as she pitched forward.

A shattering sound beat her eardrums. Droplets of wine bespattered her. The ogre rose from his chair with a howl.

"Look what you've done!"

Aeolia scurried to her feet as the ogre swung his cane. It missed her head by an inch.

"I'm sorry, Master! I'm sorry, I tripped."

The ogre began chasing her around the table. He limped and she hobbled in her shackles, and both sloshed through the wine.

"I'll get more!" she said. "I'll get more wine!"

The ogre swung his cane. Aeolia ducked and it whistled over her head.

"The peddler comes once a week," he thundered. "How will you get wine before that?"

The cane came down and Aeolia jumped aside. The vase of dry roses shattered.

"I'll go to town, Master! I'll get wine there."

The ogre paused. Slowly he lowered his cane. Aeolia stood panting and watching him expectantly. The ogre rubbed his jaw and stared back through narrowed lids.

"You want to go to town...," he said.

"Unlock my shackles and I'll go now. I'll be back by noon tomorrow with your wine, and work into the night to finish my chores."

"How do I know you'll return?"

"My tattoo, Master. Anyone who sees it will return me."

The ogre stared at her a moment, but then snorted. "Bah! I cannot trust you carrying wine so far. You are too clumsy. No, you will stay here and spend the night licking the wine from the floor."

Aeolia lowered her head and fought down despair. So he would not let her go. She could still try sneaking away.

The ogre, however, had not finished speaking.

"You are so clumsy," he continued, tapping his chin, "you might fall into the fireplace or well, yes indeed. Safest if after you've cleaned the wine, I chain you to the cherry tree, at least for the next few days."

Aeolia's mouth fell open. For a moment she could not breathe and stood gaping, shaking her head. Then she spun around and fled into the pantry, where she fell to the floor, scraping her knees. The rows of shelves, hanging bent under their burdens, seemed to close in on her, ready to overflow and drown her. She could hear the ogre's wheezing in the other room, and she had to cover her ears, so jarring the sound suddenly seemed. He knew, she realized, he knew, he knew, he had seen Joren and he was hiding her. Why hadn't she just run? Now she couldn't even sneak away.

"Girl!" came a grunt from the living room. "Cease this foolishness and come back here. I want my foot rub."

Aeolia wanted nothing more than to stay in the pantry, hidden in the swirling shadows, but fear of the ogre's cane had long been pounded into her, and she could not fight it. She rose to her feet and shuffled toward the door, barely able to drag her irons, barely able to stand upright at all.

"I must be strong as stone, like Joren said," she mumbled, but the sweet thought of her brother made her eyes moisten, and her mouth curved bitterly in preparation for weeping. *No!* she scolded herself. *The ogre mustn't see me cry.* She shut her mouth determinedly, knuckled her tears away, and banished Joren from her thoughts.

In the living room the candles had burned to stubs, and wax hung over their holders. The fire still crackled, and leftover goulash bubbled in the pot. From outside came the sounds of whistling wind and rapping rain. The ogre sat with a checkered blanket pulled over his knees, puffing on his pipe and filling the room with green, fragrant smoke. His bare feet rested on the table, warming in the fire.

He clucked his tongue, and Aeolia nodded briskly, climbed onto the tabletop and sat beside his feet. Each foot was long as her leg, with toes as big as her feet. Sweat glued dirt, grass, and crushed insects to the soles. Aeolia reluctantly laid her hands on a rough, clammy foot. Breathing through her mouth, she began to rub. The ogre shut his eyes, let out a long moan, and leaned back in his seat.

While Aeolia's fingers worked, so did her mind. If she'd soon be chained outside, she could still wait for Joren to arrive. But what if Joren never found the farm? There was too much at stake to leave for chance and hope. Surely there was something else she could do, Aeolia told herself, but she could think of nothing. She stubbornly quelled a cloud of despair. *I can't give in to despair now,* she told herself. *I must think rationally, rationally....*

Aeolia furrowed her brow. What if she spoke rationally to the ogre? What if she made a deal? She tossed the idea back and forth as she kneaded. She had been sold for money; perhaps she could be bought back. Would the ogre be willing? Surely he would, Aeolia told herself. Besides she had nothing more to lose by asking.

"Master...," she began.

One beady eye cracked open. "Yes, girl? Speak up."

Aeolia licked her dry lips, suddenly hesitant. *I'll simply say what I have to say,* she told herself. *The rest is up to him.* She took a long, deep breath.

"Have you seen my brother?"

The ogre pulled away his feet and placed them on the floor. He laid down his pipe, put his hands on his knees, and spoke slowly. "My daughter told you, didn't she?"

Aeolia nodded hesitantly.

"And have I not told you she is mad?"

Aeolia stared at her toes. "Master, my brother will pay everything he has for me."

The sofa creaked as the ogre leaned forward. "Have I not told you she is mad?"

Aeolia's voice was barely a whisper. "I know my brother is here."

"Some things are best left unknown, yes indeed. Some things are best pounded out of memory."

Aeolia knew that if she failed, her every word meant another cane's blow, but still she spoke again. "Master, my brother will pay to buy me back. He will pay you twice what you had paid."

The ogre regarded her for several moments. Finally he leaned back, scratched his chin, and said, "Six golddrops?"

Aeolia nodded. Surely Joren had been saving for that very purpose.

"But you are not worth six golddrops," the ogre said.

"I am to my brother."

The ogre pursed his lips. "I would be able to buy two servants," he mumbled into his beard.

Aeolia felt excitement wiggle in her belly. "Then will you do it?" she asked. "Will you tell him where I am?"

The ogre slowly nodded.

Aeolia gasped. "You will? You truly will?"

The ogre bent forward, causing the firelight to paint his face a sinister red. He narrowed his eyes, slammed the butt of his cane against the floor, and when he spoke his voice was hard as iron.

"I will tell the Stoneson where you are," he said. "I will tell him I had sold you to my cousin, who took you a hundred leagues south, beat you to death, and buried you at sea."

The ogre cackled, leaned back in his chair, and banged his feet back onto the table.

"Now rub!"

Aeolia looked away from the feet, her eyes blurry. She had lost her chance to escape. She had lost her chance for rescue. She could not have raised her arms had she wanted to, so crestfallen she was. From swaddling clothes to shroud, would her life be only sorrow?

"Rub!"

Aeolia looked down into her lap, at the tattoo on her hand, at the overworked and dirty fingers. She could no longer think, she felt so numb, and as she stared her hands became small and soft, a child's hands, clutching a rag doll. She heard her brother's laugh. She tasted warm milk on her lips. She barely saw the giant hand swing through the air.

Pain exploded on her temple. She slid across the table and crashed onto the floor by the hearth, in the heat of the burning logs and bubbling broth. From the corner of her eye she saw the ogre pointing his cane at her, shouting words she could not hear. She saw him as she first had, a vacuous beast, a monster with no thoughts or pity, a terror from her deepest nightmares.

She stood up, eyes unfocused, and gazed into the pot. *Bones and blood are not food,* she thought. *I'm tired of bones and blood.* She heard the ogre rise from his chair behind her, she heard him tapping toward her. There was only one thing left to do. Her trembling fingers danced over the pot's handles, hesitating. She had to think of Joren's smile to make them close.

"I'm coming to you, Joren," she whispered.

The cane tapped, the floor creaked, the fire crackled and the broth bubbled—a deafening air that clouded all her thoughts. She took a shaky breath, tightened her lips, spun around and tossed the pot at the ogre.

The pot clanged against him. Goulash spilled with a hiss. Aeolia grabbed a stick from the fire and held it before her as the ogre howled and sizzled. She could not outrun him in her shackles, she knew. She had to face him. She lashed her torch forward, but the ogre grabbed her arm and wrenched it free. He yanked her into the air, and Aeolia screamed and slashed her nails across his face. With a roar he tucked her under his arm, pinning her arms to her sides. She screamed and struggled wildly, but could not free herself.

Through wincing lids she saw him push his sofa aside, and horror surged inside her till it spilled from her eyes. He pulled a round of keys from his pocket, containing the key to the barn, the key to her fetters, and the green, old key she had never seen him use until now. He leaned down and began unlocking the trapdoor, and Aeolia found herself shaking her head, crying her brother's name.

The ogre swung the trapdoor open. The stench of rot was unbearable. It overwhelmed Aeolia, making her sick. She wanted to throw up. She trembled violently. In the second before the ogre tossed her in, sealing her in darkness, she saw it all, saw the secret in the basement, saw why she could never hope to escape.

Down in the darkness, shrouded in cobwebs, skeletons littered the floor, all in fetters like her own.

The ogre's arm opened. The ground rushed up to meet her. Pain exploded and dust rose in a cloud, filling her eyes and mouth. The trapdoor boomed shut above her, rats screeched, bones rattled, and darkness, complete darkness such as she had never known or imagined, fell over Aeolia. She covered her head with her arms, crushed by its weight, and wept onto the floor until she had wept all thought away.

Chapter Two
Heland

Dusk.

All things settled to sleep. The sun slumbered behind the mountains, snug under a blanket of clouds. The trees and hills reposed, tucked into a bed of shadows. Birds and beasts nestled in hidden places. Crickets chirped lullabies amid stalks of ripe wheat. Sickles dropped, oxen stopped, peasants lumbered home. Farmwives tucked babes into quilt and crib, stroked downy heads, whispered hushaby and summoned enchanted kingdoms. As stormy clouds gathered, doors were barred and shutters tightened. Fireplaces blazed. Under wool and down, husbands and wives cuddled, warming each other until cold night would pass. All things slept.

All things but Roen Painter, that is. *He* was crawling outside, leagues from any bed or hearth, digging through leafmold and dirt.

He'd been crawling for hours, as the clouds thickened and the storm brewed. Finally, his stockings torn and his embroidered sleeves muddy, he stopped under an apple tree. Shaky wisps plumed from his mouth. With numb fingers, he rummaged through fallen leaves. *There.* There it was, cradled between the tree's roots. The small, silky plant he sought. *Laceleaf.* Roen let his head fall into the mud, laughing and shedding tears. There was hope now. The laceleaf shivered, fragile as life, and Roen dug into the dirt, loosening its bulb. The plant came willingly into his hands.

"Rest easy, Father," he whispered. "Soon I'll be home."

He straightened, pocketed the plant, tightened his blue cloak, and looked around him. He had crawled far. Not a farm could be seen. Hills rolled endlessly, spotted with fallen, rotting apples and mossy boulders forlorn as old tombstones. Trees stood swaying, branches bobbing like disapproving fingers, tossing dry leaves that swirled and danced. The wind was cold; the storm was close now. Roen glanced at the sky. The clouds churned like paint in oil, eddies of purple and pewter and dark angry crimson, weltering over patches of starry black. But still not a grumble. The night was silent as secrets.

But if all secrets erupt in a tempest, so did this night. Roen had scarce hitched his belt when, with a thunderclap, the storm broke.

Roen pursed his lips. The clouds had been gathering rain for hours, and it was all falling now. The drops burst against his plumed hat, soaking through the felt to dampen his yellow curls. He winced. His velvet tunic and pointed shoes were thin, and it was a long walk home. With a sigh, he shoved his hands into his pockets and started moving. The storm seemed intent on stopping him. The mud sucked his feet, the wind pushed him, and the darkness blindfolded him. Even the fireflies did not come to glow. Roen had never seen them not rise. *Surely,* he thought, *this is an evil omen.*

He shivered. This night was unholy. The storm danced like ghosts, clamoring and howling. Roen's clothes clung to him, and his teeth chattered. He had been cold all day, but this was worse. He was wet now, and struggling, and he could feel the beginning of fever on his brow. He knew he needed rest. Caves dotted the hills, beckoning. *They would be nice and dry....* But Roen tightened his lips and looked away. He could not stop. The laceleaf must be brought home.

With stiff fingers, he caressed his ruby ring, tracing its engravings. The ring his father had given him yesteryear, on Roen's eighteenth birthday. His father, who now lay abed, sick because of Roen.

The memories filled the darkness. Roen could see his father again, face drawn as parchment, paintbrush shaking in wispy fingers. One week, Duke Hyan had said. One week for a painting that would normally take moons. But the price was too tempting: enough gold to build Roen's own workshop. Smerdin Painter loved his son too dearly to refuse. He labored that week, hardly eating or sleeping. He had completed the painting that morning, and then collapsed. The demons of disease had fattened on his exhaustion, the doctor decreed. Only laceleaf, grown from rotting apple leaves, could banish them.

A flicker of light tore Roen from his thoughts. He narrowed his eyes. There, he saw it again: an orange glint like a lighthouse. Roen lengthened his stride. Arms outstretched, he trudged through a copse of pines, branches snagging his cloak. Sap smeared him, its smell thick and cloying. It seemed miles before the trees finally parted, revealing the orange flicker's source. A mountain, sparkling with city lights, rose into the clouds like a jeweled pillar of heaven. Brownbury, capital of Heland. Roen's home had never seemed more beautiful. *Soon, Father,* he thought. *Soon I'll be home with the laceleaf, and we'll sit by the hearth, drinking hot cider and eating hot, hot toast.*

He plodded for what seemed an eternity, over uprooted trees and windblown scarecrows, before he reached the city gates. The iron-studded doors sat in their granite walls, lionhead knockers glowering. Roen stood a moment, catching his breath. He was not used to cold or physical exertion, and in the icy rain, his skin and throat burned. If exhaustion had claimed his father's health, the storm was claiming his. *Funny,* Roen thought. *I'm falling ill for trying to save an ill man. Now what does that say about the world?*

Roen shook his head, clearing it of thoughts. They were too hazy for his liking. Quickly, he pounded with one bronze knocker. The plangent booms summoned no reply. Roen pounded again, harder. A shout came from atop the wall.

"Gates closed tonight! Come back at dawn."

Roen stumbled backwards. Through the rain he saw a sentry perched on the parapet like a gargoyle, horns and spikes protruding from his armor. A lantern burned in the man's hand, its crimson light crawling over his helm like demons. *He looks as wicked as King Sinther himself,* Roen thought.

"My father is ill," Roen called hoarsely. "I must see him."

The sentry crossed his arms. His voice echoed behind his visor. "Evil roams these hills tonight. Even the fireflies have not risen. Hyan's orders that gates don't open till sunrise."

Roen felt a surge of panic. He swallowed it and raised his voice again. "Duke Hyan is expecting me! I'm a painter in his service."

Armor chinked as the sentry shifted his weight. "You have a ring of guild?"

Roen raised his hand, letting the lamplight glimmer in his ruby ring.

The sentry tapped his cheek. "Well, suppose you gift me that ring, might be I'll go rummage for the key."

Roen's eyes burned. "I'll report you!"

"Then you'll have to do so tomorrow morning."

Roen tightened his lips. The sentry stared down defiantly. Lightning flashed and the sky spewed icy pellets. Slowly Roen lowered his glare to his toes. There was no time for honor or stubbornness, he knew. Smerdin could not wait. Roen looked at his ring. He let his fingertip circle the rim, trace the words engraved into the gold: *Master Painter.* Inside, he knew, were smaller letters: *I'm proud of you, my son.*

Roen heaved a deep sigh. Slowly, he slipped off the ring and raised it overhead. A moment later the gates were open, and Roen was rushing through the city.

The wooden houses huddled over the narrow, twisting streets, their eaves almost touching. Rainwater gurgled in roadside gutters. Lanterns hung in most street corners, but half had been snuffed out by the downpour. The darkness was thick as lies. Roen walked quickly, his blisters chafing, his skin hot. He was definitely ill. But worse than the pain was his worry. *Soon,* Roen thought, *soon I'll be home with your medicine, Father. Soon we'll sit by that fire, drinking that warm, warm cider....*

At last he saw their small house from a distance. The iron paintbrush hung skewed over the door, the pots of cyclamens lay toppled on the porch, the shingled roof dripped rainwater. Orange light flickered behind the closed shutters, which meant Smerdin was well enough to kindle a fire, or was, an hour ago. Roen found himself close to tears. *Everything will be fine now,* he thought. Finally the terrible night was over. Roen knuckled his eyes, climbed onto the porch, grabbed the doorknob... and paused.

Muffled voices were arguing inside. Roen could hear them despite the wind and thunder. A sudden chill gripped him. Shaking, he placed his ear against the door and listened.

"Sorry, Your Grace, but we searched everywhere," rasped a coarse voice. "The son's not home."

A nasal voice answered. "Not home, you declare. This is... incommodious. 'Twould be untoward if Ketya finds him first. The waif might desire to presage him. That would be even more niggling. And as we all know, so much upset can prove deleterious to certain incompetent people. So what say you take these portraits off the wall and go comb every cranny of this noisome, verminous city until you unearth the boy, what?"

Roen heard armor chinking and boots stomping. Before he could back away, the door opened to reveal two burly soldiers, clad in mail and crimson surcoats. Roen took a step back. The soldiers stared at him, stared at the parchments they carried, and then stared at each other. Slowly their faces split into dumb grins. Roen spun on his heels, but before he could take a step, gloved hands grabbed him. The soldiers' grip was iron, and Roen struggled uselessly as they dragged him inside.

The workshop was a mess. Tables had been overturned, paintings pulled down, and shelves toppled. Jars of pigment, rolls of canvas, and dozens of paintbrushes cluttered the floor. Amid all the disorder, surrounded by more soldiers, stood Duke Hyan Redfort, warming his pudgy hands before the hearth. Roen stared at him through drooping wet curls. Pink, plump, and pug-nosed, the head of Heland's armies looked like a pig in samite.

Hyan was a great general, Roen knew. He protected Heland's borders from Stonemark's Sinther, stood stalwartly against the mad stone king. But right now, his father's porcine patron was the last thing Roen wanted to see.

The soldiers tossed him free, and Roen almost collapsed. He took a ragged breath, steadying himself. Water pooling at his feet, he managed to sketch a clumsy bow. He could not guess what was happening, but knew he must tread carefully.

"Your Grace," he said. "What a pleasure to see you—"

The duke interrupted him, his fat lips pouting into a smile. "We would propound you save your, hum, sweet talk for the court, what? You are, you see, under arrest, and about to join your father in prison."

The words sank in slowly. Roen felt a chill run through him, colder than his icy clothes. He blinked sweat out of his eyes.

"But we've done nothing wrong, Your Grace."

Hyan raised his eyebrows, his mouth forming a surprised circle. "Oh? We do believe you took our gold and, hum, frittered it away without painting our portrait. We would call that 'something wrong', no?"

Roen shook his head. "What are you talking about? Your portrait *and* your gold are both safe upstairs."

The duke began to chuckle. For a moment, his jowls quivering, he *did* seem a pig. A wet snout trembled in his face, floppy ears dangled from his head, and when he opened his mouth only a squeal came out. Roen rubbed his eyes, and when he looked again, Hyan was once more human, and talking to his guards.

"The boy is impertinent, what?" The duke dabbed an embroidered handkerchief against his forehead. "Incarcerate him in a solitary cell until his trial. We don't want him in any propinquity to his father."

The soldiers reached out to grab him, their armor clanking, their gauntlets opening and closing like mandibles. Roen could only stare and shake his head. The hunks of metal loomed over him. More armor clinked at his sides. Roen took a step back out of his puddle. The soldiers came chinking after him.

And then, one slipped in the water and crashed to the floor.

Never afterwards could Roen explain what hidden force drove his feet forward at that instant. With the gap opened in his cage, with the fever befogging his mind, Roen's body moved on its own. Over the fallen soldier, onto the staircase, and up the stairs his feet took him. Beyond the roar of blood in his ears, he heard the hiss of steel on leather as the soldiers drew swords behind him.

He reached the attic and stumbled inside. In the small room, Hyan's painting was gone from its stand, and their coffer of gold was open and empty. Roen didn't have time for surprise. He slammed open the window and tossed his hat outside, then hid under his bed. The soldiers' shadows danced over the floor as they clanked into the room.

"There, out the window!" one said.

Roen heard them clamber into the alley below. He peeked from under his bed. They were gone. Knees shaking, he crawled out and stood up. Sweat washed his hot face. *This is madness,* he thought. The painting, the gold—his father!—gone. Madness! He heard the sound of more boots thumping upstairs, preceded by a stench of oil and sweat. Roen knew it was folly to run, folly to resist arrest when the courts could prove him innocent. But he also knew that Smerdin had hours to live. Roen would not entrust the laceleaf to these brutes. Too much was at stake. Somehow, he'd have to reach Smerdin himself.

He took a deep breath, climbed onto the windowsill, reached outside and caught the tiled roof.

Something grabbed his foot before it could leave the sill. Roen glanced over his shoulder to see Hyan clutching him. Heart in mouth, Roen kicked and freed himself, spraying mud onto the duke's bald head. He hefted himself onto the roof, where the storm raged and flapped his cloak. Brownbury's roofscape sprawled around him like a field of thorns, black on black. Lightning flashed, and the roofs sparkled with raindrops.

The duke's squealing came from inside. "Catch him, you incompetent fools! Catch him and bring him hither."

Roen blundered down the slippery roof, arms windmilling. Clumsily he leapt onto the next roof, scraping his knees. He clutched the chimney, straightened, and glanced over his shoulder. Soldiers were climbing onto the roof behind him, shrugging off their mail. A lump suddenly filled Roen's throat. It was all too terrible. Eyes burning, he stumbled onto another rooftop, then another. Soon he was running, leaping headlong from roof to roof, crashing into chimneys, sending tiles cascading into the darkness. Even as the sky grumbled, he heard the soldiers following.

They seemed to be everywhere. They leapt at him from surrounding rooftops, from the streets, from inside the houses. Three scrambled onto the roof before him. Two more leapt from the roof behind. Roen stumbled onto a third roof, but there too he found pursuit. Dozens of hands reached out to grab him. Swords flashed like lightning. The sparkling roofs whirled.

Everywhere he looked were white faces, red eyes, yellow grins. Roen ran blindly, leaping, stumbling, awash with sweat.

Soon he skidded to a stop. He had reached the wide streets of the merchants' quarter. The next roof onward lay far away, before it a dark chasm. Roen hesitated. It looked too wide to jump. The height made his head spin. Panting, he glanced behind him. The soldiers were rushing forward, eyes flashing in the lightning. Roen looked into the chasm again. *You can make it,* came a thought like a whisper. *All you need to do is fly.* He took three paces backwards. His knees knocked.

"He's trapped! Catch him!" cried the soldiers behind.

Roen's fingers curled into fists. He took a deep breath. With the soldiers jeering behind him, Roen ran forward, leapt off the roof and soared, legs kicking. Time slowed to a crawl. He seemed to be forever in the air. Wind blew the curls back from his feverish forehead. Raindrops fell like snow. Everything moved so slowly. Roen outstretched his wings and flapped them, laughing. *I'm a bird,* he thought, *a bird flying to freedom, flying to its father, flying... to the ground.*

The world began to tick at normal speed again. Roen had enough time to realize he missed the roof, before he slammed into the wall beneath it. He reached out as he fell and caught a window's shutters. The wooden blinds snapped one by one, till Roen was left holding the windowsill, his fingers slowly slipping. His feet dangled. His head spun.

"Where is he?" came a voice from above.

"Fell to his death."

"You sure? I heard some strange cracking when he fell."

"His bones breaking! Come, let's find a way down to his body."

The soldiers voiced their agreement and walked away.

Roen released the cough that had been swelling in his throat. He scuffed his feet against the wall till he found a crack, and shoved his toes into it. He pushed upwards and grabbed a waterspout. After moments of struggle, his shaking limbs fueled by fear alone, he caught the eave and pulled himself onto the roof.

He collapsed over the tiles, sweat and rain pouring down his forehead. He lay sprawled and supine, too weak to lift his head, too hot to feel the cold. Tendrils of steam rose from his skin where the raindrops hit it, tiny wraiths rising to heaven. *Soon I will join them,* Roen thought, *join them where cold is warmth and pain is numbness.* The face of Death formed above him in the tenebrous sky. Eyes cracked open in the clouds, flashing with lightning, weeping icy tears. A mouth yawned open beneath it, dripping spit and laughing with deep, grumbling thunder.

In the clouds, Roen saw the stony face of King Sinther, the lord of malice. Roen knew it laughed for the end of his life, and he reached out toward it, and invited it to come.

Instead, came the fireflies.

The first one rose from an alley to bob lazily across the sky, like a wandering star. A second soon joined it, then a third, and before long the darkness brimmed with a million glowing specks that danced languidly, flickered, frolicked, hid the clouds behind their glow. Roen lay limp, watching as the fireflies swam above him, dipped down to circle his head, alighted on his fingertips and tugged at his clothes as if trying to pull him up. It was like floating in a sea of stars, an endless galaxy of glowing, swirling stars, swiveling around him, blinding him, filling his eyes with light. Even as the storm raged, the fireflies lingered, glowing like they had for every night Roen could remember, be it in summer or in winter, in country or in city, over land or over sea. Glowing, in a storm only evil could brew. Glowing, when no living thing should be outdoors. Glowing, when even the most powerful lord would bar his door and shut his shutters and hide behind thick walls.

Like Hyan was doing right now.

Roen sucked in his breath. Pictures floated across the fogs of his mind. He could see the soldiers scurrying to chase him over a field of thorns, leaving their master safe behind. He could hear the duke's squeals: *Bring him hither.* Hyan had stayed in the workshop, awaiting his underlings' return, not daring to face the storming night alone. Roen reached into his pocket and caressed the crumpled laceleaf. It was dangerous, he knew. Even with the clouding fever he knew as much. But he also knew it was his only chance to save Smerdin. He looked up at the sky, so mocking, hating, awhirl with endless glowing flecks. *The storm did not stop me,* he thought. *Nor will men. I may be only a humble painter, but I will save my father, if I have to kidnap a duke to do so.*

He sat up. The fireflies tugged at his shirt, and he rose to his feet. With weak legs, he began moving again, stumbling across the roof. The fireflies swam around him, lighting his way. The dainty, ethereal creatures took hold of his shoulders and lifted him, carrying him over the city. Roen saw all of Brownbury beneath him, tiny roofs and tiny domes, towers like sticks and streets like thread. The beauty of it brought tears to his eyes. Maybe he was dreaming. Maybe he was dead. He was too muzzy to care. The fireflies descended and lowered him onto the roof of his home. Roen stood on the wet tiles, holding the chimney for support. The fireflies swirled around him in a twister, rising and rising till they rose above his head and settled into the clouds like stars.

Roen took a deep breath. He felt dazed, but he also felt stronger, calmer. Firefly light still shining in his eyes, he crawled down the roof to peer into the attic window. The room was empty. Carefully, he lowered himself onto the windowsill, but there he slipped and crashed inside onto the floor.

"Did you hear something?" came a squeaky voice from downstairs, speaking with a foreign accent. Roen's heart skipped a beat.

"Only the thunder, dear Ketya," replied Hyan's unmistakable nasal voice.

Roen let out his breath and slumped into a chair, his face wet with rain and sweat. His head spun and he felt faint. *One more hour*, he prayed. *All I need is one more hour*. When he shut his eyes he could still see glowing orbs, floating languidly against his lids. The sight calmed him, gave him strength, parted the mist in his mind. He took a deep breath and made himself think. *How will I do this?*

Hyan was not alone. A girl was with him—Ketya—an Esiren by her lilt and name. What was one of her race doing in Heland? *Ketya might want to warn him*, the duke had said. Could there be some scheme afoot, some devilry involving more than gold and paintings? And if so, why would it involve him? Roen could not guess. He had to learn what was happening. He rose from his chair and inched along the floor, thrust his head into the staircase and peeked downstairs.

Hyan was standing by the hearth, firelight glinting off his pink head and samite robe. Before him stood a girl of maybe thirteen years, with a pale brown ponytail, protuberant ears, and an impish face. She was dressed in rags, but held an embroidered purse in her hand. Roen gasped. His purse! His stolen purse from the coffer! Hyan reached out to take it, but the girl pulled it back and gave the duke a scolding glare.

Chin thrust out boldly, she said, "You didn't tell me you wanted it stolen so you could frame the painters." Her voice was high and squeaky, almost comically unfit for her brazen tone.

Hyan steepled his plump fingers and smiled over their tips. Spit bubbled on his lips. "We seldom divulge our machinations to, hum, orphan refugees, you see."

The girl placed her hands on her hips. "You should have told me! You said you'd free my friends if I stole your gold. You said nothing about imprisoning others instead. I don't like this."

Hyan's smile widened. His lips were like two quivering, well-fed leeches. "We thought you might not, dear Ketya. That is why, of course, we cannot let you go free."

Ketya took a step back. "What do you mean?"

Hyan stepped toward her. "That you're joining your 'Esiren friends' in prison, where you'll all await Joren of Stonemark together."

Ketya paled. "Not Butcher Joren...."

Through the curtains of Roen's fever, the duke was looking like a pig again. With a fat, black trotter he grabbed Ketya's arm. She yelped and struggled, and the duke backhanded her. Blood speckled the wall.

Before Roen realized what he was doing, he was limping downstairs, leaning against the rail with one hand and holding his chair in the other.

"Leave her alone, Hyan," he said hoarsely. "It's me you want."

The girl and the giant pig holding her turned to face him. Ketya gaped slack-jawed, but Hyan only nodded slowly, all amusement gone from his eyes. He shoved Ketya to the floor and drew his sword. The blade hissed free and whistled toward Roen's belly.

Mustering his scant strength, Roen lifted his chair and swung it. The blade tangled in the oak legs and flew from the duke's grasp. Roen and Hyan stared at each other, frozen for a moment. Then, with his last drop of vigor, Roen tossed the chair at the duke and dived for the sword. He came up with his back to the wall and the sword gripped in his shaking hands. He pointed it at Hyan's chins.

"Free my father," he said.

At least, he tried to say so. It was, at best, a hoarse whisper that actually left his throat. The sword was suddenly heavy. He could barely hold it up. He tightened his grip, but still the blade wavered, bobbing like a drunkard over a cup. Roen cleared his throat and tried to speak again, but managed only an unintelligible wheeze. Sweat dripped into his eyes and he blinked it away. When he could see again the door was open, and he glimpsed Hyan fleeing down the dark road, pulling Ketya behind him. Roen bolted after them.

The small effort was too much. His knees felt as soft as rotten apples. For a moment he stood catching his breath. The fireflies swirled furiously around him. Wind and rain buffeted him, piercing his shirt. He heard a clang at his feet and realized the sword had fallen. He leaned down to lift it, but could not stand up again. Too hot. It was too hot. The road swam. His eyes lolled. He felt water flow around him, pulling him down a gutter. Somewhere in the distance a girl screamed, but her voice soon drowned under the roaring stream. All thought faded. The last thing Roen Painter felt was the pattering rain, and then nothing.

Chapter Three
Secret Gift

Aeolia slept for a long time.

It was a deep, dreamless sleep, peaceful as a midnight sea. Its black waves covered her, smoothed her worried face and washed her memories clear. She floated in this slumber, smiling, wanting never to wake, only to drown in oblivion. For ten years her hope for rescue had deprived her of rest. Now, with its demise, she slept with the calmness of surrender.

She awoke slowly, reluctantly, peeking fitfully from slumber like pebbles between waves on shore. She tried to stay asleep. She furrowed her brow, tightened her eyelids, tossed an arm over her head. She rolled over, hugged her knees, mumbled sleepy nonsense. She sucked her thumb. She moaned. But no matter what she tried, she could no longer find her slumber. One by one her senses awakened, and the world came into focus.

The stench assailed her first, a mixture of rot and mold, churning her stomach. Soon after came the cold, freezing her bones, making her teeth chatter. Next she heard the sounds: chirping, squeaking, pattering, sniffing. Aeolia shivered, not daring to open her eyes. Sight was a sense too frightening to use. Where was she? She could not remember. Finally her curiosity overcame her fear, and she parted her eyelids to slits, and peeked.

Darkness stared back, darkness thick enough to breathe, thick enough to feel, darkness blacker than the space between stars. Aeolia yelped, shut her eyes tight and covered them with her hands. Icy sweat washed over her. She could have sworn the darkness was sentient, that it scorned her. There had been hate in its stare. Aeolia vowed never to open her eyes again; the darkness within her lids seemed like sunlight compared to what lurked beyond.

As she lay shivering, her memories slowly returned. First they were murky, and she could recall only her hope and its loss. But soon she remembered the spilled wine, the rubbing of feet, the tossed pot of broth. Finally she remembered the green key, the open trapdoor, and the skeletons of former, recalcitrant slaves that surrounded her. And with her past she saw her future, saw her flesh rot and be eaten, and her dry bones dwindle to dust. She would never see Joren again.

She curled up into a ball and waited to die.

It was hard not to weep. She fought it as best as she could, biting her lip to keep her mouth shut, clenching her eyelids lest they leaked. It was all she could do to withhold total misery. She lay still with her knees to her chest, afraid to move and touch the bones. She kept her hands over her face, afraid to move even them. Sleep claimed her several times, but never for long, and it now carried nightmares. Hours passed as she lay curled up, maybe even days. Her lips and tongue parched, and her stomach cramped. It would be a hard death, she knew, and she could not wait for it.

Aeolia thought things could get no worse, and then they did.

At first they just squeaked, but Aeolia knew they squeaked for her. *I'm not dead yet!* she wanted to cry, but her throat felt too dry. She covered her ears, blocking their noise, and for a while she could imagine them gone. But soon the rats began to sniff, placing their quivering noses on her skin, tickling her with their whiskers. They were too many and too hungry to beat off. They climbed her, covering her with a blanket of coarse fur. She could not help but sniffle when their claws tickled her skin. As she squirmed, trying to shake them off, she crashed into the skeletons, scattering bones. She had never known such anguish.

Then one bit her. She yelped, beat it off, and felt more teeth sink into her thigh.

"I'm not dead yet!" she sobbed. "Wait till I'm dead!"

More teeth bit her arm. Claws ran all over her body. Her mind whirled with terror, and the rats kept biting, eating. Aeolia wanted to tell them, wanted to beg.

"I'm sorry, Joren, I'm sorry, I have to break my promise...."

Panting, she opened her eyes and stared into the darkness. She let her fingers uncurl, welcoming her gift. The old tingling filled her. She cried then, and arched her back, and clawed the air. Tears ran into her mouth. Sorry, she thought. Sorry, sorry.... The rats flurried, scratching, biting, and Aeolia reached out her mind. Buried alive, leagues from home, grown, saddened, dying, Aeolia broke her old promise. For the first time in ten years, she did what Joren had forbidden. She used her secret talent. She linked to the strongest rat.

Their minds merged.

Suddenly she was two beings. She lived inside herself, but also inside the rat. She felt the hunger in its belly, her skin in its paws, smelled her fear in its nose. She knew it experienced her senses too; their minds were one. The rat, confused, bit and clawed with more fervor. When its teeth sank into Aeolia's flesh, both felt the pain, and the rat shrieked, leapt off, and scurried away.

Overwhelmed with the sensations, Aeolia barely managed to sever the link. When she did, one half of her vanished in a blinding flash. Senses disappeared. Bits of the world shut down. She was only herself again. All the rats had pattered away, as if they knew to fear her magic, and Aeolia lay alone and trembling.

"It's okay, I'm Aeolia, I'm only Aeolia, I'm not a rat, it was just the link, I'm only me again."

She took deep breaths, forcing herself to calm down, and for a while she lay still and numb and dazed. When her thoughts finally cleared, shame inundated her. She had broken her most sacred vow, she realized, only days from her death. She would die knowing she had betrayed her brother. *It would've been better to let them eat me,* she thought.

Gingerly, she curled back into a ball and continued waiting.

The wait was worse this time. Before, death might have brought solace. Now, she knew, it would bring only perdition. She was an oath breaker. There would be no clemency for her in the afterlife. She awaited her judgment in a haze, floating between wakefulness and slumber, neither in one nor the other. She suspected she was feverish, but her skin felt cold as snow. She wondered how much time had passed. Though her tongue was parched, thirst had not yet killed her; it couldn't have been more than a day or two. Yet it felt much longer. She could hardly remember her life aboveground; it seemed distant and unreal as a dream. The darkness had become her only reality, solitude her only companion.

She thought of her homeland, of Stonemark, of her king—who also lived underground. She took comfort imagining she was him, strong as stone, not a prisoner but a ruler of men. In his subterraneous cavern, King Sinther drew magic from the surrounding rock, turning his skin to stone against which swords broke and arrows shattered. Aeolia wished her body, too, were hard as granite, unable to feel pain. She wished her heart were made of flint, unable to cry. She wanted to stop feeling, to sink into nothingness forever. With her chance for life perished, with her hope for salvation dead, Aeolia could only pray to join them quickly.

And so it was, that when the footsteps creaked above her, Aeolia covered her ears and tried to ignore the noise. She wanted silence for her death.

But the footsteps continued pacing, and try as she may, Aeolia could not ignore that something was *wrong* about them. Something alien and familiar at once. She frowned, uncovered her ears and listened. The footsteps were too light, too graceful for an ogre's stomping. And there were many of them, three or four pairs of feet.

She could also hear a chinking, almost like her shackles. *Has the ogre bought another slave already?* she wondered. No, she heard no chains dragging, and this chinking was finer, soft as summer rain. The sound tickled a childhood memory, and an image flashed through Aeolia's mind, an image of a Stonish soldier, sword at waist, clad in chinking mail.

"What are you saying, you overgrown, flea-bitten freak?" a male voice demanded above, his words muffled by the ceiling. "I can't understand your gibberish."

Aeolia's heartbeat quickened. The man spoke Northtalk, the language of her childhood, with the liquid vowels the ogres never could master with their guttural voices. She feebly sat upright and strained her ears, listening. Through the ceiling then came the ogress's voice, speaking Ogregrunt, and Aeolia could just barely hear her whispers.

"The girl you seek, she is here, beneath the sofa."

A grating sound scratched along the ceiling—the sofa being pushed aside.

"Spirit's Beard," swore the man speaking Northtalk. "A trapdoor."

Aeolia could scarcely believe her ears. She rose to her wobbly feet, leaning against the wall and trembling. Her breath came fast and shaky and her aching stomach churned. Was that Joren speaking? Had the ogress led him to her? A slam came from above, and Aeolia knew it was the lock being broken, and she tasted salty tears on her lips. She stood still, gazing at the ceiling.

Dust and beautiful light showered into the basement as the trapdoor swung open.

"Joren!" Aeolia gushed into the blinding light. "Joren, I knew you'd come for me!"

As her eyes slowly adjusted, her smile faded. Three Stonesons were gazing down from above, but her brother was not among them. Two of the men were soldiers, with cold faces under iron helms. The third man wore no armor, only a draping robe that was gray like his eyes. A long scar rifted his cadaverous face, tweaking his smile.

Aeolia took a step back, her stomach turning cold. The scarred man let down his hand for her to grasp. It was the first human hand Aeolia had seen in years, and yet it seemed cold and alien, and she could not take it. It did not belong to Joren. Joren had not come.

"Where is my brother?" she asked, her long-unspoken language tasting strange on her lips.

"In Stonemark," the man replied.

His words were a slap in the face. It was a struggle to keep her voice steady. "Who are you?"

"My name is Lale. I'm your brother's best friend. Here, Aeolia, take my hand."

Aeolia had forgotten the sound of her own name; she hadn't heard it spoken in a decade. The flowing vowels sounded sweet as wine to her ears, and she bit her lip to fight back her tears. Why wasn't it Joren speaking her name now, calling her Aeoly as he always had?

"Why didn't my brother come?"

The man's smile widened, causing his scar to crawl like a caterpillar. "Why, he is preparing your new house. You will live together now, in the richest neighborhood in Grayrock. Joren says he hopes you kept your promise, because now he sent me to keep his."

Aeolia gasped, joy blossoming in her again. *It's true!* she thought. This man knew of the promises; he truly was Joren's friend! With a wide smile and happiness bubbling inside her, Aeolia reached up and took Lale's hand.

When his hand tightened painfully, and his smile curved into a snarl, she did not understand. When he yanked her up her arm hurt, but she did not cry out, only gaped in confusion. He dropped her to the living room floor, at the boots of the soldiers, on the bearskin rug which was always the toughest to dust. When he drew his sword above her, ready to strike her dead, still she could not comprehend, only stared. Her mind blurred. It was like floating in a dream—as surely this was—and she watched, eyes wide with confusion, as the nightmare unfolded around her.

The ogress, so frail but twice a man's size, grabbed one soldier's head and cracked it against the hearth. As the second soldier drew his sword, the ogress lifted the poker and thrust it deep into his eye. Like a puppet show, Aeolia thought, everybody twitching like dolls on strings. The blood didn't even look real. She wanted to laugh. There, another splash of red paint as Lale buried his sword into the ogress's thigh. Such a realistic puppet! The wooden, yellow face, looking down at the pooling red paint, almost seemed lugubrious. Then—what wonder!—the ogress puppet looked up into Aeolia's eyes and whispered sad words.

"I'm sorry, girl, I'm sorry. I know how it feels."

Lale's blade flashed. Red liquid splashed like wine from a cracked jug. The ogress's head wilted onto her shoulder.

Aeolia stared, eyes wide and jaw unhinged. Some strange, whining whisper left her throat, like a baby's mewl. Hot, sticky droplets trickled down her face, onto her lips and into her mouth. Blood. Aeolia grimaced. She began to pant. She looked up at Lale, who stood over the body of her dead mistress, and her heart seemed to shatter inside her. Her mewl turned into a hoarse, wordless cry, and she lunged forward. Lale turned his head at her cry, amused surprise on his face, and Aeolia slammed into his chest.

The amusement left Lale's face as his heels hit the basement's opening. He stood tilted, arms windmilling. Aeolia had to shove him again before he toppled into the darkness. His hand caught the rim, and Aeolia slammed the trapdoor shut, crushing his fingers. The floor was slippery with blood, and the sofa moved easily when she pushed it. She placed it over the trapdoor.

Her ears rang in the sudden silence. Aeolia shivered and hugged herself. She gazed around her, knees quaking. The shutters were open, and it was early morning outside. So long since she had seen daylight! The sunrays slanted into the room, illuminating it with a soft glow. The room was dusty, Aeolia noticed. She should clean it. The ogre's nose was sensitive to dust, and the cane always flew with the sneeze, and—what's that?—there was no firewood in the fireplace, she'd have to chop more, and look at all those dirty dishes on the table—

Aeolia barked a laugh. She would have given the world for those old troubles again. Suddenly she felt faint. She held her head in her hands and took deep, shaky breaths. She could not comprehend what was happening. It was too surreal to accept.

A thud came from the basement, and the sofa budged an inch. The Stoneson was breaking free, Aeolia realized. She had to hide somewhere, maybe in the barn, or in the honeysuckle behind the sheep pen. She dragged her shackles two steps toward the front door, but it swung open before she could reach it. She stopped in her tracks. The ogre stood in the doorway before her.

The old shepherd stood still, gazing into the living room. His face was flushed from cold, and his hat sparkled with raindrops. The scent of sheep and grass mingled with the coppery smell of blood. The ogre passed his eyes over the room, and when his stare rested on his daughter, his face grew ashen. His fist tightened around his cane. Slowly he looked up at Aeolia, his brow pushed low over his beady eyes.

"You killed her," he said and began to limp toward her.

Hurriedly, Aeolia knelt by a dead soldier and grabbed the hilt of his sword. The ogre reached her before she could draw it. He slammed his cane onto her wrist, knocking the sword from her hand. The cane came down again, this time on her shoulder, knocking her to the floor.

Aeolia knew what to do. Eyes burning, she prostrated herself and covered her head with her arms.

Three blows were enough. She did not think she could have endured more. Three blows and she was crying, her tears spilling onto the floor. Three blows she welcomed, embracing their pain, soaking them willingly. Three blows, and she was unbroken but bruised, and hurting, hurting. And with pain saturating her, nearly wiping her away, Aeolia opened her eyes, stared at the ogre, and linked to him.

The cane dropped from his hand. Was it his hand or hers? For a moment she was not sure. *What is happening to me?* came a frightened thought. *I must have sprung my old back, how come it hurts so?* Confusion welled inside her, confusion at a whirling world viewed from two sets of eyes, the dizzying awareness of two bodies and beings merged.

Who am I? both minds thought. *Am I ogre or girl?*

Aeolia yelped as the ogre's bad leg gave way and he crashed to the floor. She shakily stood up, tears streaming down her cheeks. At the same time she felt the ogre groping for his cane, trying to rise to his old, aching feet.

What am I doing in your body?

I'm sorry, I didn't want to break my promise, I had to....

You killed my daughter!

No, I didn't know, I only wanted Joren....

Aeolia stumbled toward the dead soldier and drew his sword. She dragged it back toward the ogre. He was gritting his teeth against her pain and struggling to stand up. Mustering her scarce strength, Aeolia lifted the sword above him.

No, don't kill me!

Help, I'm killing myself, no!

Aeolia severed the link. Her one half vanished, and she was only herself again. She leaned weakly onto the sword's pommel, and her weight drove the blade into her master like a hot needle into wax. Blood bespattered her, and she blundered backwards. Her back hit the wall and she cried in pain. Her wet hands caught the windowsill for support.

Autumn was beautiful behind her. A breeze blew through the shutters and caressed her hair, kissed her skin and whispered in her ears like a lover. Golden leaves swirled into the room, and Aeolia heard the warbling of cardinals and robins, and smelled the scents of heliotropes and roses and sweet, sweet lilies. They were her favorite flowers. She grimaced, leaned over and gagged, her empty stomach heaving. Her head spun.

Another thud came from the basement, almost knocking off the sofa. Aeolia squelched forward and pushed the sofa back. But the scarred man inside, though pale and sickly, was tall and strong. Aeolia knew the prison would not contain him long.

She knelt by the dead ogre and rummaged through his pocket. She pulled out his round of keys. With shaky fingers, she found the right one and placed it in her irons. For a moment she paused, thinking of Joren's warning, of her secret gift, and mostly of her stone king whom no sword could harm.

She turned the key, and her fetters fell off like two broken promises.

Chapter Four
The Forest

The Forest had no sky. Like pillars, its boles supported a ceiling of crisscrossing branches, bronze leaves, and entrapped wisps of cloud. The forest floor was a reflection of its canopy. Fallen leaves carpeted it, and from their depths rose gnarled roots like branches. Moss covered everything. The moldy air was silent as sin.

Tracking a faint trail, Taya of Yaiyai was careful to keep this silence. So warily she paced, her moccasins did not crunch the dry leaves. These hoary oaks had been growing undisturbed for generations. It was known they disliked strangers. Like lecherous old men, they huddled around her, stretching knobby fingers over her head, brushing beards of moss against her face. Taya bared her teeth at the endless green shadows between the trunks. Her knuckles were white as she clutched her spear.

The trail was leading her far from her clan, farther than she'd ever gone. The woods here were no less dim, damp, or dense than at home, but it was whispered that where no humans dwelled, fairies frolicked free. They could be anywhere, Taya knew—peeking from behind any leaf, hiding under any toadstool, crawling along any branch.... Taya was not afraid, though. She was never afraid. At eighteen, she had already killed dozens of beasts. Why should she fear some old trees and invisible spirits? She forced herself to laugh.

Wings fluttered past her eyes, and Taya started, her heart leaping into her throat. She spun around to see a bat disappear into a hollow cedar. Bats often nested in imps' hair, her mother once said, and Taya narrowed her eyes, raised her spear and scanned her surroundings. Moss swayed like ghosts from the oaks' branches, while elf cups clung to the birches. Mushrooms sprouted from the leafmold or coated fallen logs. Above her, wind rustled dry leaves the color of her hair, and stirred moss the color of her eyes. Down where she stood, the air hung thick with the smell of humus.

Nothing, Taya thought. Nothing. No fairies, no spirits. She forced herself to smile, a savage smile, her breath fast and her jaw clenched. The spirits dared not harm her, she told herself. Who could blame them? Around her neck clinked a string of boars' tusks, wolfbone beads hemmed her bearskin mantle, and her two thick braids were strewn with eagle feathers. No sprite would dare enchant a warrior thus attired, she told herself.

Teeth bared halfway between snarl and grin, Taya outstretched her arms, flaunting a weapon in each hand. One was her knife, with its bone blade and antler hilt. The other was her flint spear, its knotty staff decorated with strings of scrimshawed snail shells.

"I cannot see you!" she announced, staring around defiantly. "I'm no shaman like my mother. But I am Taya of Yaiyai, the Forest Firechild! I killed wolves when I was eight, and bears when I was ten, and I'm not afraid of you. I'm *never* afraid!"

She stood with arms outstretched, breathing heavily, daring any spirit to challenge her. The trees were silent. Good. *Let them fear me,* she thought. *I won't fear them. I'm never afraid.* With a satisfied nod, Taya lowered her arms and placed her knife back in her belt. She snapped her teeth at the knurled boles and, feeling reassured, resumed following the trail.

It was a faint trail—too faint, Taya thought proudly, for most trackers to follow. The warrior pack had walked like ghosts, leaving no footprints, only the occasional bent fern or mud smudge, soon overlain with fallen leaves. But Taya was better than most trackers. Her cousin Talin—the Halfman of Chameleon Skin—had taught her the skill, and even without her magic, Taya walked at a quick, steady pace. It made her proud. She wished Talin were there to see.

Her mother, of course, thought woodcraft unbefitting an apprenticing shaman. Taya's lip curled bitterly at the thought. The old shaman had insisted Taya study only the invisible world. But Taya hated studying, hated being cooped up in some dusty treehouse while the village boys played outside amid the branches. What need I chants or charms, Taya would demand, I who am the Firechild? I am more powerful than any shaman. Her mother would only shake her head and mutter words about discipline, tradition, and other hogwash that boiled Taya's blood.

She was the Firechild. She was powerful. She would not spend years studying just to talk to some stupid spirits. Being shaman was fine for some, but Taya was destined for greater glory. They said Sinther of Stonemark wanted to conquer the Island, and only as a warrior could Taya protect the Forest. And as for her mother, well... as far as Taya was concerned, the old woman could catch greenskin and rot.

Taya forced her mind back to the warriors' trail. It had turned down a steep slope, between clumps of elm and dogwood with ivy hanging from their branches. It was a difficult route, strewn with roots and rocks, but full of animal prints and droppings, which meant it would not dead-end. Before long, it reached a rocky stream of silent green water. Taya walked alongside, her moccasins pushing into the moss that carpeted the bank. *Soon,* she thought. *Soon I'll be a warrior and never have to study again.*

As time went by, the trail became fainter. Unlike the leafmold, the moss was springy and did not hold footprints. Taya chewed her lip and searched for mud smears. After a while of meticulous tracking, however, it began to drizzle. The raindrops fell plump from the canopy, effacing what clues were still visible. Taya cursed softly. Doggedly, she continued moving, refusing to concede defeat. But after three dozen steps and not a clue, she was forced to stop. This trail, she suspected, would have stumped even Talin.

She sighed. She'd have to use her magic.

Fingers trembling slightly, Taya clutched her spear to her chest. She drew a long breath and shut her eyes. The first prickle of magic made her wince. Her fists clenched around her spear. Sweat dripped down her temples. The magic slowly filled her, magic such as no other Forestfellow had, magic that was hers alone. It flowed through her veins, stirred the soft hairs on her nape, made her teeth ache. Her own magic. Firefly magic. And when it saturated her, and she could soak up no more, she used it.

As if punched in the belly, she bent forward, and her hands hit the ground. She tossed back her head and howled. The surrounding bushes soared high as trees as she shrank. Stones bulged into boulders. The magic went wild, flurrying the leaves, crackling the air. Taya felt fangs push through her gums, a tail shoot out of her back, fur sprout over her body, and claws spring from her fingertips. Her clothes and weapons—parts of her no less than her limbs—melted into her skin. It all burned like a bath of embers.

And then, it ended. The magic slowly settled in the pit of her stomach. Trembling, Taya opened her eyes. The world had become a blur of blacks, whites, and grays.

But if her eyesight was weakened, her other senses had become keen as a claw. She could hear geese honking miles away, mice rustling in bushes, her own thumping heart. Every odor was distinct to her nose: every plant, every animal, the faint spoors of things that had walked by hours past. She could even smell the tangy, human scent of herself as she had been a moment ago. Taya padded over to the stream and glanced down at her blurry reflection. She was the perfect vixen.

The magic ached inside her, and she had to concentrate to contain it. If she relaxed, the magic would dissipate, and she would become human again. The constant effort was uncomfortable, like keeping tired eyes open or a stomach sucked in. Anxious to return to her true form, Taya left the stream and wiggled her nose over the ground. The scent of the warrior pack was strong. They couldn't be a day gone.

Taya leapt into a sprint, paws flying over rocks and roots. The clammy air filled her nostrils and her tail flowed behind her. The warriors' spoor led her away from the stream, along an animal path, the oaks thick as walls on her sides. Dirt and damp leaves kicked up from under her paws with a rustle. The warriors' scent intensified, till finally, beside a mossy boulder engraved with ancient runes, Taya smelled them steps ahead. She had never guessed they could be so close.

She paused, tongue lolling, her fur a tangle of burrs and leaves. She stood on her back paws and, with a sigh of relief, let go of her magic. Her limbs stretched, her fur vanished, her claws receded. She was human again.

It felt good to be herself, with her clothes and weapons and no tingling inside her. She leaned against the boulder, catching her breath. Absently, she brushed away the moss to reveal the runes. Blessings for travelers, she surmised—carved by ancient shamans. Well, Taya did not need the blessings of shamans. She had the fireflies to bless her. Her own fireflies. And if her mother didn't like that, she could eat spoiled grubs and choke. Taya was tempted to smash the runes with her spear.

The dim murmur of conversation, coming from ash trees behind, tore her from her thoughts. The warriors. Here were people who'd understand, Taya told herself. Here were people who'd respect power—who'd respect *her*. Here was where she belonged. With a deep breath, Taya brushed her deerskin leggings, tightened her lips, and stepped around the stone.

The forest leapt at her. Taya yelped and dropped her spear. The trees leaned closer, pointing spearheads, staring with slanted green eyes. *Goblins!* was Taya's first thought. She fumbled for her knife, but then noticed the tattoos on the leafy creatures' faces. Her cheeks flushed. She clenched her jaw and lifted her spear.

"Lower your weapons," she demanded of the camouflaged warriors. "I am Taya of Yaiyai. I come sent from my mother, Eeea, shaman of our clan."

"Do as she says," came a deep voice from behind the Forestfolk.

The ring of warriors parted, and a burly, bearded man stepped forward. Taya was tall as most men—embarrassingly tall, she often thought—but this man towered over her. A bear's skull topped his large head, and his red braids tinkled with bones. His cheeks lacked the green stripes of a Claw, such as the other warriors sported. Instead, they were tattooed with black zigzags, marking him the higher rank of Fang. This was Uaua of the Aaee, Taya knew—leader of the pack.

He gave her a hard stare. "Taya of Yaiyai. I left one of my warriors with your shaman to be healed. Where is he?"

Taya inclined her head. She kept her voice quiet and respectful when she spoke. "My mother used all her runes and incantations, but his wound was too festered. Even a Healer couldn't have helped him." Taya pulled a leather bundle from her belt and held it forward. "I brought you his heart and courage to eat."

Uaua took the bundle and solemnly tucked it away. He spoke with lowered eyes and the low voice meant for the dead. "We will absorb his courage tonight and remember his brave deeds." He looked up at her. "The pack thanks you, Taya of the Yaiyai, and prays the spirits grant you a safe journey home."

Taya did not move. Now was the moment, she told herself. *I was born for now.* She took a deep breath and spoke carefully planned words. "Fang Uaua, I've come with a purpose of my own, as well. With your warrior gone to the spirits, your pack is missing a Claw." Taya raised her chin. "I want to replace him."

A mumble ran through the pack. A faint smile played across Uaua's lips. "You want to join us?" he said.

"I'll make a good warrior."

"But you're a girl."

The words were a spit in the face. Taya gasped with humiliation. "So? Seever of the Nine Knives was a woman. The Rider of the Leafwolf was a woman." Taya pointed at two of the smaller warriors. "*They're* women!"

Uaua narrowed his slanted eyes. "I said 'girl,' not 'woman.' I don't care what my warriors have between their legs, so long as they can toss a spear. But *you*"—Uaua jabbed Taya's shoulder—"you are a spoiled shaman's daughter, grown aboveground where the only beasts are birds and squirrels. What do you know about the forest floor?"

Taya's tongue clove to the top of her mouth. No one had ever spoken to her thus. Blinking furiously, she swept her hands over her clothes. "Enough to claim these trophies!"

Uaua tossed back his head and roared with laughter. "You might have trapped a wolf with a carcass and rope, or even shoved a spear up a boar's bottom while he was drinking from the pond. But you're too weak to fight a man in battle."

Taya could not believe her ears. All her life, she had suffered the scorn of Yaiyai's clanswomen for being too tall and strong. And now this warrior would call her weak!

Talin had warned her against her temper, but Taya could not curb it now. It was all too impossible, too maddening, too... *unfair!* The pain and humiliation fused into anger, washing over her, burning her skin, blinding all thought. Her nails dug into her palms. Soft, hissing words slipped past her lips.

"I can beat *you*."

Uaua snorted. "Is that a challenge?"

Taya tightened her lips and managed to stare at him unblinkingly. "A test. If I best you in unarmed battle, you let me join."

Uaua regarded her in silence. Then he sighed and shook his head. "Go home," he said and turned to walk away. "I don't fight girls."

Taya could not let him leave. She would not return to her clan a failure. Death was preferable. She raised her voice and called after him. "You're not *afraid* of fighting a girl, are you, Fang Uaua?"

Uaua stiffened. Slowly, he turned to face her. He had no choice now, Taya knew. She had insulted his courage—the worst insult one could give a warrior. He would have to fight her now. To decline would be to validate her words. She leaned on her spear and gave him a small, lopsided smile.

"If I beat you," he said, "will you stop whining and go home?"

Taya nodded. "I will. But if I win, you let me join."

Uaua grunted. "All right. But I warn you, I won't be gentle."

"Nor will I," Taya said softly and tossed her weapons into the leaves.

She began rocking on her feet, sizing up her opponent. Uaua had obviously seen many battles. His beard was braided a dozen times, once for each of his kills. His chest and arms bore tiny, pink scars. Two of his teeth had been bashed in, and a finger was missing from his left hand. His muscles were very big.

Taya swallowed hard. She wasn't *afraid,* of course. She was never *afraid.* Her fingers trembled from exhilaration, she knew—not fear. So what if Uaua was strong? She was stronger. She was the Firechild. She could do more than just borrow animal traits. She could become whole animals. Even Talin couldn't always beat her. Yes, it was good that she had challenged him. It wasn't stupid at all.

The first blow struck her temple, knocking her down. Pain exploded, and blood blinded one eye. Dirt and leafmold filled her mouth. Squinting, Taya saw Uaua standing above her, his fists turned to hoofs. She rose to her feet.

Uaua smirked, and Taya tightened her lips. How dare he mock her? She'd show him. She clenched her fists and prepared to use her magic. But before she could draw it, Uaua's hoofs vanished and his fingers sprouted wolf claws. Taya leapt away, but Uaua was too quick. His claws tore through her mantle and shoulder.

An iciness filled Taya. She stubbornly ignored it. She was not afraid! Snarling, she sucked the air for magic, clenching her fists. Why did it have to take so long?

As she stood still, Uaua spun, lashing a lizard's tail. It slapped Taya to the ground. Uaua came plunging after her, an eagle's beak jutting from his face. Taya yelped and grabbed the beak an inch from her throat. Uaua struggled wildly, shaking his head, and Taya slammed her knee into his groin.

He grunted, and Taya scurried free. She needed her magic, now! But Uaua gave her no leeway to draw it. He lashed a squid's tentacle and grabbed her ankle. As she fell, another tentacle caught her. More tentacles encased her like a shroud.

Taya did not struggle. She had to concentrate. Uaua spun her slowly, till he stood behind her. Even slower, he pulled her against him. His tentacles became hard, sleek mandibles. One came clanking to her throat.

"Now," Uaua grumbled into her ear, "I eat your heart."

Taya's magic crackled the air. A wet, wiggling fish squirted out of Uaua's grasp.

Uaua could imitate animals. Taya became them. In midair, she shifted again, becoming a hawk. She flapped around Uaua's head and landed behind him, became a lioness and knocked him down. She leapt onto him, stretched into a python, and began constricting him.

When she heard him crying yield, she resumed her human form.

The warriors were gaping. Taya gave Uaua a hand and helped him to his feet.

"Th-the Firechild," he stammered.

Taya could barely stand upright, but she would not show him her exhaustion. She ground her teeth and managed a bow and lopsided smile.

"And your new Claw."

Chapter Five
Curing Chameleon

After running all morning, Aeolia felt ready to collapse.

She blundered down a dewy hill, her head spinning, mist swirling round her blistered feet. She had drained a waterskin and swallowed a bread roll back at the cottage, but what vigor that had given her was fading. Once again her stomach clung to her back, and her tongue felt dry and brittle. Her knees wobbled, she stumbled and fell. The tall foxtail brushed against her bruised back, and she cried in pain. Grimacing, she pushed herself up and kept running.

At the bottom of the hill she glanced over her shoulder. A weak cry fled her lips. The Stoneson was close now, so close she could see the scar that rent his face. Tears welled in Aeolia's eyes. She wanted to lie down in the mist, shut her eyes, and wait for the man to end her pain. But her legs kept running, even as they ached. She had to find Joren. She had to hear him say it wasn't true, that he hadn't betrayed her, hadn't broken his promise like she had broken hers.

Pebbles littered the valley, jabbing her soles. Thistles scratched her ankles, where once her fetters had been. A second hill rose ahead from the mist, and Aeolia struggled up its steep incline, knowing her legs would soon buckle. Hoary birches with bronze leaves crowned the hill, shadowing a cairn of mossy stones. Surmounting the crest, Aeolia thought she saw a man in the copse, and hope sprung inside her, but when she looked again the figure was gone. There would be no help for her here, and nowhere to hide. Somehow she'd have to hamper her pursuer, or die.

Panting, she dashed behind the cairn. With shaky arms she pushed one mossy stone, to roll it over Lale. The stone went loose, rolled down the cairn, thumped into the grass and stayed there. Whimpering, Aeolia whipped around the cairn. Lale was steps away. Aeolia shoved the stone, wincing. She gasped with relief when it began rolling downhill. It hit Lale in the shins.

Lale screamed, and Aeolia whooped with triumph. She returned to the safe side of the cairn and pushed another stone. This time it fell easily and rolled on its own. Lale, now limping, jumped aside belatedly, and the stone ran over his foot. His curses echoed in the valley. Heartened, Aeolia began pushing another stone.

This stone, however, did not budge. It didn't matter, Aeolia told herself; she had a whole arsenal. She pushed another stone. It didn't budge either. Urgently, she tried a third. This time, the stone seemed to... push *her*. The entire cairn, Aeolia noticed in alarm, tilted in her direction, as if being pushed from the other side. Aeolia glanced over the top. Lale had his arms outstretched in the air, his eyes shut tight as if in effort. He *looked* as though he were pushing, but he still stood paces away.

"This is impossible!" Aeolia cried. Regardless, the cairn tilted further. Aeolia tried pushing back, but to no avail. The entire heap threatened to crush her. Loose stones tumbled. Aeolia rose to flee, and as soon as she let go, the cairn collapsed. Stones buffeted her, knocking her down. She tried to rise and found her leg trapped under the stones. She pulled frantically, but her leg would not budge.

From the corner of her eye, Aeolia saw something move, a figure in the trees, but she could not turn to look. Lale's gray robes rustled above her, so close she could smell the ogress's blood on the hem. He reached for his sword, and Aeolia saw that his hand was bandaged, the cloth bloody. She had crushed those fingers,

Aeolia remembered, but it was a small triumph now. Steel hissed on leather as Lale drew his blade.

"At last," he said. "The Esiren Firechild, the one who can hurt him. I have come a long way to find you."

It was all over, Aeolia knew. For whatever reason, he would kill her now. She thought of the ogress, who had died to save her, and she thought of Joren, whom she would never see again. She shut her eyes and mumbled a prayer.

A voice, coming from behind Lale, answered it.

"Still beheading defenseless girls, are you, Lale?"

Hesitantly, Aeolia opened her eyes. The voice had come from the copse ahead, but she saw no one. Lale searched in bafflement as well.

"Old Lale didn't scare you, did he, girl?" the voice said, and it was as if the birches spoke. Aeolia strained her eyes, and then she saw the man. His clothes, his hood, and the scarf around his face were all speckled white and bronze, the same color as the birches. He blended into them like a chameleon. Even his drawn sword was the same color.

"Who are you, Forestfellow?" Lale demanded.

"An old friend," the chameleon man replied, stepping out of the trees. He removed his scarf, revealing a young face, green eyes, and short auburn hair.

"Spirit," Lale swore softly, paling. "Talin Greenhill, whom I carried over my back so many times.... You were but a boy last time I saw you."

"And I've been watching you since," said Talin, "waiting to catch you alone and unguarded."

Lale presented his bandaged fingers. "You challenge a man with a battered sword hand?"

"Better than slaughtering a boy's family before his eyes."

Lale took a step toward the younger man. "I should never have spared you that day," he hissed. "A mistake I don't intend to repeat."

"So we fight," Talin said and raised his thin, speckled blade in salute. Lale raised his own sword—a wide weapon of dark steel, the word "Bloodtalon" engraved upon the pommel—and the two men began circling each other.

Aeolia lay, her leg trapped under the stones, and for a moment she could do naught but take deep, dazed breaths. She was still breathing. Her heart still pounded. She might yet see Joren again. Steel rang, and Aeolia tilted her head and saw the two men dueling, dirt kicking up from under their boots. Lale's Bloodtalon slammed against Talin's thinner blade. Aeolia could scarce believe how close it had come to beheading her.

As her heart slowed, she realized the chameleon man had created the perfect distraction. If only she were free! She pulled her leg gingerly, expecting the pain of broken bone. Miraculously, her leg felt only bruised. Aeolia mumbled a thankful prayer. With trembling hands, she began removing the entrapping stones. They tumbled away, rolling over the grass.

She was dimly aware of the fight behind her, a hubbub of grunts and curses and ringing steel, of raining dirt and tearing grass. She could not judge swordplay, but when she glanced at the fray she saw smugness in Lale's eyes. She tightened her lips and tumbled the rocks with more fervor. If Talin lost she would have to run again. She only hoped he could occupy Lale long enough to let her flee.

Her leg could move now. When she pulled it hard it budged an inch, and the rocks above it shifted. A hot droplet splashed against her face, and Aeolia lifted her eyes and saw Talin retreating toward her, his shoulder pinked and bleeding. She pulled with all her famished body's might. Her leg moved an inch. And another inch. A scratch appeared on Talin's arm. And another scratch. Stones rolled across the grass. Steel clanged. Dirt rained.

Lale's onslaught was a terrible thing, and Talin fell back step after step, till he stood above Aeolia, with the tumbled cairn behind him and nowhere to retreat. His blade whirred, and it was all he could do to check Lale's blows. Aeolia could not bear to watch. She tumbled rocks with a fury, mumbling fervent prayers. She was almost free now, a speck away. Just one more tug, she knew, and she'd be free. Just one more tug. She pulled, and....

Talin slammed into the cairn. New stones showered onto Aeolia's leg, trapping her anew. She blew out her breath with frustration.

Talin rebounded, trying to escape the stones. He spun in a semicircle, blocking Lale, and fled into the open. It bought him a moment's respite, but no more. Lale's offensive continued unabated, and another scratch bled on Talin's shoulder. Aeolia frantically tossed the rocks, her fingers raw. The new pile was not heavy, and once again her leg was a tug away. She took a deep breath, preparing for the last, freeing pull.

She pulled.

Lale slashed.

She was free!

Talin's blade flew from his hand.

Aeolia stood up.

The sword clanged down at Talin's feet.

She had to run, now! Lale approached Talin slowly, savoring his victory. The Stoneson's back was turned to Aeolia, and she knew it was her last chance to flee. Lale raised his blade to strike Talin down.

Will my troubles never end? Aeolia wondered as she lunged at Lale. She hung onto the crook of his arm, and clung.

Talin scurried for his weapon, but Lale was quicker. He grabbed Aeolia's hair with his left hand, and pulled her head under his right arm. As Talin swung back his sword, Lale brought his blade to Aeolia's neck. Talin froze.

"Kill me and you've killed her!" Lale screamed.

The steel was cold against Aeolia's skin. She held her breath, her heart thumping.

"Kill her," Talin grunted, his speckled blade held above them, "and you've killed yourself."

Lale smirked. "It seems we're at a deadlock."

He tightened his grip on Aeolia. His arm pushed against her bruised back, but she was too frightened to feel pain. She stared pleadingly at Talin, and for a moment their gazes locked. His eyes were liquid green, and they somehow soothed her fear.

Talin returned his eyes to Lale. "So we drop our blades together."

Lale laughed—a sound like crackling ice. "Pitiful, that your pity should foreswear your revenge."

The two swords clanged against the ground. Aeolia fell to her knees. She touched her neck and breathed in relief finding it unscathed. Her heart still pounded, and she drew a long, shaky breath. Noting the lack of ringing steel, she raised her eyes. Lale was gone, running downhill.

"Why does he run?" Aeolia asked, Northtalk still strange to her tongue.

"To fetch reinforcement," Talin said. "Safer than dueling me alone, when you might sabotage him again. Lale has ever been the coward." He knelt beside her. "Poor child... what have they done to you?"

Aeolia realized how she must look: her skirt tattered, her hair tangled, her body bruised, her hands still stained from the ogre she had killed. She looked down into her lap with shame.

"Here, drink," Talin said, handing her a flask from his belt. Aeolia took the flask gratefully. She drank, the water running down her chin and dripping onto her neck. She had never known water to be so sweet, and she shut her eyes to enjoy it. When she felt a soft touch on her back, she looked over her shoulder. Talin was kneeling behind her, caressing her.

"Don't move," he said, stroking her slowly. His touch was sweet and cool, flowing like the water, melting her pain. Aeolia pulled away.

"Why are you touching me?"

He said nothing and continued caressing her. It frightened her. A man should never touch a girl, she knew. It was sinful. And yet she did not resist. His touch was too soothing. He lifted her hair and rubbed her back. His second hand caressed her leg. Aeolia swallowed. What was he doing?

"We shouldn't," she whispered. She had heard that if a man caressed a girl long enough, a baby grew inside her.

But again he said nothing. Aeolia shut her eyes. Something was happening to her. Soothing waves were flowing through her. She rocked slowly to it. The pain in her bruised back faded. Her head stopped spinning. Strength filled her again. She panted.

Talin removed his hands, and Aeolia ached for the loss of them. She opened her eyes. She felt healthy, restored. Even her empty stomach no longer hurt.

"Put this on," Talin said and wrapped his cloak around her. When the fur touched her back, it didn't hurt. Aeolia reached over her shoulder and touched her skin. She gasped. The cane's open wounds were now nothing but three more scars. She lifted her tattered skirt and looked at her leg, which had been battered by the rocks. Her skin was white and clear with not the slightest bruise. She rose to her feet, looking at Talin in astonishment.

"You're a Healer!" she said. She had heard of Healers. But then she frowned. "Why did Lale call you Forestfellow?"

Talin cleaned his sword with a handkerchief, revealing the word "Stormshard" filigreed in golden wire. "My mother was a shaman in the Forest, my father a lord in Heland," he said, keeping his eyes fixed to the blade. "I am of both bloods and yet of neither. I can heal bruises and cuts, but not mend broken bones. I can emulate a chameleon, but no other animal."

Aeolia pondered this a moment. A Healer and a Forestfellow. That would explain his accent, she supposed. Joren had once told her Healers spoke the same language as Stonesons, but she had never guessed they would speak it so differently, with vowels choppy rather than smooth, and r's that rolled on the tip of the tongue. Of Forestfolk Aeolia knew even less, not even what language they spoke. She hadn't even known they could emulate animals, only that they were wild and fierce, that they forged no metal and did not worship the Spirit who had created All Things. She knew so little about the Island's kingdoms.

"I'm sorry," she said. "I know so little about Forestfolk, you see."

Talin shrugged. "You'll be seeing many soon."

"What do you mean?"

"We're going to the Forest."

Aeolia cocked an eyebrow. "We are?"

Talin nodded. "Lale has a dozen soldiers in every town in the Beastlands. No doubt he is leading them here as we speak. To beat him now, I must face him where he is weak and I am strong, where he is alone and I have friends. The Forest. Lale will be unable to bring his army there; the Forest's border is patrolled. That's where I'll kill him."

"So what do you need me for?" Suddenly the Forest didn't sound so tempting. Aeolia did not wish to be anywhere near fighting; she did not think she could bear the sight of blood again. Besides, she was headed to Stonemark to find Joren, and that was in the other direction.

"What do you think I need you for?" Talin produced a stone from his belt and gave Stormshard two quick licks. "Lale followed you here all the way from Stonemark. He will follow you into the Forest as well."

Aeolia understood. "I'll not lure a man who wants to kill me, just for your revenge!"

Talin gave her a steady look. "Lale has been hunting you for ten years, girl. He will keep hunting you until you're dead. So you can either keep running till he kills you, or you can come with me." His voice softened. "We'll catch him together. You'll be the worm, I'll be the hook."

A shiver ran through her. A worm. Bait. But Talin had saved her life, and Aeolia could not bring herself to refuse him. It seemed she would still see blood before she saw Joren again.

She sighed. "All right."

"Good!" Talin slammed Stormshard back into its scabbard and straightened his baldric. "Now, are you hungry?"

The thought of food made Aeolia's mouth water. Before she could speak, her stomach grumbled embarrassingly.

Talin smiled. "In that case, I'll build a big fire, lots of smoke for Lale to see. We'll cook rabbit stew while we wait for him to catch up."

Talin turned to walk into the copse of birches. Aeolia stared at him a moment, then followed. If she feared luring Lale, her hunger overpowered that fear. Together they walked amid the white trunks, collecting dry branches and twigs from the moist earth. The hill ended abruptly with a steep slope, as if some huge beast had bitten off its eastern side. They descended the declivity slowly, holding hands for support. In the grassy valley below, the last wisps of mist were dispersing in the breeze, and there they set camp and built a fire.

Aeolia tossed twigs and leaves into the flames, creating abundant smoke for Lale to see and follow. When the flames were lower, Talin cooked a skillet of rabbit and roots. The smell made

Aeolia's mouth water. When the stew was ready and Talin handed her the pot, she forgot about the world, and ate.

"You must have been hungry," Talin said a moment later.

Aeolia glanced into the pot and felt herself blush. The pot was empty and glistening clean. "I'm sorry!" she said. "I didn't even notice...."

Talin tossed back his head and laughed. "Don't worry about it," he said. "I've got plenty more. I'll cook another pot. We'll see how fast you can wolf it down this time."

Aeolia squealed. "I didn't *wolf* it down!"

"True. Wolves chew."

She bit her lip. "I was hungry, all right? And you're a good cook." The ogre used to give her only turnips and sometimes pepperwort soup or porridge.

Talin filled a second pot. "What's your name?" he asked as he stirred.

"Have I not told you yet? It's Aeolia."

He frowned. "But that's a Stonish name."

"Of course it is. What else would it be?"

Talin shrugged. "Well, Lia, Esiren or Stonish, you have the appetite of a troll."

Esiren? That was what Lale had called her. What did it mean? Aeolia was meaning to ask, but then the second pot was ready, and all thoughts but of food left her mind. One pot more, and they doused the fire and set out east.

They ambled between the hills, walking slow enough to make sure Lale followed. Aeolia took care to shove her feet deep into the soil, break twigs, bend branches, and flatten grass. At one point, she tore off a piece of her skirt and hung it on a hawthorn. They walked so slowly, and their trail was so blatant, Aeolia expected to see Lale appear any moment. But he never did. By late afternoon they reached a river, and when the sun touched the craggy chalk horizon, they set camp on the bank, under an old hickory.

Talin caught a trout and sat to build a fire. Aeolia left him and ambled along the riverside, over the slippery stones. She had never before just walked for pleasure, and she wanted to feel what it was like. It felt strange. Even the physical act itself, walking without her fetters, still felt odd. But the ability to go wherever she wished and when she wished it—that was nearly unfathomable. She had never imagined it could feel so odd, having no chores, no daily routine, to look at the setting sun and not know what the morrow would bring. Aeolia smiled softly. Freedom. And yet.... The longing for a home, for a brother, for somewhere to belong—these were still her companions. She sighed. No, this was not how she had envisioned her freedom.

The music of the river grew louder as she walked, splashing like rain. Ahead grew an alder, stretching its branches over the river like a gateway. Daisies grew amid the tree's roots. Aeolia thought to pick some of the flowers for Talin, or perhaps place one in her hair like she used to as a child. She skipped over the mossy rocks toward the tree, held onto a branch, and swung around the trunk. She found herself staring down a waterfall.

For a moment she could not breathe, and her heart stopped in her chest. She stood frozen, numb fingers still hooked around the alder's branch, staring into the churning basin below. She saw the foam welter, the waves crash against boulders, the spray rise in a cloud. She had never been so terrified. She whimpered and blundered backwards, where she tripped on her skirt and sat down hard.

For several moments she sat dazed, her legs spread out before her, her arms hanging limp at her sides. And then, strangely, she began to cry. The tears just formed and flowed down her cheeks and fell into her mouth, and she could not stop them. Once her life too had flowed straight, to Joren, to

Stonemark her home. But her beautiful alder had hidden a waterfall of its own, and now she was falling, tumbling, crashing against boulders that altered her course. If only she could say that somewhere, however far away, was a brother who loved her, she would have been content. But she could not. Joren had promised to save her, but only his friend had come, and he had tried, for reasons she couldn't guess, to kill her. Had the ogress been right? Had Joren betrayed her?

"Lia! The fish is ready!"

Aeolia knuckled her tears away, embarrassed by them. She turned her head and saw Talin, the setting sun at his back, motioning her to return. She moved hastily over the boulders, and together they sat by the fire he had kindled. Aeolia nibbled at her meal; she was not hungry. They sat together and watched the flames as gloaming spread around them.

The fireflies came with darkness, as always. The first dot of light rose from the grass to swirl lazily in the sky. A second soon joined it, then a third, and soon the sky swarmed with numinous specks of floating, flickering light. Aeolia sat and watched them, and as always the sight calmed her. Fireflies are the stuff of magic, Joren would say. It is magic that glows inside them. Aeolia smiled softly. Magic fireflies. If she looked carefully, she could see four different colors of light. Some of the fireflies glowed white. Others glowed orange, and others red. The prettiest, Aeolia thought, were the fourth kind of fireflies, those that glittered like gold. Each color was a different magic, Joren would tell her. Four different magics, one for each of the Island's human countries.

"Are you finished eating?" Talin asked, tearing her from her thoughts.

"Yes, Mas—" she began, caught herself, and blushed furiously. "Yes," she finished hastily.

Talin wrapped up the remaining fish and placed another log in the fire. "Lale isn't yet in sight," he said. "We can afford a short rest."

"Is it safe letting him get so close?" she asked hesitantly.

"We can move as fast as him if we need to. As long as he remains behind us, we're safe. Sleep. I'll stay up and watch."

"You should sleep, too."

"You need it more. You've had a rough day."

She *was* tired. At the thought of sleep, her lids drooped as if pulled by weights. And so she did not argue. Talin leaned against the hickory, and Aeolia curled up in his cloak. She tucked herself in like Joren had always tucked her in, with the blanket folded under her like an envelope, to contain her warmth. She lay wiggling her toes, watching the fireflies and listening to the gurgling river. She remembered how she used to sleep back at the cottage, in the old barn with the cow and the goat and her dreams, and soon she found herself thinking of her former mistress. *Without her,* Aeolia thought, *I would not be here now.* She shut her eyes and mumbled a prayer for the dead ogress's soul. She considered for a moment, then prayed for the ogre as well. He had been cruel to her, but he had also fed and clothed her, had given her a roof when her father would not. She felt she owed him as much, at least. There was no one else to pray for his soul now.

Eventually her tiredness became too strong to resist, and it pulled her into a deep, dreamless slumber.

She awoke at dawn.

She pushed herself up, blinking feebly. Talin still sat under the hickory. He smiled at her.

"You let me sleep too long," she said.

He frowned. "Excuse me?"

Aeolia realized she had spoken in Ogregrunt. She felt her cheeks flush. So clumsy she was!

"I meant to say: You let me sleep too long." Her tongue still felt awkward around Northtalk's smooth vowels.

"Lale never showed up," Talin said. "He must have been tired, too. I didn't want to get too far ahead of him."

Aeolia shrugged one shoulder. Lale had seemed determined, but he had a clear trail to follow, after all, so he had time to spare. Aeolia rose to her feet, shivering in the brisk air. She walked to the river and knelt on the bank, and where the water pooled in a cradle of stones, she gazed at her reflection. What she saw surprised her. Her hair used to be straight and fine, its color a brown so pale it was almost blond, like almond peels or the fur of a mouse. Caked with mud as it was, it now looked dark as cinnamon, and tangled as an ogre's beard. Her face, once round and soft, now had a hollow look, which made her eyes seem too large. Was this who she was—a dirty, haggard vagabond? Was this how Talin saw her? She plunged her head into the cold water, scrubbing her face and hair till it hurt.

They continued their journey, eating a breakfast of grainy bread, riddled cheese, and leftover fish as they walked. Aeolia was careful to step around the fairy rings in the grass, even though Talin said that was only superstition. Why else should she be so cursed, she reasoned, if not for having stepped in one once as a child? As time went by, however, Aeolia found herself burdened by heavier concerns. Lale still had not appeared. They walked even slower that day, leaving a trail a blind man could follow. Every once in a while, Talin climbed a tree or crested a hill, gazing west. But the scarred Stoneson was nowhere to be seen. It seemed unlikely he'd lost their trail or given up. Perhaps he was so confident, he moved even slower than they did.

By noon they left the river, and Talin announced they were only a day away from the Forest. Aeolia had never imagined it could be so close.

They climbed a rocky hill, pebbles cascading beneath them. The waterfall still rumbled faintly in the distance. They ascended the scree slowly, using their hands for support. Several fallen firs, bedecked with moss and snails, littered the slope, giving them further handhold. Boulders crowned the hill, big as a man, and they reminded Aeolia of her old king in Stonemark.

She said, "My brother used to tell me King Sinther is made of stone."

Talin nodded. "Both in skin and heart."

"So it *is* real, not just a fairytale. I was never really sure."

Talin nodded. "You see, Sinther is a Firechild."

"A Firechild?"

Talin looked at her, and Aeolia thought she saw sadness in his eyes. She bit her lip and lowered her head.

Talin spoke softly. "Every kingdom has its own color of fireflies, with its own magic. Once a century, there is born someone blessed by the fireflies, someone able to wield their magic more than his kin. Such a person is called a Firechild. For him the fireflies glow."

"For him they glow?"

Talin climbed over a fallen log. He gave Aeolia his hand and helped her over. "When no Firechild lives the fireflies of that magic sleep," he said. "When a Firechild is born they begin to glow at night, and glow every night until their Firechild dies. Nobody truly knows why."

Blessed by the fireflies, Aeolia thought. It sounded enchanting. "But Sinther is cruel; his heart is made of stone, you yourself said. Would the fireflies truly bless him, if he is... wicked?"

"They say he was not always wicked," Talin said. "When Sinther was young, he used no more magic than any Stoneson—shaping stone, creating stone, but no more. But when he discovered his talent, Sinther moved underground, where he drew power from the surrounding rock and turned himself to stone. So much magic he used, they say his heart and sanity turned to stone with his flesh. As long as he's underground, nothing can harm him, and so he remains there and sends Lale to do his killings."

Aeolia pondered this for a moment. Could all Stonesons truly control stone? True, she had left Stonemark at age six, but she was still Stonish, and she had no power over rock. Perhaps the magic required special training.

"So Sinther is completely invulnerable?" she asked. "No one could ever hurt him? I've heard of a legend...."

"Yes. There is one special person, with a special power, who can hurt him. Just one."

Aeolia laughed. "I wouldn't like being that person! Imagine—Sinther would never let someone like that live. He'd send Lale across the Island to hunt him if—"

She froze in her tracks.

"She too is a Firechild," Talin said, looking into her eyes. "But her fireflies are of another color, another kingdom. She is an Esiren, and hers are the golden fireflies. All Esirens can share thoughts, but this one can also share senses, even pain. She is the only one able to hurt Sinther past his stone skin."

"Me?" Aeolia asked incredulously, and gave a mirthless laugh. She shook her head. "No, it can't be."

"Lale obviously believes you are."

Aeolia remembered how she had hurt the rat, how she had hurt the ogre. She remembered what Lale had called her: the Esiren Firechild. Fear twisted in her gut like a knife. No, she told herself. It was impossible. She came from Stonemark! She was Stonish, not Esiren! Wasn't she...?

"Lale is crazy," she said decidedly.

"May be," Lale answered her, "but a madman with a sword can still cut."

Aeolia screamed.

They emerged from behind the boulders above them, Lale and a score of Stonish soldiers, all with drawn swords.

"Run, Lia!" Talin cried, and together they stumbled downhill, pebbles avalanching beneath them. It came clear to Aeolia with a flash: Lale had never followed them; he had flanked them. Sharp bolts whizzed by as they ran, and one sliced Aeolia's sleeve, scratching her arm. She cried out in pain and terror. Another dart scratched Talin's cheek.

They leapt over a fallen log, crouched and pushed themselves against the rotting wood. Darts peppered the other side, jolting the log violently. Aeolia grimaced and covered her head with her arms. The log shook behind her, and she heard more darts whistle overhead.

"What are they shooting?" she cried.

"Stone splinters," Talin said grimly, drawing Stormshard. Blood trickled down his cheek. "They shoot them from their fingertips."

"We must run!"

Talin shook his head. "They'll catch up, if they don't shoot us down first."

As the soldiers neared, the barrage intensified, the stone darts buffeting the fallen log with a deafening rattle. Woodchips and tufts of moss flew. Tears burned in Aeolia's eyes.

"But we can't stay here!" she pleaded and grabbed Talin's arm, knowing only he could save her now. She saw him tighten his lips and glance around nervously, and she realized that he, too, was helpless.

Suddenly the log creaked, tilted, and nearly rolled over them. Aeolia glanced up and saw a Stoneson's boots above her head. With a grunt, the soldier pushed himself over the log and landed before them on the pebbly hill. Aeolia whimpered and cowered back against the wood. Blood bespattered her face as Talin ran the soldier through.

She leaned her head against the bole and shut her eyes. She heard more soldiers crashing down the hillside. One soldier dead, Aeolia thought, and twenty more above. She knew Talin could not fight them all. The rumble of falling rubble and charging boots roared in her ears like a waterfall. She sought Talin's hand and squeezed it.

"Talin...." She spoke hesitantly.

"What?"

"Do you think.... You said that... Lale will truly follow me anywhere?"

"Yes, Lia! But—"

The log above them creaked again, and two more soldiers leapt over. As they stood balancing on the slope, Talin slammed into one and sent him clanking down in his armor. He clashed steel with the second, kicked the man's stomach and opened his neck. More soldiers came crashing down from above.

Shakily, Aeolia stood up, her arms wrapped around her stomach. Stone darts whizzed around her head.

"Lie down!" Talin said and reached out to grab her.

Aeolia stepped back, looking at him. The soldiers rushed down toward her, shooting stones. One dart sank into her thigh, and she gazed at it numbly. She raised her eyes to look at Lale, who was sauntering downhill, smiling. Their eyes locked. Lale's smile widened. Aeolia stared at him, tightened her lips, then tore her gaze away. She turned and began moving downhill.

"Lia, where are you going?" Talin called. "Come back!"

Aeolia ignored him. He tried to grab her, but more soldiers came leaping over the log and engaged his sword. Aeolia continued descending the slope. She glanced over her shoulder and again her eyes caught Lale's. He was following, a thin smile on his lips. Aeolia widened her stride. Scree cascaded beneath her bare feet. She began picking up speed, until she was running, racing down the hillside. A stone dart sank into her shoulder, but she barely felt it.

"You wanted me!" she cried, surprised at the strength of her voice. "Come get me!"

Wind roared in her ears. Her skirt and hair billowed. The surrounding trees and boulders smeared into blurry lines. She heard Lale running behind her, felt his eyes on her back, his smile cutting into her head. The wind seemed to lift her as she ran. Her arms pumped at her sides. Her feet barely touched the ground.

She heard the roar of the river ahead. Cold spray wet her face. Her feet pushed off the rocky bank, and with a great, cold crash, icy water flowed over her head. The current caught her at once, pulling her at breakneck speed. She flapped and kicked underwater, eyes open and stinging. She saw fish shoot by, stoneworts, mossy boulders... and Lale, swimming behind, still smiling, his silver hair sticking to his scar.

Aeolia's lungs ached for air. She flapped mightily and her head bobbed over the surface. She drew a deep, ragged breath. The riverbanks rushed by her sides, all blurry lines of green and gray. The rumbling of the water grew louder, so loud it hurt her ears. A cloud of spray rose ahead. Aeolia saw the alder rushing toward her, daisies amid its roots. She took a deep breath and reached up as high as she could. As the current pulled her over the waterfall, she hooked her fingers around the alder branch, and clung.

Her feet pulled out from beneath her and dangled over the fall. She held onto the branch with one hand. Fifty feet below, the water crashed against boulders, foam swirled, spray rose in a cloud. Aeolia felt warm liquid trickle down her thigh.

In a flash, Lale came shooting beneath her, tumbling over the waterfall. In midair his hand lashed out and caught her leg.

Aeolia screamed. Dangling over the pit, Lale dug his fingers into her flesh. The branch Aeolia held creaked and bent.

Tears sprung into her eyes. The height laughed beneath her. Lale swung up his second hand and grabbed her waist. Aeolia cried and let him climb her, too terrified to resist. The height was too awful. She couldn't move for fear.

She shut her eyes, and behind her lids she saw fireflies, a million specks of swirling golden light, blinding her.

Her eyes snapped open. She kicked, and her foot found Lale's face, and she felt his nose crush beneath her sole. She kicked again, and his fingers slipped down to her ankle, tearing her skin. She kicked a third time, and then, in a great relief, she felt his weight let go. His scream was lost beneath the roaring water.

Shakily she pulled herself onto the tree trunk. She lowered herself onto the bank and crawled into a myrtle. It was not long before the soldiers arrived, and Aeolia peeked between the leaves to see them gazing down the waterfall. She heard them conversing but could not grasp the words. When they left she crawled out of the bush. She felt faint.

"Lia!"

Talin caught her before she collapsed. She leaned against his chest.

"I can't believe it," he breathed.

Aeolia blinked at him. She looked back at the waterfall. She felt confused.

"What happened?" she asked.

Talin lowered her onto her back. "You've lost blood."

Aeolia laid her head in the grass. *More blood,* she thought. *But this is the last I'll ever see.* She leaned her head sideways, gazing into the spray. When she shut her eyes and listened carefully, she thought she could hear, behind the roar of crashing water, a man laughing.

Chapter Six
The Rooftops

Roen dreamed he was turned to stone. His muscles were frozen and he could not move, not even breathe. He stood helpless, staring into darkness, yearning for death, knowing it would never come. Statues could not die. Blood did not course through them. They were immortal. Fear filled Roen, an ineffable, nightmarish fear, so thick it was almost tangible. His stone eyes couldn't even cry.

A Forestfellow woman stood beside him. She was nearly as tall as him, with slanted green eyes and two thick orange braids that fell over her shoulders. Roen thought her beautiful. As he watched, she too became stone, the grayness spreading over her, flowing into her mouth, turning her hair solid. Her eyes locked on his just before they, too, froze. Roen and she stood, gazing at each other, two sentient statues.

In the surrounding shadows, an echo laughed. There was no voice to it, only an echo, reverberating in the stone chamber where they stood. It was the laughter of King Sinther, Roen knew. He wanted to scream, to run, to hold the woman beside him, but he could not move. From the mists of terror inside him a single word solidified, a single word to somehow save his sanity, to cling to with the sliver of hope still throbbing in him. He grasped it with the tendrils of his mind. *Aeolia.*

"Aeolia!" he cried, and bitter fluid filled his mouth.

"Hush," said a woman's voice. "Don't try to talk or you'll choke."

Roen grimaced at the bitter taste. He grimaced! Urgently he kicked and thrashed, reveling that he could move. Had the beautiful woman returned to flesh as well?

"Calm down, son! It was only a dream."

Roen opened his eyes. Disappointment filled him. It was not the beautiful Forestfellow who gazed down at him, but a skinny, homely woman like a starving rat, with dusty yellow hair and a mug held in her bony hands. *Only a dream,* Roen thought, and then: *where am I?*

He surveyed his surroundings in the flickering candlelight. Walls of cloth draped around him. An old, ornate rug covered the sloping floor. He was lying in a bed of straw, and he wore strange clothes: baggy pants, a yellow woolen shirt, a rough-spun vest with big brass buttons. A pair of pointed leather shoes stood beside him.

"Where am I?" Roen asked. His voice was rusty. He remembered the stormy night when he had fainted feverish into a gutter. It was a wonder he could speak at all.

"Somewhere safe," replied the woman and brought the mug to Roen's lips. Again the bitter liquid filled his mouth. Again Roen grimaced.

"What is this stuff?" he asked, wiping his mouth with the back of his hand.

"Laceleaf tea," said the woman. "I found some in your pocket, I did. Lucky thing too, or the fever would've claimed you."

Roen sat up in bed. "Is there any left?" he asked urgently. There might still be a chance to save his father.... "Spirit, is there any left?"

"Calm down, son. You're still convalescing. Don't worry, Smerdin is recovered."

"You saw him? Where is he? Is he safe? Is he well?"

"Hush, Honeycomb! You'll bring the fever right back, you will. Smerdin is well, but still imprisoned in the Dungeon. I am a cook there." The woman grinned. "I smuggled him some laceleaf with his meal."

Roen shut his eyes. His father was imprisoned, but alive.

"I don't know how to thank you," he said.

The woman touched his cheek. "You don't need to, Roen."

Roen opened his eyes. The woman smiled at him. *I have judged her too harshly,* he thought. She wasn't as old as he had first guessed. She was probably closer to thirty than to forty. And she wasn't even all that homely, if you ignored the frowzy hair, and her smile was pleasant.

"How do you know who I am?" he asked.

The woman laughed. "All of Heland knows you, Roen Painter. Your posters are all over Brownbury. There's a twenty gold reward on your head, there is."

At that moment the tent flap opened. A man of about thirty years stood at the entrance, the sun at his back. He had a hard, grim face covered with yellow stubble, and a patch hid one of his eyes. His good eye fixed Roen with a cold, blue stare.

"So the ground man is awake," he said.

"He's as much a rooffellow as us now, Grom," the woman returned.

Grom ignored her and spoke to Roen. "You're lucky you are still alive, ground man. We wanted to throw you back whence you belong. If it weren't for Nepo here we would have. We might yet still."

The man let the tent flap drop. Roen heard his footfalls walking away.

"Are you Nepo?" Roen asked the skinny woman.

"Aye, and that was my brother, Grom. You must forgive him. The Redforts nearly caught us the night they followed you here."

"Followed me? What do you mean, where am I?"

"Go see," Nepo said and opened the tent flap.

Roen pulled on his shoes and stood up. His knees wobbled slightly, but he felt strong enough to walk; a cup of laceleaf gave more strength than any meal. He shuffled outside, blinking in the sunlight.

When his eyes adjusted, his mouth fell open.

He was standing on a roof, and more rooftops spread all around him. He remembered fleeing the Redforts here in stormy darkness. The roofscape looked so different in daylight he could scarcely believe it was the same place. It no longer looked like a field of black thorns. It was now a colorful jumble of maroon tiles, bronze rooster vanes, redbrick chimneys, gilded domes, granite turrets, and below it all the narrow, twisting streets. The variegated patchwork spread for leagues around, flowing across the mountainsides. The height and colors made Roen's head spin.

Scores of motley people crowded the roofs. There were elderly men with long white whiskers, pregnant young women, dour young husbands, frolicking children, even dogs and cats. Everyone was dressed in scraps, but decorated with tassels, scarves, kerchiefs, and baubles of scavenged junk. Some of the faces Roen recognized. There was One Toothed Ok, who years ago had escaped a public hanging, never to be found. Not far behind stood the buxom Friendly Fara, who had once owned Brownbury's most expensive brothel, until customers started complaining about missing jewelry. Next to Fara, a gaggle of children clutching her skirts, stood the famous Liz Purplerobe, who had yesteryear embarrassed her lord husband by fleeing his fists and taking his heirs with her. Roen even saw Burnface Bas, whose fearsome countenance had graced wanted posters when Roen had been a child.

An outlaw community, Roen realized—right above the law's nose. He had to lean over and hold his head. Unbelievable. And he had always thought it rats padding over his rooftop at night. No wonder the cheese always disappeared without springing his traps. And no wonder he never saw anything when he climbed up to replace it. Half the steeples and chimneys around him, he now saw, were actually tents painted with mock shingles or bricks. If he had not just stepped through one, he wouldn't have believed it anything but limestone.

"So what do you think of our kingdom, ground man?" Grom asked, leaping over an alley to come stand before Roen.

"Impressive," Roen confessed. "Do you lead it?"

The one-eyed man shook his head. His long, glass earring tinkled. "Every man is king of his own roof here above Brownbury, ground man. There is no queen and no law. There was no Guard until you led it here. If it hadn't been pitch black, we'd have all been hanged by now."

The surrounding men and women muttered agreements. The children made faces at him. They hated him, Roen realized, and for good reason. *Twenty golds,* he reflected. Even an outlaw would risk approaching the City Guard for such a sum.

"I'm an outlaw, too," Roen said. "I'm one of you now."

Friendly Fara laughed out loud. Grom spat.

"Up here we have only one rule," the one-eyed man said. "If you bring the Guard, you fall to the ground. I let my sister tend to you for a while, but now your time is up."

"Then I will leave," Roen said.

Again Fara laughed, and even Burnface Bas snickered.

"You have seen our haven," Grom said. "You cannot leave alive. You leave by falling."

Grom snapped his fingers, and the burly Bas grabbed Roen and pulled him toward the roof's ledge. Nepo rushed to stand before them.

"Stop, Bas!" she said and turned to face her brother. "Please, Grom. He's one of us now. Can't you see? I found him in the same place you found Ketya. It must mean something."

Roen gasped. The girl who'd robbed his workshop! "You know Ketya?" he asked incredulously.

"You leave Ketya out of this!" Grom snapped.

Roen now noticed that while most of the outlaws had the blue eyes and blond curls of Healers, others had fine brown hair and amber eyes. Esirens. Like Ketya. Were they all refugees, fleeing Esire's war with Stonemark? What were they doing on the rooftops?

Nepo put a hand on Roen's shoulder. "Ketya used to live with us," she said. "Her family had been slain by Butcher Joren, but she had escaped. For weeks the poor child crawled through Esire's snowy mountains, living on bugs and worms and Big Brown bark, till she reached Heland half-starved. Grom found her sleeping in a gutter. I found you in the same place." She turned to Grom. "You see, Grom? It must be a sign."

"It means nothing!" Grom said. "It's because of the ground man that Ket is now in prison."

Nepo looked sad. "I know it's hard, Grom. I love her too. She's like a daughter to me. But you can't condemn the boy to death for your grief. It's not his fault."

Grom turned his back on them. His fists clenched at his sides. "You did not see her when I found her, sister. You did not see how wet and frightened she was. I made a vow then. I vowed I'd kill anyone who harmed her again."

Roen took a deep breath. "Then you must kill Hyan Redfort," he said.

Grom spun around, his one eye blazing. "You speak high words for a ground man. Dangerous words. You will yet bring the Guard upon us."

"Are you afraid, Grom?" Roen asked. "Are you such kings of the rooftops that one of you is now in prison? But I'm not afraid, Grom. I want to free my father just as you want to free Ketya."

The crowd had grown silent around them. Roen feared he had gone too far, but then, he had nothing to lose now.

"What are you saying, ground man?" Grom demanded quietly.

"Only this: I will kidnap Hyan Redfort and make him free his prisoners. Then I will give him to you to deal with as you like."

The crowd stared at him.

"You're lying," Grom said.

"There are plenty of Esirens here. Ask any one to read my mind. I am not lying."

Grom drew a curved, silver-handled knife from his belt and leaned close. "If any harm comes to Ketya, ground man, if so much as a hair is torn from her head, don't think I'll be afraid to descend these roofs to find you. I will make you wish we had thrown you to the ground."

With that, he slashed his knife across Roen's cheek. Pain blazed and blood trickled. Grom grunted, turned around and leapt onto another roof, where he disappeared into a camouflaged tent. The rest of the outlaws dispersed to their own tents, until only Nepo and Roen remained outside.

Roen shut his eyes and mustered his magic. It tingled inside him. Shakily, he passed his hands over his cheek, healing it.

Nepo looked at him. "That's some healing. Didn't even leave a scar."

Roen shrugged. "I've always been good with magic." *If only we could heal illness like wounds,* he added silently, *I wouldn't have been in this mess.*

Nepo stared at him a moment, but then she sighed and smiled. "Now, that much magic probably made you hungry. I'll get you something to eat."

He followed her back into her tent, where she fetched him a wheel of cheese, three grainy rolls, and a jug of milk. Roen realized his stomach ached with hunger. He took the knife Nepo offered him, sat down, and began to eat voraciously.

Between mouthfuls he asked, "Why do *you* live here, Nepo? You're obviously not an outlaw if you work in the Dungeon."

"No, I'm not an outlaw," Nepo said. "But after my husband left me for my barrenness, I decided that life with my brother was preferable to life alone. I work at the Dungeon so I can spy on the Redforts and smuggle things to our imprisoned folk. I bring Ket candy sometimes, and candles. The poor thing. She only tried to save her Esiren friends."

Roen chewed his bread-crust thoughtfully. He was still not sure how he felt about the Esiren girl. Why had he tried saving her that day? What did he care about her? She had robbed his shop! And yet... Roen had to admit that he, too, would probably rob strangers if it could save his father. Ketya had only tried to save her fellow Esirens.

He swallowed the last roll. "Many Esirens are outlaws, I see."

Nepo poured him a mug of milk. "A moon ago, Hyan decided to arrest all Esiren refugees in Heland. He never explained why. Some Esirens returned to Esire and its war against Sinther. Others fled into the Forest. Some fled up here and live with us now. But many were imprisoned in the Dungeon."

"Maybe we can save them yet." The milk was cold and thick.

Nepo sighed. "You truly do intend to fight the Redforts, don't you?"

"The law is corrupt. I want to resist it."

"But mostly you want to stop Grom from throwing you off the roof."

"Mostly I want to save my father."

Nepo touched his hair. "I know, Roen. But it will be difficult. Hyan is powerful, and the rooffolk don't trust you yet. You must be careful what you say to them; they have been living this way for years. Some have had children born here. They don't want trouble. And Grom still blames you for Ket's imprisonment."

Roen swallowed the last drop of milk and rose to his feet. He wiped crumbs off his knife, then began to crop his yellow curls. Stubble already covered his face. *Good.* He wanted to be hard to recognize.

"Is Hyan still in the city?" he asked as he worked.

"He's been spending the last few days in the palace, the turnkeys whisper. They say the queen and he are going to make a speech off the balcony today."

Roen nodded. "Then I'll go there now. I want to see him. Do you have a hood or a scarf—something to hide my face?"

Nepo opened an old chest, rummaged through a pile of clothes, and finally produced an old cloak with a long hood. The brown thing was shaggy and moth-eaten, but when Roen donned it the hood pulled deep over his face.

"It belonged to my husband," Nepo explained.

Roen brushed off the dust and stepped outside the tent. He crept down the sloping roof till he stood on the ledge, above an empty street below. *Leather Lane,* he thought with a thin smile. He had bought parchment there many times, never thinking to look up. Before jumping over the narrow street, he turned to face Nepo. He opened his mouth to speak, but found himself lost for words. *This woman saved my life,* he thought. *Twice. How can I possibly thank her?*

Nepo seemed to read his thoughts. "I know," she said, smiling. "Go. And be careful."

Roen nodded. "I will."

He took a deep breath and leapt into the air. He landed on the next roof, scraping his knees on the tiles. His head spun. Not long ago he had leapt over these roofs heedlessly. Now, in daylight, the height churned his belly. The next roof was easier, though, and soon Roen found that, as long as he didn't look down, jumping became natural as walking. He became stronger as he leapt, and the brisk autumn air seemed to cleanse his illness away.

But if his body felt healthy, his heart was heavy. If he failed to rescue the prisoners, Grom would hunt and kill him. And Roen couldn't flee the city, not with his father in prison. Roen didn't know if Smerdin had been tried yet, but he suspected it made no difference. Hyan had been too clever. Legally, Smerdin *was* guilty; he hadn't granted Hyan a painting, and hadn't returned its price. Even if the Queen's Court hired Esirens to read Smerdin's mind, they would learn the same. So what if Hyan had arranged for the money and painting to disappear? The only person who knew it was Ketya, and she too was imprisoned. And who would listen to a refugee thief anyway?

The late afternoon sun hung low in the sky, gilding the thin clouds. Roofs, spires, and domes sprawled ahead, basking in the metallic light. Half a league east, Roen recognized the roof of his workshop. He forced his eyes away. The sight was too painful. He raised his head and looked up at the palace, which perched on the crest of Brownbury's mountain, soaring above the city. Sunlight glinted off its teardrop domes, so bright Roen squinted. In one tower's wall ticked a large clock with brass hands. From the crest of another tower flapped Heland's flag, the red firefly on a cream field. Roen had painted these towers dozens of times, always in awe. Today the sight rankled him. In this grand palace Duke Hyan was a guest of honor. It made all the gilt and marble worthless in Roen's eyes.

Why had Hyan framed them? What were simple painters to him? Roen could not imagine. In truth, he did not care. All he wanted was his father free. And his workshop back. And to paint again. As he traversed the rooftops, a plan formed in his mind. Hyan had to leave the palace sometime. Roen would watch until he did. Then, he would follow Hyan along the rooftops. At the right moment he would jump down, place a knife on the duke's throat, and force him to free the prisoners. Roen tried to convince himself it was possible. Noblemen had been assassinated or kidnapped before. Why not again? And after all, Roen had almost kidnapped Hyan once before.

Closer to the palace, the roads widened, and the jumps between roofs lengthened. Here lived the rich merchants and minor nobility. Their fine, paved streets were too broad to jump over. Roen would have to walk. He found an empty alley between Wool Walk and Scribe Street and climbed down a spout, glancing around furtively. The road was empty.

Pasted on the wall beside him was a poster with his portrait. Roen recognized the drawing; he had sketched it last moon. For a moment he stared at the serious, soft-cheeked boy in the poster, with the wide plumed hat. Had this truly been him only a moon ago? Roen felt like he had aged years since. Words were scribbled beneath the sketch: *Wanted, dead or alive (preferably dead), twenty golds reward.* Roen glanced around him. He saw no one. Hurriedly, he tore off the poster.

He began to walk, hood tugged low. He tried to seem casual, but his legs were stiff as logs, and he couldn't help but clench his fists. When he turned off Wool Walk onto busy Main Avenue, he held his breath. Nobody, however, spared him a second glance. They didn't recognize him.

After what seemed an eternity, Roen finally reached the palace gardens. They were fringed by a row of cypresses, beyond which sprawled grassy blankets that sprouted not a tree, bush, or flower. The palace glistened ahead. Roen soon found the main path—a wide marble lane stretching through the sward. He walked it quickly, shoes clanking against the marble. White statues speckled the grass around him, likenesses of past monarchs. Roen could almost imagine them glaring at him.

Townsmen walked the road with him, flocking to hear the queen speak. The Royal Guard was keeping order, men in burnished hauberks and purple surcoats, filigreed swords at their waists. Roen followed the flow of people into the courtyard—a wide, cobbled square beneath a balcony in the palace wall, in the shade of a gilded tower. The crowd was thick, and Roen tugged his hood lower. No one paid him any mind. To them he was just another townsman.

Up on the balcony, the purple curtains opened. The crowd below fell silent. Two servants in lavender rolled a red carpet onto the balcony, then straightened and blew golden trumpets. One of the men announced, "Her Royal Majesty, Healer of all Hurt, Sovereign of all Heland, Elorien Purplerobe!"

The queen stepped onto the balcony, and Roen and the crowd bowed.

At over fifty years of age, Queen Elorien was still beautiful, standing regally straight and tall. Pearled nets held her hair in buns and supported her brittle crown. Emeralds and sapphires speckled her flowing purple gown. A single lapis lazuli twinkled in the center of her forehead. Roen found himself thinking how he would love to paint her.

"Rise, my people," the queen said. Her voice quivered slightly.

The crowd straightened, and Roen noticed that the queen's face sagged, and that her eyes glistened with tears.

"I have an announcement to make," she said. "It might not be easy to hear."

The queen paused, and Roen felt dread curl in his belly. He did not like this one whit.

"For years," Elorien said, "I've been harboring a lie. It's time to reveal the truth. The children of my womb, the royal princes and princesses, are bastards." A murmur swept over the crowd, and Elorien continued speaking. "They aren't the children of the late king, as I've led people to believe. The late king, may the Spirit protect his soul, was sterile. My children are of a lover, a commoner like yourselves."

Roen released his breath with relief. For a moment, he had expected calamity. The news was shocking, to be sure, but not disastrous.

But then the queen continued. "Since my children were improperly conceived, they cannot succeed me. I therefore name my new heir Duke Hyan Redfort."

Roen's mouth fell open. For a moment he could not breathe and stood gaping, shaking his head.

"How can this be?" he whispered. "The Purplerobes hate the Redforts."

It made no sense. Even if the princes were bastards, there were still other Purplerobes, or even Greenhills. Why would Elorien name Hyan, a Redfort, her heir? Everyone knew the two houses detested each other.

Up on the balcony, the servants trumpeted again, and Hyan came stepping outside, smiling and waving. The fat duke wore enameled scales, and garnets studded his carmine robe. He began a speech, but Roen was too rankled to listen. Hyan, who had ruined his life, heir to Heland's throne! But soon Roen was stung by a deeper consternation. Now that Hyan was heir, he would leave the palace rarely, and only in a carriage, under heavy royal guard. If once he had been well-protected, now he would be unreachable.

How would Roen kidnap him now? If he did not, Grom would kill him, and Smerdin would languish in prison. Roen knew he had a choice. He could either storm the palace to kidnap Hyan, or storm the Dungeon to rescue its prisoners.

He needed an army, he knew. But could he convince the outlaws to become one?

Chapter Seven
Betrayal

Aeolia's clothes dried slowly in the dim, damp woods.

The Forest was a strange land, she thought, gazing at it silently. Cold, rotting leaves murmured beneath her bare feet, the only sound to disturb the silence. The clammy air hung foglike, smelling of lichen and humus and age. Trees huddled around her, dense as darkness, growing tall and twisted and bearded with moss, hiding the sky behind their foliage. *Everything is alive here,* Aeolia reflected, *even the boulders are more lichen than rock. And yet it's so lonely here, and so sad. Like me.*

She still shivered when she remembered how close to death she had come. Whenever she shut her eyes she saw the waterfall rushing toward her, felt the water flow over her head, heard the dizzying laugh of the terrible, terrible height. But she had lived, and now she was fleeing again. She hadn't seen Lale since his fall, but she had seen his footprints trudging out of the churning pool. And Aeolia knew he was following her. She could feel it.

She looked at Talin, who walked beside her, and drew reassurance from his presence. The half-breed had used his Forestfolk magic earlier, blending into his surroundings, and his clothes were now earthy green and brown. Aeolia felt safe beside him. Soon, she knew, she would be even safer. Talin's cousin, he had promised, was the finest hunter in these woods. Soon, Aeolia dared to hope, they would catch Lale. Soon she'd be able to go find Joren.

"Is your cousin's village still far?" she asked.

"We should reach it soon, I think," Talin said. "It's hard to remember. I haven't been here in several years."

Aeolia plucked some bark off a birch and juggled it idly. There was so much of Talin she did not know. He was a lord's son, and the son of a shaman. He had probably traveled all over the Island, having adventures like in the fairytales.

"Where have you been these past years, then?" she asked.

"In prison."

Aeolia looked at him. "You were a prisoner?"

"In Brownbury, capital of Heland."

Aeolia felt strangely ashamed. "Oh," she said quietly.

Talin nodded. "I escaped just last year, and have been hunting the prince since."

Aeolia gave him a sharp stare. "What prince?"

"Why, Prince Lale, of course."

Aeolia dropped the bark. Her tongue clove to the top of her mouth. It was a moment before she could speak. "Are you telling me that that scarred, sickly, *beastly* man is the *Crown Prince of Stonemark?*"

Talin shrugged. "I thought you knew."

"No!" she said, shaking her head. Lale, King Sinther's son! Aeolia lowered her head in despair. Suddenly her struggle seemed hopeless. What chance did they have, an escaped slave and an escaped prisoner, fighting an entire kingdom? She was only a callow girl. She could not fight such power. She could not kill her own prince.

She took a deep breath and opened her mouth to tell Talin no, she could not continue their quest. But before words could leave her throat, the shadows darkened, and she looked up, and her jaw unhinged, and all words escaped her.

A village loomed above her. It clung to the treetops like moss, a hodgepodge of rope and wood and grass, of bone and vines and leather. People scurried about the jumble, crossing swinging bridges, climbing rope ladders, swinging on logs tied to vines. Round huts speckled the branches like acorns. Water gurgled through twisting wooden pipes. Gardens grew on jutting ledges. It looked like something out of the fairytales Joren would tell her. Aeolia gaped, her head tilted back, feeling dizzy.

"I can't believe it," she said. "It's a village in the air."

Talin nodded. "All Forestfolk villages are."

"I get all dizzy looking at it."

"That's because you're a plainswoman, used to thinking horizontally. The Forestfolk think vertically. Rather than cut down trees and live side to side, they live up and down."

"Is this Yaiyai, your cousin's clan?"

Talin nodded. "Come, let's go find her."

Aeolia followed him around a clump of gorse and mushrooms, and there she saw a rope ladder that dangled from a swinging bridge two dozen feet above. Talin began to climb and motioned her to follow. Aeolia stood still, her belly roiling.

"What's wrong?" Talin asked.

"I don't think I can climb that high."

"Don't worry, it's safe. These ropes have been hanging here for generations."

Aeolia swallowed. "Somehow that doesn't make me feel better."

"Do you want to wait here while I fetch my cousin?"

Aeolia shook her head. Lale was following her, she was sure of that. She dared not stay alone.

"I'll climb," she said. If she had managed the waterfall, she would manage this.

She climbed the first rung. The ladder swung. Aeolia quickly pulled herself up another rung, then another. Cold sweat beaded on her brow. *I can't do this,* she thought. *It's too scary.* Only the memory of Lale's sword on her neck spurred her onward, and she climbed quickly, her heart hammering. The rope ladder swayed like reeds in a storm. Tears budded in Aeolia's eyes. *I can go down now,* she thought. *I can still climb down. How high am I?* She glanced down to check.

The whole earth spun. She clenched her eyes shut and clung to the ladder, frozen. Even Lale's Bloodtalon now seemed benevolent. How had she ever survived the waterfall?

"Are you all right?" came Talin's voice from above. "Do you need help?"

"No!" Aeolia squeaked. If he came to help, he'd only make the ladder swing. "I'm fine. I'll be right up."

She opened her eyes to slits and climbed another rung, stubbornly stifling the thought of the distant ground. With every rung surmounted, the ropes creaked like coffin doors. Aeolia held on so hard her fingers turned raw. She felt her heart would stop beating. Nothing mattered now, not Lale, not Talin, only getting *off that ladder*. And as the closest end was now the top one, Aeolia climbed, biting her lip so hard it bled.

Talin grabbed her wrist. He was leaning from the bridge.

"Here, let me help you," he said.

Aeolia gripped him, digging her fingers into his hand. With his help she climbed the last rungs onto the bridge. She breathed in relief and stood shaking.

"I guess I'm still thinking horizontally," she said.

Talin smiled. "You did very well. Come, let's go find my cousin."

They walked along the bridge. It swung with every step, and Aeolia kept her fingers twined around Talin's. Traversing the village, they crossed bridges, climbed ladders, swung on swings, and tiptoed across branches. Aeolia moved slowly, her head spinning. Wooden pipes wound around them. Treehouses clustered in branches high and low. Little clay bells, scrimshawed bones, and other charms hung from every branch. Aeolia spared these marvels little attention. She thought only of not falling.

Forestfolk scurried around them like squirrels. They were a slender people with reddish hair and slanted green eyes. The children frolicked naked, while adults wore deerskin and fur, and sported trinkets of feather, bone, and snail shells. Their language, which Talin called "Woodword", was quick and tinkly as jingling copper. Aeolia wondered how they heard words in its music. She must have appeared as strange to them as they to her, for many stared at her curiously. Aeolia lowered her eyes, feeling out of place with her mousy hair, round honey eyes, and ragged woolen dress.

Finally Talin stopped before a rope bridge lined with wooden spikes. Aeolia was appalled to see animal skulls surmounting the spikes, crystals set in their eye-sockets. At the bridge's far end sat a house even more horrid. The roof was woven of grass, but the walls were built of bones, row after row of them, held together with vines. Strange icons were painted onto the bones with what looked like blood.

"What is this place?" Aeolia asked, clutching Talin's hand.

"The clan's Core," he replied. "This is where my aunt and cousin live."

"Your cousin lives *here?*"

"It's a holy house for the clansmen. They believe the spirits of their dead inhabit it. The shaman lives here so she can talk to the spirits and learn the future."

"I don't believe in spirits," Aeolia said, more to herself than to Talin.

Talin smiled. "Nor do I, but to Forestfolk the supernatural world is as real as the tangible one. Come, let's go see my cousin."

They began crossing the bridge, holding hands. It swung with every step. *I don't believe in spirits,* Aeolia told herself. *I don't.* The animal heads, lining the way, gazed down with their crystal eyes. *They are dead,* Aeolia told herself. *They're just dead skulls, they're not really looking at me. Talin too said there's no such thing as spirits.* She squeezed his hand just a little tighter.

As they neared the house, Aeolia got a closer look at the bones. They were human bones, she saw with a shudder. The door of the house too was built of bones, but leather was stretched over it. Strange pictures were painted onto the leather, pictures of animals and hunters and strange symbols she did not understand. Talin opened the door slowly, and Aeolia found herself holding her breath. *I don't believe in spirits. I don't, I don't, I don't.*

Talin stepped into the house, and she followed him gingerly. She found herself in a dark room. The air smelled of incense, dust, spices, and sundry other smells she did not recognize. In the center of the room was a heap of small, arcane objects. Every curiosity imaginable constructed the pile. Aeolia saw batwings, crystals, horns, painted shells, gnarled roots, wood and bone carvings, balls of cobwebs, braids of grass, fur tassels, even insects in amber.

Then the junk pile spoke. "Your name is Aeolia."

Aeolia started. The pile of bric-a-brac was a woman, she realized, a woman so bedecked with charms she was unrecognizable as such. The strange objects covered her hair, hung around her neck, pierced her nose and ears. Slanted eyes, set in a face painted green, peered out of this jumble, all knowing. Fingers long and thin as twigs, with painted curly nails, tapped against one another. Indeed these were the only parts of the woman visible. It was impossible to tell her age for the clutter covering her. She could have been thirty, and she could have been three times as old.

"H-how do you know my name?" Aeolia stammered.

The woman's accent was heavy. "The spirits know, child, yes.... The spirits know everything. Shaman Eeea knows everything. The spirits tell her, they whisper in her ears the words of Northern talk. They are in this room with us, you see, touching you with their fingers...."

"Now that's enough, Eeea," Talin interrupted. "There's no need to frighten the girl."

The strange woman looked at him. "Ah, my nephew, the half man. You have returned to your clan at last? You have tired of your northern kith?"

"I'm here hunting the man who killed Mother," he said.

Eeea folded her hands in her lap. "An old grievance, half man. My sister has long joined the spirit world. She is at rest. So should you be."

"Not until I kill the man."

Eeea shut her eyes. "He is following you now, the scarred Stoneson. I can see him not far from here. He is alone, following your trail like a wolf...."

"I've come seeking Taya's help," Talin interrupted her again.

"Then I cannot help you," Eeea said tersely. Aeolia discerned bitterness around the woman's mouth. "My daughter has defied me. She has forsaken tradition, abandoned her studies, and left to join a pack of warriors." The shaman spat the word as if it tasted foul.

"Warriors?" Talin exclaimed. "The thickheaded mule! What was she thinking?"

"But Talin," Aeolia ventured, tugging meekly at his sleeve. "This is wonderful news."

"It is?" Talin asked, perplexed.

"Don't you see? If Taya helps us now, she'll have a bunch of soldiers with her."

Eeea turned her slanted eyes upon her. "What need you warriors, you who bask in firefly glow?"

Aeolia lowered her eyes. That green stare was too intense to look into. She could imagine the spirits hovering about the shaman, whispering into her ears.

"I-I need their protection," she said.

"Protection?" Eeea echoed. "What need you protection when no one can hurt you?"

"I don't understand. People *can* hurt me, I—"

Eeea smiled, showing large, glistening teeth. "Yes, child, you are young, you do not yet know your power. But the spirits know, child, yes.... The spirits know everything. Shaman Eeea knows everything. If you like, she could tell you more."

"You mean... my fortune?"

Eeea grew solemn. "Would you like to hear it, child? Would you like to hear what the spirits whisper?"

"No," said Talin.

"Yes," said Aeolia at the same time. She raised her eyes for just a moment, and Eeea's intense, green stare caught her. Aeolia tried looking away but could not. There was real knowledge in those green eyes, real power. Though fear swirled within her, Aeolia longed to hear what this strange woman had to say. Maybe, she dared to hope, maybe she knew something about Joren.

"Leave us, half man," Eeea said to Talin.

"Lia, are you sure—"

"Leave us," Aeolia said, never removing her eyes from Eeea's.

She heard him shuffle out of the room. She could not turn to look, could not tear her gaze from Eeea's eyes. She was transfixed by a power she could not plumb. The shaman reached out and took Aeolia's hand. The thin, coarse fingertips prodded her palm.

The shaman spoke. "You are confused now, child, but soon things will come clear. Soon you will be happy, safe as a grub in a log, yes.... You will wear the Northerners' gowns and perfumes, and sapphire and topaz and diamond.... I see flowers and friends and peace. You are so happy, a queen in the North. But then...." The painted face became concerned.

"What?" Aeolia asked. "What do you see?"

"It is best not told."

"Tell me. I'm not afraid."

Eeea spoke slowly. "I see the flowers wilt, child, and I see pain. Heat. A terrible land of flame, flames engulfing you, burning your hair, burning your heart. And then...." Eeea grimaced.

"What is it?"

The shaman's fingers twined together. She shut her eyes, and Aeolia could see her eyeballs moving behind her lids. "And then the flames die, and... it is cold, so cold and dark. There is a dark place, child, a cold and lonely place, and you are walking into it alone, leaving everyone you love behind. There is a man calling you to return, but you ignore him, though he is a man you love deeply...."

"What does he look like?"

"His hair is silver, his eyes gray—"

"Joren! He's my brother!"

"Brother? Yes, he is your brother, but not in blood, no.... He loves you, though, loves you like a brother. I feel great pain in him, great shame. He has done you much harm, and he is sorry. He regrets his wrongs...."

"Tell him I forgive him!" Aeolia cried, grabbing Eeea's shoulders. "Tell him!"

Eeea's eyes opened. After a brief moment of silence she smiled. "I cannot speak into the spirit world, child, only listen. And now the spirits have silenced and returned to their frolics. And so should you, child. It is never good to know too much of one's future."

"Tell me more."

Eeea sighed. "All I can tell you is this: one day you will have a choice, child, two paths to choose from. One path will lead to peace and safety, to friends and family and flowers. The other path will lead into darkness, into pain and lonely death. And you will have to choose."

"But that is an easy choice," Aeolia said.

"Then I have nothing more to tell you. Now go, return to sunlight, leave this place of shadows."

Aeolia left the room quietly. What did Eeea mean, Joren was not her brother in blood? And what was this 'cold, lonely place'? She shivered.

Talin stood outside, leaning against the house. "How did it go?" he asked.

Aeolia forced herself to smile. "You were right, it's fake. There's no magic here."

"I told you," Talin said.

"Now let's go find your cousin. I want to leave this village."

* * * * *

Aeoly was home alone.

Her daddy and brother had gone to the graveyard, to talk to her mommy in heaven. Aeoly was never allowed to go with them. Clutching her doll, she went to the window, stood on tiptoe and laid her nose on the sill. Snow covered the city of Grayrock like a sheet. Aeoly wanted to go out and play, but knew it was forbidden. She was never allowed outside. Daddy said she had no business there. Joren said it was too dangerous.

Big boys were playing in the snow. Aeoly watched them longingly. The sun sparkled on their silver hair and their gray eyes gleamed. They were having such fun, Aeoly ached to join them, laugh with them, feel the snow in her hands. Maybe they would play dragons-and-damsels with her. It was her favorite game.

She hopped away from the window and tiptoed outside. The snow crackled under her shoes. She leaned down and touched it, marveling at how white and cold it was. When she straightened, a snowball hit her face.

"Go back to Esire where you belong!" cried one boy.

A snowball fight! Happily, Aeoly scooped up her own snowball and threw it. It hit the boy's shoulder. He cursed and called his friends, and they all threw snowballs at her together. Soon she was soaking wet, and she decided she did not like this game. She tried fighting back, but more snowballs hit her face. Inside some were rocks. Her eyes welled with tears.

"Mind reader, mind reader!" the boys chanted, and one boy cried, "Joren should've left you in the gutter where he found you."

One of the bigger boys grabbed her hair. "Look at this hair!" he said. "Like a dog."

His friends laughed, and the big boy dumped snow over Aeoly's head, smearing it into her hair.

"Now this is the color hair should be!" he said triumphantly, inducing more laughter. What was wrong with her hair? Joren said it was the color of almonds, and her eyes the color of honey. She was crying violently now, the shame of her strange colors stinging more than the snow. She wanted to run home, but the big boy held her fast.

"Now," he said, lifting a handful of dirty, gray snow. "We must do something about the eyes...."

Aeolia woke up with a start. She opened her eyes but saw only darkness, darkness awhirl with a million specks of golden light, encircling her head, blinding her.

"Talin!" she called.

She reached for him in the darkness and felt him at once, wrapped her arms around him and clung. His body was warm against hers.

"I had a nightmare," she mumbled. "No, a memory, but it was like a nightmare, it was...."

Suddenly she realized what she was doing. She drew away from him, her face hot.

"I'm sorry," she said, so embarrassed she could hardly speak. "I was dreaming. I'll go back to sleep now."

She could not see him for the darkness, but she felt his fingers touch her hair, moving through it. It surprised her, even frightened her that he should touch her so. It was wrong, she knew. It was sinful. She knew she should stop him, but did not. His hand felt too good, a kind of strange, tingling good. It was different from when he had healed her. She had never felt anything quite like it. She sat still, letting him stroke her. The fireflies danced lazily around them.

He said, "Your hair is soft."

"Do you like it?" she asked dumbly.

His hand paused, then drew away.

"I'm sorry," he said.

"No, don't be. It feels good, so warm...."

There was a moment of silence. Finally he spoke, and it was as if he spoke to himself. "I am of two races, and all my life I've carried this burden. But a mix of three races, at a time of war and hate such as this.... It would be cruel."

"What? I don't understand...."

She realized she could see now. Dawn was breaking through the canopy, spilling over their camp. Aeolia saw the outlines of the twisted oaks, the tall mushrooms, the leafy forest floor. The fireflies slowly retreated into the gray boles, or glided down onto the fallen leaves to extinguish like sparks. As Aeolia watched one golden firefly glide into the trees, she thought she could discern movement amid the boles. She narrowed her eyes. She could almost see a white, scarred face, smiling at her.... But when she blinked the vision disappeared.

"Dawn," Talin said. "We should keep moving. I'll turn my back, and you can get dressed."

He stood up and turned his back. Aeolia stared at him, feeling strangely cold and empty. But with the night and fireflies gone, what spell there had been between them was now broken, and could not be retrieved.

She rose out of her fur blankets, shivering in her underclothes. She had left her tattered rags in Yaiyai and taken from Eeea some of Taya's old clothes. Aeolia unfolded the bundle, inhaling the scent of fur and leather. She began to dress quickly. The first item was a mantle of raccoon pelts, which Aeolia tied around her waist with a pouched belt. Next she pulled on doeskin leggings, which went up to her thighs. Finally she slipped on soft moccasins rimmed with fleece. The clothes were large on her, but they felt warm enough for a snowstorm.

The thought of snow reminded Aeolia of her dream. Esiren, the boys had called her. Mind reader. Joren found you in a gutter. Could it be she'd been adopted, was not Stonish at all? She could, after all, read minds instead of controlling stone.... No, Aeolia told herself, shaking her head. It was just a dream, just a stupid dream, not a memory at all. So what if she lacked stone magic? She came from Stonemark. She was Stonish. Sinther was her king, and Joren her brother. If Talin, Lale, or Eeea thought otherwise, that was their problem.

"I'm done," she said quietly.

Talin turned to face her. "Then let's keep walking. Maybe we'll find Taya today."

Aeolia nodded and they began to walk, leaves crunching beneath their feet. Gnarled roots hid inside the leafy floor, threatening to trip them, and so they moved slowly. Colors emerged with sunlight. The gray boles became brown, their leaves turned bronze, the rocks once more became green. Curtains of moss, hanging from curly branches, brushed against Aeolia's face, wet with dew, and she was reminded of Talin's hand in her hair.

Her heart thumped at the memory. She could still feel his soft touch. She recalled his words and pondered their meaning. Had he meant he could love her... like a man loved a woman? Aeolia did not think of herself as a woman. She was only a simple girl, slavery tattooed onto the back of her hand. She did not deserve these warm furs, let alone a man to love her. She had her brother to love her, and that had always been enough. He *was* her brother.

Suddenly she stopped in her tracks, her breath leaving her lungs with a short *oof.* A creature unlike any she had ever seen stood on a fallen log before her, staring with yellow eyes. The thing looked like a cat, but was much larger, sleek and black.

"Talin!" Aeolia cried, clutching his arm.

Before he could reply, the most remarkable thing happened. The great cat stood on its hind legs and seemed to... change, to melt into another shape. It all happened so quickly, Aeolia could hardly believe her eyes. Where the cat had been now stood a Forestfellow woman, tall as a man, with slanted green eyes and two thick, orange braids that fell over her shoulders. Her cheeks were tattooed with green stripes, and two large, green acorns were her earrings.

"Taya!" Talin called.

The woman jumped off the log and hushed him with a finger to his lips. She whispered something in Woodword.

"What did she say?" Aeolia whispered.

The woman turned to face her. "There is man following you," she said in clumsy Northtalk, her accent heavy.

Lale! Aeolia thought. *So I really did see him!*

"We know, Taya," Talin said. "He's been following us for several days. I came here for your help catching him."

Taya became solemn. "He Lale, no? The man who kill my aunt."

Talin nodded, and Taya touched his cheek. She mumbled something soothing in Woodword.

"Come," Taya said, turning to Aeolia. "I help you catch him. I warrior now. Other warriors help too. I show you to pack."

She spun around and disappeared into the trees. Talin and Aeolia followed. Taya walked with wide strides—like a man's—and Aeolia could barely keep up. She tried to doff her fear. Her plan was working. Lale was alone, Eeea had said. He had sparked violence in the Beastlands, and no doubt feared doing the same here, what with warriors like Taya, and so he had brought no soldiers. Now they would catch him. *And then I can stop running,* Aeolia thought. *Then I can go find Joren. My brother. He* is *my brother, and I don't care what anybody says.*

Taya stopped in a patch of beech. At first Aeolia was perplexed. Why had they stopped there? Then she saw movement in the trees, and she gasped. Forestfolk were standing all around, camouflaged in grass and leaves, blending into their surroundings. Aeolia had never seen such strange men, with tattoos on their cheeks, bones in their red beards, and flint spears in their hands.

Taya approached one of the warriors, a burly man with a bear's skull on his head. Aeolia knew at once this man was the leader. He was the strongest and tallest, and he beamed with the aura of command. When Taya finished talking to him, the man walked to stand before Aeolia. His chest and arms were very muscular, she thought, and his braided beard was thick.

"Greetings, travelers," the man said, his accent heavy.

"You speak Northtalk!" Aeolia said, delighted. She was not surprised Talin's relatives spoke the tongue, but she hadn't expected other Forestfolk to know it.

The man shrugged. "Clan once had Healer slaves, bought from troll for piles of fur, talk all the time." He smiled. "Me is Uaua of the Aaee, Fang of this pack. And who you be, sweet girl?"

Sweet girl indeed! No man had ever called her that before. But then, Aeolia had never met such a man as this chieftain, who stood as if his bare chest and wild braids were not animal but noble. And if she found his bold, approving stare embarrassing, she also found it heady. A giggly smile crept to her lips.

"My name is Aeolia," she said, "but no one calls me that, really. Talin always calls me Lia, but my brother, he always said Aeoly, and, well... you can call me whatever you want, I don't mind, I—"

Talin interjected in a dry voice. "I doubt our secret follower cares much about his quarry's diminutives."

Aeolia bit her lip. She had forgotten her purpose completely. She nodded briskly. "We're luring Lale, you see," she explained to Uaua. "You know, the prince of Stonemark. I thought maybe, if you let us join you, you can catch him for hunting your guests. He's worth a fortune of ransom, you know, and—"

Uaua leaned close and hushed her with a finger to her lips. "Ransom money is good," he said. "But sweet girl's smile is gooder. Me bring for sweet girl Lale's heart to eat, if only it make sweet girl smile."

Aeolia could not help but grin dumbly. "Isn't that wonderful, Talin?"

He said nothing.

* * * * *

He continued saying nothing most that day. The half-breed seemed to avoid Aeolia, and when she tried talking to him he answered laconically. Aeolia remembered what he had said, how they could never love. She wondered if that was the reason for his indifference. She watched him walking with the warriors, conversing with them heatedly in Woodword and not sparing her a glance. *He's probably planning how to catch Lale,* Aeolia thought. *After all, that's why he's with me. I am bait for him, that's all. Bait and not a jot or tittle more.* She felt a lump in her throat.

When she heard crunching leaves behind her, she turned to see Taya regarding her with cool, green eyes. Aeolia had to tilt her head back just to see the tall woman's face. Feathers were strewn through the warrior's two orange braids, and boars' tusks hung around her neck. Aeolia had always envisioned beauty as gowns and dainty jewels, but she could not deny there was a certain untamed charm to this woman's garb and bold carriage.

Taya said simply, "You is loving my cousin, yes?"

Aeolia furrowed her brow. "Love Talin? What do you mean?"

"You not know it yet. But you is loving him. I see."

"I'm sure I don't know what you're talking about."

Taya smiled lopsidedly. "You will."

"You sound like your mother."

Taya laughed. "I nothing like my mother."

"More than you know!"

Taya shook her head. "Our paths in life are different. My magic different."

Aeolia remembered how Taya had been a large cat. She asked, "How do you... become animals?"

"I am Forest's Firechild."

Firechild! Aeolia opened her eyes wide. A Firechild was blessed by the fireflies, and had magic tenfold stronger than others of the same race. Like Sinther, for the Stonesons, able to become stone instead of merely controlling it. Like Lale claimed her to be for the Esirens....

"It must be wonderful," Aeolia said, "becoming animals."

Taya shrugged. "It useful for warrior."

"You mean useful for fighting?"

Taya nodded and told Aeolia a story of how she had joined the pack, besting Uaua by using her magic. She told it so funnily, that soon Aeolia was laughing.

"And you turned into a *fish?!*" she asked, gleefully wrinkling her nose.

"And remember," Taya said, "he was... how you say? Half crab. I was ascared he is wanting to eat me."

Aeolia laughed, but then fell silent. Hesitantly, she asked, "What about the Esiren Firechild? Do you know what he or she can do?"

Taya seemed startled. "You not know?"

"No, I'm... kind of ignorant... in the ways of the world."

Taya glanced at the tattoo on Aeolia's hand, and comprehension softened her eyes. Aeolia quickly withdrew her hand and lowered her head in embarrassment.

Taya broke the awkward silence. "They can... how you say... merge minds. All Esirens can share thoughts. Esiren Firechild can share senses too. Big weapon."

"Why is that?" Aeolia asked.

"You cannot hurt Esiren Firechild. You only hurt yourself."

Aeolia felt fear trickle into her belly. Pictures flashed through her mind, of a rat fleeing its own bites, of an ogre feeling his own blows. The only one able to hurt Sinther past his stone skin, Talin had said. No, it was impossible! Aeolia tightened her lips stubbornly. Impossible. She was Stonish, and Joren was her brother. He was!

"Well," she said to Taya, forcing a smile. "Tell me more of your adventures. Have you ever tried turning into a bird and flying?"

"Ah, that is interesting story—" Taya began.

"Taya!" The shout came from behind them.

Aeolia and Taya turned to see Uaua approaching. The Fang stopped before Taya and spoke to her in Woodword. Taya nodded, smiled apologetically at Aeolia, and walked away into the trees.

Uaua put his hand on Aeolia's shoulder. "We go hunt Lale now," he said. "Don't worry, sweet girl, we catch him for you."

"Thank you," she said. She found his smile pleasant, but his hand was a little heavy on her shoulder.

He touched her hair, much like Talin had, only Uaua's touch was rough.

"You know," he said, "I can bring you back to clan. Make you concubine. Many women would be honored."

Aeolia cast down her eyes. "Thank you," she said, "I'm really flattered, but I'm going to live with my brother in Stonemark, you see."

Uaua moved closer. His stale breath blew against her face. His coarse fingers rubbed her cheek. "You are like real woman. Small. Quiet. Not like that Taya, who thinks herself a man."

Aeolia did not like his voice; it seemed almost dangerous. She was glad when Uaua turned and walked away, giving her a small wink as he left. She watched him disappear into the trees.

Suddenly she noticed that Talin had disengaged himself from the warriors and stood under a hazel, watching her. Finally! Aeolia had thought he'd forgotten she existed. She ran through the fallen leaves to stand before him in a patch of mushrooms.

"Talin!" she said. "Have you been avoiding me? I've hardly seen you today."

"Perhaps you were busy looking at someone else."

Aeolia frowned. "What do you mean?"

"We all need you, don't we, Lia? For revenge, or for money." He looked at her. "But you were more to me, Lia. You were more than bait. But you only wanted my sword, didn't you? And now you want his warriors. You find a stronger man to charm and leave the other with the bat of an eyelash. I saw how he touched your hair, Aeolia. Was it also 'so warm'?"

Aeolia understood, and it pinched her heart. What a fool she had been!

"No," she whispered. "No, I didn't... I didn't try to charm you, I... thought you liked me."

"I thought I did too."

His words hit her like a slap. She turned around lest he saw the tears that sprung into her eyes. By the time she dried them and turned back, he was gone.

* * * * *

Uaua returned the next day. Three of his warriors did not return with him.

Aeolia quietly asked Taya what had happened.

"He take us one by one," Taya said, her voice flat. "Alone. Slice necks so quick no scream. But no worry. We hunt him again, this time all pack. We leave only some warriors here to protect you."

Aeolia stood watching as the warriors fixed their camouflage and hefted their spears. *Spirit,* she thought. Three people dead—because of her. It chilled her stomach. She saw Talin sharpen Stormshard, and realized he meant to go with them. Trepidation filled her. If something happened to Talin.... Aeolia wanted to beg him to stay, but knew he would ignore her. This was the moment he'd been living for since his childhood, his moment of revenge.

And also the moment he ceases to need me, she thought. It filled her with a strange and poignant sadness.

Within seconds the pack had vanished into the trees. Only five warriors remained to guard her. Before she could object, the five surrounded her, leaning on their spears, forming a cage around her.

"There's no need to be so protective," Aeolia said.

"We need protect you from Lale," said one of the warriors, an albino with one ear. As Aeolia watched, he pulled a skin from his pouch and took a draft. Aeolia smelled spirits.

"I need to go make water," she said.

"Then go here," said the albino.

Aeolia tried to push through the ring of warriors. They kept her safe inside.

"Please let me go," she said. "I want to go."

"We need protect you," said the albino. He seemed to be the only one who spoke Northtalk.

"I'll be safer with Talin," she said. "I want to go join him."

The warriors passed around the skin, taking long swigs. They muttered amongst themselves in Woodword. Aeolia heard the word "Esiren" interspersed in their conversation. Go to Esire where you belong, she could imagine them saying. Just like the boys. Just like her father, who had sold her.

"Talin will hear of this," she warned.

"Talin never hear nothing again," said the albino.

"What do you mean?"

The warrior produced a scroll from his pouch. "We find this on third dead warrior," he said, and read slowly from the parchment. " 'A sack of golddrops for the Esiren.' " He grinned wickedly. "Much money."

Aeolia's stomach knotted. Again she tried pushing past the circle, but the warriors held her fast.

"Leave me alone!" she cried.

Drooling, the albino drew his bone knife.

Aeolia steeled herself, mustered her magic, and linked to the warrior. It was easier this time than the last two. She was too scared to have any qualms. Their minds merged, and she bit her cheek, hard. The albino screamed and dropped his knife into a pile of leaves. The other warriors unsheathed their own blades and drew closer. Aeolia released the link and stood firmly, prepared to fight as best she could.

"Cease this!" Uaua commanded, emerging from the trees.

Aeolia breathed with relief. Uaua had come to save her, just in time!

"I told you no hand her in yet," the Fang told his Claws, speaking Northtalk for her to understand. "Leave me and sweet girl alone. When I done with her, then we sell her."

Aeolia watched the warriors disappear into the trees. When they were alone, Uaua paced toward her, loosening his belt.

"No," Aeolia said. "No, Uaua, I don't—"

He slapped her. "You no talk."

Her cheek burned. Hissing words slipped past her lips. "Talin will kill you."

"Talin and Taya sent to be dead. They like you too much, make too much trouble. Now, now... calm down, me no hurt you. Me like Esirens. Like very much...."

He shoved her to the ground. Aeolia suppressed a scream, knowing it would only alert Lale. She tried to fight, but Uaua pinned her shoulders down. She tried to reach the albino's fallen knife, but it was too far. She arched her back, struggling wildly. She freed one arm and slashed her nails across Uaua's face. He struck her backhanded, loosening a tooth in her jaw.

Sudden rage filled her. She drew her magic. When Uaua slapped her again, Aeolia linked to him. He grunted, not understanding where the sudden pain came from. He hit her again, grunted again. Aeolia released the link and raised her knee into his stomach. As he doubled over she punched his nose.

Suddenly, Uaua's skin greened. His irises yellowed and his pupils narrowed. His arms slimmed and grew scales. His fists shrank and hardened, becoming snakes' heads. Aeolia bit her lip with horror. Uaua wrapped one snake-arm around her throat, slowly constricting her.

"Try that again," he hissed in a buzzing, inhuman voice, "and I break your neck."

His forked tongue shot between sharp fangs and licked his chops. Aeolia grimaced in disgust. She tried wrestling, wishing she were strong as Taya, but her soft limbs could not resist him. Uaua's one arm coiled around her thigh, spreading open her legs. The other snake tightened around her neck. She saw spots dancing before her eyes like fireflies. Blood dripped from his nose onto her chest. The fight began ebbing out of her. If only she could reach the knife!

Then Aeolia had an idea.

She feigned a submissive face. "Okay, Uaua, I give up," she said.

He leaned back, his slit pupils focusing on her.

"Then why you still struggle?"

"Because here are rocks and roots that hurt my back." She tried to look shy. "Please, take me over there, in the pile of leaves." The leaves where lay the blade....

Blood dripped into his mouth as he grinned. He brought his jaws to her ear, and his forked tongue touched her when he spoke.

"I knew you want this," he hissed.

He lifted her and tossed her into the leaves. She spread her arms over her head, waiting for him. Uaua lowered himself slowly. The albino's knife entered his heart quickly.

The blood washed her hands, like the blood of the ogre only half a moon ago. Aeolia winced. Again she had killed. But there was no time for guilt or mulling now. She rolled the dead man away and retrieved the knife. She allowed herself only a brief moment of relief before fear swept over her again. Talin and Taya were in danger. Lale was hiding in the trees. Aeolia stood, her feet wide apart, staring around wildly.

"We are alone at last," came a voice from the woods.

Aeolia started with a yelp. She dashed into the opposite trees, her heart thrashing.

"Why do you flee me, Aeoly?" The voice came from in front of her.

Aeolia spun around, running madly, her hope trickling away. He was toying with her. A desperate cry fled her lips.

"You have run too long," the voice said soothingly. "You are tired. Come to me, let me relieve your weary head."

"Leave me alone!" she cried. "What do you want from me?"

"Your life," he answered, his voice coming from in front of her again.

Aeolia turned and ran, stumbling over roots and rocks. The woods became tangled as ogres' hair. Branches snagged her, roots tripped her, but still Aeolia ran, never looking back. On and on she raced, crashing through the foliage, swimming through an orange sea. Up ahead she saw a cluster of laurels. She dashed into one and hid in its leaves, panting.

"Where are you hiding, little Aeoly?" she heard him say.

Aeolia peeked through the leaves and saw him, his gray robes moving amid the bushes, gliding like a ghost. She remained still. He couldn't see her. She dared hope he'd miss her and walk on.

"Do you know how I first found you?" Lale asked, walking amid the bushes. "A man turned you into me, the only man who knew you are a Firechild."

Aeolia winced, his words like the blows of a cane.

"He tells me many things, you see," Lale said. "I am his best friend. He loves me better than he loves you, who had once been his fostered sister."

Tears burned in Aeolia's eyes. Her mouth curved bitterly. Was it true? She remembered her dream. In that dream she had been adopted (found in a gutter?!), raised Stonish, and sold before discovering her true heritage. She remembered Eeea's words. Not your brother in blood... Joren was not her brother. He had lied to her. Aeolia bit her trembling lip not to cry out loud.

Lale continued speaking. "They call him Butcher Joren, I am told. Do you know how many thousands he's killed? I have long lost count. He told me where you were, and do you know why? Because he will never find peace, Aeoly.... He will never find peace until you die."

Aeolia's heart seemed to shatter inside her. "NO!" she screamed. "You lie!"

Lale's sword whirred at her. Aeolia leapt aside, and the blade caught in the bush. She began fleeing through the thick flora. Branches and bushes slapped her, cutting her face and arms.

Something grabbed her ankle and she pitched forward. She felt a hand pulling her leg. She kicked wildly, wailing. Her foot hit something and she heard Lale grunt. She kicked again and freed herself. She scurried to her feet and glanced over her shoulder.

The sword swung at her. Aeolia ducked, and the blade whistled over her head and sunk into a tree. She lashed her knife and scratched Lale's stomach. Bloodtalon flashed down, and Aeolia rolled aside. The blade hit the ground, severing a strand from her hair. Aeolia lashed again, slicing Lale's leg, and then she scrambled up and ran.

She knew she couldn't run forever. Already she felt weakness slowing her. Her plan had failed. Lale had outsmarted her again. And now she was going to die. She'd never even see Talin again.

And then, a miracle happened, and she did.

Talin stood amid the trees ahead, Taya and the other warriors around him. Aeolia had found the hunting expedition.

She rushed to Talin, blubbering with fear. "He's right here, right behind me, he grabbed my leg...."

Talin was about to reply, when the Forestfolk swarmed over them. A dozen hands grabbed Talin and yanked his sword away. Two warriors grabbed Aeolia and bent her arms behind her back. When Taya tried to stop her comrades, they did the same to her. Soon the three were held helpless, like sheep to be shorn.

Lale stepped out from the trees. Blood trickled from his scratches, but he was otherwise unharmed. He *tsk*ed, shaking his head.

"So innocent, girl, trying to sell me for ransom," the prince said and smiled sourly. "If you knew my father, you'd know the Esiren Firechild is worth more golddrops to him than his son."

He paced toward her, Bloodtalon in hand.

Aeolia knew she was going to die. She wiggled her head free and looked into Talin's eyes.

"I'm sorry, Talin," she whispered, and words just slipped out of her mouth. "I love you so much."

She didn't mean to say that. She could not guess why she did. *I barely know him; how could I love him?* She opened her mouth to take it back, but Lale interrupted her, tapping his cheek.

"And after all," the prince said, "there is nothing worse than watching the deaths of your beloved. Isn't that so, Talin? I think we both learned that lesson. Spirit, did we learn it." He turned to face Aeolia. "That is why, Aeoly, before you die I want you to watch me kill your two friends. Starting with the woman."

Aeolia opened her mouth to scream, but the Forestfolk's palms muffled her cry. She watched, tears burning down her cheeks, as Taya was led forward. The warrior woman walked straight, not suffering herself to be dragged.

Lale placed his hands on Taya's shoulders. Slowly he spun her around, as in a languid dance, till he stood behind her. Graceful as a lover, he pulled her against him, his arm across her chest. Gently he laid his blade on her neck.

Aeolia linked to her. *Turn into a fish!* she pleaded in Taya's mind. *Turn into a fish and squirt away!*

Taya gazed at her, green eyes sangfroid. A droplet of blood trailed down her neck.

"Release the link," Taya said calmly. Trembling, Aeolia obeyed.

Taya smiled at her—a small, lopsided smile. And then she grabbed the blade. Blood flowed between her fingers. She winked. Then, in a sudden movement, Taya pulled down, plunging Bloodtalon into her stomach, through her and into Lale.

Lale screamed behind her. Blood filled his mouth.

"Help me!" he screamed. "I'll pay anything! Just help me!"

Aeolia fell crying as the Forestfolk rushed forward. Through her tears she saw them lift Lale, Taya pinned to his stomach. She saw Talin fighting the Forestfolk, trying to reach the skewered bodies, but the Forestfolk fled into the trees. Everything was red. She shut her eyes, but only saw Taya wink, Taya bleeding, Taya pinned to Lale like a collector's butterfly.

"I killed her," she cried as Talin knelt beside her. "I killed her, Talin, I killed her."

He held her, and she sobbed against his chest.

* * * * *

Aeolia and Talin fled deep into the forest, where no foot had ever stepped, where only loneliness dwelled. They sat in an ocean of orange leaves. A soft breeze blew and the trees swayed like waves, whispering. Dry leaves glided and danced. Aeolia thought of all the horrors she had seen, how Lale was hunting her, how Joren had betrayed her, how Talin and she could not consummate their love—and her life seemed lost. Her tears fell into her lap like little jewels. She let her hair drape over her eyes, to hide them.

She felt Talin near, his body warm, his hand once more smoothing her hair. He held her fingers, and her heart fluttered so hard it hurt. His hand was so warm, her fingers felt more alive than her entire body. She looked up at him. His eyes were soft, deep green like fathomless wells. He held her. She parted her lips. They kissed in the saddest and most tender moment of her life.

She wondered if she'd ever see Joren again.

Chapter Eight
Awakening

Earth enveloped her, pushing against her skin. It felt cool and good. She took a mouthful of the nourishing moistness and swallowed, as if she could swallow life itself into her belly. The pain was gone now. For a long time it had been with her, making her twitch and wiggle. But now it had faded, leaving only a hazy contentment in her mind, a kind of languor halfway between wakefulness and slumber. It became hard to think. It was easy to forget, to burrow deeper into the cool soil of life and never reemerge. And yet... something disturbed her, some tingling in her belly. It meant something, she knew. She strained to remember. She had not always been this long, soil-eating strip. Once she had had a form and a name. Taya. Yes. Taya of light and leaves, not of dirt and darkness. Slowly the memory flooded her.

Aeolia had seemed so frightened, her lips trembling like a child's. Turn into a fish and squirt away, the girl had pleaded, and Taya had been tempted, but now she had Lale alone. If she changed shape the Forestfolk would surge. And so Taya stayed human, smiled and grabbed the blade. It was so sharp she felt nothing when she impaled herself, only satisfaction hearing Lale scream behind her. The warriors carried them away, skewered together. Then the pain came, sharp and blinding, and weakness replaced her draining lifeblood.

"Get me a Healer!" Lale screamed beneath her. "Get me a Healer, you louts, I'm dying! I'll pay anything!"

"What do we do?" one warrior asked.

"The Aaee clan has a Healer slave," another replied. "His wound is a slow death. He might last the journey. He'll pay a fortune if he lives."

"I'll pay anything!" Lale screeched. "And get this strumpet off me!"

Taya's eyes were lolling. She felt herself slipping away. She took a painful breath and tightened her lips. Pain exploded as she mustered her magic, more than she'd ever used, so much magic it almost burned her away. She screamed as she morphed, turning into the smallest animal she could manage, smaller than she'd ever gone before, smaller than she'd ever thought possible. She turned into a worm.

Thus diminished, the impaling blade split her in two. Her halves fell to the forest floor. Writhing in pain, Taya crawled away, leaving her tail behind. Her mind fluttered with fear and disgust. She burrowed into the moist soil, crawling deep into the ground, down into the nourishment. She'd be fine now, she knew. As a worm, she would heal. Calmness swept over her, and she slept.

How long had she lain here, convalescing underground? Taya did not know. It felt like long. *Why not stay longer?* came a thought like a whisper. She could stay forever vermian, curled in the damp softness, eating, letting the soil filter through her. It was nice here, so cool....

But no. She could not. The magic would not let her. She felt it inside her, tingling, like an elusive sneeze. The more she thought of it, the more unbearable it became. She had mustered much magic, and it had lasted long, but now it was itching. She would have to release it sooner or later, she knew. But was it time? Was she healed yet? Was her... tail grown back? She didn't want to become human and find she was missing her feet.... She tried a wiggle. She felt whole enough. There was only one way to find out.

She wriggled up through layers of loam, humus, leafmold, moss, rotting leaves, and finally into sunlight. She lay a moment, hesitating. Then she let go of her magic. It was a great feeling of relief, like a breath of air to a drowning man. She bulged and swelled, felt bones form within her, sprouted limbs and hair. She thought she felt feet, but she wasn't sure.

When all magic left her, she lay still. Damp leaves murmured beneath her. Sunlight fell on her shut lids. And she felt no pain. In fact, she felt healthier than she'd ever felt. But there was only one way to be sure. With a deep breath, Taya opened her eyes and looked down.

Her leggings were torn, her moccasins were tattered, but her lower half had not a scratch. She was whole again. And strangely, she did not feel glad.

She stared at her new legs and felt only a lump in her throat. Her body was whole again, but she was not the Taya she once had been. She touched the tattoos on her cheeks. Suddenly she loathed them. Shame and humiliation rose like bile in her throat. She had been a fool, thinking she could become a warrior. Uaua had been right. She was only a spoiled girl. All her dreams had been built on nonexistent frameworks.

She thought of Aeolia her friend and of Talin her cousin. They, at least, had each other, and a purpose to their lives. But she, Taya, had been left here, alone, not dead, but with no life to live.

Slowly she rose to her new feet. She brushed dirt off her bearskin mantle and heaved a deep sigh.

"It's time to go home," she said and started walking.

* * * * *

She reached Yaiyai four days later.

She climbed the rope ladder and entered the airborne village. She walked along its bridges, amid the clusters of tree houses, while children scuttled underfoot. Water gurgled in wooden pipes that wound around her. Woodsmoke curled out of grass roofs. The smell of fresh and spicy food filled the air. Taya sighed. Living here would be dull, but not a bad life. She would become shaman in time, and if she had no adventure or glory, at least she would have respect and power in her clan. Perhaps she would even marry. A dull but peaceful life. And if it did not fit her, Taya knew it was her destiny.

"Hello, Blueberry!"

Taya turned her head. The call had come from a group of aging men sitting in hammocks that hung from a branch.

"What do you want?" she demanded.

"Some of those sweets they say you've been handing out," one man said. His friends' laughter was not avuncular.

"What are you talking about?"

"It's the whole village that's talking. Come on, sweet berry, give us a sweet time."

Taya walked away in disgust. She had grown up knowing those men. They had been friends to her father before he had died of bluebone several winters past. How dared they talk to her like that! She had been away fighting Lale in the woods, and they treated her like a trollop. It offended her but mostly made her sick.

She crossed several swinging bridges, climbed a series of ladders, and gradually forgot the men. She found herself anxious to see her mother, despite their recent disagreements. How she'd surprise her! Perhaps Eeea would make her a plate of roasted grubs and mushrooms, Taya's favorite, and some honeycombs and berries for dessert. Taya licked her lips.

Imagining the taste of food on her tongue, Taya spied Ooor standing ahead on a branch. Ooor was the strongest and handsomest bachelor in the village, every girl's dream. His teeth were white and straight, his muscles were corded, and he had three braids in his red beard. He was two years older than Taya, and had always ignored her when they were growing up. Now, however, he smiled and waved.

"Hi, Taya!" he called.

"Hello, Ooor," she replied, and was surprised to find a small, lopsided smile on her lips. She had always told herself she wasn't interested in men, but Ooor's admiring gaze felt good on her.

"I missed you," he said. His teeth sparkled.

"Really? Well... I missed you, too."

Taya Tomboy, missed by Ooor! Imagine that. Perhaps things at home weren't so bad, she thought. If Ooor liked her, things might turn out fine. That would show those cub-eyed, empty-headed girls who had always called her a hoyden. Yes, perhaps things weren't so bad at all.

"Tell me," Ooor said, "what are these stripes on your cheeks?"

"Do you like them?" Taya asked.

"I'll tell you what I like." He leaned closer. "I liked it yesterday, when you wiggled your tongue in my ear."

Taya stepped back. "What do you mean?"

Ooor pulled her close and stuck out his tongue. "Let me show you."

Taya shoved him away. "You're crazy," she said and walked away.

The whole clan was losing its mind, she thought. She was surprised to find herself close to tears. Was she welcomed nowhere, not even at home? Why was everybody acting so strange, taunting her so? What had she ever done to them?

Her spirits low, she reached the clan's Core, where she had lived with her mother. The house looked dreary as ever, with its bone walls and skull bridge. But home was home, and Taya drew comfort from the sight. She told herself that when she is shaman she would spruce up the place. Smoke was rising out of the grass roof, and as Taya crossed the bridge she could smell her mother's cooking. She swung open the door.

Her mother stood inside, bedecked as ever in batwings, cobwebs, dried leaves, gnarled roots, crystals, shells, and endless other clutter that covered her head to toe. The only parts of her visible were her eyes, which now blazed, and her knotty fists, which rested on her hips.

"So there you are!" the shaman said and slapped Taya across the face.

Taya stared in shock, her cheek burning.

"What—" she managed stuttering. "What—"

"Don't dare talk to me after how you've shamed me, dallying with your clansmen, letting them touch you.... And now you're getting tattoos! After all the years I've been a mother to you...." Eeea looked ready to cry. "Just get out. Get out and don't come back."

Taya fled as Eeea tried slapping her again. She raced along the bridge, tears welling in her throat. She stood outside, legs shaking. What was happening? Was this all some terrible dream?

Ooor! It must be him! He was always bragging about girls, he must have been telling stories about her. Taya's rage flared. How dare he! She'd show him. She'd rip his lying tongue out!

She marched back through the village, enraged enough to shed blood. When she reached Ooor, she paused, steaming. The lying boar's-dropping stood before her, fondling a scantily dressed girl. Their mouths were glued together, and neither noticed her. Taya clenched her fists. *He flirts with me, and a minute later he's petting some trollop! I'll turn into a ferret and bite off his lousy—*

The girl looked up, and Taya felt the blood leave her face. Looking at the girl was like looking into a mirror. They had the exact same face.

The girl smiled and winked, then stuck her tongue into Ooor's ear.

Taya let out a strangled yelp, turned around, and ran.

She fled down swinging bridges and rope ladders, and all but crashed to the forest floor. She ran between the boles as if all the horrors of the world were following. She left Yaiyai far behind, running deep into the silent woods, running till she could run no more. She fell panting into the moss.

"It's just a dream," she told herself. "It's just a bad dream. I never met Lale, I was never a worm, I was never...."

…split in two.

Taya moaned. Split in two!

Of course! After becoming a worm, she had been cut in half. *Both* her halves had grown. And now her twin was ruining her reputation, upsetting her mother, and taking over her clan.

Taya's anger bubbled. Yaiyai was *her* clan. She would not share it. Not with that cheap, sleazy, cunning, darned... *Ayat!* Her twin had grown warped, not like her at all. The girl's brains were in her pants. Lower half indeed! She'd have to get rid of her, Taya decided. And if she couldn't, she herself would leave. Yaiyai was too small for the two of them.

Fists clenched, Taya marched back to the village, prepared to confront her evil twin.

* * * * *

She found Ayat in the center of the village, flirting with some young men. Her blood boiling, Taya marched up to her twin and grabbed her arm. The young men stumbled back, eyes and mouths wide with shock.

The twins stared at each other, and Taya shuddered. They looked frighteningly alike, though Taya now noticed that Ayat, grown from her lower half, was missing the green stripes on her cheeks.

"Hello, Taya," Ayat said calmly. "You look upset. Were you surprised to find me here?"

"Get out," Taya hissed. "This is my clan."

"I got here first. If anyone should leave, it's you."

Taya saw Ooor standing among the surrounding men, rubbing his eyes. His friends gaped and muttered amongst themselves. How many of them had Ayat bedded already?

"You're not me!" Taya shouted at her twin. "You're nothing like me."

Ayat smiled. "You mean I'm not a lonely virgin? I'm doing a better job being you than you ever had. People *like* me."

"They like your body, maybe."

"It's your body, too, you know."

"You disgust me."

Ayat's smile was condescending. "Look. Why don't we live here together? We'll have fun. Many boys dream of twins, you know."

"I'll never live anywhere with you." Taya pointed at her twin and spoke to Ooor and his friends. "This woman is an imposter!"

Ayat smiled sadly. "I'm sorry it has to be this way," she whispered. "We could have made a fine couple."

Saying that, Ayat faced the young men and pouted like a baby. "Please help me," she said. "She thinks I'm not Taya, and I'm really scared."

Taya blew out her breath. "You're not fooling anyone, you know."

Ayat spoke tremulously. "I know I've sinned, running off into the woods. And now the spirits are punishing me, sending this ghost whose cheeks are marked with evil. And I know, I deserve it! I've been such a naughty girl. I need a strong man to take control of my life."

To Taya's dismay, the clansmen's faces softened. Taya felt ready to explode. Smoke was almost coming out of her ears.

"She's lying! How can you believe her? You know me, I never talk like that."

Ayat clung to Ooor, pressing her body against him. "This is so scary," she said. "Please, Ooor, make the ghost go away. I'd be *so* grateful. I'll do *anything* if you make it leave."

"Anything?" Ooor asked dumbly.

"Ooor, you dolt," Taya snapped. "Think with your head, not your pants! How can you believe her?"

"Silence, devil!" Ooor said. He drew his knife and stepped forward with his friends.

"Don't you touch me," Taya warned. "If you touch me, I'll have your heads off when I'm shaman."

Ooor spat. "The Taya I know loathed the idea of becoming shaman."

"Well, I've changed my mind."

"Changed your form, more like. Come, friends, let's drag this doppelganger out of here. And don't dare show your tattooed face here again."

Ooor and his friends grabbed Taya's arms. She was too dumbfounded-mad to resist. She was expelled from Yaiyai! They'd recognize her tattoos and she'd never be able to return, she realized with cold dread.

As the men led her away, Ayat shifted close.

"You should have agreed to share the village," Ayat whispered into her ear. "I'd have gotten bored sooner or later and left, anyway. But now with you gone I think I'll stay." She smiled wickedly. "You wanted to get rid of me, and now you'll pay."

Chapter Nine
Greenhill

The ground shook with thundering hoofbeats.

Aeolia pointed gleefully. "Ooh, look, knights!"

Talin grabbed her arm and pulled her into a bush. When she tried to protest, he placed a finger on her lips.

"Hush and keep still," he whispered and wrapped his cloak around them. Aeolia watched him use his chameleon magic, which turned his cloak green as the bush they hid in.

"Who are they?" she whispered in his ear.

"Redforts."

Aeolia peeked through the leaves. Stocky horses thundered by, kicking up dirt with shaggy hoofs big as her head. The knights' crimson capes billowed, and sunlight glinted off their armor. Aeolia thought they looked almost as scary as Stonesons.

When they were gone, she and Talin climbed back onto the road.

"Now we're hiding from Healers?" Aeolia asked, brushing off leaves. "I thought we came to Heland to be safe."

"We're going to Greenhill Dukedom, to my lord cousin, to be safe. That's still a week away. This land belongs to House Redfort."

"And they wish me harm as well?" Aeolia asked wearily. After all she'd been through, she wouldn't be surprised.

Talin laughed. "No, they wish you no harm. This time it's me."

"Healers are after *you?*" she asked skeptically. Talin was half Healer himself.

"The Redforts are. You see, Heland has three noble houses. House Greenhill rules the farmlands. House Redfort rules the armies. House Purplerobe rules the throne."

"And you're a Greenhill."

"Half of me, at least. My father was the former duke, exiled by the Redforts after wedding a Forestfellow."

"They exiled him for *that?*"

"Miscegenation is illegal in Heland. Marring of the magic, they call it. Even the queen had been unable to deny the Redforts' accusations."

Aeolia bit her lip. "I'm sorry. I never knew. Is that why you were imprisoned here?"

Talin smiled thinly. "I was a foolish youth, certain that righteousness would always overcome. I had marched back to Heland and found the man who had demanded us exiled. Hyan Redfort is his name, and when I challenged him to a duel, he ordered me imprisoned."

A foolish youth, Aeolia thought. Like her. She remembered Talin's words in the Forest, how he would never beget a mixed child. She gazed over the rolling hills, the apple trees, the dots of bluebell and goldenrod. So often she had prayed to see this beautiful world, where lived no ogres, where everything was the right size, where she could finally belong. Such a fool she had been to imagine all humans lived in love. In some ways she had felt better in fetters, when ogres were bad and humans were good, when her brother still loved her and everything made sense. Apple leaves glided into her hair, and she thought of how Talin had touched that hair, how he had kissed her but could never love her more.

The fairytales were all lies. The heroes never won. Her hero, too, was not a noble prince, only an outcast sojourner. And if Aeolia had felt a spark of love for him, she was wise enough already to douse it and let it kindle no more. *Not in this world,* Aeolia knew. *Not in this world I am seeing truly for the first time.*

And so it was, that she spent all of next week walking in near silence.

For the first few days, they walked through Redfort land, where forts rose like hills, and walls snaked like rivers, and everywhere were knights, soldiers, and bushes to hide in. Then, on the fourth day, they crossed a river into Greenhill land. It was, in truth, not green at all, but golden with prairies of wheat, sprawling endlessly. Here there were no forts and no soldiers, only fields and farmers. Aeolia and Talin walked through the tall stalks for several days before reaching Greenhill Castle, which stood on a knoll above a village.

A stream encircled the village, lazily spinning a great wheel. Talin told her the wheel was a mill, but Aeolia didn't believe him. She had always ground wheat with stones at the ogre's cottage. The village houses, too, were strange. In Stonemark houses were made of stone, in the Beastlands they were wooden, and Forestfolk only had huts of branches and grass. Here in Heland houses were built of "wattle and daub" (Talin taught her those words), with crucks that slanted all the way to the ground. The Healer peasants were as strange as their houses. They were large, for one—taller than Forestfolk, and wider than Stonesons—and their hair was yellow, and their eyes blue. Their clothes were odd, too. Men wore tunics and hoods, women wore skirts and kerchiefs—all in browns and yellows. In Stonemark everybody just wore gray robes. As she had in the Forest, Aeolia felt foreign and self-conscious.

The castle rose behind the houses on a grassy hill. Vines bedecked its marble walls, and its green towers touched the sky. Aeolia thought it pretty, not at all like the squat Redfort strongholds. This was a land of farmers, she reminded herself, not soldiers.

A round wall, with a single portcullised gateway, surrounded the castle. Up on the parapet, the guards waved at Talin and cried his name. Five men gathered to turn a winch and raise the portcullis. Aeolia marveled at such a mighty protection, that five men were needed to lift it. She followed Talin through the gateway into a courtyard beneath the castle towers. She was delighted to see colorful fish swimming in pools amid the cobblestones. She also saw doves nesting in cotes, rabbits peeking from warrens, and even several peacocks roaming aimlessly about.

They did not wait long, and the castle doors slammed open with a boom. Aeolia shied back and hid behind Talin. Standing in the doorway was some great, tow-headed ruffian—probably the village drunk—roaring at them. To Aeolia's dismay, the roaring man charged forward, crashed into Talin, wrapped his huge arms around him and squeezed.

"You leave him alone!" Aeolia cried. She grabbed a branch from the ground and began beating the man on the head.

"Lia, stop!" Talin said. "This is my cousin, Duke Wilon Greenhill."

Aeolia dropped the branch. The large man rubbed his shaggy head, grumbling.

"Wil, this is Aeolia, my friend and companion," Talin said, smiling.

Wilon touched the bump on his head and winced. "Forgive me, miss," he said. "I didn't mean to scare you."

Then, to her surprise, the duke bowed before her and kissed her hand, as if she were a lady. It made her blush.

"I'm sorry I hit you," she said. "I guess I'm just... used to people trying to kill us!"

Wilon grinned. "Well, my lass, you needn't worry about that here. The only thing dangerous in Castle Greenhill is me when I'm drunk, and I make a habit of getting drunk loud enough to send everyone a-hiding."

Talin laughed, and Aeolia smiled hesitantly. *Finally,* she thought, *I'm safe.* No one would try to kill her here. Finally she had escaped Lale.

So why don't I feel happy?

Wilon showed them into his castle, and Aeolia gaped at its wide halls, with their tapestries, portraits, suits of burnished armor, and sparkling chandeliers. She had never imagined such wealth. She felt as if she were tainting this sumptuous abode with the dirt of her journey. When she voiced her concern, Wilon laughed and fetched her a maid and a clean, new dress. The maid took Aeolia's hand and began leading her down a corridor.

"Where are we going?" Aeolia asked.

"To give you a bath," the maid said.

A bath! Aeolia caught her breath. The maid took her to a stone chamber, where stood a cauldron of hot water, a copper bath, and a stool with towels and soaps. Aeolia suddenly felt very dirty. When the bath was ready, she climbed in with a long moan. She sat in the hot water for a long time, eyes closed, lips curling with pleasure. She hadn't had a bath in... well, never, really; she would just use buckets, brushes, and coarse soap at the cottage. This was how queens washed, Aeolia told herself. She imagined herself a queen and giggled. That would be the day—her, a queen! Everything was so strange. Just one moon ago she had been a slave and thought herself Stonish. And now... who was she now?

She climbed out of the bath and wrapped herself in a towel. She must have been in long; her toes were wrinkled as raisins. As she was drying her hair, she caught glimpse of herself in a tall bronze mirror. She had regained what weight she had lost in the ogre's basement, she saw. Her limbs were rounder, and her face had lost its hollow look. It was the face of a girl, round and soft. Aeolia bit her lip. She thought of Talin, how he had kissed her, and suddenly she wished she were as beautiful as Taya.

A wooden hairbrush hung on one wall. Aeolia took it gingerly, as if touching it were sinful, and for the first time in her life she brushed her hair. It came out smooth and thin and very straight. She braided it twice, once over each shoulder, and examined herself in the mirror. Her braids were thin as twigs, she noticed sadly, not half as thick as Taya's. They made her feel strange besides. She undid them with numb fingers and brushed her hair straight and to the sides.

She folded her towel and slipped on the pea-green dress she had been given. It fit her embarrassingly well, snug-tight in just the right places. Used to baggy clothes made for comfort, Aeolia blushed wearing a dress sewn for beauty. She thanked the Spirit that the neckline, at least, was topped with silky ruffles. She fluffed them up as best she could.

Still blushing, Aeolia stepped outside to find Talin wearing a doublet and hose of the same green cloth as her dress. Hand in hand, they set toward the main hall, to dine. Trestle tables were already set up when they arrived, people taking their places. Dogs lay slumped on the floor, lazily flicking their tails. Duke Wilon Greenhill sat alone at the head table. When he saw Talin and Aeolia, the bluff man rose to his feet.

"Come, my friends," he called and slapped the tabletop. "Sit beside me."

Aeolia and Talin obeyed, and soon liveried servants handed out large, flat pieces of bread. Aeolia licked her lips and sank her teeth into hers, but paused seeing everyone giving her startled looks.

"Lia," Talin whispered, "you're eating your plate."

Feeling herself redden, Aeolia laid down the trencher. She was thankful when another servant relieved her embarrassment by pouring her a goblet of wine. She brought it hurriedly to her lips. When she lowered the cup, she noticed Wilon quickly averting his eyes, and she realized he had stared at her tattoo. She pulled her hand to her lap, abashed.

Luckily, yet another servant then arrived, carrying steaming plates of fowls. The smell made Aeolia's mouth water. The servant filled her trencher with the spiced meat, and Aeolia surrendered to the food, taking hearty bites, gravy dripping down her chin. Before long, she was surprised to see the servants bringing more and more dishes, loading her plate with carrots, mushrooms, watercress, hazelnuts, pies, and meats of all sort. She ate what she could, and secretly fed the rest to the dogs. She was thanking the Spirit it was all finally over, when more servants regaled her with a series of strange, sweet foods Talin called "dessert." Aeolia thought her dress might burst. No wonder Healers were so big.

When the feast finally ended, Aeolia trudged outside and flopped down under a basswood. The dogs followed her, curled up at her feet, and licked her fingers. She sat with them as the gloaming spread and fireflies came to glow. The airy orbs swirled around her, dancing their lazy dance, filling her eyes with multicolored light. White, red, orange, gold. Four colors, for four Firechildren, one in each kingdom of man. Talin had taught her which color glowed for which magic, and Aeolia watched each in turn.

First she watched an orange firefly hovering over a patch of mallow. Orange fireflies glowed for the Forest's Firechild. If they still glowed, that meant Taya still lived. Aeolia wondered where her friend was now. Taya had saved her life, nearly dying in the doing. No one had ever done anything like that for Aeolia. Taya was a real heroine, she thought. She was the bravest person Aeolia knew.

Next, Aeolia watched several red fireflies that swirled around a wisteria. Red fireflies glowed for the Healer Firechild. Talin said no one knew who the Healer Firechild was. Aeolia wondered where he might be and what his magic was. Perhaps he could cure disease as well as heal wounds, or even resurrect the dead.

She turned her gaze onto several white fireflies dancing in circles around a boulder. Aeolia shuddered. These were Sinther's fireflies. These were the fireflies that turned his skin to stone, rendering it impenetrable to sword or arrow. They frightened her. She wished they were all extinguished.

Hurriedly, she looked up at the golden fireflies, which glided around her head. Golden fireflies. Esire's fireflies. Aeolia tried to count them, but they were too many. As they danced around her all other colors disappeared, till she saw only them, drenched in golden light.

All Esirens can share thoughts, Talin had said, but this Esiren can share senses as well. Only she can hurt Sinther. Aeolia thought of her dream, and of Eeea's words, and of the secret gift she had promised never to use. Joren had known. He had known and tried to protect her from Sinther. But he had betrayed her at the end, like the ogress said he would, like Lale said he had. Tears formed in Aeolia's eyes. She was not Joren's sister. She was not even Stonish. Adopted. Esiren. Alone. Who was she? Who was she now?

She remained under the tree until the darkness became complete, and the fireflies burned so bright they hurt her eyes. A servant finally arrived to lead her to her room, a chamber frightfully high up one tower. Small and round, it commanded a view of the entire village. Fireflies shone at the window. The bed was snug, but Aeolia tossed and turned for hours. She finally fell asleep with golden light on her face.

* * * * *

Blaring trumpets woke her at dawn.

Aeolia blinked in the sunlight and shut her eyes again. She was still sleepy. The trumpets continued blaring, however, joined by shouting soldiers, clinking armor, and neighing horses. Aeolia flipped onto her stomach and pulled the pillow over her head. But still the din increased, and the drumming hoofs seemed loud enough to topple the tower. Aeolia reluctantly climbed out of bed, rubbing her eyes. Curious to see what the commotion was about, she swallowed her fear and peeked out the window.

Her breath died in her throat.

Down in the courtyard, green-clad soldiers were mounting horses and galloping toward the village bridge. There, on the far side of the stream, stood maybe two hundred crimson-clad Redforts. Aeolia winced. What were Redforts doing here? This was Greenhill land. Aeolia descried an armored Talin riding a destrier toward the bridge. She recognized him by his green blade. Could the Redforts have come to claim him?

Aeolia pulled on her dress and dashed down the tower stairwell. She burst out into the courtyard, her skirt flapping. The sentries called her to stop, but Aeolia ignored them and ran into the village, to Talin.

She reached him by the bridge. He dismounted and took her hands. He looked strange and cold in armor, truly like a duke's son.

"What's happening?" she asked.

"I don't know," Talin said. "Wil is talking to them."

The duke of Greenhill sat mounted next to Talin, clad in plate armor, bellowing at the Redforts.

"Be gone, Lord Hyan! I rule farmlands, not armies."

Aeolia felt sorry for the Redfort leader's horse. The poor thing looked ready to collapse under its master's weight. Its saddle—pommel and all—were lost under the man's corpulence.

"Our dear Duke Greenhill." The fat man spoke in a honeyed, nasal voice, his lips pouted into a smile. "From your vociferation one would assume you suspect us warmongers." Hyan's jowls quivered as he chuckled. "We assure you, we seek no fray; messy business, that. Blood leaves such frightful stains. We desiderate only the girl, you see. The Esiren Firechild."

Aeolia shied back a pace. She squeezed Talin's hand.

Wilon guffawed. "The Esiren Firechild? You think this girl is the Firechild? Duke Hyan, the fat has finally suffocated your brain!"

As Hyan's soft cheeks flushed, Wilon roared with laughter. Carefully, Talin laid a hand on the large man's knee. Wilon, still laughing atop his horse, looked down at his cousin. Talin stared into his eyes. Slowly, Wilon's smile faded.

"Are you telling me," Wilon whispered, "that she...."

Talin nodded. "She is, Wil."

Wilon went pale. He snapped his head around to stare at Hyan. "What need you her, Redfort?" he demanded. "I thought it is Sinther who wants her."

Spit bubbled on Hyan's smile. "And we shall give her to him."

Wilon's face went from pale to red. "Traitor! What has the stone tyrant promised you?"

Hyan dabbed his forehead with an embroidered kerchief. "Enough worth storming your castle for, hum?"

Despair filled Aeolia. Must she bring ruin wherever she went? Would anyone who helped her be cursed? Her belly knotted. Hyan wanted to storm the castle. With her life she could stop him. What was one girl's life?

"Let me go to him," she whispered to Wilon.

Wilon looked down at her, his eyes hazy. He opened his mouth, hesitating. Before he could speak, Talin did.

"Wil, listen to me," he said. "We must keep Lia safe. She's the only one able to defeat Sinther and save Esire from his claws."

Wilon spoke carefully. "That is not Heland's quarrel. Heland has always been neutral."

"All the Island has been neutral until Sinther arrived. Can't you see, Wil? The five countries have always been balanced. But if Esire falls to Stonemark, if the traditional balance of power is disturbed...."

Wilon nodded slowly. Even slower, he wheeled his destrier to face the bridge. Then, in a sudden movement, he kicked the beast so it bucked, and raised his sword overhead. He bellowed at the top of his lungs.

"Today Greenhill goes to battle!"

Shouting erupted, horses whinnied, armor clanked. Aeolia grabbed Wilon's leg.

"I'm not worth it!" she cried, tears in her eyes. "Let me go to him!"

Talin grabbed her waist and pulled her back.

"Tell him, Talin," Aeolia pleaded as he pulled her away. "Tell him...."

"Hush, Lia. We must get you to safety."

He pulled her through the village and into the castle walls. The courtyard was deserted, everyone gone to battle or into hiding.

"Stay here behind the walls," Talin told her.

"Talin," she cried, "I can fight!"

"No! I can't let them get to you. Stay here, in safety."

He turned to leave, then paused and looked back. For a moment he hesitated. Then he stepped forward, lifted his helmet's beaver, and kissed her lips. It caught Aeolia by surprise, for he himself had spoken of such acts as sinful.

"I love you too," he whispered, left her dazed, and marched outside into the village.

Aeolia slumped to the ground, dazzled. Behind her, a man was sending doves into the sky, notes tied to their legs. But it was too late for help now, Aeolia knew. Men were dying, and for her. She could hear them scream. She rose to her feet and paced the courtyard, the sound of battle like hammers in her skull. She stopped under the castle wall and stood still, staring upwards.

After nearly fainting at the waterfall and in Yaiyai, Aeolia had sworn never to go near heights again. But then, breaking promises was nothing new to her. She must see what was happening. Slowly, she climbed the stairs up the castle wall. Her head spun as she stepped onto the wall-walk. She tightened her lips, clutched a merlon, and ignored the dizzying height.

She could see the battle clearly. The dead were already piling up, most of them wearing the green. As Aeolia watched, the Redforts forced their way across the bridge and into the village. Aeolia wrung her hands. She couldn't just stay here in safety while men died for her! Was there nothing she could do? What if Talin got hurt or... died.

She grabbed one sentry's arm.

"Where's the armory?" she asked.

"Left room off the main hall, down the stairs," the sentry said. "Why?"

Aeolia did not answer, but scrambled down the wall, stumbling the last few stairs. She ran across the courtyard, dashed into the castle, veered left and scurried downstairs. The armory was empty.

From a rack of weapons, Aeolia chose the thinnest sword, a silvery weapon with "Firefang" engraved into the blade and a firefly in amber upon the pommel. She used the blade to split her skirt down the sides. She tore the lace off her bodice and used it to tie her hair behind her head. Hurriedly, she rummaged through piles of armor. No breastplate seemed her size, but she found a small shield that wasn't too heavy. She slipped on the smallest basinet. It wobbled on her head, but she decided it would have to do. To finish, she donned a heavy, green surcoat. With the helmet's visor down and the surcoat slung over her, Aeolia was certain no one would recognize her. She suspected she looked ridiculous, but she didn't care.

Sword and shield in hand, she rushed outside and into the stables. Only one horse remained, a sorrel filly with a pink nose. She was no warhorse, but Aeolia knew that little, frightened females could sometimes beat the fiercest foes. Only after the stable boy had saddled the horse and Aeolia set her feet in the stirrups, did she realize she had no idea how to ride. She took a deep breath, mustered her magic, and linked to the filly.

The link confused the horse. She bucked and snorted. The double eyesight frightened her. She had never seen color before.

It's okay, Aeolia thought to her soothingly. *I know it's scary, being in two heads. I'm scared too. We're going to do this together.*

The horse calmed slightly.

Good girl, Aeolia thought. *Now, please take me outside into the village.*

The horse obeyed, gingerly trotting out into the courtyard, under the portcullis, and into the village. The battle raged around them. Riders and footmen thundered between the houses, children screamed, peasants fought with pitchforks. Archers crouched in thatch roofs, shooting an incessant rain. Knights in carmine torched granaries and houses. Black smoke billowed skyward like devils unfurling from slumber. Aeolia's horse whinnied, rolled her eyes, and pawed the air. Next to the huge destriers, the filly seemed smaller than a pony.

It's okay, it's okay. Aeolia tried to allay the horse's fear. *Be a brave girl. You can do this.*

She spotted Talin fighting fifty yards away, and her heart skipped a beat. Talin's armor was splashed with blood. She had to reach him! Aeolia urged the filly onward. The horse took hesitant paces.

Before she could reach Talin, a Redfort rider came charging toward Aeolia, brandishing his sword. Aeolia reared her filly and raised her shield. The Redfort's sword slammed into the wood, nearly dislocating Aeolia's arm. She wobbled in her saddle, breathless. The Redfort lifted his sword again.

Hurriedly, Aeolia severed her link with the filly and linked to the Redfort's warhorse.

Turn around! she thought forcefully.

The great beast spun around. Aeolia sliced its rider's stirrup.

Jump! Aeolia commanded.

The warhorse jumped, and the Redfort hit the ground. Aeolia linked back to her terrified filly, and before her foe could rise, she ran him over. He lay still.

Talin still fought ahead. Aeolia drove her filly onward between a swarm of footmen. She parried attacks, sliced at footmen, wounded one by nearly severing his arm. She did not allow the horror to overwhelm her; she had to reach Talin. At last, winded and shaking, she did.

She urgently examined him. He was covered in blood, but he sat straight in his saddle. The blood wasn't his. Aeolia breathed in relief.

"Rather small for a soldier, aren't you?" Talin asked her grimly.

"Talin, it's me!" she said.

Talin's mouth fell open. "Lia!" he whispered. "What are you doing here?"

"I've decided to come fight."

"You don't know how to fight! Get back inside."

Aeolia shook her head. "Sinther may stay in his fortress while others fight for him, but I will not."

A Redfort soldier came snarling between them. As Talin engaged his sword, Aeolia turned away to fight. Fight.... She looked at the blood around her and suddenly felt hesitant. Could she truly fight? How did one exactly—

A footman slashed at her, and Aeolia reared back. The soldier's sword sliced through her filly's breast. Aeolia screamed in pain, clutching her own chest, and hurriedly released the link. Her horse bucked madly, and Aeolia hit the ground.

The soldier stood above her. He swung his bloody sword. Aeolia parried, and the two blades locked. Before the soldier could attack again, she kicked his groin. As he whimpered, she stood up and ran him through.

Once more, she drew blood. Once more, she had killed. Aeolia stifled the guilt. No time for that now. Wildly, she looked around her. Her horse was gone. Talin was far away. The Redforts were undoubtedly winning. Dead Greenhills sprawled around her in pools of blood, stiff hands reaching up like tombstones. The smoke of the burning village filled her helmet, burning her eyes. She coughed violently.

"Into the castle!" she heard Wilon bellow behind her. "Into the castle!"

The rout caught her like a current, sweeping her through the castle gateway into the courtyard. Slowly, the portcullis began to descend. Aeolia noticed in alarm that there were still green soldiers outside.

"Talin!" she cried. Her feminine voice drew puzzled stares, but Aeolia didn't care. "Talin, into the castle!"

Green soldiers surrounded her. Aeolia was too short to see who was entering the gates. She heard the portcullis slam shut. She elbowed through the crowd, seeking Talin. If he had not managed to enter.... But finally she found him atop his horse, and she rushed toward him. He dismounted and she clutched him.

"I thought they locked you outside!" she said.

Greenhill archers were already shooting off the walls. Through the portcullis's spikes, Aeolia glimpsed Redforts fall dead.

"Come," Talin said. "We must help."

Aeolia gripped his hand, and they climbed the wall. On the wall-walk, soldiers were preparing cauldrons of boiling oil.

"Here, help me with this!" one soldier called to Aeolia, tilting a cauldron between two merlons. Aeolia helped him pour the oil, then watched it sizzle over the Redforts, like the goulash had sizzled over her master. Someone handed her a torch, and Aeolia tossed it over the battlements. The oil burst into flames. Redforts screamed, burning, pierced by arrows. The survivors tried to organize an escalade, but Aeolia was now tumbling boulders, knocking the invaders down like skittles. The green soldiers hooted and waved their fists.

Over a hundred Redforts died that morning at the wall, forming a heap of bodies. The several dozen survivors, seeing new oil pots ready to spill, spun on their heels and fled. The Greenhills roared and rushed down the wall. Five strong men began winching the portcullis open.

"What's happening?" Aeolia yelled.

"We're going after them," Talin said.

"They're retreating. Must we truly butcher them?"

Talin's eyes shone. "We cannot live in fear of them forever. Now we will destroy Hyan Redfort once and for all."

"Then I come too."

"No, and this time I mean it. You've done your share, now stay here in safety."

"But I'm worried about you."

"I'll be safe; the real battle is over."

He hopped onto a horse, brandished Stormshard, and joined the army storming out the gates.

Aeolia watched him leave. Soon the courtyard emptied of soldiers. The silence was eerie. A cold wind whistled. Dry leaves skittered over the cobblestones and flurried around Aeolia's feet. She was alone.

She gazed through the open gateway at the pile of dead Redforts. So many of them, seasoned warriors, fallen to peaceful farmers like ants to cruel boys' heels.... Aeolia shakily climbed up the wall. She saw Wilon's army chase the Redforts out of the village, into the golden fields.

Suddenly she started. Something was moving below. She glanced down, her pulse racing. But it was only some of the Redforts, shifting and groaning. Aeolia rubbed her temples and took a deep breath. They were dying. No reason to be afraid. She was just skittish after the battle, she told herself.

But the Redforts kept moving, undulating like a heap of snakes. Then one soldier stood up. Then another. Aeolia shook her head, her jaw unhinged. Before her eyes, half the dead bodies rose to their feet: fifty healthy Redforts, who had all played dead.

Aeolia was too terrified to scream.

The portcullis was open, and she alone. As the Redforts approached the gateway, Aeolia dashed down the wall. She slashed Firefang several times, severing the rope that held the portcullis. The iron spikes slammed down, impaling one Redfort and blocking the rest.

Aeolia panted, trembling. She forced herself to take deep breaths, to calm down. The portcullis was sturdy. The Redforts could not pass through it. She was safe.

"I have nothing to worry about," she told herself shakily. "Talin will be back soon. All I have to do is wait."

She climbed back up the wall, praying Talin returned soon. She gazed into the fields, where the Greenhills were catching up with the fleeing Redforts. There, in the wheat, she saw something that froze her blood.

As one, the Redforts stopped fleeing and turned to face their pursuers. From the tall stalks, a thousand more Redforts rose to their feet. The Greenhills were surrounded.

Aeolia watched helplessly as Wilon's army crumbled. The wind slammed the screams against her. Some of Wilon's riders broke an opening through the entrapping Redforts, and the green soldiers began routing back toward the castle. Aeolia saw Talin riding at their lead, clutching his wounded chest.

Tears flowed down Aeolia's cheeks. The wind was blustering, and she covered her ears, but still she could hear the Greenhills' cries.

"The portcullis is down!"

"Spirit, pull it up!"

"The rope is torn, we're trapped!"

The Redforts were cutting them down one by one. Blood splashed against the castle walls like waves against a pier. Aeolia could not bear to watch. She trembled from guilt and horror. Because of her, because of her....

She tore the helmet off her head. She ripped the lace from her hair. She tossed off her surcoat.

"Here I am!" she cried. "You want me! Here I am!"

They could not hear her; the battle was too loud. *Is all lost?* Aeolia wondered... and then the fireflies emerged. They swirled around her, haloing around her head. She glowed above the battlefield.

Both armies turned to stare, and for a moment the battle froze. The wind was the only sound, streaming through Aeolia's hair. *I must be brave like Taya,* she told herself. She shut her eyes.

"Take me, but spare my friends," she said. "I give myself to you...."

Wreathed in fireflies, Aeolia spread her arms to her sides. The wind whipped at her sleeves, flapped her torn skirt, roared in her ears.

Why, Joren, why have you betrayed me?

She jumped off the wall.

Chapter Ten
Stonemark, Ten Years Ago

Joren sat on the stone floor, waiting for his father to return with supper. The silence hurt his ears. Only a week had passed since Sem had sold her, but a week was a long time for an eleven-year-old, and this week of silence had been an eternity. Joren missed Aeoly's laughter so bad he ached.

Hunger had also ached. There was always food now, of course: fresh bread, fish, turnips, salty shallot soup. But last week there had been none, and the memory of hunger was still ripe in Joren's mind, so vivid he could almost understand his father. Not forgive, not accept. Understand. As long as he brought food.

The door slammed open and his father stepped in.

Something was wrong, Joren saw at once. Sem's hair was disheveled, and his clothes were torn. A bruise covered his left eye, and his face was puffed a drunken red. And he carried no food. *He carried no food.*

Joren rose to his feet. "Father, are you all right?"

Sem ignored him and began pacing the room, clutching his head and mumbling to himself. "Damn thief... I'll show him.... Cheating at dice.... Stealing people's hard-earned money...."

"Father! Is the money—"

Sem backhanded him. "Yeah, the money's gone, are you happy?" He shoved Joren to the floor. "I bet you are, you ungrateful bastard." He kicked Joren in the ribs. "You didn't like me selling her, did you?"

Sem grabbed Joren's collar. He lifted him so their noses almost touched. Joren winced smelling his father's drunken breath.

"I sold her for you, boy. Better one child with food than two without, huh?" He threw Joren to the floor. "Now get out of my sight."

Joren scrambled up into the loft, tears blurring his vision. He crawled into his bed of straw. Both his food and his sister—gone. Joren gazed at the straw pile beside him, where Stuffings now lay alone. She had lost the doll when the monster grabbed her. Would she ever see it again? The loft was so cold and empty without her, yet Joren could almost hear her laughter, see her smile.

Six years ago he had found her, while visiting his dying grandmother in southern Stonemark. Drawing water from the river one evening, he saw a crib floating toward him, fireflies hovering over it. A pink little creature lay inside: an Esiren baby, a note tied to her leg, sent from the Esiren hell while her parents awaited execution. The child was half dead; it was a miracle she had survived so far. Joren warmed the baby, fed her milk, and when his grandmother died he brought the child back to Grayrock. Sem wanted to give her to an orphanage, but Joren cried and begged till his father agreed to adopt her.

But that had been before Sem lost his job, before he surrendered to the drink. He had been a different man then. Suddenly rage filled Joren: against the war, the poverty, the soldiers who had killed Aeolia's parents. But mostly, Joren raged against his father, a father who did not bring food, who had sold his daughter, who had gambled away the money she had fetched. Swallowing his tears, Joren fell asleep. He dreamed a sweet dream, that he was adopted like Aeolia, and that his real father was a handsome prince.

* * * * *

Next morning, Joren climbed downstairs to find Sem holding a knife.

Joren cowed back, his chest pounding.

Sem smirked. "Don't worry, son. It's not you I'm after. It's the dice-cheater I'm going to kill."

Grim determination in his eyes, Sem stepped out of the house.

Home alone, Joren paced the floor.

An hour later, an officer of the City Guard came to the house. A gruff-looking man, he wore chain mail beneath Stonemark's royal gray uniform, the chest emblazoned with the white firefly of Sinther.

"Is this Sem's house?" the man asked.

Joren nodded, dread curdling his belly.

"Are you home alone?"

Joren nodded again.

"Where's your mother?"

"She's dead," Joren said. She had died years ago.

The officer put a hand on Joren's shoulder. "Sorry there, boy, but I'm afraid your father's just joined her."

"Is he dead?"

The officer nodded. "Got into a brawl. Died a quick death—the other man's knife in his heart. Didn't feel a thing."

Joren stood silently, not knowing how to feel. His father—dead. He felt nothing.

"Do you have any kin, someone to go to?" the officer asked.

Joren shook his head.

The officer shifted his weight. "Well, look, kid. The temples take in orphans. The clerics will care for you."

Joren was indignant. "I don't want to become a cleric!"

The officer shrugged. "It's not a bad life, clerichood."

Joren shook his head violently. "They aren't allowed any women."

The officer laughed and jabbed a finger against Joren's chest. "Got me there, you did." He grew serious. "But that's where you're going. Grayrock has enough street urchins. A temple it is for you, Joren Semson."

Joren had heard tales of temple orphanages. It was like living in prison. They whispered that the clerics beat the children.

"Now come on, lad," the officer said, reaching out to grab him. "Off we go."

Joren dashed away and scrambled into the loft. He heard the officer following, clumsy in his armor. Joren grabbed Stuffings, shoved the doll into his shirt, and jumped out the window. He landed in a puddle outside, scraping his knees. He scurried up and ran down the alley, rain matting his hair. The officer followed behind. Joren clenched his fists and ran harder. *I won't become a cleric,* he thought. *I won't!*

Skirting the corner, Joren emerged into crowded Limestone Lane. He dashed into the throng and hid between the people's legs. Peeking around one man's robes, he saw the officer scan the crowd, sigh, then turn back into the alley.

Joren let out a thankful breath. He was saved.

He didn't need any temple orphanage, he told himself. He'd live alone, finally free of his oppressing father. He'd be able to do whatever he wanted. It was actually a good thing, Sem dying. He was a strong and clever boy. He'd survive, get a job somewhere. Yes, it was a very good thing.

Joren allowed himself a tentative smile.

* * * * *

A moon later, he was begging on the streets.

He had found no job, and *had* found he was a poor thief. He ate rats and pigeons when he could catch them; when he could not he went hungry. His flesh was slowly melting, leaving him dizzy and weak and thin, like a stick figure etched in dirt. He was on the brink of starvation, he knew. Perhaps he was starving already.

He had exchanged his boots and hat for bread, and so he was always cold. It rained every day, the icy drops soaking him to the marrow. Joren knew he wouldn't survive winter. He regretted refusing the orphanage, but doubted he'd be offered it again. He was just another ragamuffin now, like the hundreds that infested Grayrock, grand city of stone, capital of Stonemark, Jewel of the Island.

He missed Aeoly more than ever. He dreamed of her every night, as he lay curled up in some dark alley, and would awake shivering and crying like a baby. The loneliness was unbearable. It became a tangible thing, a dim nausea in his stomach. But still Joren spurned the other beggars. Their dirty, emaciated faces frightened him. Their snaggletoothed grins seemed to mock him: *You're one of us now, boy, just like us....* And Joren believed them, and saw his face reflected in their own.

If it hadn't been for the parade, one early winter morning, Joren was sure he'd have died that year.

He was lying slumped in Chalk Corner, palm outstretched, when he heard the trumpets and drums. He rose to his bare feet, smoothed his rags, and crept into wide Slate Street. A crowd was amassed there. The throng blocked his view like a wall. Joren hopped up and down, trying to see.

"What is it?" he asked one woman.

"A parade," the woman replied. "Prince Lale has come of age today."

Joren had never seen his prince before. Who was the man, he wondered, who ruled this ragged hive of squalor? Would he wear silver and gold while his subjects ran barefoot through filth? Joren decided that today he would see. He burrowed through the crowd, crawling between people's legs. Finally he reached the front edge of the crowd, where he stood up and watched.

The royal band was marching by, playing huge black drums and silver trumpets. Dancing women followed them, flapping banners of gray and white silk. Behind the women, frolicked jesters with bells in their hats, juggling iron balls and making funny faces at the children. Next marched helmeted knights, gray surcoats hanging over their armor. Joren gazed in wonder at this grand cavalcade, both awestruck and sickened by such wealth and fanfare.

Behind the knights, girls were flowering the street with white stock petals. The crowd bowed in a great wave. Everyone fell silent. A carriage came trundling down the street, over the petals, but its curtains were drawn. Marching before the carriage, surrounded by guards, four burly men carried a palanquin over their shoulders. Atop the palanquin, waving to the crowd, sat Prince Lale.

For a moment Joren could not breathe.

The prince was beautiful. His teeth sparkled like pearls, and his silver hair was silky as summer clouds. He wore unadorned gray, and only a plain, silver coronet proclaimed his position. His regality shone not from his costume, but from the depth of his gray eyes, the strength of his jaw, the whiteness of his unblemished skin. *So this is my prince,* Joren thought. *This is beauty I can follow.* The prince smiled and waved at him, and Joren's heart overflowed with admiration and love.

Suddenly, Joren's eye caught a glint of metal coming from a house on the opposite side of the street. He glanced up, and his heart missed a beat. In the house's window, a man was aiming a crossbow at Prince Lale.

Joren gave a wordless cry. Before he could think, he was lunging forward. He slid under a guard's legs, bounded up, and pounded into Lale's throne.

The throne tipped precariously. A quarrel whizzed and rebounded off the prince's coronet. The throne, with the prince on it, crashed down.

The guards were immediately atop their prince, shielding him with their bodies. Other guards dashed into the assassin's house. The flower girls were screaming. The crowd rustled. Lale was pulled into his carriage. Joren tried to slink away, but a guard grabbed his shoulders.

"You're coming with us, runt," the soldier growled. "You don't attack the prince of Stonemark and get away with it."

Joren stared with indignation. *Attack* the prince of Stonemark?

"Stop that, Gawm!" came a clear voice from the carriage. "That boy saved my life. Bring him here. I want to talk to him."

Joren's heart took to flight. With a grunt, the guard lifted him, tossed him into the carriage, and slammed the door shut.

Joren sketched a deep bow.

A beautiful woman sat on Prince Lale's lap, showering him with kisses. She had curly auburn hair and round green eyes. She was not Stonish, obviously, but Joren couldn't pinpoint her race. Probably a crossbreed, with some Forestfellow in her.

"Are you hurt, my prince?" the woman pouted between kisses.

"Thanks to this young fellow, I am well, Ness," the prince replied. He turned his gray eyes on Joren. "Rise, my friend. What is your name?"

"Joren, Your Highness," he said, straightening.

"You saved my life, Joren. Tell me your father's name and I'll make him a rich man."

"I'm an orphan, Your Highness."

Ness's eyes softened. "And you have no home? Such a poor thing...." She looked at Lale. "Isn't he a poor thing? Look how thin he is. We must help him."

Lale was solemn. "Is that true, boy? You live on the streets?"

Joren nodded, ashamed.

"This cannot be, no...." Lale tapped his cheek thoughtfully, then seemed to have an idea. "I am in need of a groom," he said. "You seem a dashing fellow, quick of body and mind. I like that. You are obviously loyal; you risked your life saving mine. What say you take the job?"

Ness beamed. "Hooray!" she cried and kissed Lale's cheek. "My noble prince."

Joren, however, only lowered his head. "Your Highness, you honor me, but I am only a commoner, unworthy of serving you."

"Nonsense," said the prince. "I say who is common and who is not. And you, my friend, are anything but common. My bravest knight wouldn't dare topple my chair like that."

Ness and Lale laughed, and Joren couldn't help but smile.

"Be my servant," the prince said.

Joren bowed. "I am honored, Your Highness, and swear to serve you as best I can."

"Good lad," said the prince. "Here, come sit beside me."

Joren's head clouded with joy. It was like a dream. He would serve his prince with all his heart, he vowed, no matter what. His life had purpose again. Once more, he had someone to love.

* * * * *

Lale ended the parade early. The people shouldn't expect parades, he reasoned, when they harbor assassins. The audacity rankled. With brisk commands, he dispersed the performers and ordered his carriage to Ness's home.

The boy came with them, his face suffused with joyous awe. It made Lale smile. He liked the kid. He had spunk—unlike those boring, docile servants normally inhabiting the Citadel. The old fortress was such a dreary place, it could use a spirited lad to liven things up. Scrub him up, dress him nicely, and the boy would be fine.

The carriage stopped on Onyx Avenue, outside Ness's house. Lale squeezed her thigh and kissed her lips.

"Good-bye, my love," he said.

"You will tell him today?" she whispered.

"We can no longer keep it secret. You are my love. I wish to marry you. I must tell him."

Ness nodded, her eyes round and afraid. She looked so helpless and innocent, it stirred Lale's blood. Spirit, he loved her when she was frightened.

"Go," he said and gently shoved her off the carriage. She alighted, gave him one last look, then turned around and ran into the house. Such a pretty sight. Lale licked his lips.

He turned to face Joren.

"You," he said, "will accompany me to the Citadel, on what will be either the greatest or worst day of my life."

The boy nodded, his eyes still sparkling. Lale allowed himself a smile. The boy worshiped him. He barked an order, and the coach whipped the horses into a trot. The carriage trundled over the stone roads, heading toward the Citadel.

Lale watched it approach from his window. The Citadel. Stonemark's ruling seat. The most fearsome fortress on the Island. Its spires and turrets pierced the sky. Its granite walls brooded like the gates of afterlife. Gargoyles perched atop its crenellations, twisted sentries with eyes of black jet. Created by ancient Stonish magic, the edifice was now home to a Stonish Firechild: Lale's father, the king of Stonemark. Sinther, the man of stone.

The carriage passed beneath thick outer walls and entered a vast courtyard. So huge was this courtyard, armies could muster on its ground. The fortress proper loomed above it, like a tombstone for a god. The carriage crossed the courtyard and stopped before a round, stone stage lying like a porch under the fortress doors. Lale and Joren alighted, climbed onto the stage, and approached the huge doors.

Lale motioned the bowing guards to rise. They pulled the doors open.

"We'll go see the king now," Lale told Joren.

They stepped through the doorway into a large, shadowy hall. It was the last large room they would see. The next doorway led them into a maze of coffin-like cells and narrow corridors. The place was twined, windowless, and bleak as a morgue. The torches were far-spaced. The air was cold and musty. Lale scorned extravagance, but this place chilled him to the bone. He walked quickly, tapping his thigh. They climbed down endless, curving stairways, plunging into a subterraneous kingdom, down and down into the belly of the earth. *What a cozy home,* Lale thought with a wry smile. *I wonder what my boy thinks of it. He's probably scared witless. Spirit, this place terrified* me *at his age.*

Finally, after what seemed like miles, they stopped before a simple door.

"There is a secret behind this door," Lale told Joren, "a secret no one but my father and I know."

The boy nodded. He was shivering. It was probably from the cold.

"No one is allowed into this room," Lale continued in a soft voice. "No one. The penalty is death."

Sweat rolled down the boy's forehead.

"You saved my life," Lale said. "And you will be my most personal servant. Therefore I will trust you with this secret. But once you behold it, you are forever bound to my service."

"I'm not afraid, Your Highness," Joren said. His voice cracked only slightly.

"Then you wish to proceed?"

Joren nodded. "I swore to serve you completely, Your Highness, and that is what I'll do."

Lale smiled. The boy's bravery was soothing. Lale wished he himself were as brave; his impending task was unenviable. With a sigh, he pulled the door open, and they walked in.

The room inside was empty. The stone walls were bare and dank. In the wall across from them, gaped a large hole—the opening of a tunnel. A second hole lay in the center of the floor. This bottom hole was the opening of a stairwell, though its steps were cloaked with darkness.

Lale pointed at the tunnel before them.

"This tunnel is the secret in the room," he said. "It leads outside the Citadel, into an alley in the city. My father, though invulnerable to all but one person, built it as an emergency egress. No one knows of it but he, I, and now you. You must swear never to tell of it to anyone."

"I swear, Your Highness!" Joren said.

"Then come, we'll go see Sinther."

Lale realized his heart was racing. His palms were sweaty. He took a deep breath, trying to calm himself. *I am twenty-one today,* he told himself. *A grown man. Go down there and do what you must, like a man.*

With tightened lips, he led Joren into the hole in the floor. The narrow, corkscrew stairwell was dark and slippery. It had been carved from the solid flint, and its walls were rough and dank. Torchlight flickered against the stone.

Their descent ended abruptly at a stone door. Lale steeled himself and knocked.

"Enter," boomed the king.

Lale shivered. No matter how many times he heard his father speak, it always chilled him. It sounded like an echo, but without a voice. If stone could speak, Lale thought, that would be its rumble.

Lale opened the door, and he and his boy stepped in and bowed.

The chamber was like a cave, roughly hewn, tar black but for the light of a single torch. The air was cold and wet. Lale saw the king walking towards them—an animated statue of stone. From the corner of his eye, Lale saw Joren shivering.

"You brought a boy," Sinther rumbled with his terrible echo.

Lale straightened. He gently touched Joren's back, signaling him to straighten as well.

"He's my groom, Your Majesty," Lale said. "I thought he should know the room."

"You did not consult me on this."

"I am sorry, Your Majesty. I did not wish to trouble you."

The king spat a pebble. It clanked against the floor. "No one may know of the room. Kill the boy."

Lale heard the faint trickle of Joren wetting himself.

"Father, please," Lale said. "I beg of you. The boy saved my life."

"Saved your life?"

"There was an assassin on Slate Street."

Sinther grunted. "I'll have the street torn down. Fine, you may keep the boy. Consider him my birthday gift."

Lale breathed out with relief, only to let a deeper fear seep in.

"Your Majesty," he said, aware that his voice was quivering, "there is something I must tell you."

"Speak then."

"I have chosen a bride."

Sinther bunched his eyebrows. "Who? Duke Gorze's daughter?"

"No, Your Majesty."

"Who, then?"

Lale took a shaky breath. "She is Greenhill's daughter."

Sinther was silent for a long moment. The only sound was the crackling torch. Finally the king spoke. "Greenhill the exiled Healer?"

"Father, I love her," Lale blurted out, and then cringed, expecting his father to bawl, even beat him for loving a half-breed.

Instead, Sinther gently laid a stone hand on Lale's shoulder. His touch was cold and hard.

"I understand, son," he said.

"You do?" Lale asked tentatively.

Sinther nodded. "You cannot choose who you fall in love with. But you see, my son... sometimes she can choose you."

"I don't understand."

"I know you don't, son. You are young and innocent. All your life I have shielded you from the cruel, outside world. I will explain. You see, these half-breeds... they are not like us. They are cunning, only seeking to destroy. This girl you love, she has wooed you for your power. She is using your naivety to reach the throne, to be queen, to spawn impure heirs for Stonemark."

Lale shook his head. "Father, no.... She loves me."

"It seems so, son, I know." Sinther's voice was so gentle, it brought a lump to Lale's throat. "But you are a prince. People fear you, respect you, admire you—but they do not love you. No one loves you, my son. No one but I. This mongrel girl loves only your power. She wants to steal it from you, to taint your royal blood."

Nobody loved him, Lale thought. Nobody but his father. It had to be true; his father would not lie. Lale's fear slowly ebbed away. It felt good to believe, to please his father, not to have him yell.

"I never thought of that," he said hesitantly.

"I know, son. I know. It's hard to see past their cunning; a crossbreed is the most devilish creature after an Esiren. Don't let this girl use you! Go to her house and tell her you know her plan. Tell her you won't be used!"

"Yes...," Lale said, his confidence slowly mounting. "Yes, I will do that."

The stone king smiled—a loving, fatherly smile. "Good, son. Show her who the rightful ruler is! Secure our mighty reign, don't let impurity weasel in."

"Yes, yes! I'll do just that. I'll tell her the prince of Stonemark must breed purely. I'll tell her I can't see her anymore, and that she must leave the city."

"Yes, that is good, son." The king's voice was reluctant. "But the penalty for treason is more severe than banishment."

"Treason? Father, but—"

"Is this not treason? Did the Greenhills not try to use your innocence to overthrow us? This is treason, and like in every kingdom that ever was, so in Stonemark is the penalty for treason death."

"But, no... this can't be."

"Oh, my son, I know how hard it is. You are enchanted by her. The charm will break when you bring your sword down onto her neck."

"What are you saying?" Lale asked with horror.

"In your blindness, son, you have almost ruined us. It is most right that your hand should be the one to annul the sin."

"Father, please!"

"I shall not hear your whining. You have shamed me, and you must mend what you have broken and restore my trust. Go to the girl's house and execute her and her family. Return to me with their heads."

"Father!"

"Do as I command, or I will kill the girl myself. The death I'd grant her would be less pleasant, I assure you."

"I cannot...." Lale wept.

The echo rose to a howl. "Cease this groveling, you are a man today! Do as I command, prove yourself a worthy heir. If you cannot, by the Spirit I'll find another successor! Now go, tonight!"

Lale fled the room. He rushed upstairs, blinded by tears. When he reached the top and entered the antechamber, he stood with shoulders heaving. Joren emerged from the stairwell. Lale turned his head away, lest the boy saw the turmoil in his face.

I must control myself, Lale thought. *This is pathetic. I am a man today.*

He took several deep breaths, then spoke, trying to sound gruff. "You heard the king, boy?"

"You will do as he said, Your Highness?"

Lale lowered his head. "I have no choice. He'll disown me if I don't, and kill her himself." He turned around and looked Joren in the eyes. When he spoke again his voice was gentle. "Do you regret being my groom, child?"

Joren puffed his chest. "I'm not afraid. My own father was pretty tough."

Lale's laughter took him unexpectedly. It snorted out of his nostrils and then seized him completely, and he laughed harder than he had laughed in a year. It was a minute before he could speak again. "I like you, Joren."

The boy beamed with pride.

"But we must do as he commands," Lale added gravely. "And you, Joren, will help me."

*****

In the quiet evening, man and boy slunk out of a carriage. Silently, they paced across paved Onyx Avenue, casting shadows long and thin as daggers. The sun melted into the horizon, dripping red paint over the stone city. *Or red blood,* Lale thought as he and Joren approached the house.

The gates' metallic spikes, painted with sunset, reminded Lale of gory spears. They screamed when he pulled them open.

Fingers tapping against Bloodtalon's pommel, Lale stepped into the garden, his boy following. They crept over the violets and forget-me-nots and crouched behind the lavender. The flowers were gray and cloying. A cloud of red fireflies swirled away to flee across the grass, like droplets of blood.

Lale peeked through the leaves. A light shone in one of the house's windows. Lale heard the dim murmur of conversation. He could smell food: garlic beef, mushroom soup, bread, cheese.

"Looks like they're having dinner, Your Highness," Joren said.

Lale nodded. "That means they're all home."

"Do you...." Joren choked, swallowed hard. "Do you have a plan, Your Highness?"

"I want her never to suspect. We'll walk in smiling and ask to speak to her alone in her chamber. We'll let her think the king has approved of our marriage."

"A clever plan, Your Highness. She will be put off guard."

"That's not my intention," Lale snapped. "I simply... want her to be happy."

Joren had the grace to look ashamed. "Of course, Your Highness."

Lale continued. "In her chamber, I will do the deed, quickly and painlessly. When I am done, you will enter the main hall and direct the family's attention out the window. I'll surprise them from behind."

Joren nodded. Lale took a deep breath, trying to calm his heart. This had to be done, he told himself. Better he killed her than his father's assassins. A thought flitted through his mind: he could warn her, let her flee the city. But Lale dismissed the idea as fast as it had surfaced. If he saved Ness, the king would disown him. Was one girl worth the throne? One girl who loved only his power? Lale tightened his lips. He would not let her ruin his birthright. He'd do his task.

"Come," he said to Joren and rose to his feet. "We go."

They walked the cobble path up to the house, fireflies swirling around them. It was not a small abode; the exiled duke's magic earned plenty of money in a kingdom where Healers were rare. *Soon,* Lale thought grimly, *they will be even rarer.* He smoothed his gray robes, straightened his coronet and sword, and knocked on the door.

The Greenhills' young boy opened the door.

"Your Highness!" the boy peeped happily as he bowed.

"Rise, young Talin!" said Lale, forcing himself to smile.

Talin bounced up and hung onto Lale's neck.

"Give me another dragon ride, Your Highness!"

Lale feigned a chuckle. "You're getting too heavy for this, Talin. Maybe later. First show me in."

Talin sighed and turned to lead Lale and Joren into the house.

The Greenhills sat around a dinner table in the main hall. For a moment, the family didn't notice its visitors, and Lale stood and watched them. Ness was volubly telling a story, her auburn curls bouncing. Her Healer father, his blond beard grizzled, nodded as he listened. Her Forestfellow mother gazed at the two fondly with slanted green eyes.

"His Royal Highness, the prince of Stonemark!" Talin announced, disrupting the perfect picture. Lale experienced a pang of regret; that perfect family picture will never more return.

As the family made obeisance, Ness glanced up nervously. Lale swallowed his bile and winked at her. A smile spread across her face. *She thinks the king has approved of our marriage,* Lale thought. *Good. I want her to die happy.*

"I'm sorry to interrupt your dinner," Lale said, motioning the family to rise. "But I bring happy news that I am anxious to tell."

Ness was beaming, her smile sparkling like sunlight on water. "Then tell us, my dear prince!"

"First I must speak to you alone," Lale told her, the words stale on his lips.

"Why, certainly, my lord prince," she said and gave him her arm.

Leaving the others to their meal, Lale and Ness left the hall. Joren trailed humbly behind.

"Joren, light some candles," Lale said as they entered Ness's chamber.

The boy obeyed, and soon candlelight danced over pale pink curtains, ebony nightstands, and a silk bed. Shadows swirled like nightmares. An owl hooted in the distance, and Lale started. He realized he was clammy with sweat. *I must not let her see I'm anxious,* he thought.

He took her hands. "Ness," his whispered, "I love you."

He leaned forward and kissed her lips, forcing her mouth open with his tongue.

She pulled her head back with a giggle. She spoke over Lale's shoulder. "Joren, why don't you leave us?"

No! Lale almost yelled. He needed the boy to later create the distraction.

"Let him stay and watch," Lale said, trying to sound easy-going. "He needs to learn these things somewhere."

"How much is he to learn tonight?" Ness asked quietly. "A good-bye kiss, or an engaged couple's lust?"

"I will show you," Lale whispered and kissed her neck. She smelled of milk and clove and passion. He brushed his lips over her skin while his hands caressed her. She moaned.

"Now close your eyes," he whispered. "I have a surprise."

"What is it, Your Highness?" She giggled.

"You'll see. But you must keep your eyes shut until I say you may open them."

She smiled and shut her eyes. A cold breeze ruffled the pink curtains. The candlelight flickered. Shadows crawled over Ness's skin like demons.

"Here, lie down," Lale said softly, gently pushing her onto her bed. She lay down slowly and placed her head on a pillow. Her red hair settled around her head like a pool of blood. The sheets suddenly looked like shrouds, the bed a coffin, and Ness a corpse. Lale turned his head away.

"Well, where's my surprise?" Ness asked.

"Soon, Honeycomb. Just don't peek."

Lale's fingers closed around Bloodtalon's hilt. Slowly, silently, he drew the blade. The dark steel gleamed in the red candlelight. The curtains swayed in the breeze, and Lale saw the fireflies swirl furiously outside. He raised the blade above Ness's neck.

Talin appeared at the doorway.

"Why is your sword drawn inside?" the boy asked.

Ness opened her eyes. For a second, she blinked confusedly. Then she began to scream. Her brother's face suffused with horror and he fled the room.

"Spirit's Beard!" Lale swore, his stomach churning. Ness rose to her feet and tried to flee. Lale grabbed her. She struggled, crying. Why did this have to happen? Lale wanted to scream. He wanted to give her a good death.

"Help, Papa, help!" she cried.

"Quiet!" Lale shouted. He shoved her to the floor and knocked Bloodtalon's pommel against her head. She slumped down unconscious.

"Watch out!" Joren called from behind.

Lale spun around. Ness's father was rushing into the room, a dagger in his hand. Lale jumped back, and the dagger slashed through air. The Healer slashed again, and Lale but barely parried the blow. The old man was a seasoned fighter. Lale felt fear knot his belly. Suddenly he was afraid for his life. He fled around the bed, but the Healer pursued him viciously. Lale saw Death's grin.

Suddenly the old Healer stumbled facedown. Joren had grabbed his legs.

Lale slashed his sword. Blood bespattered the curtains and doused one candle.

Lale had scarcely taken a breath, before Ness's mother peeked around the doorway. The Forestfellow's eyes widened, and she began to scream.

"Silence!" Lale shouted. The woman's screaming made his blood boil. "It was not supposed to be this way!"

She began to flee. Lale chased her into the hallway and cut her down. He had to strike her twice more to silence her infuriating caterwauling.

Trembling, Lale blundered back into the room. Joren was heaving in a corner. Ness was mumbling groggily, still half unconscious, her white skin bespattered with red droplets. Lale approached her and raised his dripping sword.

"I'm sorry, I'm sorry," he blubbered, suddenly weeping. He shut his eyes and swung the sword. Hot liquid splashed against his face.

There, he thought, his eyes shut. *The deed is done.*

A shriek came from behind. Lale turned his head. Talin was charging at him, holding his father's dagger. Lale raised his arms, but Talin leapt up, hung onto his neck, and shoved the dagger down Lale's face.

Pain exploded, and everything turned red.

* * * * *

An hour later, Lale and Joren were still combing the city, searching for the boy through every twisted, rat-infested ally.

"Your Highness," Joren begged, "you're wounded, you've lost much blood."

Lale waved him silent and moaned through the wet bandages wrapped around his face. The pain burned, but Lale ignored it. Pain was trivial now, and blood could no longer disturb him. He had to find Talin. The half-breed would grow and want revenge.

Joren must have read his thoughts. "Your Highness, if you don't return now, the boy will have no need for revenge, for you'd have killed yourself. You must return to the Citadel and see a doctor."

Lale grumbled. Joren was right. The hunt was over. Talin had escaped him. He could be a cunning lad, that Talin. *He'll never understand why I did it,* Lale realized. All's the same. Nothing mattered now.

Lale shook his head violently. His thoughts were rambling, incoherent. Perhaps he had lost too much blood. Perhaps he was losing his mind.

"Come, Your Highness," Joren pleaded. "We must return."

Lale nodded weakly. He hefted the sack of heads over his back and continued trudging down the street. Joren walked beside him, supporting him as best he could. Cold wind howled between the stone houses. Rats shrieked. The starless sky rumbled. Lale could barely see his way, and he stumbled every few steps. Blood from the sack dripped down his back. His own blood trickled through his bandages and down his neck. His head spun and his knees trembled. Bloodtalon, hanging at his waist, was heavy as guilt.

Eternities passed before they finally reached the Citadel. They stumbled across the vast courtyard, onto the stage, and through the doorway. The guards recognized Lale's coronet and bowed bewilderedly.

"Your Highness," Joren said, "let's find you a doctor."

Lale shook his head. He had to see his father first. Leaning on Joren's shoulder, they began their descent. They spiraled down,

down into the rock, an endless plunge into the underground, the vast bowels of the Citadel. And finally, into the secret room, with the secret tunnel, and the stairwell carved into the floor. Lale could hardly hold himself upright now, and his head seemed ready to split. Leaning onto Joren, he limped down the corkscrew stairwell, into the king's black tomb.

Lale bowed before his stone father. Joren held him from falling.

"My poor son," Sinther said in his echo without a voice. "Look what they did to you...."

Lale straightened, swaggering, and handed his father the bloody sack. The stone king examined its contents briefly and seemed satisfied. He didn't know there was a boy, Lale realized thankfully. *He thinks I killed them all.*

The king tossed the bag aside, and a head rolled out. Lale felt his gut rising. He fell to his knees.

"Now, now," the king said soothingly. "Have heart, my son. You did the right thing. I'm proud of you."

The warm words soothed Lale. He looked up through his bandages at the stone face, like the face of a roughly hewn statue. Was that a glimmer of love that flitted across the king's stone eyes? Lale thought it was, and his own love for his father bloomed inside him. His father said he had done right. His father knew. Lale's heart calmed. He had not sinned.

"Now," said the king, "I am afraid I have another task for you."

Lale nodded. Anything. He no longer cared.

"You know, of course," Sinther said, "I am not... completely invincible."

Lale nodded. His father's bane, his nightmare. The reason for the escape tunnel. The whole Island knew of Sinther's weakness. Sinther was the Stonish Firechild. His stone skin was immune to any weapon. Only one person could harm him. The

Esiren Firechild. Able to merge mind and body, the Esiren Firechild could reach past the stone skin. Lale had grown up hearing tales of this horrible demon and the wicked race that could spawn it.

"You have shamed me," said the king, "by nearly tainting our royal line. The only way for you to fully propitiate me is to hunt this Esiren Firechild. When the golden fireflies no longer glow, then you shall have proved yourself a worthy heir."

Lale heard Joren gasp beside him.

"How can I kill the Esiren Firechild?" Lale demanded through his bandages. Fresh blood gushed from his split lips. "He can link body like mind. Anything done to him is done to me. Killing him would be killing myself."

Sinther shook his head. "As I, the Stonish Firechild, have a weakness, so does the Esiren Firechild. He can share only senses. He can share pain, but not the actual wound. A slow, painful death—yes, that can be shared through a link. If the mind feels itself die, it will stop working. But a quick, painless beheading—that will snap the link and leave the killer safe."

Lale cackled. "But how can I find him? Am I to behead every Esiren on the Island?"

Sinther gave him a sober stare. "Trial and error is the safest method."

"You want me to kill an entire race single-handedly?" Lale cried, choking on the blood. "Am I a prince or butcher?"

The king shrugged. "Why, your groom will help you. He will be your royal executioner. Now leave, go see a doctor."

Leaning on Joren, Lale limped away. The king waited till they reached the door before speaking again.

"And by the way, my son: happy birthday."

* * * * *

Joren knocked on the door.

"Who is it?" came an irritable reply from within.

"It's Joren, Your Highness," Joren said.

After a moment of silence came the reply. "Come in."

Joren smoothed his livery and opened the door. Lale sat slumped inside on a stone chair, his bandages finally removed. Joren felt the blood leave his face. He bowed hurriedly.

"Am I so hideous?" Lale asked dryly.

Joren straightened slowly. "You... look better than last time I saw you."

Lale laughed. "A tactful remark, my friend. I told you on the first day your mind is quick." He sighed. "I wish I never did hire you that day. Look at what trouble I've gotten you into."

"No, Your Highness!" Joren said indignantly. "I'm glad to serve you, and will continue doing so."

"I take my words back, you're a fool!" Lale snapped. "Run while you can! You heard my father. If you serve me, it won't be as groom, but as executioner."

Joren took a deep breath. *What matters whose hand wields the blade?* he thought. *A hand will always be found. It might as well be mine. My life is over, let me bear the curse. I will do this for him.*

"Your Highness," he said, "as I have saved your life, so have you saved mine. I'd have starved on the streets had you not taken me in. You're like a father to me."

Lale sagged in his seat. "I'm too young to be your father, Joren," he said softly. "But we will be brothers, bonded in blood. And Joren, my dear friend Joren, the blood shall wash and blind you, until the golden fireflies glow no more."

And Joren thought: *Forgive me, Aeoly, for I can never bring you home.*

* * * * *

"This is so strange, Aeoly. It's like... being two people."

Aeolia nodded. *Try closing your eyes,* her voice said in his head.

Joren shut his eyes, and everything came into focus. He could see himself through his foster-sister's eyes. He shared all her senses, as if he were in both bodies at once. He was as much Aeolia as Joren.

Now let's play a game, she thought. She took from her pocket a crumb of bread, a crumb of cheese, and a piece of turnip. She laid them on the floor before her. She closed her eyes too, and finally everything went black.

I'll eat one, she thought. *Guess which it is.*

Joren felt her hand lift one of the items and put it in her mouth. He tasted the tangy goat cheese.

"Cheese!" he exclaimed. "I can't believe it. I can actually taste it."

Neat trick, right? she thought, and then she opened her eyes.

Joren opened his eyes as well...

...and found himself a grown man, lying in a tent, curled up in his cloak.

He moaned. Only a dream. Grumbling, he rubbed the sleep out of his eyes and wiped cold sweat off his brow. It was his twenty-first birthday, he remembered. The year his promise to Aeolia was due. And he was in Esire.

Dawn's red light oozed through the tent's flaps, accompanied by the stench of blood and fire. Joren tossed his cloak aside and rose to his feet. The same dream, over and over again. Would it never leave him? He uncorked a flask and splashed water onto his face. That had been the day, he remembered, the day he had learned who she was. The one he now hunted.

Aeolia hadn't known she was adopted. She thought herself Stonish, just like her adopting family. She didn't even know what an Esiren was. But Joren knew, and knew his foster-sister's magic was more powerful than any other Esiren's. A link capable of sharing not only thoughts, but senses too—even pain. A link powerful enough to hurt Sinther.

Joren pulled out his razor and began shaving. His hands shook and he cut himself. He brought a towel to his bleeding cheek. Lately his hands shook whenever he held a blade, be it his razor or his ax. He was ill, he suspected. But there was no remedy for his illness.

Joren sighed, pulled on his black mask, and lifted his ax. He opened the tent flaps and stared outside. Nestled between the mountains, the border town lay in a heap of smoldering ashes. Big Brown trees lay tumbled. Ravens picked at blackened bodies. Flies bustled in pools of congealing blood. *Esire,* Joren thought. *We have made it so ugly.*

Long ago, he had accepted that he was a bad person, that his heart was rotten, dank, murderous. He was a liar. A butcher. He had not kept his promise, had killed countless innocents. *And yet, I still love her.* He reached into his pocket and felt Stuffings, her old doll. *I hate myself, but I still love her.*

He stepped outside, blinking feebly in the light. He made his way between the bodies and ruins till he reached the town square. The Esiren survivors were amassed there, shackled around a barrel, guarded by Stonish soldiers. Lale stood grinning beside them, wearing a conical party hat.

"Happy birthday to you," the prince sang. "Happy birthday to you...."

"Your Highness." Joren bowed his head.

"My dear executioner," Lale said. "Good morning! So, today you become a man, what? Ah! I remember my own coming of age as if it were yesterday."

"It was the day we first met," Joren reminded him. "Ten years ago."

"So it was. The years have passed quickly."

"We've been busy."

Lale gazed at the Esiren prisoners. "And getting busier. Four scores of them today, huh?" The prince sighed. "I'm working you too hard. I wish that damned Firechild would just turn himself in so we can end this mess."

Joren nodded and swallowed a bitter taste in his mouth. A Firechild appeared only once a century; as soon as they killed the Esiren one, as soon as they doused the golden fireflies, the nightmare would end. Joren grimaced. Could he truly bring himself to do it? No. He loved her too much.

"Well!" said Lale. "Begin then. Let's see the royal executioner at work." He rubbed his hands together eagerly.

The guards pulled forward the first Esiren: a little girl, no older than six, tears streaming from her honey eyes. For a terrible instant Joren was sure the girl was actually *her*, but no... Aeolia must be sixteen now. Joren lowered the girl's head onto the barrel. He raised his ax, ready to strike the quick, painless blow that would sever a link safely.

"Joren!" Lale said. "Are you all right? Your hands are shaking."

"I think I might be ill."

Lale sighed. "It's because you're always moping. You are too serious, Joren. You know, I don't think I've ever seen you so much as smile."

Joren lowered his ax. "Lale, I...."

"You want to rest. I understand. Hey, it's your birthday! Go, get some sleep. I'll do this bunch for you. Even the prince needs to get his hands dirty every once in a while, huh?" Lale laughed, but became solemn when Joren only nodded gloomily. "Joren, is something else wrong?"

"Lale, we need to talk."

"All right. Want me to finish these off first?"

The girl's pleading eyes were all Joren could see. "I'd rather we talked now. Alone."

Lale nodded slowly. The two stepped aside, leaving the Esirens out of earshot. Snow fell softly around them.

"You know you are more than a prince to me," Joren began. "You are like a brother."

"And you to me," Lale said.

"Well, you see, as you are my brother, so there is a sister."

"A sister?" Lale smiled.

"She is a girl I love deeply, more than anything, more than life. I love her... with a passion you cannot imagine."

Lale grinned and nudged Joren with his elbow. "Maybe you want more than sibling relations then, huh, you devil?"

"Lale, this girl... she's an Esiren."

Lale's smile faded. "An Esiren...."

"You know how it is," Joren said in a cracked voice. "You know how hard it can be...."

Lale became solemn. He placed a hand on Joren's shoulder. "Yes, my friend. I know how it feels to have to kill a girl you love. Who knows better than I? And so I understand why you hid her from me. Don't worry! I'm not upset. Let's just not mention her anymore, all right?" Lale winked. "I'll pretend I never heard this."

"You are very kind to me," Joren said, "but I'm afraid you haven't heard all. This girl, she lives far away. She's a slave in the Beastlands."

"So what are you worried about?" Lale exclaimed with a smile. "That's out of our reach anyway."

I am a man today, Joren thought. *I must act like one. How many more little girls.* He took a deep, shaky breath.

"Lale," he said, "this slave girl is the Esiren Firechild."

Chapter Eleven
Brownbury's Burrows

Aeolia seemed to fall forever.

Tumbling, gliding, like a feather, like leaves from a tree. There was no bottom, only endless air, and she showered down in an eternal rain. Dark clouds surrounded her, Death's gentle breath, collecting her to its bosom.

Again you call me, old friend..., Death murmured.

"No, I... don't want to die."

You taunt me, it said. *You taunt me over and over.*

Pictures floated up from the clouds. Aeolia saw herself a little girl, throwing a snowball at big boys. The snowball became a pot of goulash in midair. It spilled over an ogre, whose blows Aeolia welcomed like long-lost friends. To soothe her burning back she plunged into a waterfall, where swam a snake that wanted to choke her, but she only batted her lashes at it.

"I just wanted to make everything right," she pleaded. "I promise I won't taunt you again."

Promise, do you? We know all about promises....

The clouds darkened, swirling around hazier images of a dourer her, honey eyes grim, pacing through lands of flame. She saw the tongues of fire lick the hair off her head, the flesh off her bones, leaving her a blackened skeleton. She saw herself moving, walking on fleshless limbs, descending into the belly of the earth, where she looked into a stone mirror, her reflection bloody.

"No!" Aeolia cried. "No, that's not me! I don't want to die, let me live, let me live!"

Death laughed, and its breath assailed her face like cold wind, reeking of darkness and sweat and horse. The clouds below her parted, and Aeolia fell, shooting down into the maw that opened beneath her. She cried and tried to flap her arms, but they would not budge. Death swallowed her and pushed her down its throat, down and down into the darkness, where she tumbled, flipping like a tossed coin, falling and falling until finally, rumpled and dazed, she fell no more. She had landed.

Hesitantly, she opened her eyes.

She saw endless grass, which wasn't exactly how she had envisioned the afterlife. And she felt pain. Her muscles ached, and her wrists, bottom, and inner thighs burned. She was being jostled up and down, which increased the pain. She was tied to a horse's saddle, she realized, her arms bound behind her, her head resting against a man's back.

I'm alive, she thought, *and the pain I feel is not crushed limbs, but saddle sores and cramped muscles. But where am I?* She raised her head. The man on whose back she had leaned glanced over his shoulder, his face puffed red.

"You're awake at last!" he said in glee, spit bubbling on his lips.

Aeolia recognized him at once. Duke Hyan Redfort, the man who had attacked Greenhill. The memory of the battle hit her like a cane. Glancing around her, she saw a dozen more riders cloaked in Redfort's sanguine.

"How long have I been asleep?" she asked in a small voice.

"A week," Hyan said. "You were wounded, hum, direly. It took that long to heal you. We feared you wouldn't wake at all."

A week! Aeolia looked down at her body, still half-expecting to see broken bones and mangled limbs. But she seemed whole enough, if somewhat thinner than she remembered. Instead of her green gown she wore a simple linen dress.

"We saved your life," Hyan said. "We can take it back again. So be a good girl, hum? None of those Esiren mind tricks."

Aeolia scarcely heard him. A week.... She must be so far from Greenhill now. Far from Talin.... If he was even alive, that was. If any of them were alive.

"What happened to my friends?" she asked.

Hyan shrugged and turned back forward in his saddle. "We spared them, as you requested before plummeting down to probable demise. They live in Greenhill Castle's Dungeon."

Aeolia let out her breath. She had saved her friends, at least.

Plummeting down to probable demise, she thought and shivered. Had she truly jumped off a castle wall? Suddenly she felt dizzy, and had to lean her head back against Hyan's back. She could still not fathom how close to death she had brought herself.

But for now she had greater concerns. She had saved Talin, but he was still imprisoned. She herself had not died, but she was bound and captured.

"You're taking me to Stonemark?" she asked quietly. It hurt to speak much louder; her tongue and lips were parched and felt ready to crack. She considered asking for water, but decided against it. Hyan knew she was thirsty. She would not give him the satisfaction of seeing her beg.

"We're taking you to Brownbury," Hyan answered, "where you'll await Lale's escort to Grayrock. We believe you are, hum, already acquainted with the prince."

So Lale is alive, Aeolia thought. Somehow she was not surprised. The prince, too, had a talent for weaseling out of death.

"What will he pay you for me?" she asked in disgust.

"A kingdom," Hyan said, and said no more.

Aeolia licked her dry lips. *What does it matter what he'll pay?* she thought. *The only thing that matters is that he'll have me soon, and finally be able to kill me, like he always wanted.*

Suddenly Aeolia frowned. Something made no sense.

"Why did you heal me?" she asked slowly. "Why does Lale want me alive?"

Hyan chuckled. "When Lale discovered you and his archenemy are, hum, lovers, well... let's just say he has more in store for you than mere death now."

Aeolia shut her eyes and fell silent. She winced with every jostle, thinking of the pain to forget her despair.

* * * * *

A week later, the city of Brownbury loomed before them.

Aeolia sat on her own horse now—a small piebald palfrey tethered to Hyan's courser. Her arms were still bound behind her back, the rope biting her skin, and now her mouth was gagged as well. A hood shadowed her face and a cape concealed her arms. Her muscles were so stiff, every step of her horse made her wince.

The capital of Heland was a jumbled monochrome of browns sprawled over a round mountain. Aeolia thought it looked like some huge anthill lined with labyrinthine streets and straggles of wooden houses. Perched on the mountaintop, rising above the rest of the city, glistened a palace of marble walls and gilded towers. *That must be where the queen lives,* Aeolia thought.

The road toward the gates teemed with travelers rushing to enter the city before dark. Aeolia saw knights and clerics, peasants and merchants, beggars and tatterdemalions and lepers. As her palfrey trotted closer to the gates, ramshackle huts sprouted along the road, a second city outside the walls, where lived the sick and poor and unwanted. From knight to ragamuffin, no one spared Aeolia a second glance, seeing only a cloaked rider, not a prisoner.

Hyan drew rein outside the city gates. The gatekeepers wore lavender surcoats over burnished breastplates. Queen's men, Aeolia surmised—Purplerobes. But even so, these guards of another house bowed before the duke of Redfort, and humbly let him pass. As Hyan pulled her into the city, Aeolia stared pleadingly at the purple guards from the shadows of her hood. If they noticed she was gagged and bound, however, they were careful to ignore it.

Inside the walls, wooden houses huddled over narrow, winding streets. Sloping roofs and awnings blocked the evening sun, shadowing the roads. The thick crowds parted before the Redforts' coursers. Some faces in the throng, noticing Aeolia's gag, gave her pitying looks. But no one offered any help. Hyan was too puissant, Aeolia realized downheartedly. No one would challenge his right to take a simple sixteen-year-old girl prisoner. An entire city, Aeolia thought, and she was all alone.

It had been so long since she'd seen a city, she suddenly reflected. It was a strange reflection, perhaps, for a girl awaiting her death, but still Aeolia found herself watching her surroundings with interest. These streets were nothing like the stark stone boulevards of Grayrock. Here everything was wooden and ramshackle and chaotic. The first few streets especially were jumbled and foul. These were the city dregs, with streets so narrow the houses' roofs touched. But as Hyan and she progressed further up the mountain, the streets widened. Here they passed merchants' stalls, bakeries, fruit vendors, and workshops. The smells of breads and candies filled the air, and the stench of squalor faded. Houses became larger, streets cleaner. The palace peeked above the shingled roofs.

Finally, with the first fireflies come to glow, Hyan drew rein by a simple tower in an empty square. The corpulent duke dismounted clumsily and helped Aeolia off her horse. Gripping her shoulder, he led her toward the tower. Aeolia trembled. The tower's guards, bowing ingratiatingly, wore crimson. This was the Dungeon, Aeolia knew. Talin had told her the Redforts ruled it. She felt her lip quivering beneath her gag. *I must be brave like Taya,* she told herself. Taya never cried.

Hyan ordered the guards to straighten.

"Yes, Your Grace," they chimed obsequiously, and as they straightened Aeolia noticed them giving her hungry glances.

"We want you to take utmost care of our prisoner, what?" Hyan said.

"We take utmost care of all our prisoners, Your Grace—" one guard began.

"Incarcerate this one in a solitary cell," Hyan said. "Have your fun, but see that she comes to no harm. Prince Lale of Stonemark himself will be arriving to fetch her."

"Yes, master! Very important guest, very good care...."

Hyan dabbed his forehead with a handkerchief, mounted his horse, and cantered away.

Two guards grabbed Aeolia. Their bony fingers dug into her flesh. She tried to struggle, but soon capitulated; she was too weak. Head hung low, she walked with them into the tower. Inside, a tunnel spiraled down into darkness. Shivering, Aeolia trudged down with the guards, plunging into a black, underground city.

If Brownbury was an anthill, these were its secret caverns. The fuliginous tunnel wound downward, burrowing into the mountain, craggy walls dripping moisture and mold. Muffled screams echoed in the darkness. Rats pattered across the floors, screeching. Aeolia saw one rat carrying a skeleton's hand in its mouth. She whimpered through her gag, only joining the prison's chorus of crazed, desperate wails.

Cells lined the walls, and famished people languished inside. Some people were chained to walls, moaning, covered in cobwebs. Others hopped about like animals, madly cocking their heads, gawking with wild eyes. In one cell, Aeolia saw a group of prisoners with pale brown hair and gloomy honey eyes.

Esirens, she realized with a gasp. Her kin. She had never seen other mind readers before, but she recognized them instantly, like a newborn babe recognizes its mother. She had once had such a mother, Aeolia suddenly thought—a mother she had never known, a family she had somehow lost. Esirens. Her true people. What were they doing in Heland? As the guards pulled Aeolia by the cell, she felt a prickling in her head. One of the prisoners was linking to her, a girl two or three years her junior.

Here, take this, the girl thought to her. As the guards escorted Aeolia past the cell, the girl reached out through the bars and placed something in Aeolia's bound hands. The guards didn't notice.

And be brave, friend, the girl thought as Aeolia was pulled away. *The golden fireflies glow. Our Firechild will save us in time.*

Save us in time..., Aeolia echoed hollowly, when the guards rounded a corner and the link snapped.

The guards dragged her onward. For a long time they walked, plunging deeper into the Dungeon. It seemed hours that they descended, down dingier tunnels where the rats grew larger and the screams grew louder, where writhing vestiges of men dwindled to dust. Aeolia thought of the girl as she walked, and held her gift tight in her fists.

Finally, when she was surely beneath the mountain, the guards stopped. They unlocked an iron-studded door and shoved Aeolia inside. She fell to the floor, scraping her knees. The door slammed shut behind her, and she was enveloped in darkness.

It was like the ogre's basement, the darkness so thick she could feel it—touching her skin, filling her lungs. It reeked of smoke and mold and waste. A muffled scream came from somewhere far above, and Aeolia began panting. Her eyes began to burn. *No!* she told herself. *Don't cry. Be brave. Like Taya.*

Sniffing back tears, she sought distraction by rubbing the Esiren girl's gift. A waxy cylinder, a cold, hard cube.... A candle and tinderbox! Aeolia whimpered with joy. Funny, she thought, how just the promise of light could comfort you in the blackness. She stood up, leaned down, and passed her bound wrists under her legs. After ripping off her gag, she sat down. She played with the tinderbox till she managed a spark, and lit her candle. The small flame flickered into existence, and Aeolia lifted it, surveying her prison.

The sight was not heartening. The cell was narrow like a closet. Cobwebs and soot upholstered the cracked granite walls. The door was heavy and studded with iron. Aeolia saw no escape this time. There was no ogress to save her in this strange city. There wasn't even a wall to jump off of. This time, Aeolia knew, all was truly lost. Despair inundated her, but she shook her head, stifling it. *Don't cry,* she told herself. *Be brave. Talin had been imprisoned here before. I must be brave like him.*

Talin. She longingly recalled his kind face, his erudite eyes and gentle lips. It was a mistake. At the tender thought of him, her eyes moistened and her mouth curved bitterly. Aeolia forced her mouth shut, rubbed her eyes determinedly, and banished Talin from her thoughts. She would not submerge in grief and longing. *Don't cry. Be brave.* Perhaps the queen had received Wilon's doves and was arranging Aeolia's rescue. Yes, yes! A jailer might come any minute now, sent by the queen to free her. Any minute, that jailer might appear....

A peephole in the door rattled open. A jailer's red eye peered in.

"Hey there, girlie," the man rasped. "At dawn the shifts change, and then us free turnkeys will give you a little welcome party. One by one. All day long." He smirked. "Just thought I'd let you know. Have a good night."

The peephole slammed shut.

For a long moment Aeolia stared in numb shock, not comprehending, not feeling, just staring blankly. Then she slumped to the floor and surrendered to her tears. She cried violently, the sobs racking her body. The tears claimed her completely, all her unshed tears, from all her tribulations. They soaked her hair, soaked her dress, and still they flowed. She wept for hours, like she had never wept in her life, crying and crying until she could cry no more.

She lay sprawled on her back, cried dry. Her mind was befogged and thoughtless. In numb, hopeless misery, she gazed up at the ceiling. In the flickering candlelight, she thought she could discern letters carved into the granite. Two letters. Initials.

Aeolia blinked, raised her candle, and strained her eyes. Though neither of them could read very well, Joren had once taught her the Northern letters. And so, recalling her lessons, Aeolia concluded that these letters carved into the ceiling were a T and a G.

At first she thought it was just her imagination, but slowly Aeolia came to realize it was true, had to be true. She lay in the same cell where Talin Greenhill had been imprisoned.

It must be a good omen, she told herself. She felt she must touch the letters, caress them, borrow from them strength. That would help her for the morrow. She put down the candle, rose to her feet, and shoved her fingers into the cracked wall. Clumsy in her bonds, she climbed to the ceiling. She reached out her tied hands and touched the letters.

The ceiling bent like a blanket.

Aeolia fell to the floor, but she hardly felt the pain. *Chameleon magic....* Shaking, she climbed back up, let go of the wall, and grabbed the ceiling. The camouflaged blanket came into her hands. She fell back down, coughing as soot showered onto her. Gazing up, blinking the soot away, Aeolia saw a large hole.

A trembling seized her. A crawlway concealed by Forestfolk magic! She lay a moment, crying and laughing, then climbed up and grabbed the hole's rim. Leaving the candle behind, but dragging the magic blanket with her, Aeolia wriggled inside.

The thin burrow wound like a wormhole, rising four feet and then curving to the left. Aeolia crawled along, coughing at the smoky smell. She imagined Talin digging the tunnel for long moons, planning his escape. She promised herself she'd give him a thousand kisses next time she saw him. She *would* see him again, she decided stubbornly.

The crawlway ended at a vertical, bricked shaft—a chimney, Aeolia surmised. She took a deep breath and squeezed inside. She barely fit. The chimney was so tight, the walls pushed against her, trapping her in midair. Her feet dangled. How would she climb? The chimney was too narrow. Slowly she released her breath.

She slipped down two feet.

She inhaled sharply, and immediately found herself stuck again. The chimney was so narrow, she realized, it trapped her while her lungs were full, but let her climb when they were empty. And so Aeolia began to climb, moving breath by breath, marveling how Talin, bigger than she, had ever squeezed through. Soon she was covered with soot, coughing, blinking it away. The chimney seemed to wind up forever, curving in crazy angles. Aeolia plodded upward, praying no one lit a fire below.

Finally, sooty as charcoal, she saw moonlight and fireflies above. Tears wet her face. She climbed with more vigor and soon reached the top of the chimney.

The opening was wide as her palm.

Her spirits crashed. She could not exit. But Aeolia refused to despair. She would find another way. Lips tightened, she climbed back down the chimney, down all the twists and turns. She passed her old cell and continued descending. Finally, after what seemed like miles, she saw light beneath her. She glanced down. A hearth lay below her, with a maid stacking firewood. As Aeolia watched, the maid took a flint from her pouch and prepared to light a fire.

Heart racing, Aeolia began scrambling up the chimney. But in her rush she slipped, yelped, and crashed down into the fireplace.

Nearly fainting, Aeolia spun around. The maid was gaping, jaw unhinged. Aeolia rose to her feet, holding her blanket over her bound wrists. She glared at the maid.

"What are you looking at?" Aeolia demanded, trying to sound as stern as Taya could be.

"I.... That is, you...," the skinny maid stuttered.

Aeolia frowned. "Don't tell me you were going to *light* that fire."

"Well, I kind of...."

"Didn't anybody tell you the chimney was being cleaned today?"

The maid shook her head, her eyes wide.

Aeolia scowled. "You can get in deep trouble for this."

"No, no," the maid pleaded, waving her palms. "I didn't know. Nobody told me...."

"This is very severe," Aeolia said, quivering beneath her stern facade. "I'll need to talk to the cellarer. Go fetch him at once."

"The cellarer?" The maid seemed confused. "You mean Old Tawm?"

"Of course I mean Tawm," Aeolia snapped. "Go get him at once, or there'll be trouble."

The maid spun on her heels and fled the room.

Aeolia breathed shakily and stepped out into the empty kitchen. She reviewed the shelves quickly. Her eyes landed on a bread knife and she breathed with relief. She took the knife and cut the ropes off her arms. Her wrists were a bloody mess, but she spared them not a second glance. Holding the knife in one hand, the magic blanket in the other, she tiptoed out the door.

A dark tunnel stretched before her. Aeolia entered it warily, holding her knife before her. She began to walk. The narrow, twisting passageway sloped steeply upward, with not a single intersection. Aeolia was thankful; with any hope, the tunnel led straight to an exit. She rounded a corner, then suddenly reeled back. Behind the corner, the maid and an old man were returning to the kitchen. Heart in mouth, Aeolia lay down in the shadows where wall met floor and tossed the blanket over her.

The maid and the cellarer walked by.

Aeolia rose to her feet. They had not seen her. She mumbled a thankful prayer and continued creeping up the steep tunnel, away from the kitchen. Soon she reached familiar grounds—the rat-infested, scream-permeated place she had been dragged down that evening. Had it all occurred only several hours ago? It seemed an eternity.

After walking for several minutes, Aeolia heard footfalls approaching from ahead. She peeked around a bend in the tunnel to see a group of crimson-clad jailers sauntering her way. Again, Aeolia hid in her magic blanket. Apparently, however, her luck had run out. Rather than pass her by, the jailers paused at the corner where she lay and leaned against the wall. One stood so close, her nose almost touched his heels. They began to talk.

"Boy, she's a cute one, isn't she?" one jailer said. "Large honey eyes...."

One of his comrades smirked. "Honey eyes? Me, I'm after more than just her eyes...."

The jailers laughed.

"I hear Prince Lale is coming to fetch her himself," one said.

"Yeah, but you heard the duke—keep your mouths shut, and don't let the purples find out. Apparently the queen wants the girl just as bad."

"Oh, yeah? What she want of her?"

"Who knows? The girl is probably some runaway Esiren princess, a pawn in the war. Who cares, as long as we can dip into her?"

"But still, you don't want to anger the queen."

"Bah! The queen'll be dead soon. And then, all of Heland will be ours!"

The jailers roared their approval, and Aeolia's nervousness mounted. They seemed intent on staying a while. How long before they noticed her lying concealed at their heels?

Then, as she was becoming certain her escape had failed, she heard footfalls dashing up from below.

"The duke's girl!" a new voice panted. "She's gone!"

The tunnel erupted with curses. Aeolia heard the jailers clanking away, running down whence she had come. She peeked from under her blanket to see them gone.

She leapt to her feet and began running up the tunnel. She remembered the way; the exit was not far. She heard the jailers shouting and cursing somewhere below, and she quickened her step. The tunnel twisted upward like a streak of lightning. Aeolia ran fast as she could, past the prisoners' cells, toward the exit.

Suddenly, she skidded to a stop and fled behind a corner. Not a dozen paces up the tunnel, another turnkey was leaning against the wall. The man had not seen her, but still he blocked her way. How would she creep past him?

Then Aeolia realized what cell the man was guarding. The Esiren cell, crowded with her kin. Esirens. Mind readers.

Aeolia swallowed. She peered around the corner, took a deep breath, and shut her eyes tight. She linked to the guard.

Hey, ugly! she thought. *Here, inside the cell.*

The jailer reeled to face the cell. He pounded against the bars.

"Stop linking to me, you rats!" he shouted.

As he roared, Aeolia severed the link and began creeping past him. But as she was slinking by, she caught the eye of one of the prisoners—a young, ponytailed girl with protuberant ears. Aeolia recognized her: the girl who had given her the candle.

Esirens, Aeolia thought again. Like her. Like the true family she had never known. For all she knew, the mother she had never met, the mother she had lost for reasons unknown, might be there in that cell. For all she knew, this girl with honey eyes and almond hair might be her younger sister.

The jailer, muttering, was slowly turning away from the bars. If Aeolia wanted to flee, it would have to be now. So instead, she lunged forward and knocked the butt of her knife against the jailer's head.

Rather than passing out, the man turned around, eyes widening.

"Outbreak!" he managed to cry, before Aeolia plunged the knife into his throat, silencing him.

Clanking footsteps began approaching from below.

Fingers shaking, Aeolia grabbed the jailer's keys. So many! She frantically tried them in the cell's lock, one by one. The footsteps grew closer. Finally one key fit, and the cell's door swung open.

The Esiren prisoners gazed at her in awe.

"I'm the Esiren Firechild," Aeolia said. "I'm here to rescue you."

"Don't mock the Firechild!" the ponytailed girl demanded. Her voice was bold but squeaky. She couldn't have been older than thirteen.

"You don't believe me?" Aeolia asked. "I'll prove it." She linked to the girl.

The girl's eyes moistened. "It's true," she said. "I see through her eyes, I feel her body. We share senses...."

The jailers came clamoring into the hall, emerging from both sides as one, trapping the prisoners in the middle.

"Fight them!" Aeolia said.

The Esirens rushed out of their cell and crashed against the jailers. Blood splashed like wine from a drunkard's cup. A jailer came snarling at Aeolia, and she shrieked and opened his neck with her knife. A second jailer lunged at her, and she sidestepped, raising her blade into his face. The prisoners fought alongside her, grabbing the dead jailers' weapons. They were weak but fueled by desperation. The sounds of battle shook the walls.

"Send reinforcement!" the last living jailer called, before Aeolia slashed him silent.

She surveyed the scene quickly. The Esirens had suffered only several casualties and stood beaming, weapons in hands, over the dead jailers.

"Run!" Aeolia said, pointing her bloody knife toward the exit. "Follow me!"

The sound of more jailers came from below. Aeolia leading, the prisoners began to run. They stormed like an underground river, raging through the caverns, gushing toward the surface. Aeolia opened the cells she passed by, freeing more prisoners. Joyous wails echoed through the dark halls.

"What's your name?" asked the ponytailed girl, running beside Aeolia.

"Aeolia," she said.

"You saved us, Aeolia," the girl said, diamonds twinkling in her eyes. "We knew you would. And you'll save us from Sinther, too."

Jailers came charging from ahead, waving swords. The prisoners crashed against them. Steel rang. Blood flooded the floors. The jailers fell dead and the prisoners ran on, sweeping Aeolia at the crest of their wave. Sweet air and firefly light swirled ahead. The prisoners burst into the moonlit streets, erupting like a spring.

Aeolia squealed in surprise as the Esirens lifted her onto their shoulders. They rushed through the city, chanting at the tops of their lungs. "Our Firechild has come! Our Firechild has come!"

Chapter Twelve
Hideout

Roen dreamed of the green-eyed woman again.

This time, she was not turned to stone, but was of warm flesh and silky hair and soft, soft lips. She fell through the air, tumbling down and down. The furs she wore flapped, and her two braids streamed like comet tails. Her lips were slightly open, as in the middle of an unuttered word, but her slanted eyes were shut. Like a fallen angel she tumbled, outcast from heaven, flipping, gliding. Falling.

Roen stood watching from a field of blood. Death and misfortune sprawled around him, but he was only dimly aware of it. His eyes were transfixed to the falling beauty above, this woman he did not know and yet had known forever. Tears streaming down his cheeks, he reached up his arms. She landed light as leaves into his grasp. He held her limp body and looked into her face, at the tattoos on her cheeks, at those parted, soft lips.

"Who are you?" he whispered.

Her eyes opened and she spoke.

"Hyan Redfort."

Roen jerked up in bed. A dream. He exhaled slowly. He was still on the rooftops, fireflies around him. The voice had come from below, he realized. As he listened, a second voice joined it.

"That is my name, Lale, you know it as do I. So spare me your tedious greetings, what? The sun will presently ascend, and we have, hum, much to discuss."

The duke's nasal voice was unmistakable. The sleep left Roen and his pulse quickened. Hyan Redfort, back in the city! Roen shrugged out of his blankets, crawled to the roof's ledge, and peered down. Soldiers stood at the alley's ends, maybe twenty men in all. In the middle, right under Roen, stood two figures cloaked in shadows. One was thin, the other round.

"There is nothing to discuss," said the thin man, speaking with the soft, hissing accent of Stonemark. "You have the girl. I want her."

"Tut tut, Lale. I do believe we've never agreed on a price, hum?"

Roen wanted to leap down and throttle the fat duke. But something Hyan had said made Roen stay still and listen. Lale. Could this tall Stoneson truly be the prince of Stonemark? Roen felt icy fingers running down his spine.

"Name your price," said Lale.

Hyan answered: "I want to be king."

Lale snickered. "I'm afraid that's out of my power, Duke."

"Not necessarily. I am royal heir. You need simply kill my queen."

"I am a general, Redfort, not an assassin."

"Exactly. No assassin could kill Elorien. She is too well guarded. I need an army to kill her."

"Then use your own."

"And have Heland see me as a usurper? Nay, Lale. If you want the girl, you shall obey my words, hum?"

Lale was silent for a moment. Then he spoke. "What exactly brews in that twisted mind of yours?"

"I want you to conquer Heland and execute the queen."

"You are mad."

"I am also head commander of Heland's armies. As such I pledge you: not a sword will hamper your conquest."

Lale barked a laugh. "What good is your crown without a kingdom?"

"I will have my kingdom, Lale. I will not let you keep it. Conquer Heland. Execute the queen. Then leave."

"Humph! On what pretext?"

"I will pretend to chase you. I can be quite the actor, you know. After you execute the queen, I will feign some grand show of bravery, storming over the palace walls with my men. Your part in the play will be to flee before me."

"I will not be made a fool of."

"Oh, you will, Lale. You will if you want the girl. Conquer Heland. Execute the queen. Let me chase you away. As soon as you've left Heland, and I am rightful king and hero besides, then you shall have the Esiren Firechild."

"You ask too much! You are mad! You're asking me to feign a war!"

"You've been fighting a real war over the girl for ten years. What's a fake war in comparison, hum?"

"You are madder than my father, Hyan Redfort. But I will do as you ask. I have business in the Forest first—the tree dwellers cannot wound a prince of Stonemark and go unpunished. But then I will return. In one moon, I will expect Heland's borders empty of swords, and a clear passage to Brownbury. You ask a high price, Redfort, and a humiliating price. But for my father's sake I will pay it."

Hyan clapped his hands together. "Splendid! Then we shall meet again in one moon, with you fleeing before me. Guards!"

As the soldiers approached their duke, Lale turned to walk away. But at the mouth of the alley, the prince paused and looked back. "Oh, and Hyan?"

"Yes, Lale?"

"I was wondering. How did you get that old prune of a queen to name you her heir?"

"Why do you care?"

Lale's voice was chilly. "Because you are a hornswoggler, Redfort. You revel in treachery, like a pig in filth. But I warn you, Hyan Redfort: if you try to hoodwink me, if for some reason I don't get my girl, it will be *your* head I put on a spike."

Before Hyan could reply, Lale vanished around the corner. The fat duke dabbed his forehead with his handkerchief, mumbled something under his breath, then walked the other way with his men.

Roen crawled back up the roof. Dawn was rising over the city, gilding the roofscape. Roen's mind pounded with what he had heard. Lale and Hyan conniving a mock war to kill the queen. Hyan—king. The mere idea sickened Roen.

He stood up. Hyan Redfort would not see the sunset, he vowed. The rooffolk had waited long for the duke to return from Greenhill. Now they would catch him. They were ready. Roen felt excitement tingle through him.

He crept to where Nepo slept, knelt by her, and touched her shoulder. The spindly woman opened her eyes, blinking sleepily. Slowly her gaunt face split into a smile.

"Roen!" she breathed.

"Nepo," he said. "Hyan is back in the city."

For a second, Roen thought he saw disappointment in Nepo's pale blue eyes. Before he could ponder it, a hand clutched his arm from behind. Roen turned to see Grom, Nepo's younger brother, staring at him with his one eye.

"You saw him?" Grom's voice was cold and slow. "You saw Hyan?"

Roen nodded. "In the alleys with his guards."

Grom's grip tightened. "You sure, ground man?"

"Does pigment blend in oil? Come, Grom, today your Ketya comes free."

Grom nodded and released his grip. "We wake the rooffolk."

The two men moved from blanket to blanket, waking the outlaws. They told the news to each in turn. Before the palace bells peeled dawn, three scores of outlaws stood amassed on the roofs, each with a sword in hand.

For every sword there was a dead Redfort, Roen knew. For the past moon the rooffolk had been fighting a war of shadows against the City Guard. Redforts were found dead in dark alleys and darker taverns, knives in their backs or garrote marks round their necks. More weapons had been robbed from Redfort barracks, along with chests of food and wine and oil and cloth. These folks had been cutthroats and thieves in their former lives, and they fought as such. The Guard was helpless against them.

They each had their reasons for fighting. Roen fought for his father. Grom fought for his Ket, whom he had sworn to protect. Burnface Bas and One Toothed Ok each had children in Hyan's Dungeon, and Friendly Fara, Roen had learned, had once been raped by a Redfort. Others fought simply because Hyan had set prices on their heads. By naming their common cause aloud, Roen had turned them from runaways into savage fighters. And that common cause was catching Hyan Redfort.

And today was the day, Roen thought. *By the Spirit, today we roast the pig.*

He climbed onto a pointed steeple.

"Rooffolk!" he said. "Today our friends and family come free from the Dungeon. Today the prices lift from our heads. To catch the duke we must spread over the city, a man on every roof. Sooner or later he'll pass beneath one of us. When you see him, alert the others, and together we'll leap down onto his guards and—"

Suddenly, Roen fell silent and frowned. The crowd too frowned and rustled. Something was happening below in the streets. Roen heard a commotion of falling feet and clanking armor, like an army running. He heard shouts, grunts, singing, and above the din another noise—a girl's voice. A familiar, squeaky voice. Roen could just barely make out the words.

"Spirit help me, descend from heaven!" the girl cried. "Spirit help me, descend from heaven!"

The clamor grew closer. Roen looked down between the overhanging awnings. In the street below, leading a group of ragged Esirens, ran Ketya. Pursuing the group were scores of armored Redforts.

All around Roen, the rooffolk began to run. Swords drawn and faces grim, they leapt from roof to roof, following the escaped prisoners who ran below.

"Spirit help me, descend from heaven!" Ketya cried.

"What does she mean?" Roen asked Nepo, running beside her.

They jumped over an alley and continued running along the long roof of a tavern.

"When an outlaw is pursued by the Guard," Nepo explained, "she doesn't climb onto the roofs, so not to lead the Redforts to our camps. Instead she goes to a hideout, where we can 'descend from heaven' to help her."

Roen glanced down. The Redforts were many and armored. Roen did not see how the rooffolk could defeat them. The outlaws were stealth warriors; they could not face a real army in daylight. Roen's stomach knotted. It wasn't supposed to be this way. They were supposed to kidnap Hyan, not face his Guard in battle. Roen considered calling his comrades to stop, but knew they wouldn't listen. They were savage people, too given to their rage to heed reason. Roen felt his plans and hopes collapse.

The outlaws stopped atop a wide, dilapidated building, which might once have been an inn, but now seemed to host only rats. Grom was the first to enter, crawling down the spout and into a window. Burnface Bas entered next, and after him One Toothed Ok. The rest of the rooffolk lined up to follow. Down in the street, the escaped prisoners entered the building and slammed the door shut.

It was Roen's turn to enter the window. He paused above it, hesitating. This was not the way. Entering this house would be entering a coffin. And yet... it was Roen who had convinced the outlaws to fight Hyan in the first place. If he backed down now, they would never trust him again. With a heavy heart, Roen slung himself over the roof and entered the window.

He landed in a dusty attic. The single door was open, revealing a staircase. Roen climbed down the stairs into a large, cobwebbed room cluttered with broken furniture. The outlaws and freedmen crowded the place. Roen saw Grom embracing Ketya, mumbling, tears in his one eye. The gamine was splashed with blood. Many other escaped prisoners were just as bloody. Their clothes were torn and their faces dirty.

The dirtiest prisoner, a girl of fifteen or sixteen years, stood on a table in the center of the room. She was so covered with soot, her skin and hair were black. Only her golden eyes marked her as an Esiren. Roen surmised from the way the freedmen surrounded her that she was their leader.

"What do we do now, Aeolia?" one man said.

Aeolia! Roen furrowed his brow. Where had he heard that name?

The sooty girl bit her lip. "I don't know," she said, sounding abashed and distraught at once. Strangely, her accent was Stonish. "Why do you ask me?"

"You came here to save us, Aeolia!" Ketya piped, detaching herself from Grom's embrace. "You are our Firechild. You must lead us!"

The Esiren Firechild! Roen caught his breath. Could this girl truly be her, the one Sinther was hunting? The golden fireflies had begun glowing sixteen years ago, and this Aeolia looked about sixteen. It was possible. Roen remembered the conversation he had overheard. Yes, it all made sense. This was the girl Lale agreed to kill Queen Elorien for. This was the girl who would make Hyan king.

Aeolia wrung her hands. "The men, grab tables and blockade the door. And guard the windows! Upstairs too. Um... the women and children, you search the building, look for slats of wood, sturdy chairs, anything that can be a weapon."

The escaped prisoners rushed to their tasks. The men and women collected chairs and tables. The children scurried for stools and broken slats of wood. Roen spotted an old, feeble man with long white hair struggling to drag a table. Roen rushed to help him, and the old man looked up.

He was Smerdin.

Roen dropped the table. For a moment he could not move. Then he cried and embraced his aged and whitened father.

"Father! I thought I'd never see you again."

"My son, Roen, I can't believe, I thought they got you too, I...." The old man's words blurred into weeping.

Before Roen could say more, booms rattled the blockaded door. Roen glimpsed the crimson uniforms of Redforts behind the wooden blinds. The building shook as the soldiers pounded against it.

"Quick, more tables!" Aeolia cried. "Bring anything you can. Secure that door!"

More tables were heaped. The door creaked, splintered, but held. Roen didn't think it would hold long. He shuddered. The soldiers outside were armored and trained, and they outnumbered the outlaws.

They won't burn us out, Roen thought. *They won't risk hurting Aeolia.* No, they would break in. The siege might last fifteen minutes, Roen reckoned. An hour at most. After that it would be a massacre.

Smerdin seemed to have reached the same conclusion. "Roen," he said, "is there another way out?"

"There's a window upstairs. You can climb onto the roof."

"Then go," Smerdin said. "You must seek help."

"Help, where?"

"From Elorien."

Roen laughed. "The queen? What do you mean? She won't defy the Redforts' right to claim escaped prisoners."

A window smashed open. A soldier slung a crossbow over the sill and shot. A woman clutched her chest and fell. Hurriedly, the Esirens slammed a table over the window, blocking it. The Redforts' swords smashed at the table from outside.

Smerdin held Roen's head and looked into his eyes. "Elorien will do as you say. Trust me."

As crazy as it sounded, something in his father's tone made Roen believe him. And so, with the sounds of splintering wood behind him, Roen turned to rush upstairs.

"And hurry!" Smerdin called after him. "We won't last long."

Roen dashed into the attic. Two Esirens stood guarding the window.

"I'm going to get help," Roen told them. "Let me out the window."

One of the men shook his head. "There are Redfort archers outside. You'll be killed."

"I'll climb onto the roof," Roen said. "I'll be fine."

"You'll be shot dead."

"If I don't get help, we'll all be dead."

Roen laid his foot on the windowsill. He paused and looked back.

"This Aeolia," he asked. "Is she truly a Firechild?"

The Esirens nodded. "True as they come."

Roen pursed his lips and pushed himself out the window.

He saw them at once, two archers in the alley. Heart racing, Roen spun, jumped, and caught the roof. Bowstrings creaked below. Pain exploded in Roen's thigh. He gritted his teeth and heaved himself onto the rooftop. Before he could duck, another arrow slammed into his shoulder. Jaw clenched, Roen ran, stumbling across several rooftops before he slumped down panting. He was out of range now. He only hoped the Redforts wouldn't follow. If Aeolia was their main quarry, perhaps they'd let him flee. Roen didn't think they had seen his face.

He hurriedly reviewed his wounds. Blood soaked him, but no internal organs seemed to have been hurt. Healing would be quick. He took a mouthful of shirt and yanked out the arrow in his thigh, then the arrow in his shoulder. They came out with gushes of blood. Shakily, Roen ran his hands over his wounds. They closed perfectly, leaving not a scar. With a deep breath, Roen stood up and glanced behind him. The hideout was surrounded by a small crimson army like a puddle of blood. Fifteen minutes. An hour at most. Roen turned away and hopped onto the next roof.

The domes and spires of Brownbury sprawled leagues ahead. The palace, glistening on the mountaintop, was agonizingly far. Roen moved as fast as he could, leaping heedlessly. But as he drew closer to the palace—higher up the mountain—the streets became wider, and the roofs farther apart. At Brewer Road, Roen was forced to climb down.

It was afternoon—market hour—and the entire city thronged the streets. Roen wrapped his cloak around him, concealing the bloodstains and his face. He tried running, but the crowd was too thick. When he tried elbowing, the crowd jostled back. It seemed for every step he gained, he was pushed two steps back.

"Let me pass!" he shouted. "I'm in a rush!"

Faces in the crowd smirked.

"We're all busy," one man said.

"You're no better than anyone else," said a woman.

Roen clutched his head. This couldn't be happening, not now! He tried shoving harder. The crowd resisted him. Roen felt sick. He was stuck, his father was minutes from death, and the Redforts were about to make Hyan king.

And then Roen heard a nasal voice from behind. "Out of our way, peasants! Coming through!"

Roen turned his head and froze. Clad in enameled armor, sitting atop a chestnut destrier, Duke Hyan Redfort came riding down the street. The crowd fled from his horse's hoofs.

Roen knew what to do.

He elbowed toward a fruit stall and climbed up. The vendor tried pushing him off, but Roen held his balance. When Hyan came riding by, Roen took a deep breath and leapt onto the duke's horse.

Hyan gaped, so stupefied he could utter only one word.

"You!"

If I had a knife I could have kidnapped him now, Roen thought ruefully. Then, with a sigh, he punched Hyan's nose. The fat duke tilted in his saddle and crashed to the ground.

Roen tried to control the bucking horse. He had never been much of a rider, and the destrier whinnied and kicked beneath him. Hyan rose cursing to his feet and drew his sword. Roen kicked the horse madly. Be it his urging or the sight of Hyan's steel, the horse broke into a wild gallop. People scurried out of its way.

"Whoa, hold it, hold it!" Roen cried, clinging for life. The horse only galloped harder. At the end of the road it turned the wrong way, onto Market Street, heading away from the palace.

"No, you fool!" Roen shouted. "Stop!"

He pulled the reins mightily, and finally the horse slowed. Roen wheeled it around and began leading it in the correct direction. The horse moved leisurely, as if strolling in a park.

"A little faster...," Roen urged, kneeing gently.

The horse burst into a wild gallop, crashing into everything. People screamed and fled. Stalls overturned. Fruit rolled. Dogs barked. Behind him, Roen saw Hyan lolloping in pursuit. But soon the duke vanished from sight. The galloping horse was nearing the palace. Before long, Roen was riding on Purple Lane, outside the royal gardens.

The horse, however, galloped alongside the gardens, refusing to enter them. Roen cursed. How did anyone ride such a beast? He yanked the reins, trying to stop the animal. The horse seemed content at galloping full speed. No matter how hard Roen tugged, the horse wouldn't slow. A vision of the hideout, its inhabitants dead, shot through Roen's mind. He rose in his stirrups as the horse galloped under a sycamore. He reached up and grabbed a branch.

The horse galloped out from under him. Roen was left dangling. Then the branch snapped, and he fell to the cobblestones. Muttering, Roen rose to his feet and ran into the gardens. The grassy sward sprawled all the way to the palace. Roen raced down the main path, his shoes thumping. Scores of marble statues, the likenesses of erstwhile monarchs, frowned as he ran by.

The palace grew closer, looming above him. It was built of white marble, and its teardrop domes were gilded. Embedded in the widest tower was a huge, round clock with brass hands and golden numbers. Roen had painted these towers a hundred times. The thought that Hyan might soon rule them was unbearable.

Finally Roen reached the end of the path, where a pair of wiry gates broke the palace wall. Behind the gates, a staircase stretched up to the palace. Before the gates, loomed the gatekeeper. Roen gulped.

The gatekeeper was huge, maybe ten feet tall, with fat arms like pillars and a chest like a wagon. Seeing Roen, the brute's pendulous lips opened in a slobbery grin. He scratched his belly.

" 'ello," he said gleefully, drool dripping between his fangs.

An ogre! Elorien had hired an ogre to guard her gates! Roen said, "I need to see the queen."

The ogre chortled. "Huh?"

"I need to see Queen Elorien."

"Who?"

Roen tapped his foot. He spoke slowly and clearly. "I need to see her majesty, Queen Elorien Purplerobe."

The gatekeeper clapped his huge hands together. "Oh! Grumbolt understand. You want see Urmajesty."

Not just an ogre, Roen thought, but a half-witted one. "Excuse me?"

"Urmajesty. That her name. Urmajesty." The ogre became wistful. "She Grumbolt's true love."

"I see," Roen said. "Well, I have urgent news for her. I must see her at once."

"Oh no, Urmajesty busy lady. You tell news to Grumbolt."

"No, look, I really need to see the quee—uh, Urmajesty."

Grumbolt chuckled. "You funny little man."

"Yes, and I must enter the palace. Now."

Roen tried to step around the ogre, but Grumbolt stopped him with his hand.

"Oh no, don't be naughty. Grumbolt not allowed let strangers in."

Roen stepped back quickly. The simpleton's palm was big as a watermelon, and could no doubt crush Roen like an egg.

"Look, Grumbolt, you must let me pass. Every man has the right to request audience with the queen."

"Huh?"

"Everyone is allowed to see Urmajesty," Roen said.

"Ah...," Grumbolt said cunningly. "You must wait till Urmajesty calls you."

"Well, will you tell her I'm waiting to see her?"

"Tell who?"

Roen clutched his head. "Urmajesty!"

Grumbolt frowned. "And leave gate alone?"

Roen felt his control slipping. He had no time for this pettifogging. "Please, Grumbolt! This is important, don't you understand?"

"Grumbolt understand very good. Grumbolt told you wait in garden until Urmajesty calls you."

"But you won't even make the appointment!"

Grumbolt shrugged. "Grumbolt busy guarding gates."

"Grumbolt! Listen to me. The Redforts will catch the Esiren Firechild if you don't let me in, and if Hyan captures the Firechild, then Lale will conquer Heland, and if Lale conquers Heland, he will... kill Urmajesty."

Grumbolt frowned. "Kill Urmajesty?"

"Yes, Grumbolt! If you don't let me pass, Urmajesty is going to die!"

Grumbolt scowled. "That bad thing to say. Urmajesty is Grumbolt's true love."

"But it's true! I must pass, or Urmajesty will be killed."

"That bad thing to say!" Grumbolt growled. "You go away. Grumbolt no like this game anymore."

Roen found himself close to tears. "Game? Is that all this has been to you—a game?"

Grumbolt nodded hotly. "At first, game be fun. You say you want pass, Grumbolt say you can't. Very fun. But now game no fun anymore. Now you say bad things about Grumbolt's true love."

"But bad things are going to happen!" Roen said desperately. "This is crazy. You must let me pass."

Then Roen made the mistake of trying to walk past the ogre.

Grumbolt grabbed him and tossed him like a rag doll. Roen flew off the path and hit the grass with a thud. The breath was knocked out of him. Groaning, he lay on his back beneath one of the statues. The marble monarch gazed down at him disapprovingly.

"You go away and don't come back!" Grumbolt rumbled. "You *never* pass gates now."

Roen remained lying, gazing up at the statue. His mind was racing. "This might work," he mumbled. He rose to his feet and trudged away, between the rows of statues. "Yes, this might definitely work."

* * * * *

A short while later, Roen paced back toward the palace, his cloak covering him. When he was close enough, he doffed the garment. Whitewash covered him, painting him a solid white.

Roen stepped off the path and stood among the statues. Painted, he looked just like one of them. At least, Roen hoped he would to Grumbolt's eyes. He crept forward and soon saw the huge gatekeeper standing before his gates. Roen froze. But if Grumbolt noticed an extra statue, he conveyed no sign of it.

Roen began inching forward, moving only when Grumbolt looked away. Luckily, there were many birds, ants, and clouds for Grumbolt to gaze at, and soon Roen came very close. So close, he could hear the ogre's breath, smell his sweat, see the veins on his arms. *If he catches me now,* Roen thought, *he won't just toss me away. He'll crush my head.* Slow as melting wax, Roen crept closer, till he stood in Grumbolt's shadow.

The ogre jerked his head around and stared right at Roen. Roen froze. Sweat ran down his back.

"Duhh... Grumbolt don't remember no statue here." The gatekeeper scratched his head, then shrugged and turned away. "Must be new one."

When Roen's pulse had slowed, he took another step. Grumbolt stared at him again, frowning.

"This new statue very close...."

Grumbolt paced forward and thrust his face close. His small eyes narrowed. His brow furrowed. His huge, round nose sniffed suspiciously. Roen remained still, breath held, belly knotted.

"Hello!" Grumbolt demanded. "Hello!"

Gingerly, the ogre touched Roen's nose. He pulled back his hand as if bitten.

"This statue soft...," he mumbled. "Hello! Can you talk? Hello!"

Roen's lungs ached for air. Desperate prayers skittered through his mind.

"Grumbolt don't like this," the ogre muttered, his face suffused with confusion. "Grumbolt think he smash this statue."

He pulled back a huge fist.

Roen started moving. He whipped around the gatekeeper and bolted for the gates. He grabbed the handle as Grumbolt howled behind him. The gates swung open, and Roen shot onto the stairway, Grumbolt pursuing. The stairs seemed endless. Roen heard Grumbolt grunting behind. He glanced over his shoulder. The gatekeeper was gaining on him. Roen lowered his head and leapt three stairs at a time. But he couldn't outrun Grumbolt's huge stride.

The ogre grabbed Roen's shirt. The cloth ripped, leaving a clump in Grumbolt's hand. Roen ran for his life, heart thrashing. Grumbolt reached out again, and his fingers grazed Roen's back. Roen's feet scarcely touched the stairs. Grumbolt's snorting came closer, stirring Roen's hair.

But the gatekeeper's breath was wheezing. He was tiring. He was lagging behind. Hope filled Roen. The palace doors were but paces ahead. He was going to make it!

Then the palace doors opened, and the queen came stepping downstairs.

Roen skidded to a stop, so not to crash into the woman. As soon as he stopped moving, Grumbolt's arms wrapped around him.

The ogre lifted him in a crushing hug. A beefy palm slammed over Roen's face.

"Who is this, Grumbolt?" the queen demanded.

"A bad man, Urmajesty!" Grumbolt exclaimed. "He say bad things about you. He say Grumbolt let him pass gates, he say Urmajesty going to die!"

The queen paled. "Dear Spirit, an assassin."

Roen tried to scream, but he couldn't even breathe. Grumbolt's palm covered his mouth and nose. Dots danced before his eyes.

Grumbolt smirked. "Don't worry, Urmajesty. Grumbolt take care of this 'sassin."

Ruffled, the queen nodded. "Yes, take him to the Redforts."

Grumbolt turned and began carrying Roen downstairs. The ogre chortled. "Grumbolt teach you a lesson, you 'sassin. Grumbolt cut off your tongue for saying bad things."

Roen's lungs felt ready to burst. He struggled to open his mouth behind the fat fingers. Darkness fell over him, blinding him. He had seconds to live, he knew. The muscles of his jaw strained. He managed to open his teeth and fit between them a fold of Grumbolt's flesh. He bit down with all his strength.

Grumbolt dropped Roen onto the stairs and burst into tears. The darkness lifted as Roen took grating breaths, like a rusty saw in oak.

The queen knelt beside him. She wiped the paint off his face.

"Roen, is it really you?"

Roen stood up and managed a bow. "You know me, Your Majesty?"

Before Elorien could reply, Grumbolt grabbed Roen again.

"Now Grumbolt break your neck!" the ogre blubbered.

"No, wait, Grumbolt. Let him go."

"Urmajesty?" Grumbolt asked, sniffing back tears.

"I said let him go."

Grumbolt grunted and dropped Roen again.

"Why did you come?" the queen asked, touching Roen's hair.

Roen rose to his feet. "A painter named Smerdin sent me, Your Majesty. He needs your help."

Elorien gripped Roen's shoulders. "Where is he?"

"He's in an abandoned building on Cooper Corner. The door's blocked, but the Redforts are trying to break in, and—"

"But he's fine, isn't he? The Redforts don't have him yet?"

"Not the last time I was there, Your Majesty."

The queen began rushing down the stairs. "Then we must save him!" she said.

* * * * *

Roen and Elorien rushed around the palace to the barracks. The queen slammed the door open, revealing scores of armed soldiers with purple mantles thrown over their hauberks. This was the queen's personal guard, Roen knew, rarely seen outside the palace. Seeing their queen, the men stood up and bowed. A tall, square-jawed knight stood among them, golden wings protruding from his helm. Roen recognized the man—Sir Grig Purplerobe, the Winged Knight, nephew to the queen and hero to every boy in Heland.

"Sir Grig," barked the queen, "come here please."

The tall knight stepped forward eagerly. "Yes, Your Majesty!"

"The Redforts are besieging a building downhill. I want you to stop them, with swords if you must." Elorien gestured at

Roen. "Roen Painter here will show you the way. I will go alert the other guards."

"Yes, Your Majesty." The knight bowed, and the queen hurried away. Sir Grig turned to face his soldiers. "Men, two lines!"

The guards—there were about three scores—formed two orderly rows. They looked like a formidable force, and Roen just hoped they weren't too late.

"All right, painted boy," Grig said, grinning. "Take it from here."

"Follow me," Roen said and left the building. The soldiers marched after him, boots drumming. As Roen led them through the gardens, he glimpsed Elorien rushing about, whisking more guards out of their barracks. By the time Roen reached the gardens' end, his force had doubled in size.

They entered the city. Roen ran, his heart pumping. If they were too late, he'd never forgive himself. Behind him the soldiers clanked, a purple stream flowing through a wooden canyon. This time, the crowd parted before Roen, gazing curiously.

When they reached the hideout, Roen cried out in dismay. The door and windows had been smashed open, and Roen saw Redforts crowding the room inside. They were too late. The Redforts had taken the building.

Sir Grig stepped forward, coned his hands around his mouth and bellowed. "Clear out, by order of the queen!"

The Redforts ignored him. Roen noticed they were engaged in something inside, flurrying and hacking. He heard thumping and booming and grunting. There was still fighting inside, Roen realized with renewed hope. Some outlaws still lived.

"If you do not step outside," bellowed Grig, "we will remove you by force."

The Redforts paid Grig Purplerobe not a second glance.

"Right!" spat the Winged Knight. He faced his men. "We're going to get those blasted reds out if we must chop them first to pieces. Squads one and two, you enter the door. Squad three, come in through the windows. Squad four, find any back entrances, you enter those. You, painted boy, help squad four. Squad five—you stay out here as reserve." Grig drew his sword and flashed a wild grin. "Let's go!"

With a great roar, the soldiers rushed to their tasks. Roen ran with his group around the building to the back window. The Redfort archers were still there, covering the escalade of a dozen red soldiers. Roen glimpsed Esirens in the window, fighting off the reds.

"Drop your weapons!" cried the Purplerobe squadron leader. The Redforts ignored him.

"Attack!" cried the purple, and the soldiers stormed forth. The Redforts retreated from the window to defend themselves. Steel clanged. Blood splashed. Grunts and moans echoed in the alley.

Roen was only an artist, not a warrior. But he refused to let fear wash over him. His father was in there, possibly still alive, and Roen had to help. He knelt by a wounded red soldier and wrenched free the man's sword. It felt clumsy and heavy in his hand.

Soon enough, a red soldier rushed at him. Roen waved his sword wildly. The soldier seemed surprised by such an unorthodox attack, and Roen's blade severed one of the man's fingers. The soldier screamed and swung his sword. Roen parried, only partially diverting the attack. His foe's blade sliced Roen's arm, and a flap of skin unfolded. Roen cried out and parried a second blow. His feet sloshed through his own blood. His head spun. Suddenly he knew he was going to die. His foe raised his sword for the final strike. The man was smiling when a bloody blade burst out of his chest.

"You all right, lad?" asked Grig, wrenching his sword free.

Roen nodded feebly. He gazed around him and saw the red soldiers lying dead in pools of blood. The pain then came, strong and burning. Roen flapped his wound shut, mustered his magic, and healed himself. The wound closed. The surrounding purple soldiers gasped.

"That's some healing, son," said Grig. He whistled softly. "It would've taken most men an hour."

Roen shrugged. "Come, we must enter the window. They need help in there."

"Right," said Grig, nodding. "Men, form a pyramid. We're climbing in."

With the sounds of affray above, the purple soldiers heaped themselves together. Roen, the only man not wearing armor, climbed on top and entered the window first.

A score of outlaws crowded the room, ashen and bleeding, holding the door. Thuds shook the wood as the Redforts pounded from outside. Roen breathed in relief, seeing Smerdin safe and whole. Ketya and Aeolia stood there, too. Aeolia bled from a gash to her forehead.

"We're coming to help," Roen said as the purple soldiers came climbing in. "It's going to be okay."

Aeolia gazed at him blankly. Her eyes were glazed, and beneath the soot and blood she was pale. "So many died...," she said hollowly. "So many died for me."

"You're bleeding," Roen said. "Let me heal you."

He passed his palm over Aeolia's forehead, closing her cut. He wiped her blood away.

Meanwhile, the purple soldiers had opened the door and were driving the reds away. The fight gradually moved downstairs, leaving the upper room empty. Only Smerdin, Roen, and the two girls remained.

Aeolia lowered her eyes. She said to Roen, "I was so afraid. I thought they would all be killed. I caused so many deaths...."

"You caused no deaths," Roen said. "Hyan Redfort did that."

Aeolia raised her eyes, and Roen saw in them a deep, determined blaze. "Where is Hyan?" she asked, her voice taut.

"I saw him outside. He was heading toward the palace."

Aeolia nodded. She grabbed Ketya's hand. "Ketya, you come with me. Show me the way."

"Right!" Ketya squeaked. "Follow me."

Ketya leading, the two girls climbed out the window onto the roof.

Roen and Smerdin watched them leave. Smerdin sighed and put a hand on Roen's shoulder.

"I would go with them," Smerdin said, "but my old legs can't keep up. And, well, also I'm ashamed to see the queen. It was, of course, all my fault. We kept it secret so many years, Elorien and I, but I grew careless. I came to the palace too often, visiting my children or bringing Elorien portraits of you. Someone was bound to notice, and Hyan did...." Smerdin covered his eyes and fell silent.

"What do you mean?" Roen asked. "What secret, Father? What children?"

Smerdin smiled sadly. "Elorien and I have been lovers for decades."

For several long moments Roen could not speak. Finally he managed uttering, "So the princes' real father... it's you!"

"Elorien raised most of our children," Smerdin said quietly, gazing out the window. "I kept only the youngest."

Chapter Thirteen
Homecoming

Aeolia and Ketya ran through Brownbury's narrow streets. The entire city bustled around them. Red and purple soldiers marched in troops. Families scurried into their houses and barred the doors. The air smelled of fear and war. Aeolia bit her lip; she knew that smell too well. She tightened her grip on her bread knife.

She was exhausted. Her head pounded and her arms shook with weakness. Chimney soot still covered her, sticking with sweat, and her rags were on the brink of collapse. Her mind felt scarcely sturdier. Now that she was free, she thought only of Talin imprisoned in Greenhill Castle. It was her fault, Aeolia knew. She had to save him, or she'd die of guilt and pining. And the only man who could save Talin now was Hyan Redfort.

"Are you all right, Lia?" Ketya asked as they ran. "You look tired."

"I'm fine."

"Want to lean on me as you run?"

"No, I'm okay, Ketya, honestly."

"Are you sure? Do you want me to carry you?"

Aeolia laughed. "I doubt you'd be able to. But thanks anyway."

Ketya opened her mouth to say more, but Aeolia silenced her with a smile. The young girl had been awestruck by the prison break, and hadn't left Aeolia's side since, serving her with religious devotion. It made Aeolia uncomfortable. After all, she was only a couple years older than Ketya, and never thought herself anyone inspiring.

"It's right here," Ketya said, leading Aeolia past a wall of cypresses into a vast lawn speckled with white statues. Aeolia saw the palace ahead, its golden towers twinkling. A large, round disk was set into one tower, ticking rhythmically. A clock, Aeolia surmised; she had heard of such mechanisms. She experienced a moment of insecurity. The grand building, with all its gilt and wonders, made her feel small and insignificant, a mere fledgling girl, not a warrior woman like Taya. What chance did she have saving her friends from an entire army? Still, she had to try. She had to rescue Talin.

The girls skidded to a stop before the palace gates. Aeolia felt herself go cold, seeing the huge gatekeeper.

An ogre.

This ogre was younger, cleaner, and thinner than her old master, but still Aeolia trembled with fear. Memories of her slavery rushed back into her, and she could feel the cane all over again.

"Hello!" the gatekeeper said gleefully. He giggled. "You funny ladies, all dirty."

This ogre seemed harmless, childlike. But weren't all ogres monsters? Weren't they all cruel? Aeolia held her spinning head. So many old truths were shattering around her.

"Hello," Aeolia said to the beast hesitantly, speaking Ogregrunt.

"You speak Ogregrunt!" both Ketya and the ogre said, mouths dropping open.

Aeolia nodded. "Is Hyan inside?" she asked the ogre.

"Grumbolt think so, but Grumbolt not allowed let strangers or statues in."

Ketya linked to Aeolia and thought, *He seems weak in the head.*

Aeolia nodded, thought back, *He's like a child, I think*. Ketya released the link and turned to face him. "Listen, Gatekeeper, you must let this girl in. She's *very* important."

The gatekeeper rubbed a bandaged finger. "Oh no, oh no, Grumbolt learned his lesson, never let anyone in again."

Truly, this ogre was different from the ones who had enslaved her. He did not seem like something that would beat her. Aeolia's fear eased somewhat. She said gently, "Is that your name—Grumbolt?"

The gatekeeper nodded.

"Well, why can't you let us in, Grumbolt?"

"Last time Grumbolt let in statue, he bit Grumbolt!"

So that was why the young Healer was painted white, Aeolia realized and suppressed a smile.

"Listen, Grumbolt," she said. "That statue only wanted to help, he is a friend of ours, and—"

Grumbolt scowled. "He friend of yours? Then you go away! Grumbolt no want you here."

The gatekeeper took a threatening pace forward, and Aeolia and Ketya scurried backwards.

"I think it's hopeless, Lia," Ketya sighed.

Aeolia chewed her knuckle, considering. "Wait. I think I have an idea."

She took a deep breath and shut her eyes. Her magic tingled through her. She reached out her mind and linked to Grumbolt.

Grumbolt, she thought, *do you hear me?*

The gatekeeper looked around wildly. "Who's that?"

This is your conscience speaking, Aeolia thought.

"Who...?"

Your conscience, Grumbolt. That means your brain.

Grumbolt scratched his head. "Really? Grumbolt no think he had one of those."

Listen to me carefully, Grumbolt. You must let the girls in. Do you hear me? You must let the girls in.

"Duhhh... you sure?"

Positive.

"Oh, all right."

Mumbling beneath his breath, Grumbolt swung the gates open. He called out to Aeolia and Ketya. "Okay, funny ladies, Grumbolt's brain says let you in, so go quickly before it changes its mind."

"Why, thank you, Grumbolt," Aeolia said as she walked through.

Grumbolt muttered something in reply, but Aeolia and Ketya were already climbing the marble stairs. Butterflies fluttered in Aeolia's belly; it was not every day a slave girl dashed uninvited into a palace. If it weren't for Talin, she'd have turned around and fled. As she forced herself onward cold sweat beaded on her brow. She reached the top stair and paused outside the oak doors. Her hands shook slightly as she laid them on the doorknobs. With a deep, shaky breath, she swung the doors open and stepped inside.

The main hall was a vast, glittering cavern. Gilded columns supported a round ceiling like a second, golden sky. Between lavish tapestries, parti-colored light slanted from tinted windows, falling upon scores of sumptuously dressed nobles. At the hall's far end sat the queen on her begemmed throne. Beside her sat Hyan Redfort. As the two dirty, shabby girls stepped inside, all eyes turned to stare. A hush fell over the crowd.

"Stay here," Aeolia whispered to Ketya.

She began walking down the opulent hall, her footsteps loud in the silence, echoing in the painted ceiling. Golden sunbeams showered over her, glistening like fireflies. Dressed in rags, covered with cinder, battered and flustered and bloody, Aeolia paced toward the throne, hundreds of eyes following her in silent shock. Aeolia felt tears burn in her eyes. She bit her lip and clasped her soiled hands behind her back, but she never slowed.

Queen Elorien spoke softly, her voice clear in the silence. "Who are you?"

Hyan rose to his feet. "She's my prisoner, that's who! Guards, catch her!"

The queen stopped the guards with her hand.

"I'm no longer your prisoner, Hyan," Aeolia said, her voice quivering the slightest. "Nor are the others. I freed them, Hyan, and I will free my friends as well."

"I'll kill you!" Hyan screamed, but did not move.

Her heart hammering, Aeolia turned to face the crowd of nobles. She spoke for them all to hear. "This man is a traitor. When he held me captive, I read his mind, and heard him plotting to assassinate the queen."

Hyan grabbed Elorien's arm and hissed into her ear. "Arrest her! I'll kill Smerdin if you don't."

"Smerdin is free," Aeolia said. "I have freed them all."

"It's over, Hyan," said Elorien. "You no longer hold my lover, the father of my children. You can no longer threaten or blackmail me. You're finished, Hyan. Guards, seize this man."

When the queen's guards moved toward him, the fat duke drew his jeweled sword.

"Stand back!" he screeched, waving his blade. "You'll have to kill me before you touch me."

The purple guards drew their swords and approached slowly. The Redfort nobles in the court drew their own weapons and surrounded their duke protectively. They were about to fight, Aeolia knew. She could not allow that. Too many people had died for her already.

"Stop!" she cried, and was surprised at the power of her voice. Everyone paused and turned to stare. Swallowing hard, Aeolia slowly paced toward the duke, her bread knife in hand. With every step she felt calmer, stronger. Hyan blanched and sweat rolled down his face, but he managed puffing his chest.

"I'm not afraid of you," he said and clumsily brandished his sword.

"I know you can't hurt me," Aeolia whispered. "I know that now. No one can hurt me anymore."

She took another step forward and slowly raised her knife.

Hyan cowed back in his chair. "Help me, help me! Kill her!"

His men did not move, just stared silently. *They fear the Firechild now,* Aeolia knew. Hyan blubbered incomprehensibly, his jowls quivering. Aeolia raised her knife above him. She slammed it down, knocking the butt against his head. Hyan slumped unconscious in his chair.

Aeolia breathed shakily and realized her hands were trembling. She let her knife drop to the floor. She heard a sound behind her and turned her head. One noble, a Redfort, was running to the doors. A moment later, a second red knight followed. Soon all the Redforts were fleeing the palace.

The remaining nobles, Purplerobes and Greenhills all, began to clap. Aeolia blushed and smiled hesitantly. The queen rose from her throne, stepped forward, and hugged Aeolia.

"Please don't, Your Majesty," Aeolia said, lowering her eyes. "You'll dirty yourself."

"Oh, fiddlesticks," said Elorien. "Now tell me, girl, who are you?"

"I'm... Aeolia."

Elorien smiled, her face creasing warmly. "Is that all you can tell me, child?"

Aeolia sheepishly lowered her head, lost for words. Ketya rushed up the hall, bobbed a curtsy, and answered for her. "She's the Esiren Firechild, Your Majesty!"

The queen smiled at the vivacious girl. "And who might you be?"

Ketya squared her shoulders. "Why, Your Majesty, I'm her loyal servant."

* * * * *

"Get out, get out!" Ketya said, shoving maids out the bathing chamber's door. "*I'm* the Firechild's servant—and *only* servant."

The palace maids tried to protest, but Ketya slammed the door in their faces.

"Pushy bunch...," she mumbled.

Aeolia laughed from her copper bath. "Ketya, they only want to help."

Ketya shook her head violently, her ponytail flicking from side to side. "You don't need no Healers to serve you." She grinned. "That's what you have me for."

Aeolia sighed. Healers, Esirens, Stonesons—what was the difference? Once she would not have known. If all were humans, would that not suffice? Now Aeolia was not so sure. She could see the differences between the races now. Stonesons were pale with silver hair and gray eyes; Healers were large and blond; Esirens had eyes of honey and hair like almond peels. And though they all spoke the same tongue, their accents were different: Stonesons spoke with a drawl, Healers' vowels were brisk, and Esirens had a slight lisp and no true r's to speak of. Forestfolk, meanwhile, spoke another tongue all together. And, most importantly, their magics were different: stone, body, mind, animal. Aeolia remembered what Talin had said in the Forest, about crossbreeds leading difficult lives. She had not understood his words then.

She wrung water out of her hair, and as she stood up Ketya wrapped a towel around her.

"Really, you don't need to serve me," Aeolia said, stepping out onto the parquetry. The girl's alacrity was unsettling. Only weeks ago, Aeolia herself had served the ogress similarly.

"Oh, don't worry, I like to serve you," Ketya chattered. She lifted Aeolia's hair to wrap it in a smaller towel. "Your hair is so pretty.... But oh—your back."

Aeolia turned to face her and took the small towel away. Ketya glanced at Aeolia's tattooed hand and raised her eyes in wordless question. Aeolia nodded.

"Lia," Ketya said, shaking her head. "That—that doesn't matter, I.... Listen. When Lale conquered our towns, we fled to Heland, thinking it safer than inland Esire, little knowing the Redforts worked for Sinther." She grabbed Aeolia's hands. "Hyan was saving us for Butcher Joren to come behead us because we are Esirens. Our only hope was that you'd come save us, Aeolia."

Aeolia bit her lip. Butcher Joren. "But... it's all my fault," she said. "It's me Sinther is after, it's me Joren is killing you for. Can't you see? I caused your misfortune, I'm so sorry." Aeolia felt a lump in her throat. "I should hand myself in. That's the only way I can truly save you."

Ketya shook her head. "We never thought so, Lia. We love you too much. And Sinther hates us too much; even now he continues his conquests in Esire, even as he knows you are here in Heland. We don't want to surrender, Aeolia. We want to fight. We want you to fight for us, to save us from the stone tyrant."

Aeolia turned away and shut her suddenly-burning eyes. "I don't know who you Esirens are! I don't know who Sinther is. I—I'm just a slave girl. I don't give hope to anyone, I don't want to fight anyone.... I can't save anyone."

"You saved *us,* Lia. You saved me. Our savior...." To Aeolia's surprise, tears swam in Ketya's eyes, and her squeaky voice quivered. "Some people imagined you'd be a tall, powerful knight. Others envisioned the Firechild as a wise old hermit. I never thought of you like that, Aeolia." Tears streaming down her cheeks, Ketya smiled. "You look exactly like I always imagined."

"Scrubbed red and with wrinkled toes?"

Ketya laughed and wiped her tears away. "We'll fix that in a second. Here, let me help you with your gown."

Aeolia approached the stool where lay the azure gown the queen had given her. She caressed the embroidered silk, gingerly fingered the pearls fringing the laced bodice. *It's too nice for me,* she thought. *It'll look silly on me, like a golden saddle on a donkey.* But she had no other clothes, and so she dressed quickly, as the steam from her bath dissipated. When she had finished, she gazed into the mirror. The gown fit awkwardly, too tight around her hips. The maids had wanted to send in a dressmaker, but Aeolia had refused; she had no time to dawdle with gowns and servants, not with Talin imprisoned, Talin who had loved her in rags and didn't care for dresses and primping.

"Come, Ketya, let's go to the parlor. Queen Elorien wanted to see us there."

The two girls stepped out the door. They walked down a corridor, between suits of filigreed armor, portraits of old monarchs, and gilded candelabrums. After climbing a staircase, they entered a small chamber, its brocade curtains pulled back from the windows. A woolen rug covered the floor, surrounded by carved cherry chairs. On a marble table stood a compote of dusty fruit, while smaller ebony stands held seashells, statuettes, and pots of daphne and gillyflower. Aeolia thought of a certain turnkey who had only been doing his job when she had plunged a knife into his throat. Why should she live in such wealth while he lay dead?

The chairs proved hard and uncomfortable, and the girls sat in the soft rug instead. Aeolia was absently fingering her dress, remembering the taste of Talin's lips, when the door opened.

"Grumbolt!" Aeolia said with a smile. "Hello." She was glad that she no longer feared him.

Bowing under the lintel, the ogre clumsily entered the room. "Hello, ladies. Ooh! You all clean now."

Ketya nodded. "Isn't Lia's dress beautiful? Blue suits her so well."

Aeolia lowered her eyes, abashed. "Your dress is nice too, Ketya."

Grumbolt furrowed his brow. He said to Aeolia, "*Her* dress don't have pearls and ruffles on it like yours."

Feeling her cheeks redden, Aeolia changed the subject. "Say, Grumbolt, what are all those crumbs on your shirt?"

Before Grumbolt could reply, the door slammed open. The queen stood at the entrance. Aeolia and Ketya stood up and curtsied, but the queen seemed not to notice them.

"Grumbolt!" she said. "Have you seen the baron's wedding cake?"

The ogre looked sheepish. "Duhhh, what wedding cake?"

The queen rushed forward and plucked a crumb off his shirt. "*This* wedding cake! Grumbolt, you dolt, the wedding is half an hour from now. Where are we going to get another cake?" Elorien sighed and turned to face Aeolia and Ketya. "If I were you I'd be careful; he eats everything sweet he sees. You should come to the wedding, by the way. There'll be many young bachelors."

Aeolia said, "Well, Your Majesty, I...."

"Already have a sweetheart?" Elorien said. "I supposed you might. A girl so lovely, you must be surrounded by suitors. Ah, innocent youth... a pretty sight on dark days like these. Dark days.... Civil war rages throughout my kingdom, just a week after that darned pebble-brained king conquers the Beastlands."

"What?!" Aeolia gasped, flabbergasted, then recovered herself. "I mean: Your Majesty, has Sinther conquered the Beastlands?"

"Aye," said Elorien. "Last moon some ogress kicked Lale in the rump, or so I've heard, and his daddy ordered the place conquered. The Spirit knows what that whiny, scar-faced boy was doing down there in the first place." The queen sighed. "They're invading the Forest now, and I shudder to think who next. Just when I need an army, that pillow of a duke Hyan starts with his little tricks. By the Spirit, tomorrow noon I'll stretch his fat neck—if I can find it!"

All those wars, Aeolia thought. All her fault. She had lured Lale into the Beastlands and the Forest, in both places sparking violence. It was to kill her that Sinther had declared war on Esire. And now this—civil war in Heland, again her doing. She wreaked havoc wherever she went. Perhaps she *should* be locked up.

"Why so sad, girl?" Elorien asked.

Aeolia shrugged one shoulder and said nothing.

The queen took her hand. "I'll tell you what," she said. "Follow me to the balcony. I've got a little something to cheer you up."

Leaving Grumbolt behind, Aeolia followed the queen out of the room. Ketya trailed inconspicuously behind. They passed through more lavish corridors, all lined with tapestries, jeweled chalices, and marble statues. Soon they reached a balcony, its purple curtains closed.

"Go on," said the queen, nudging Aeolia forward.

Wondering what lay behind the curtains, Aeolia stepped out onto the balcony.

Wild cheers assailed her, coming from scores of Esirens in the courtyard below. Aeolia shrieked and fled back into the palace.

"Why are they following me, Your Majesty?" she asked in alarm.

The queen smiled. "You saved them, Honeycomb."

"Saved them? But there are so many more now...."

"Of course. The city was full of Esirens, hiding in every alley while their families languished in prison. With Hyan gone and you here, they all emerged from hiding."

"But what do they want, Your Majesty?"

"Why, they want you to lead them."

"Me? I don't know how to lead people!"

"You did a good job of it up till now. These people adore you, child. Take them off my hands; the Spirit knows I have no use for them. As for me, I must be off. Grumbolt is loose, the wedding feast is cooking, and I forgot to post guards at the kitchen door."

As the queen hurried away, Ketya touched Aeolia's shoulder.

"Talk to them," the girl urged.

Aeolia nodded timidly. "All right, Ketya, I'll try."

She parted the curtains and gingerly stepped onto the balcony. The crowd cheered. Aeolia twisted her fingers, quelling an instinct to flee back inside. Her knees quaked. Tentatively, she raised her hand, and the crowd fell silent.

She licked her suddenly dry lips and spoke in a small voice. "Hello."

The crowd erupted in wild acclamation.

She said hesitantly, "My name is Aeolia."

They began to chant her name.

Aeolia looked back over her shoulder in distress. Ketya gestured her on. Aeolia returned her eyes to the crowd.

"It seems I am the Esiren Firechild," she said. "I understand you want me to save you from Sinther."

The crowd roared even louder. These people worshiped her blindly, Aeolia realized. They were fools if they adored her so! She was nothing but bad luck. In the past few weeks she had sparked several wars, had killed more men than she could count. She looked down at them—thin, woebegone people, with almond hair and honey eyes, as her brother would say. Her foster-brother, who had betrayed her. Her foster-brother, who had beheaded Ketya's family. Her foster-brother, Lale's best friend, from the land she had once so craved, from the land that wanted her dead.

Mind reader, the boys had chanted. *Mind reader, go back to Esire where you belong.* Almonds and honey, scores of them, millions of them. Her kin.

"Could it be?" Aeolia whispered. "Could I have finally found myself?"

Looking down at them she knew it was true. Esirens, her kin, her true parents.... Homeland....

She realized tears were streaming down her face, fear and love swirling in her breast. She took a deep breath. *If I do this*, she thought, *it is not for glory, it is not for hate, it is not for a million pleading strangers. I will do it for one orphan refugee, for one half-breed outcast, for one butchered ogress, for one pinned butterfly. And for one very frightened sixteen-year-old girl, who has finally found her home. Like fireflies, we will light the darkness, together.*

"I will take you to Esire!" she said. "I will save you from Sinther!"

Even as they roared, Aeolia heard Ketya sobbing behind her, and she too cried for Esire, for a new home.

She said, "We leave tomorrow."

* * * * *

Milky dawn poured through the window, spilling over the room, outlining bed and wardrobe, chest and rug, washstand and mirror. Aeolia stood still amid the furniture, as if she too were one. She had stood thus most of the night, eyes drooping, not daring to sleep. She needed to be tired today.

The sun soon peeked over the horizon, dim behind gray clouds. The fireflies fled from its light and disappeared. When the last had vanished, a rap came on the door.

"Who's there?" Aeolia called.

"It's Ketya," came the reply.

Aeolia smiled. The long night had been lonely; it would be nice to see her young new friend. She opened the door.

Ketya greeted her with a sober nod. She wore a woolen riding skirt and carried another over her arm. Her normally effervescent face was pale.

"Is something wrong, Ket?" Aeolia asked.

Ketya nodded and stepped inside. "Elorien wants to meet us by the stables before we leave. She wants to give us horses for our journey."

"Really? That's very nice of her. She already gave us dresses."

"Dresses don't eat people."

Aeolia smiled. "You're afraid of horses."

Ketya shook her head violently, her ponytail flicking. "I'm not afraid of anything."

"Good, because today I have a scary task for you. While our people are gathering to leave, I want you to help me save Hyan Redfort."

Ketya's mouth dropped open. "Save that fat pig?"

"Steal him, rather. I have use for him."

Slowly, Ketya nodded. "This has to do with your beloved, doesn't it?"

"Will you help me, Ket? Say you will."

"I'd do anything for you."

Aeolia smiled. "Thanks, Ket. Here's what I need you to do. Go to the dressmaker and get a big gown, the biggest they have, with matching shoes and a wide-rimmed hat. I will be sleeping under a tree outside Old Raven Tower. Bring me the gown and wake me silently."

Ketya nodded. "Got it."

Aeolia dressed swiftly. The gray woolen dress was thick and warm.

"Okay, let's go, quickly."

The girls stepped out into the corridor. There they parted, each heading in her own direction. At the end of the corridor,

Aeolia hurried down a carpeted staircase. She passed through the library and exited a pair of bronze doors. Morning mist was rising from the grass outside. Aeolia walked quickly, past marble dragon fountains, through flocks of meandering peacocks, along flowerbeds and topiary. With each step another butterfly took flight in her belly. If her plan failed....

She crossed a small stone bridge, over a bubbly stream where goldfish swam, and entered a courtyard. Gaunt men in chain mail fenced over the gravel, filling the air with clanging steel. The men waved at her, and Aeolia reluctantly waved back. It seemed the whole palace knew her already, which meant her movements were observed, which meant her plan might be uncovered. Aeolia did not fear returning to prison. It was the thought of never seeing Talin again that was unbearable.

Past the courtyard and the soldiers' barracks lay a barren lawn. Several naked trees rose from the yellow grass, shivering in the wind. A tumbledown tower rose above them, piercing the gray sky. Unlike the rest of the palace, this tower was cold and sinister and dank. Holes honeycombed its brick walls, and its tiled roof looked ready to collapse. The roiling clouds made it seem to tilt. Old Raven Tower, it was called. The palace prison. Aeolia shuddered at the thought of entering it.

The turnkey at the tower door—a wiry man wearing ringmail and a leather skullcap—eyed Aeolia suspiciously.

"A dreary place for such a lovely girl," he observed.

"A quiet place," Aeolia said.

"They making you crazy in the palace?"

Aeolia nodded. "I came here to lie under the trees and nap."

The man smiled. "You can be sure no one will bother you here. Sleep tight."

"You too," Aeolia mumbled and lay under a nearby cottonwood. She folded her arms beneath her head and shut her eyes. Having stayed up half the night, tiredness soon overcame her, and dreams began to float behind her lids.

Before sleep claimed her completely, she summoned her magic and linked to the guard. Sharing all feelings, Aeolia's weariness overcame the guard's vigilance, and as she fell asleep, so did he.

The link disappeared as she slept, and dreams came to haunt Aeolia. They were strange dreams, of a cavern where friends lay frozen and cold, and death lurked in shadows, reeking of evil. Talin and Joren, the two men of her life, stood behind her, calling her to return. Aeolia ignored them. She walked into the darkness, forsaking light behind, till the shadow engulfed and claimed her.

"I'm here, Lia," a voice whispered.

"No, no, I'm sorry," Aeolia mumbled. "I'm sorry, Talin, I had to go, I had to leave you, Joren, I'm sorry...."

Hands clutched her shoulders and shook her. "Lia, you're dreaming. Wake up."

Aeolia opened her eyes. Ketya was kneeling above her, her face drawn with concern.

"You had a nightmare," the girl said.

"No... it was not like a dream, it was...." Aeolia blinked and shook her head to clear her thoughts. "Yes, a nightmare, that's all."

She rose to her feet. The turnkey lay snoring on the ground beneath the tower. Her plan was working.

"Here, tell me if this is all right," Ketya said. She unfurled a pink gown, wide as a sail, with matching slippers and a plumed hat.

"It's perfect," Aeolia said and took the outfit. "You did well, Ket, thank you."

Ketya beamed with pride. "What should I do now?"

"Stay here and wait for me. If the turnkey wakes up, hit him over the helmet with a rock."

Ketya nodded. "Sure thing!"

Aeolia smiled; it felt good to have such loyal help. She stepped toward the slumbering turnkey and knelt beside him. Carefully, she unslung the keys from his belt and drew the dagger from his boot. Holding the keys in one hand, dagger in the other, Aeolia entered the tower.

A rickety staircase wound upwards, missing a wooden stair here and there. Sunbeams slanted from holes in the round wall, falling over cobwebs, dust, and mice. A raven burst to flight from a rafter, flapping in circles while crowing raucously, shedding feathers. Aeolia swallowed. *It's too high,* she thought. Then she smirked. *I jumped off a wall to save Talin. Surely I can climb this.*

She placed her foot on the first stair. It creaked menacingly. Cold sweat beaded on Aeolia's brow. She paced up slowly, the stairs creaking. Spiders and mice fled from her feet. The floor dwindled into a small, gray coin. Aeolia's head spun, and her breath came fast and shaky. She forced herself to stare straight ahead, never down.

The next stair cracked underfoot and plummeted down. It crashed against the floor. Aeolia recoiled and stood trembling. She swallowed and took several deep breaths. Gingerly, she stretched her leg over the gulf, reaching for the next stair. If this one fell, she knew, she would fall with it. She breathed in relief when it held, and kept climbing.

Soon she heard moaning from above. It sounded like a lost soul, the wretched whimper of a caged beast. Aeolia banished sudden pity. She wanted him to suffer, she told herself. He deserved it. And yet she had to cover her ears, for his mewling pinched her heart. She cursed herself for her compassion.

"You'll be free soon enough," she muttered and took another step.

Before her foot had fallen, a rat leapt at her. Aeolia screamed and covered her face. The rat landed on her arms and jumped over her head. Aeolia lost her balance and wobbled, fell back a step, slipped and stumbled. Her head dangled over the pit. The tower spun around her. Panting, she groped for support. She caught the corner of a stair and shakily pulled herself upright.

She breathed deeply for long moments, her heart hammering. The rat was gone. It was several moments more before her heart slowed. She resumed climbing, wondering if her scream had woken the turnkey or alerted other guards. If she was caught here, sneaking into Hyan's prison, she might be hanged with him.

Finally the stairway ended at an iron-barred door. The moaning came loud and heart-wrenching through it, along with the stench of sweat and garbage. Aeolia unlocked the door and opened it.

Hyan sat blubbering inside in a pile of straw. The only item in the room was a small water dish. There wasn't even a slop bucket. When the fat man noticed Aeolia, he knuckled his eyes and glared.

"What do you want? Have you come to gloat?"

"I've come to save you," Aeolia said.

Hyan snorted an oink. "Get out of here. Save me. Save me indeed!" He laughed, his jowls quivering, spit bubbling on his cracked lips.

"They plan to hang you today," Aeolia said, annoyed. "I'm your only way out. You have nothing to lose by coming with me."

Hyan gave her a shrewd, slanted stare. "And why would you wish to extricate me, hum?"

"Does it matter?"

Hyan heaved a long sigh. "I suppose not, hum.... You have some sort of plan, I assume?"

Aeolia nodded and tossed him the pink outfit. "You wear this."

Hyan's laughter snorted out of his nose before seizing him completely. It was a whiny, squealing laughter, containing more misery than mirth. The tower shook with it.

"Will you be quiet?" Aeolia demanded. "Someone might hear."

Hyan slapped the dress with his palm. "Are you trying to make a fool out of me?"

"Undoubtedly. But I'm also saving your life and returning you your dukedom."

"Bah! I am a duke. I shall wear no woman's accouterments. I shall not be put to laugh."

Aeolia sighed. "You make me sad." She turned to leave.

Hyan grabbed her arm. "No, wait!" There was panic in his voice, and he blinked furiously. "Don't leave me here, please! It's so dark at night, and there are rats, I hear them. There isn't even a chamber pot. Oh, Spirit...."

Though he obviously struggled to stifle it, the duke broke down and wept.

Aeolia had not guessed her bluff would work so powerfully. Hesitantly, she touched Hyan's shoulder.

"I'm sorry," she said. "I didn't really mean to leave you here, I—"

Hyan shoved her hand away. "Don't touch me, waif. I am a duke, by the Spirit." He straightened and smoothed his clothes. "Fine. I shall don the dress. My subjects await me appetently, and I must escape hastily for their sake. Even if that entails unmanning myself. A duke must make certain sacrifices, for the good of the people and all that. But, hum...." Hyan went from condescending to sheepish. "Truth be told, I've never seen a woman with stubble before."

"That's why you'll shave," Aeolia said and handed him her dagger.

She waited, tapping her foot, while Hyan fumbled with the blade. She thought of all the things that could go wrong. Elorien might notice she was missing and look for her. The sleeping turnkey might wake, and Ketya be unable to knock him back to sleep. A second jailer might come to change shifts. Anything like that, and her plan was doomed, and she would never see Talin again.

Finally Hyan was done, wiping away specks of blood and muttering. "This is no way for a duke to shave, hum.... You are fortunate I'm in a magnanimous mood, or I would have sent you to the stocks for this blunt blade...."

"Are you done?" Aeolia asked. "Good. Now into that gown."

Hyan ponderously obeyed. Aeolia stuffed his old shirt into the gown's bodice, enhancing his bosom. When Hyan set the plumed hat on his head, Aeolia couldn't help but laugh.

"That's it!" Hyan said. "I'm not doing this."

"No, no, I'm sorry," Aeolia said. "It was mean of me to laugh. You look very nice."

"Really?" Hyan looked over his body. "Well, I do look rather fetching, don't I? I suppose I could get used to this, hum...."

Aeolia sighed and began pacing downstairs. Hyan followed in his slippers, cracking several stairs on his way down, and punching one hole in the wall in an effort to steady himself. Finally they reached the ground, and Aeolia breathed in relief finding the turnkey still asleep.

Upon seeing Hyan, Ketya fell into the grass with laughter, rolling around and struggling to breathe.

"Come, Ket, don't laugh," Aeolia said. "Our people are waiting, and we are ready to leave. Let's go."

Ketya rose to her feet, still giggling, and the three walked away from the tower. They took an inconspicuous route, passing around the winery along the palace's outer wall, where roses grew tall and thorny. The clouds thickened as they walked, drizzling icy drops. Aeolia shivered and hitched on her dress as if she could make it warmer by wishing it so.

The Esirens stood waiting outside the stables, dressed in rags, their scarce belongings slung over their backs. They began to cheer when they saw Aeolia approach. As she waved back at them shyly, she experienced a pang of guilt. They all adored her so, but if they knew who her foster-brother was.... Even Ketya, Aeolia suspected, would hate her if she knew. She bit her lip. She would have to keep her love for Joren secret. She would not bear it if they knew.

Queen Elorien stood amid the crowd in embroidered lavender and a wide headdress against the rain. Aeolia and Ketya curtsied before her. Hyan bowed.

Elorien frowned. "Who is this woman who bows before me?"

Ketya was quick to reply. "She's my mother, Your Majesty. She knows little of the ways of the court."

Elorien wrinkled her nose the slightest. "I dare say you have more of your father in you."

Aeolia felt it safest to change the subject. "Ketya told me about your gift, Your Majesty. I'm very grateful."

"Ah yes, the horses. Come along, girls, and choose the ones you like."

Aeolia bit her lip and smiled. She followed Elorien into the stables. The huge wooden building was full of hay, horses, stable boys, and swallows peeping in the lofts. At the doorway Ketya froze, her face pale, and refused to enter.

"Come, Ket," Aeolia said. "Don't be afraid, they won't hurt you."

Ketya shook her head. "They'll eat me alive. I hate them."

"Well, *I* like them," Aeolia said and began ambling amid the horses, searching for a favorite. All manner of horseflesh crowded the stalls: big shaggy warhorses, slim shiny coursers, palfreys and hackneys and even several ponies. Aeolia patted each one, fed them chaff, scratched their ears, let them sniff her palm. She thought them all lovely, and couldn't find one she especially favored.

"Have you made up your mind yet?" asked a stable boy.

Aeolia hadn't, but she hated to keep the queen waiting. She laid her hand on a shiny black gelding. "I kind of like this one."

"That's the one, then."

"I guess so," Aeolia said, when she heard a familiar whinny. She furrowed her brow, unable to place the sound. It had come from behind a pile of hay, from a stall she had missed. Aeolia walked toward it, stepped around the hay, and gasped in surprise. The hidden horse was a sorrel filly with a pink nose and a long, thin scar on her chest. Seeing Aeolia, the horse tossed her head happily and stomped her hoofs.

"Stable boy," Aeolia said, "where did you get this horse?"

"It's a strange story," the stable boy said. "We found her only yesterday, hanging around the Dungeon as if her master were imprisoned inside."

"I'll take her," Aeolia said.

The stable boy released the filly, and Aeolia hugged and linked to her.

You followed me, girl, Aeolia thought affectionately. *Thank you.*

Aeolia showed her horse to the queen, and led her to the door.

"Do you like her?" she asked Ketya.

"She's not as big as the others," Ketya said.

"No," Aeolia agreed.

"What will you call her?"

Aeolia thought a moment. "I'll call her Acorn, because of her color, and because she's tough."

Ketya smiled hesitantly. "I guess she isn't that bad."

Elorien patted the girl's head. "Are you sure you don't want a horse, too?"

"Oh, I'd be too frightened," Ketya said.

"How about a pony, then?"

"Maybe, if its teeth weren't so big."

Elorien turned to a stable boy. "Go fetch our finest pony."

"Your smallest!" Ketya peeped after him.

The stable boy disappeared and soon returned with a very small beige pony. Ketya gingerly patted it.

"Are you going to keep him?" Aeolia asked.

"I'll need something to ride, so I can keep up with you when you're on Acorn."

"What are you going to call him?"

"Well, if your horse is Acorn, my pony will be Peanut."

The two girls smiled.

"I'm glad you chose the horses you like," Elorien said. "The rest will go to your men."

Aeolia shook her head indignantly. "Your Majesty! All the horses? It's too much."

"An army should have horses, Honeycomb."

"But I don't have an army, Your Majesty."

"Your men are an army, child, an army to fight Sinther."

Aeolia wanted to remind Elorien she was just a girl, not a general. The queen seemed so convinced, however, Aeolia hated to disabuse her, so she simply said, "Thank you, Your Majesty, you are very kind."

The queen shrugged. "I want Sinther dead as much as anybody."

Aeolia lowered her eyes. "I guess." *I guess that is my destiny,* she added silently. *Spirit help me, I had promised so myself.*

Elorien leaned toward Aeolia and whispered in her ear. "There's one gift yet, one gift that can help you in your struggle. Everyone knows you can't face Stonemark on land; their infantry has never been beaten. That is why I give you my fleet. Move your armies in my ships anytime. Take them all the way to Grayrock. That should surprise old stone-face plenty."

Even if she was not a general, Aeolia understood the significance of this offer. It meant that Esire was no longer landlocked, and that it now had a direct path to the city of Grayrock. It also gave Esire a secret weapon, enabling it to surprise Stonemark at least once. She was thinking like a soldier already, Aeolia realized with a shudder. Had all her battles trained her? Could she truly save Esire from Sinther's claws, like she had saved its refugees from Hyan's?

The stable boys began saddling the horses, and before long Aeolia sat mounted outside with her followers. Hyan was given the oldest cob, which Aeolia tethered to Acorn. Ketya sat tremulously on her pony, clenching her fists to control her shaking. Aeolia looked at her, and again she felt the burden of shame. If Ketya knew who her foster-brother was, Ketya whose parents had died at Joren's hand.... No, Aeolia would not bear it. It would be her secret. She would never tell a soul.

She was hugging herself against the cold, when Aeolia noticed a shadow stir in the rhododendrons behind Ketya. As she watched, a tall figure approached the girl, cloaked in a dark hood with a long liripipe. Ketya turned to face him, and the man removed his hood, revealing an unshaven face with a patch over one eye. Aeolia recognized him as one of the outlaws from the hideout yesterday. The man mumbled something, and Ketya answered. He tried to kiss her lips, but Ketya turned her head, and the kiss landed on her cheek. The man bowed, pulled his hood up, and disappeared back into the bushes. Ketya watched him leave, a single tear trailing down her cheek. Aeolia watched but said nothing.

Elorien returned from the stables, her skirts rustling in the wind. She gave Aeolia two wet kisses, one on each cheek. "I wish you could stay longer," she said.

Aeolia smiled and lowered her eyes. "So do I. You've been very kind."

Elorien became solemn. "But these are cruel days, child, and I foresee crueler ones ahead."

Aeolia remembered her dream, and she remembered Eeea's words, and she shuddered. Could she truly leave love behind to tread into the darkness? It began to drizzle again, and steam rose from the horses' hot backs. Acorn snorted and tossed her head. Aeolia ran her fingers through the filly's mane, and the winter rain seemed to chill her heart. *No, I will never leave Talin,* she thought. *It was just a silly nightmare.* She kneed Acorn into a light clip, and Ketya and the others followed. Elorien stood behind, waving. Aeolia waved back.

Then, although there was no breeze, the queen's headdress flew and landed in the mud. She looked old. Aeolia turned her head away.

* * * * *

They journeyed south through Heland's countryside, over undulating hills, through shadowy copses, along wide rivers, and across cropped fields. The sky brewed with winter, and its winds carried word of Aeolia's advance before her. From every town she passed, Esiren refugees emerged to join her. All told the same story: they had fled war in Esire, but wanted to return under her leadership to fight back. By the time Aeolia passed through Greenhill lands, she had hundreds of loyal Esirens at her side.

Hyan's cob tethered to her filly, Aeolia led her army through Greenhill's fields, now cropped. Just last moon, she had walked with Talin through tall stalks. The shaved land now looked desolate, grim under the gray sky. As she approached Castle Greenhill, she could see from afar its battle scars: burnt houses in the village, heaps of rubble, black stains on bare castle walls.

"Spirit," Aeolia said to Ketya. "Look at that."

A crimson army was marching toward them.

"There must be a thousand of them!" Ketya said.

Aeolia trotted on, leading her followers forward. The two crowds stopped and stood facing each other across the village bridge. On one side stood armored soldiers. On the other—ragged refugees.

Aeolia trotted forward on Acorn, dragging Hyan behind her. Ketya hurried to follow on her pony. The Redfort army watched, silent. The only sound was the whispering wind, the only movement the swirling gray clouds. Aeolia quelled her nervousness and took a deep breath. She tugged Hyan forward, for all to see.

"The Esiren people have no quarrel with you," she announced loudly. "Enough have died already. I shall return you your duke, and you shall return us this castle and its prisoners."

The Redfort army rumbled with laughter.

"We shall not exchange so much," their commander cried, "for just one man!"

Aeolia frowned. She had not expected this. Her followers muttered behind her.

"Then we'll take your castle by force!" Ketya called, and the other Esirens echoed her call, shaking their fists.

Aeolia spoke loudly over her shoulder. "No! We have not gathered to fight a civil war in Heland. Our only enemy is Sinther of Stonemark."

The Redfort army leered.

"You craven Esirens!" their commander said. "This time we won't just throw you into prison. We'll squash you like the bugs you are."

Aeolia's followers seethed, and those who had weapons drew them. The Redfort army jeered and drew their own swords. Horses neighed and armor chinked. They were going to fight, Aeolia realized in dismay. She couldn't let that happen. She had caused too many battles already.

She yanked Hyan closer to her.

"Order the exchange," she whispered in his ear. "Do it or I'll cut off your private parts."

Hyan paled, and Aeolia was shocked at her own viciousness; truly, this war was hardening her.

"Men!" Hyan cried out. "This is your duke speaking."

The Redfort army fell silent and turned to watch him.

"What's wrong with you?!" the fat man said. "What's this rubbish, you're not willing to exchange many men for one? Am I not worth a thousand men?"

The reds shifted uneasily, muttering agreements.

"Then by the Spirit, get out of that castle!" Hyan sputtered.

The Redfort officer lowered his head and mumbled an apology. He barked some orders over his shoulder, and the red army began marching out of the village.

Aeolia breathed out in relief and noticed she was shaking. She and her followers moved aside to let the reds pass. She fidgeted on Acorn, twisting her toes. *Soon I'll see Talin,* she told herself, heart thumping. She couldn't wait to wrap her arms around him.

When the last red soldier stood outside in the cropped fields, Hyan demanded, "Release me now!"

"Soon," Aeolia said. She approached Ketya. "Ket, this might be a trap. Take a group of men into the castle and see that it's truly empty, and that its prisoners live."

Ketya nodded and selected a dozen armed Esirens from the group. They rode over the bridge into the burnt village.

Time passed slowly as Aeolia waited. Snow glided into her hair. Both armies rustled uneasily. Still Ketya did not return, and Aeolia's nervousness mounted. She wrung her hands restlessly. Where were Ketya and the others? Had they fallen into a trap? The thought was too dreadful to bear. If anything happened to Ketya or Talin, she'd never forgive herself.

Finally, after what seemed an eternity, Ketya and the others came riding back.

"The castle is clear," Ketya announced.

"And... the prisoners?" Aeolia asked.

"Their shackles are being opened as we speak."

With shaky fingers, Aeolia untied Hyan's cob and sent the fat duke on his way. Aeolia knew he would besiege the castle again, but this time she would defend it properly, and stay safe behind the walls until help arrived.

"Come," she said to her followers. "Into the castle."

She kneed Acorn and galloped onto the bridge. With a great rumble, the other Esirens followed. They crossed the bridge and thumped across the village, between ruined houses and heaps of cinder. They entered the castle walls and lowered the portcullis behind them. Aeolia scanned the courtyard anxiously, her heart thumping.

"Lia!"

The call came from the castle, and Aeolia looked toward it. Tears sprung into her eyes. Exiting the castle doors, trudging toward her, were three scores of disheveled but beaming prisoners.

"Talin!" Aeolia whimpered. She hopped off her horse, ran forward, and crashed into his embrace.

"I love you, I love you," she said, and her followers cheered.

Talin smiled. "Who are these people?"

Ketya leapt off her pony to answer him.

"We're her loyal followers!" she piped, her chin raised proudly. "She is taking us back home."

"I'm going to Esire," Aeolia explained.

"And you," said Ketya, jabbing her finger against Talin's chest, "are coming with us."

* * * * *

She rode into Esire with winter's first snows, leading her followers. For days they climbed the kingdom's craggy mountains, where grew the fabled Big Browns, great conifers wide and tall as towers. At every village the commoners came to cheer, simple loggers dressed in coarse goat wool, their faces rugged like their mountainous home. Home.... This was her home, Aeolia thought, these mountaineers were her kin, the family she had never known. This was who she was, a mountain dweller and logger, born in the shade of the Big Browns, this was her. She would never leave this land, she swore, for it was her own, and she loved it like her life.

All the Island, men said, was a great mountain protruding from the sea. And in that mountain's center was a wide shallow, whence once all earth had been spewed. In this deep, white valley nestled the city of Woodwall, capital of Esire. Her walls were built of Big Browns, the huge logs bonded with iron straps. Inside the walls, snow silvered sturdy houses and wide, crisscrossing streets. The palace sat in the city's center, a stout rectangle, its corners made of Big Browns fashioned into towers, its walls built of stone white as snow. The city was beautiful, Aeolia thought, so neat and clean, smaller than other cities, simpler than other cities, but prettier. *It fits me, it is like me, it feels right.*

People thronged the streets to greet her, the palace knights paraded, trumpets trumpeted, flowers were tossed, doves were sent into flight. While war waged on her northwestern border, Esire rose in song and celebration, blazing with hope, burning the cold from her heart. Aeolia had finally come home.

Chapter Fourteen
Winter

Taya took a deep breath, raised the opened skull to her lips, and drained it. The drunkards hooted so loudly, the dingy house shook and threatened to fall off its branches.

The House of Spirits was crowded that evening, smelling of sweat and drink and vomit. This was not a holy place as its name implied. No shamans prayed in this house to the souls of dead ancestors. This was not a House of Bones. In this house, the only spirits were in the drunkards' cups.

While those drunkards now cheered her, Taya's opponent—a dour, bearded warrior called Bug—did not join the revelry. His eyes were red and bleary, but he managed to fix Taya with a loathing glare as he raised his own cup—a painted human skull—to his lips. He drained it with a single swig and wiped his mouth with satisfaction.

"Give it up," he said. "I've beaten men twice your size."

Taya spat onto the floor. "And I've drunk barrels twice yours." She filled her own skull-cup with more greenroot and gulped it down.

Bug laughed. "Ah! You're so drunk, you'll be bedding the entire Stonish army when they arrive." He quaffed another drink.

Taya followed with her own, wiped her lips and said, "You're drunker than a fish, if you're imagining an invading Stonish horde."

"I've seen them with my own eyes, swarming in from the west." Bug slammed his newly emptied skull onto the table.

"Bah! Eyes full of greenroot."

"Nay, eyes full of fear."

Taya swallowed another drink. "Always thought you was too stupid to be ascared, Bug."

She expected him to redden with the taunt, but instead Bug shook his head gravely. He sounded eerily sober when he spoke. "Twenty years I've been a warrior, woman, and I don't have enough hairs in my beard for all the braids I've earned. I must have eaten more hearts than roasted grubs. But three days ago, when I saw those demons destroy us like a bird picking bugs from a log, well, I ran like a beardless boy. Only time I ever ran from battle, and I'm not ashamed of it. I'd do it again anytime."

The drunkards had fallen silent during the speech and now muttered amongst themselves. Through the greenroot mists befogging her mind, Taya felt fear's icy breath. She shuddered. Could it be that Bug was speaking truth, that Stonesons were truly arriving? No, it was the greenroot speaking through his lips.

"You was dreaming, Bug. They were only greenroot spirits you sawed."

Bug imbibed another skull. "I tell you I saw them coming from the Beastlands. They own them now. Soon will own us too."

Taya wiped another drink's remnants off her lips. The room was spinning. "I ain't afraid of them Stonesons! Ha! They won't dare come back here, not after what I did to Lale."

"What did you do?" Bug asked. His speech was slurred. "Pass out drunk at his feet?"

Taya shook her head. "I nearly killed him, I did. Stabbed him in the belly, right here."

Bug and his fellows roared with laughter. They all spun around her.

"You don't believe me, do you?" Taya demanded. She rocked closer to him and squinted, trying to bring him into focus. "I did nearly kill him, I did! An' if he ever again shows his scarred face here again, I'll do it again!"

Bug drained another drink. His eyes swam, his face flushed, and he wobbled on his log. "By the spirits," he said, "I hope you do."

With that he crashed unconscious onto the table.

Taya tossed back her head and laughed with victory. Then she noticed that the House of Spirits was unnaturally quiet. The drunkards were not cheering or grumbling or paying off their bets. Instead, they were staring out the window. The only sound was a dim *thump thump* coming from outside.

Taya wanted to ask the matter, but her tongue felt too thick. She rose to her wobbly feet. Leaning on the tabletops, she made her way to the window. The drunkards made room and Taya stared outside.

Below on the forest floor, spread evenly under the airborne village, an army of Stonesons was chopping down the trees. As Taya watched, two of the armored soldiers began chopping at the House of Spirit's foundations.

The inebriates began fleeing out the door, but Taya stood frozen, unable to move. The whole building creaked and tilted, and Taya's head whirled. She blundered several paces backwards, tripped over a stool, and fell to the floor. She tried to rise but was too dizzy. She started crawling toward the door, but the floor tilted, and she slid into the far corner.

She heard the deafening sound of wood cracking, and then the House of Spirits began to plummet. Taya screamed. The building crashed through branches. Furniture flew. The building bounced and flipped, tossing Taya around like dice in a giant hand. Her head hit the ceiling, and everything went black.

* * * * *

She dreamed of a man with yellow curls.

Somehow she knew they were yellow, and that his eyes were blue, even though the darkness was complete. She lay in a coffin, and he lay beside her, but she could hear him breathing and so knew he was alive. Her hands sought his in the darkness, and she drew comfort from their warmth. They were soft hands, lacking the calluses of a fighter or hunter or worker. Long fingers. An artist's hand.

But slowly as she held them, his hands hardened and chilled. Taya squeezed them tighter, and it was like squeezing the hands of a statue. Urgently she touched his face, and found that his beard had frozen and was now cold and hard. His curls were like ripples of stone. It frightened her, and she tried to draw her hand away but could not. It too was frozen. She opened her mouth to scream but no sound came out, and her mouth remained frozen and open. She was turned to stone. She could not move. She struggled and strained, and at last—

Her eyes snapped open.

Slowly she let out her breath. Just a dream, she told herself. Just a dream.

Or was it? It was dark where she lay, and when she tried to move she could not. Where was she? She tried to remember, but her head ached too badly. Her body also hurt. Something heavy was pushing against her chest, and her legs were numb. In the darkness she could discern only the outlines of furniture and broken wood all jumbled above her. She was trapped beneath the wreckage of a building, she realized. No wonder she had dreamed she was buried in a coffin.

She felt a pang of panic. How had this happened? She could not remember. The last thing she recalled, she was entering a drinking contest with some old, clanless warrior. Everything after that was a blur. Only a dull, nervous knot in her belly hinted that something was wrong, something terrible had happened. But Taya could not recall what. *At least I am alive,* she thought. *I must get myself out of here.*

She stirred slightly. The wreckage trapping her creaked and shifted, showering dust and splinters. Taya froze. The structure was unsteady, she realized. The pocket of air that shielded her from crushing death might collapse if she moved. She grimaced, and her head pounded harder. She felt nauseous. The structure creaked and shifted further. It could collapse any moment, Taya knew. She had to get out fast. Hurriedly, she mustered her magic, a feat that made her head explode with pain. When the tingling saturated her, she turned into a turtle.

For a second, the heap above her held, creaking. Dust rained, and the structure shifted the slightest. Taya whisked into her shell as the heap collapsed above her.

The sound was deafening. Dust tickled her nostrils. Furniture crashed against her shell. For long moments benches and stools tumbled and rearranged themselves, wooden beams snapped, splinters flew. Finally, slowly, the din died. Taya breathed out in relief. The unsteady pocket of air was gone. Now, the structure was more compact, and she could move safely, without fear of unsettling the delicate construction.

She turned into a snake and slithered past splintered furniture, dusty furs, shattered plates, collapsed walls, a broken stone oven, heavy clay churns, and naked deadfall. Finally, she emerged onto the surface of the wreckage, under a cloudy, snowing sky. She resumed her human form.

The sky.... It had been so long since she'd seen it. Taya stood breathless for a moment, gazing in awe at the cobalt clouds, the falling snow, the ravens circling the early sun. The sky. She had never seen such a clear, perfect view of it. Where was the leafy canopy she had always known?

Taya tore her gaze away from the wonder above and looked over the village. Then she understood. The trees were all chopped down. The once-elevated village lay in ruins on the ground.

Taya saw no one. Gingerly, she limped down the heap of the collapsed building, wincing from pain. Her head still pounded, and her left leg was one big bruise. She could still not recall what had happened. Holding her bone knife before her, she walked amid the fallen village—a great jumble of wood and rope, all silvered with snow. She noticed that the snow was heaped strangely in places, soft mounds like graves. Taya knelt by one such hummock and cleared the snow away.

It was a dead body. Whether it had been a woman or man, Taya could not tell. It had been too badly beaten. Taya blundered several paces backwards, fighting down nausea. Doggedly, refusing to tremble, she began moving from body to body, searching for survivors. She found none. All the villagers had been slaughtered, children and adults as one. Many of the bodies were pierced with stone splinters. Stonesons, Taya knew. Stonesons had done this.

Then, slowly, she remembered. Last evening. The drinking contest. Bug had spoken of Stonesons. So the old warrior had been right. Stonesons had come to the Forest, and had come to kill. But why? Such pointless carnage.... These Stonesons were not warriors, Taya thought in a sudden cold rage. No Forestfellow warrior would kill mothers and children. No, these Stonesons were no more than murderers.

So this is who Aeolia fights, Taya realized. *These are the beasts that hunt my friend.*

Suddenly Taya froze, fear stabbing her belly. The mad King Sinther had declared war on Esire solely to catch its Firechild. Could it be that Lale was doing the same with the Forestfolk? Had the Stonish prince invaded the Forest solely to catch Taya, she who had nearly killed him? It was possible, Taya thought. Lale might have learned she lived here and destroyed the village to find her. If that was so, he might have learned of Yaiyai as well....

Taya grimaced. Not Yaiyai, not her clan.... Taya couldn't let this grim fate befall her home. She had to warn them to flee.

Unless she was too late already.... If she was, she'd never forgive herself.

Taya summoned her magic. She jumped into the air, turned into a hawk, and began to fly, leaving the ravaged village behind.

Gliding under the snowing clouds, Taya spotted more pockets of destruction in the Forest: more toppled villages, more heaps of bodies. The icy air smelled of blood. From the distance came a rumble like thunder, and Taya saw thousands of birds fleeing. This was the Stonish host, Taya knew, the invaders who were destroying her land. She had to reach Yaiyai in time. She no longer cared that they had exiled her. They were the people she had grown up with, and she must warn them.

Finally, after an hour of flight, when her head felt ready to split with pain and magic, Taya flew directly above the Stonish army. They wore gray uniforms over the gray, hard armor of the Northerners. They marched between the trees like an oozing puddle of dirty water. Forest animals fled from their advance. Taya pulled her wings close to her body and dived down above the head of the army. There she saw him marching—Lale, prince of Stonemark.

Taya flapped and soared, caught an air current and glided forward as fast as she could. Lale had not yet reached Yaiyai, but he was less than an hour away. If Taya were to evacuate her village, she had to hurry.

Finally she reached Yaiyai, and memories of more innocent days pinched her heart, days of boredom and childhood, before she had met Aeolia and Lale, before Ayat had driven her away. She had been living in exile for weeks, and now she was back to save a home no longer hers.

She flapped down onto one of the village's bridges, just outside the clan's Core. No one was in sight. Taya turned back human. She walked briskly along the swinging bridge toward the bone house, determined to warn her mother and help her organize an evacuation. She opened the door without knocking.

Cloaked in the shadows inside, bedecked with the holy charms of the shaman, sat Ayat.

"Hello, Taya," the evil twin said with a sweet smile. "I didn't think you'd dare show your tattooed face here again."

Taya fumbled with her tongue. "W-what are you doing here? Where's Eeea? Why are you wearing her charms?"

Ayat rose to her feet. "When we heard about the Stonesons, I convinced the old woman that for the duration of the threat, I must rule the village. I do, after all, have military training."

At that moment several bare-chested clansmen, Ooor among them, entered the room carrying trays of berries and nuts.

"Ah, thank you, my servants," Ayat said with a smile. "A berry, if you please?"

Ooor held up a clump of berries, and Ayat plucked one into her mouth, sucked on it a moment before chewing and swallowing.

Taya did not know if to laugh or cry. "You're having the clansmen serve you now?!"

Ayat shrugged. "The Forest's Firechild deserves some respect."

Ooor stepped forward from the group of clansmen and pointed at Taya.

"What is she doing here, Your Majesty?" he asked Ayat.

Your Majesty?! This time, Taya knew she *should* laugh, that under any other circumstance, she *would* have laughed. But no mirth found her now. Not today.

"Listen to me," she said to Ayat. "The Stonesons will be here any minute now, and they will destroy the village. We must flee."

Ayat raised an eyebrow. "We? Since when do you include yourself as part of this clan?"

"Enough of your bantering!" Taya said. "This is a grave matter. The clan has only moments to flee before Lale arrives."

Ayat smiled condescendingly, like an adult at an erring child. "We will not flee. We will stay here and fight the invaders."

Taya clutched her head. "You don't stand a chance against the Stonesons. There are thousands of them, they have destroyed the Forest's western packs, nothing can stop them. Even Healers don't dare fight them. Don't you know that no army has ever faced a Stonish infantry and won?"

The men in the room shifted uneasily, mumbling. Ayat's eyes flicked nervously, but theirs was a different fear. Taya understood. Her twin was in no real danger. At any time, Ayat could turn into a bird and fly away. But the Stonish menace had given her power. Their invasion had granted her rule of the village. As long as the Stonesons threatened Yaiyai, Ayat would rule it. Evacuating the village would be forfeiting her suit of charms.

"She speaks nonsense!" Ayat said, her shoulders squared and fists clenched. "Don't listen to her, men. Remember she's an imposter!"

Taya spoke mildly to her twin. "If the Stonesons find us here, you'll have no clan to rule, for they will destroy it. Don't kill our home."

"Silence, doppelganger!" Ayat screamed. "We are not cowards like you. We will fight. We will beat the Stonesons."

The men in the room cheered. Ayat marched to the door and stepped outside. She stood on the bridge and cried for all the village to hear.

"The Stonesons are coming! We fight them now."

Taya watched in anguish. The clansmen still thought her a witch, and now they worshipped Ayat like a goddess, their devotion fueled by fear. Common sense was no match to naked emotion, Taya realized. She would simply have to fight with them.

This was her home, and she could not desert it, even if it had deserted her.

A crowd gathered around the bridge, standing on surrounding walkways, peering from windows, dangling from branches.

"Get your weapons!" Ayat called. "Climb down to the surface. We face them there."

Taya rushed forward and grabbed Ayat's arm. "We'll be butchered on the surface!" she said. "If we fight, we must fight from the trees, shooting arrows down onto them."

Ooor pulled Taya away. "Don't touch our shaman, witch."

Taya shook herself free. "Ooor, please, listen to me! We are tree people. We must fight from the trees. We cannot battle an army face-to-face."

Doubt filled Ooor's eyes. Before it could take hold, Ayat shoved Taya away, nearly toppling her off the bridge.

"You know nothing," Ayat said, but doubt danced in her eyes as well. "The Stonesons would simply cut the trees down."

Taya shook her head. "Not when pelted with arrows."

Ayat bit her lip, and her eyes clouded with fear. Obviously, she had realized her mistake. But instead of conceding defeat, the twin snarled and clenched her fists.

"We fight on the ground," she said stubbornly.

"Don't be so proud!" Taya pleaded. "It's okay, you made a mistake, don't let it kill our clan."

"You just want to steal my place!" Ayat screamed. "That's what you came here for, isn't it? To make everyone think you're the better shaman. Well you're not. No one will listen to your ideas, they'll listen to mine! We fight on the ground."

Taya sighed. Short of killing Ayat—which she couldn't bring herself to do—she saw no solution.

"Then I fight too," she said.

Ayat looked about to refuse, when suddenly her eyes thinned shrewdly. "All right, you want to fight? Go ahead. In fact, since you seem so eager, I command you fight in the front line." She leaned forward and whispered. "Only this time when Lale's blade pierces you, don't turn into a worm again. I think two of us is more than enough."

With that, she spun around, marched back into the clan's Core, and slammed the door behind her.

The clansmen scurried into storage huts to grab pointed sticks and wooden shields, no doubt carved only in the last day. Taya drew her bone knife and joined the men climbing down to the forest floor.

The men arranged themselves in a wall, pointing their spears west, their faces grim. Many stared at Taya scornfully. She tried to ignore them. They had all heard Ayat command she fight, so they would not try to banish her, but still their distrust hurt. *I'm here to fight for you,* Taya wanted to shout. *You can show some gratitude.* But they only glowered at her, sure she was a witch.

"Does your new shaman not fight?" Taya asked Ooor, who stood beside her.

Ooor shook her head. "The spirits have spoken to her and told her she must supervise the battle from above."

Taya was somehow not surprised.

A fluttering sound came from above, and Taya raised her eyes to see a thousand birds fleeing. Between the trees she descried routing squirrels and deer. Soon, a rumble like a storm came from ahead. The men glanced at one another uneasily, tightening their grips on their spears. Taya took a deep breath and widened her stance, ready to fight. A small voice inside her whispered that she was insane to stay, but Taya ignored it. This was her home. She had to protect it.

The rumble grew louder and louder, thousands of boots marching in unison. War drums boomed like thunder. The sound grew so loud it was deafening. Taya wanted to cover her ears to block the maddening din.

And then she saw them, gray shadows swarming from the woods. The clansmen gasped around her, but Taya barely heard them. Her gaze was locked on the advancing army. This was what a real army looked like, she realized. For the first time in her life, she saw chain mail and helmets, made from the strange, hard material Talin called "metal." For the first time, she saw thousands of men marching in perfect precision. No wonder the western clans had been crushed, Taya thought. No wonder Bug had fled. A sudden thought flashed through her mind, surprising her: *By the spirits, only Aeolia can save us now.*

The Stonish army was close now, so close Taya could count the rings in their mail. She snarled and raised her knife. The men surrounding her grunted and pointed their spears.

The Stonesons stopped. They stood silent and still as a wall. A horn trumpeted twice: two short, brisk blows. The Stonesons drew their swords as one, the unsheathing steel hissing like wind. The horn blew once more—a long, bloodcurdling blare like a scream. The Stonish army rushed forth.

Screams erupted, armor clanked, wooden spears snapped like twigs against metal. Blood soaked the leafmold. Taya became a panther, sudden battlelust consuming her. As men died around her, she leapt from Stoneson to Stoneson, hamstringing them or biting under their arms where their mail was weak. A stone dart pierced her hide, but Taya didn't notice the pain, she was so taken by feral fury.

It was only minutes into the battle, and already half the Forestfolk lay dead in their blood. Several minutes more of this, Taya knew, and there would be no clansmen left standing. The Forestfolk seemed to have reached the same conclusion. Many were fleeing, only to be shot down by stone darts. Taya had to do something.

She turned back human and shouted at the top of her lungs, *"Into the trees!"*

She hopped onto a rope ladder and began to climb. The surviving Forestfolk followed. Stone darts flew around them, and one sunk into Taya's calf. For a moment she was tempted to become a bird and flee, but then she gritted her teeth and continued climbing. She had to save her people.

When the Forestfolk were all up, and the Stonesons were climbing after them, Taya severed the rope ladder. The climbing Stonesons fell to the ground.

"Quick!" Taya commanded. "Get the hunting bows!"

As the Forestfolk rushed to do her bidding, the Stonesons produced axes and began chopping at the trees. *Hurry up,* Taya prayed, *hurry up hurry up hurry up.*

The Forestfolk returned with the bows. Poisoned arrows rained upon the enemy. At such a close range, most slammed through the chain mail. Several Stonesons fell. The clansmen cheered.

"Spread out around the village!" Taya shouted. "Shoot any Stoneson you see. Don't give them leeway to chop the trees."

Taya grabbed a bow and shot rapidly, excitement burning through her. The village women soon arrived to help, and when no bows were left, they tossed clay pots and cooking stones. Dead and wounded Stonesons began piling up. They could not approach a tree to ax it without being pelted.

On the bridge beside Taya stood a thin, wizened woman tossing down flower pots. Taya frowned. She had never seen the woman before, yet something about her intense, green eyes seemed familiar. Then Taya realized: it was her mother. She had never seen Eeea without her charms before. She looked so... ordinary.

"Mother!" she said.

Eeea turned to face her. "Hello, Taya. My *real* Taya."

Taya felt a lump in her throat. "So you believe me! You know it's really me."

Ooor, standing beside them with his bow, spoke slowly. "I think I know it too, now. Taya. The real Taya." He raised his voice. "This is the true Taya! The true Taya is saving us!"

The clansmen echoed his call. "The true Taya! The true Taya!"

Tears blurred Taya's vision. Until this moment, she hadn't truly realized how she loved her home, the home she had once thought so dull. It was both the greatest and most terrifying moment of her life.

A shriek came from behind. "No! I'm the true Taya!"

Taya turned to see Ayat. The twin's face was flushed with anger.

"You left these men to die," Taya said, "while you stayed here in safety."

"Don't listen to her!" Ayat screamed. "Men, kill her!"

The clansmen hesitated. Ooor spoke for them. "We follow her now. She is saving us."

With that the clansmen recommenced shooting arrows.

Ayat roared like an enraged beast. She hopped into the air, became a wolf, and thudded into Taya's chest.

Taya drew her magic. Before the wolf could rip out her neck, she turned into a frog and hopped away. Ayat growled, became a bear, and caught Taya in a crushing hug. The bridge swayed madly. Locked in Ayat's furry grasp, Taya became a porcupine and bristled her quills. The bear howled and dropped her hurriedly. Taya had scarcely hit the bridge, before Ayat leapt into the air above her. In midair, the evil twin bulged into an animal Taya had only heard of in the fisherfolk's tales: a walrus.

Taya became a grasshopper and leapt away, and the walrus slammed into the bridge. The bridge collapsed in an explosion of splinters. Walrus and grasshopper crashed down onto the ground. Around them the Stonesons gaped. Arrows rained.

Taya turned into a hawk and soared, crashing through the boughs into the sky. She glanced behind her to see an eagle pursuing. Taya flapped madly, flying as fast as she could. In the clouds, her twin's beak caught Taya's talon. Taya screamed and slammed her neck into Ayat's body. Ayat opened her beak to squawk, and Taya's talon came free. The two birds battled. Claws slashed, scratched, yanked feathers, tried to catch an eye. Shrieks echoed in hollow beaks. Flapping pinions churned the clouds. Wind roared in Taya's ears and filled her nostrils. Earth and heaven spun around her.

Ayat tore a clump of feathers from Taya's breast, and the blood fueled Taya with rage. She shrieked and lashed forth, beating Ayat with her wings, scratching her with claws. Finally, she managed to close her beak around Ayat's neck. The evil twin struggled but could not free herself. Instead, she turned into a boar.

Ripped free from Taya's grip, the boar plummeted. Just before it hit the treetops, it became a falcon and began flying again. Taya dived and thudded into the falcon, pushing it through the treetops. The two birds crashed through the branches, leaving behind clouds of feathers, and hit the ground.

At once, both sisters turned into lions. But Taya was the quicker cat. She leapt onto Ayat, pushing her to the ground, and closed her jaws around the twin's neck.

Ayat froze, not daring to move, not morphing, just lying still. Her eyes were clouded with defeat. No matter what animal she became now, Taya could kill her.

Ayat became human again.

"I'm sorry," she whimpered. "Please don't kill me."

Taya sighed inwardly. No, she could not bring herself to kill her twin, not even if that twin had tried to kill her. With a grunt she too became human. The two identical women stared at each other.

"I'm the one who should be sorry," Taya said softly. "I should have learned to live with you, not tried to exile you." She sighed. "I suppose there is no one real Taya. We are both parts of the same person."

Taya rose to her feet. She turned around and began walking away, wondering if she would ever see her twin again. A stirring in the bushes behind her made her pause and look back.

A crocodile was rushing toward her, snapping its jaws.

Taya cursed. With no time to flee, she turned into a turtle and whisked into her shell. The crocodile's teeth closed around her, but Taya's shell protected her. The crocodile, in turn, became a python and constricted her.

Taya boiled with rage, panic tickling her as her lungs began aching for air. She tried to change into a larger animal, but she didn't have the space. Stars floated before her eyes. Her lungs felt ready to burst.

Like air, all thought disappeared.

*****

Even before Taya opened her eyes, she knew with a chilling certainty that her troubles were only beginning.

When she did open her eyes, she instantly regretted it. What she saw froze her blood. Stonesons surrounded her, pointing their fingers at her. At any moment, Taya knew, they could perforate her with magical stone darts. Behind the Stonish soldiers, ruin sprawled like a nightmare. Yaiyai lay broken on the ground, its inhabitants mutilated. Ooor lay under a bush, his face kicked in. Eeea was impaled on a spike. Taya shut her eyes again.

She felt a hand caress her hair. "Now, now," said a soft voice, speaking Woodword with only the slightest accent. "Don't cry. Tears make things sadder than they truly are."

Taya recognized the voice. She kept her eyes shut as she whispered, "I should have plunged your sword into my crotch, not my stomach."

Rough fingers pulled her eyelids open. Taya found herself staring at Lale's scarred face.

"Sit up," he commanded.

Taya considered defying him, but knew it would be futile. She sat up. Lale fitted a bucket over her head.

"A precaution," he explained, "in case you turn into a bird. Do so, and the bucket will fall and trap you. From here on, you are never to so much as tilt your head. Each time you do, I will pluck off one of your toes. Try to escape, and I will cut off your lips."

Taya remained still and straight. The bucket on her head was heavy and cold. It stank like an old chamber pot. A sudden image of her without lips shot through her mind, and Taya shoved it away, her stomach churning.

"Why, Lale?" she whispered. "All this just to catch me?"

Lale laughed. "You flatter yourself, woman. You think I came here solely to catch you? No. I came to conquer the Forest, and I came to conquer Heland. In time, I will conquer Esire and behead your little slave friend. No, catching you was simply a side benefit." The prince laughed. "It was quite an unexpected surprise, actually. While we were destroying this miserable village, a bear dragged you over to me unconscious."

Taya tightened her lips. Ayat!

"I was so pleased with the bear," Lale continued, "that I killed it and turned it into a rug."

So Ayat was dead. Taya felt strangely sad.

"Why don't you kill me, too?" she asked.

"Death is too benevolent," Lale replied, "the eventual fate of every man or woman. I want you to suffer more than that. I'm taking you to my father as a curiosity. What he will do to you I cannot guess. I know only it will make you envy your wretched kin. But first we go to Heland. And you, my dewdrop, will accompany me as my pet."

Rough hands pulled her to her feet. Taya kept her head stiff, careful not to tilt the bucket. Swords poked her back, and Taya began walking, her feet trudging through sticky snow. She kept her lips tightened, forbidding despair to overcome her. She let only one question fill her mind, repeating it like a mantra, so no other thought could find its way in. One question that determined life and death, one question she dared not ask for fear of the answer she might get. One question everything now depended on.

Where in the world was Aeolia?

Chapter Fifteen
Esire

Light snow fell outside, covering the city of Woodwall with a brittle sheet. Aeolia reached out the window, letting the snow glide onto her hand. Soft as baby's breath, it melted as it touched her warm skin. She withdrew her hand, placed it in her lap, and gazed into the gilded mirror. Her cheeks were dabbed with rouge, her lips were tinged with crushed raspberries, and her eyelids sparkled with faint gold powder. She wore an ivory-colored chiffon gown and a diamond necklace.

"I almost don't recognize myself," she said quietly to Ketya.

Ketya smiled silently and continued combing Aeolia's almond hair. She frizzed the edges, fastened them down with a platinum pin and arranged the curls over Aeolia's head.

"Oh, Ketya!" Aeolia sighed. "You make my hair look so pretty. I remember times when it hung over my eyes."

"You must look like a lady now. You're going to meet a king."

"And have done nothing to deserve it!" Aeolia exclaimed and rose to her feet. She left the mirror and resignedly dropped backwards onto her canopy bed.

"Please, Lia," Ketya said. "You're wrinkling your gown."

"It's not mine, Ketya! Don't you understand? All these gowns, perfumes, jewels.... I never wanted all this cosseting, I just...."

Ketya placed her hands on her hips. "Enough you nearly gave Queen Elorien a heart attack, barging into her court in dirty rags and covered with cinder!"

The two girls burst into a fit of giggling.

"I'll never forget the look on the old woman's face," Aeolia said through her laughter.

"She nearly fell dead backwards!" Ketya wiped a tear from her eye. "She must have thought we were two beggars come to slit her throat."

"At least the rags were comfortable. I don't see how anyone could breathe in these corsets."

"I agree. Numbskulled men." Ketya sniffed loudly—a funny, nasal sound.

"Why are you oinking?" Aeolia asked, and they both burst into laughter so wild they rolled around on the bed, struggling for breath. They didn't even notice the door open until they heard a voice.

"Miladies?"

A guard stood in the doorway, wearing a golden uniform and eyeing them uncertainly. The two girls quickly gathered themselves and blinked at him innocently.

"Lady Aeolia is wanted in the king's hall," the guard said.

"I'm not a lady," said Aeolia.

Ketya nodded. "Can't you see? She can't even fit into a corset."

"I can too!" Aeolia cried. "And at least I don't oink."

Ketya hit her with a pillow. Aeolia squealed, grabbed her own pillow and hit Ketya back. The two were laughing again.

"I'll wait outside to accompany you when you're ready," the guard said, confusion suffusing his face.

"Spirit, Ketya!" Aeolia said when he had left. "I can't believe all this is happening. I'm going to see a king, and he actually wants me to...."

She fell silent, and their laughter died. Aeolia stared at her lap and twisted her fingers.

"Come," Ketya said. "Let me help you lace those shoes."

* * * * *

Esire's royal hall was an opulent place, and Aeolia gazed at it in wonder. Marble columns engraved with leaves supported a high, azure ceiling. Golden tapestries hung on all walls but one, where embedded was a huge firefly wrought of gold—the Esiren firefly. Aeolia thought the wealth excessive; that emblem could feed a town for a year.

King Reyn sat slumped in his begemmed throne. A samite robe cloaked his spindly frame, and a jeweled crown topped his hoary head. Topaz necklaces hung around his flabby throat, and agate rings adorned his bony fingers. Silver wires inlaid his lank beard. Even Lale, Aeolia reflected, for all his faults, was not so flamboyant.

"Your Majesty," she said and curtsied.

"The so-called Firechild," muttered the old king. "Rise, girl."

Aeolia straightened, and the king gave her a piercing stare.

"Prove it," he said.

"Your Majesty?"

"Go on, link to me! Show me your magic."

Grumbling under his breath, the king shut his eyes. Aeolia shrugged one shoulder and linked to him. His mind and body were tough and gnarled as an old oak.

Yes, yes, he thought, his eyes closed. *I can see myself through your eyes. We share senses. You truly are a Firechild.*

Aeolia released the link, glad to escape the king's old body. Reyn opened his eyes and frowned.

"When people link to me," he said slowly, "it is customary for them to ask leave before letting go."

Aeolia stiffened. "Of course, Your Majesty. It won't happen again."

"I hope not. We can't have you being insolent, what with all this trouble we're in. Our border towns are being lost like an old man's thoughts, and Sinther is only getting stronger. Just today we've received word he's conquered the Forest."

Aeolia winced and bit her lip. The Forest, conquered, after a war she had sparked. Everywhere she went she brought ruin.

"And you want me to fight him...."

The king leaned back in his throne. "Well, I sure can't."

Aeolia sighed. Sinther had long been killing Esirens to catch her, and by fleeing him she had only caused more destruction. It was her duty to face him, she knew.

"I will try," she said. "I will try my hardest."

"Do you have a plan?"

"Well, Queen Elorien has promised me use of her fleet," Aeolia said. "As soon as the army's mustered, we'll sail secretly into Grayrock, surprising Sinther and circumventing his infantry. We'll be in the Citadel before he's realized anything is amiss."

"And what will you do then?" Reyn asked.

"He can't hurt me if I link to him," Aeolia said, and a chill passed through her. "I guess I'll simply chain him up."

* * * * *

She didn't spend much time planning the campaign. It was too easy to put aside such scary thoughts and simply be happy. It still felt strange wearing gowns and jewels, but the winter gardens tempted her, and her friends were pleasant enough company to make her forget her responsibilities. Who could think of war while surrounded with such peace? *I had known slavery so long,* Aeolia thought. *Let me enjoy idleness.*

She walked alone through an orchard of oranges growing sweet despite the cold, their roots feeding from Woodwall's hot underground springs. She wore a blue muslin gown with a line of tiny silver bells around the waist. At times she spun with her arms spread out, just to see her dress twirl and hear it chime. She picked an orange, peeled it and bit into a segment. The sweet taste burst in her mouth. She still couldn't fathom she was allowed to eat as many fruit as she pleased, whenever she pleased.

She blushed to think of the luxuries and adulation she received in this dreamland. From the lowliest peasant to the loftiest lord, everyone adored their Firechild—except perhaps the king, whom Aeolia still thought a sour old curmudgeon. She delivered speeches every day (though she trembled each time anew), attended royal feasts, mingled with all the nobility. She might not have been a lady, but she was treated like a goddess.

Finishing her orange, Aeolia spotted Talin walking through the trees.

"Talin!" she said cheerfully, rushed forward and embraced him.

"There you are," he said. "I've been looking for you."

Aeolia noticed his face was grave. She withdrew from him and took a few sulky paces backwards.

"There is bad news," Talin said.

Aeolia looked away. "I don't want to hear it."

"What's the matter, Lia?"

"I'm tired of bad news," she pouted. "My whole life has been full of it. Go away, leave me to walk in the orchard."

"Aeolia, this is not how I know you."

"Perhaps you never knew me until now. Perhaps I never knew myself. Perhaps I was meant to be a spoiled rich girl." She smiled at him, trying to make him laugh, but he remained sober.

"Sinther is mustering an army," he said. "Larger than any seen on the Island before."

Aeolia turned her back to him and stared down the empty path. She picked an orange from a tree, held it in both hands but did not eat.

"What does he want from me, Talin? I never wished him any harm."

Talin circled her till he stood before her again. He silently took her hands.

She looked at him. "I just want to love you, Talin. That's all I want. Is that too much to ask?"

He gazed at her silently, his eyes deep green and soft. Aeolia's love for him burst in her heart like the fruit had in her mouth.

"Ask me to marry you, Talin," she said suddenly. "Ask me and I'll say yes. We don't need to have children, Talin. We don't need to if they'd suffer for their mixed blood. But if you were to love me, Talin, love me like I love you, I would not regret a thing...."

He looked at her, about to speak, but she hushed him with a finger to his lips.

"No, don't talk," she pleaded, "because I couldn't bear it if you turned me down. Here, what's this? I see you want to speak. I will kiss you lest you refuse me."

She held his head in both her hands and kissed him desperately, holding him so tightly the orange in her hand crushed and dripped juice down his neck.

* * * * *

Milky dawn poured over the stars, glittering like pearls on the snow. The palace awoke under the clear sky to blaze with its own light. Guards stood straight and proud at their posts, their armor burnished and beribboned. Servants clad in their finest livery set tables in the gardens, topped them with damask and decked them with baskets of winter flowers: pink stock and deep blue irises, violas and pansies and poppies blooming wide in the cold. The flowers' fragrance was soon joined by the smells of cakes and candies brought from the kitchens, elaborate sweets as lovely to view as to taste. The guests then arrived, lords and ladies dressed their best, bringing presents, flowers, and adoration. Minstrels played romantic tunes. Wine flowed like tears.

Aeolia's dress was white as moonlight on water. She wore her hair down, strewn with wildflowers, and crowned with a garland of wheat. Everyone told her she sparkled like the stars. For the first time in her life she felt beautiful and happy and loved, and these were new feelings for her, and they were frightening as they were tender. She sat at her window, gazing hesitantly at the celebration outside, holding her hands so hard they hurt.

"Is all this for me?"

"Don't be silly," Ketya chided. "It's for Talin too."

"I'm so scared."

"You'll do fine." Ketya patted her hand. "You should be used to a crowd by now."

"It's not only the crowd I'm scared of," Aeolia admitted. "It's when the crowd leaves. You know, I've never.... I won't know what to do."

"What makes you think I do?" Ketya cried, bristling.

"No, no," Aeolia said, laughing. "I didn't mean to imply that you.... It's just that *I*.... Oh, Spirit, Ketya, come with me!"

"You don't want me around," Ketya laughed. "Trust me. Lia, you've fought more battles than half the knights here today. You needn't be afraid of one little—"

"Yes, yes, I know," Aeolia interrupted her, her ears burning.

Was Ketya right? she wondered. Perhaps she was so inured to pain she feared joy. Sem and the ogre had embittered her life, and the scars they had given her were still healing, and screamed at the touch of happiness like a wound screamed at the touch of a balm. But wounds could not heal without pain, Aeolia knew, and Talin was giving her the courage to face her past. She recalled her old dream, how she had left him for the darkness, and banished it from her mind. She would never leave her true love.

Ketya hugged her. "Come, Dewdrop. The ceremony is about to begin."

Aeolia lifted her bouquet and stepped outside.

She could never afterward truly remember the ceremony. It passed in a blurry haze of happiness, leaving only emotions and pictures as memories. There was Talin, dressed in Greenhill's green, handsomer than ever. The picture of Ketya catching her bouquet, squealing in delight, was etched forever in her mind. The party was a feast of laughter and tears and kisses, there and gone like summer rain. Aeolia emerged from the wedding as from a dream, and only the ring on her finger, a thin band of white gold, testified its realness.

Drunken on joy, she let Talin carry her back to their bedroom. Butterflies fluttered in her stomach as they entered the door. A dozen honeycomb candles flickered, and flames crackled in the hearth. The valance was pulled back from the canopy bed, and rose petals sprinkled the blankets. Talin placed her on the bed, and Aeolia sat, the butterflies turned to galloping horses. Talin stood watching her, his green eyes warmer than the fire.

Aeolia was suddenly overcome by a fit of giggles.

"I'm sorry," she said, "I can't help myself...."

Talin knelt and kissed her lips, and Aeolia's giggles died, and she stared at him silently. He sent a hand to her hair, but Aeolia stopped him.

"Wait," she whispered, then linked to him. "Now."

They were tentative at first, moving slowly, still clinging to themselves. But their bodies guided them, and soon they could merge, flowing into each other. She wrapped her arms around him and lay back, pulling him down beside her. They felt his hands caress her, his lips brush over her neck, blowing warm breath. He kissed her skin, and she buried her hands in his hair. They became as one body.

It wasn't frightening like she had thought. Not as they were. It hurt only briefly, and it was a good pain that was soon replaced with maddening pleasure. He left her on time, would not risk a child of three bloods, but Aeolia did not care, she felt no loss, only joy and love that flooded them until they lay still.

He lay atop her, his chest heaving, his warm breath on her face. Aeolia leaned her head sideways and saw that the candles had burned low, and their wax hung in pretty forms. Talin and she must have made love for an hour, though it felt like minutes. He rolled away and Aeolia nestled against his chest, running her fingers over his skin. Talin took her hand, kissed her fingertips, brushed his lips over the tattooed letters.

"What does it say?" he asked softly.

"My master's name."

"I wish I could erase it."

"You do, Talin." She kissed him. "You do."

He did not reply, only turned his head away and lay still. When Aeolia reached over and touched his cheek, she felt that he was crying.

Chapter Sixteen
Blood and Steel

Roen stood behind Brownbury's gates, feeling as inept a soldier as ever was. His sword was rusty, and his wooden shield was cracked. His helmet was too big. His ringmail was torn, and the boiled leather beneath it stank of old sweat. He had been among the last drafted, so his equipment was old. But his purple surcoat, hanging over his armor, proudly proclaimed him a queen's man. That was enough to send him to battle.

He pulled a roll of parchment from his pocket. One of his drawings. A beautiful woman, with two orange braids and slanted green eyes. Whenever he sat down to paint lately, he found himself painting her, the Forestfellow from his dream. Roen sighed. Suddenly he felt foolish. All the other soldiers carried locks from their beloved's hair. Nepo had offered him a lock of her hair, and Roen had refused. Instead, he took a painting—of an imaginary woman, no less. He sighed again. The siege must have affected him. He was addled from weakness.

His comrades, standing around him, were also frail. Their eyes were hollow with privation, and their faces seemed too gaunt for their helms. Even Sir Grig Purplerobe, their commander, sat slumped upon his destrier. The siege had weakened them all. When the waters had been poisoned, they turned to drinking cows' blood. When rotting meat had been tossed into the city, they all fell ill. But now, salvation had arrived in the form of Wilon Greenhill and five thousand green-clad men, marching toward Brownbury to banish its besieging Redforts. Now, the queen's purple army would fight.

The queen. His mother. Two moons after the breathtaking discovery, Roen's mind still boggled. In truth, he still barely knew her. His parents wished to keep their relationship secret, and Roen was glad to oblige. He would rather be a painter than a bastard any day. But if he had hardly talked to her, Roen had grown to admire the woman, and was proud to fight for her. He swore he'd get to know her better after the war.

If he survived, that was. Roen tapped his fingers against the pommel of his sword. Who would win the day? he wondered. The Greenhills and Purplerobes together equaled the Redfort force in size, but the reds were healthier and better trained. But then, the purples, after weeks of siege, were more desperate, and would fight harder. Roen rubbed his chin. It would be a tough battle of uncertain outcome. Only one thing was for sure: today's victor would claim the throne. Today the civil war would end, for good or bad.

Up on the wall, the sentries flurried. One turned his head and called down: "Duke Greenhill is approaching!"

Roen licked his lips. Now, for the first time in weeks, Brownbury's gates would open and the purple army emerge. And, Spirit help him, he among them. The muffled sounds of agon came from behind the wall: war horns blaring, horses neighing, armor chinking. Roen could imagine the relief force: thousands of green-clad soldiers, led by the exiled duke of Greenhill.

Sir Grig stood up in his stirrups. He drew his sword. "Open the gates!" he called.

Slowly, the gatekeepers heaved the large, oak gates open. Beyond them, out in the countryside, Roen saw the green army crashing against the red. Droplets of blood flew.

"Draw!" Sir Grig commanded.

The air whistled as Roen and his comrades, three thousand men in all, drew their swords.

"Charge!" Grig cried and spurred his destrier into a gallop.

With a great roar, they followed. Roen's helmet wobbled up and down as he ran, alternately blinding him. The rumble of charging soldiers deafened him. The man behind him kept stepping on his heels, and Roen feared he'd fall and be trampled. They ran into the gateway, passed under the wall, and burst out into the countryside.

Hurriedly, they formed into rows and began marching. The first row of purple soldiers, several rows ahead of Roen, crashed against the reds. The sweet, sickly smell of blood filled the air, accompanied by screams, grunts, and clanging steel.

Roen's heart pounded. Meanwhile he only waited, surrounded by his comrades, not fighting. Soon his turn would come. He knew the battle plan. The purple army would advance row by row, slamming itself into the reds. When a man in the row ahead fell, the man behind would move up to replace him. Wilon's green army would be doing the same on the other side, trapping the red force in the middle. This would continue until all the red soldiers were killed. It was a simple, brutal plan.

The purple rows ahead of Roen were falling quickly. More soldiers kept moving up to replace them. Soon Roen was only one row behind the action. He tightened his grip on his sword. He was deathly afraid, but it was a determined, exhilarated fear. He knew he might die, but he was determined to fight for his life rather than flee for it. Too long at siege had given him this desperate bravery.

The man before him fell, and Roen moved up to fight. He stood in the front row now. A red soldier stood before him. Roen tightened his lips and brandished his sword. The red soldier began to retreat, slowly pacing backwards. Roen breathed in amazement. Was he so daunting? Then he noticed that the entire red force was walking backwards. Roen frowned. Were they all fleeing?

Then he understood. The Redfort army was changing form. Roen watched indignantly as the rows of red soldiers folded backwards to form, instead of a straight line, an arrowhead. The arrowhead began marching, pushing its point forward, splitting the purple army in two.

A red soldier slashed at Roen, and he raised his shield. Splinters flew. Roen thrust his sword and punctured his foe's chest. The man fell. It was the first time Roen had killed a man, but he was too frightened to muse upon it. Hurriedly, before another red could arrive, he glanced around him. The purple formation had crumbled. The red infantry had split it in two. The red cavalry was flanking the two halves from the sides. Blood splashed.

A red footman rushed at Roen. They began to clash blades. The red's blade sliced skin off Roen's shoulder, but Roen kept fighting till he killed the other man. He was panting now, and more afraid. His force was divided, he was bleeding, and he could only imagine how the greens were faring on the opposite side. His helmet and armor were heavy and stifling.

At his right, Roen glimpsed a fat horseman crashing into the purple troops, slamming a heavy hammer onto infantrymen's heads. The fat man's visor was down, but his coat of arms marked him as Duke Hyan Redfort. Two mounted bodyguards surrounded him. Roen watched in disgust. Instead of fighting other armored horsemen, Hyan was cracking the heads of footmen. The duke knew no light infantryman could harm an armored rider. He simply enjoyed the killing.

The only rider in Roen's army was Sir Grig Purplerobe, sitting atop his own barded horse. Seeing Hyan's butchering, the Winged Knight galloped toward the fat duke and his mounted bodyguards.

Another soldier attacked Roen, diverting his attention. Sweat dripped down Roen's face as he fought. He suffered another nip, this time to his thigh. His opponent was better than he, and Roen would surely have died had not one of his comrades helped him slay the red.

Roen glanced back at Hyan. Sir Grig had just finished slaying the second of the duke's bodyguards. The Winged Knight was wounded, though. Blood flowed from several joints in his armor. His horse was lame. But still he rode forward, toward Hyan. Unperturbed, the fat duke swung his hammer into Grig's head. Red and gray spilled from the winged helm, like paint from a cracked jar.

"No!" Roen cried, the death of his commander chilling him to the bone even in the heat of the battle. He began to run, elbowing his way between his comrades towards Hyan.

"Mob him!" Roen shouted. "Now, when he's unguarded!"

He reached Hyan's horse and swung his sword, hitting Hyan on the knee. The blade rebounded off Hyan's armor, doing the fat man no harm. Several other purple soldiers, following Roen's example, began to slash at Hyan as well. None of their blows could penetrate the plate armor, but Hyan was confused, slamming his hammer down left and right. Roen and his comrades wouldn't stop harrying, and soon Hyan's destrier lost its legs, and Hyan must fight on foot. Swinging his hammer, the duke began fleeing toward his own army. Snarling with surprising rage, Roen chased Hyan and caught him on the red army's fringe. Roen began to slash his sword. Hyan turned to face him, parrying.

"You again!" Hyan hissed, his eyes narrowing.

Suddenly fear washed over Roen. He had hoped to catch Hyan surrounded by purple soldiers. As it was, Hyan stood with his back toward his own troops, Roen with his back to his. The two of them dueled alone. For the first time in the battle, Roen truly feared for his life.

Hyan's hammer was heavy. As Roen blocked with his shield, he thought his arm might dislocate. He slammed with his sword, but Hyan's fine, filigreed armor seemed impenetrable. Roen knew that although Hyan was older and fat, his armor and weapon gave him the advantage. Unless Roen thought of something, he would die.

And so, Roen pretended to slip. He fell to one knee, leaving his shoulder open. Hyan slammed his hammer down. Roen thrust his sword up. The hammer connected with Roen's left shoulder, shattering bone. The sword slipped through the chain mail in Hyan's armpit. Both men gasped with pain. Tears spilled from Roen's eyes. He pulled out his sword, rose to his feet and slammed the blade onto Hyan's helmet. Hyan looked stunned; he made no effort to resist. Roen slammed down again and again, with all his might, until Hyan's helmet caved in and leaked blood, and the duke slumped to the ground dead.

Squinting in pain, Roen looked around him and saw that everyone was staring. A sudden hush fell over the battlefield.

And then, the purples roared with renewed vigor and charged forward, attacking the leaderless reds. Roen retreated several paces back into his own army. He felt he would faint from pain. Shakily, he summoned his magic. He passed his hands over his shattered shoulder, healing it. He took a slow breath. He felt better.

The red soldiers were trying to retreat now, but Wilon's troops blocked them from behind. Mayhem ruled the battlefield. With the Purplerobe and Redfort commanders both dead, the battle became unorganized butchery. Trapped in the middle, the red soldiers could not escape, nor could they officially surrender for lack of command. The dead were piling up, encumbering the fighters' feet. Roen fought madly, killing several men, being wounded several times. He lost blood. He felt like he was losing his sanity. His sword became a red paintbrush, sketching death with every stroke. He had seen men die before, during the siege. This was different. This was mindless slaughter.

It was an hour past noon when the greens and purples finally met. The grand red army that had once separated them had perished.

Roen dropped his sword from his shaking hands. He tossed off his helmet and looked around him. The purples and greens numbered maybe a thousand men in all. Hills of dead rose around them. The air stank of blood and offal. Some of Roen's comrades began to cheer, but Roen did not join them, and soon they too fell quiet. The only sound was the cawing of the feasting crows. Snow began to softly fall, covering the dead in white shrouds.

Roen began to move among the fallen, searching for the wounded and healing them. His comrades joined him in silence. Many of the dead carried favors from their beloved. Some dead were no more than beardless youths. On one slain Redfort's finger, Roen saw a Master Painter's ruby ring. He recognized the sentry who had taken it. Roen knelt and meant to claim the ring, but could not bring himself to touch the dead man's hand.

He thought of himself as he had been only several moons ago: a foppish, soft-cheeked boy. Who would have thought he would stand over hills of dead, blood rather than paint on his hands? Never in his life had Roen seen or heard of such carnage, where thousands could die as one. Surely, he thought, this was one of the bloodiest days the Island had ever seen. He remembered how Hyan had escaped imprisonment two moons ago. What an evil hour that had been, Roen reflected. If Hyan had been hanged that day, there would have been no civil war.

He felt a hand on his shoulder. He looked up to see the broad, simple face of Wilon Greenhill gazing over the snowy killingfield.

"A hard sight," the duke said.

Roen nodded. "I suppose it had to be done, Your Grace."

"And you did your part well. You're the one who killed Hyan, aren't you?"

"I killed many men."

Wilon sighed. "May you never have to again. Thank the Spirit, we won our war here today. Finally we'll have peace again."

Peace.... The word drifted through Roen's mind like snowflakes. Once again, he reflected, Heland will live in peace. Water will flow freely, not blood. The smell of fresh bread will fill the city's streets, not the stench of disease. Everything will be as it had once been.

Suddenly Wilon frowned. "Do you hear that?" he asked.

Roen furrowed his brow. "Hear what, Your Grace?"

"Listen."

Roen listened. At first he heard nothing. Slowly, however, he became aware of a distant rhythmic booming and a barely audible rumble. Wilon leaned down, cleared away snow, and put his ear to the ground. Roen did the same. He heard it clearly now. The whole earth trembled and moaned with the sound.

Roen and Wilon straightened.

"What is it?" Roen asked.

Wilon's face was grim. "I don't know. But something tells me we should be behind the city walls when it arrives."

Wilon's soldiers, noticing the sound as well, gathered around their leader, awaiting commands. Their own commander killed, the purple soldiers joined them, wordlessly accepting Wilon's leadership.

"Let us enter the city," the duke called loudly. "Our troubles may not yet be over."

The soldiers followed Wilon into the city, carrying their unhealed wounded. When everyone was inside, the gates were shut and barred.

"Come with me," Wilon said to Roen, and they climbed the stairs onto the city walls. They reached the top and gazed off the battlements.

In the western distance, it looked like an oozing puddle of spilled gray paint. The rumble came loud now: war drums and hoofs and marching boots. An army, Roen realized, an army uniformed in gray. More Redforts? No, it couldn't be. This army wore the wrong color, and Roen guessed them about twenty thousand strong, a force the Redforts could not possibly have mustered.

The duke turned his head and yelled down to the weary soldiers in the courtyard. "There is yet fighting to be done. The city is being attacked."

The soldiers below, battered and fatigued, grumbled in disbelief.

Wilon shouted, "I want you to raid the city armories and fetch every crossbow you find. Then climb the walls."

Still incredulous and muttering, the soldiers went to their task.

"Stay here and keep watch," Wilon told Roen. "I need to talk to the platoon commanders. I'll make sure someone brings you a crossbow."

Roen nodded silently, too bewildered and weary to talk. A gray shadow seemed to cloak his heart, like the one cloaking the land. Just moments ago, he had been basking in the thought that he'd never see war again. Now he was not so sure. His stomach knotted.

Heland, he knew, was being invaded by Stonemark. Just like he had heard Lale promise Hyan. Only now, Hyan was not here to drive Lale away.

The Stonish army drew closer and closer. Roen could discern horsemen and chariots, hundreds of them. He had never seen an army so large. This army had conquered the Beastlands and the Forest, he knew. *Will we now follow?*

No, he told himself as his comrades returned with crossbows. This was not some backward farmland. This was not some benighted jungle. This was an embattled city with stone bulwarks and armed, professional defenders. Brownbury had withstood Hyan's siege. It could withstand Lale's. The Stonish army might be large, but it had no healing magic. Brownbury's missiles would ravage them. Roen felt even better when he was handed a crossbow. He loaded a quarrel and stood with his finger on the trigger. He felt hope of victory.

And then the Stonish army stopped. They stood five hundred yards from Brownbury's walls—just out of the crossbows' range—and did not move. Roen smiled thinly. *They fear our quarrels,* he thought.

He spotted Prince Lale among the Stonesons, robed in gray, sitting atop a charcoal courser. As he watched, the prince produced a silver horn from his belt. The prince gave a long blow like a wail. As one, the Stonish soldiers raised their arms and pointed at the city.

What are they doing? Roen wondered. *Surely they won't try shooting stone darts. We're well out of range, and besides—*

The crossbow fell from Roen's hands. His mouth fell open. He gripped the battlements. Then he knew: there would be no siege. Not behind these walls. Not against these Stonesons' magic. Roen's knuckles whitened around a merlon. He tightened his lips. Beneath him, the proud walls of Brownbury were trembling.

Around him, soldiers were blanching and dropping their weapons. The walls shook violently. Fissures formed, racing along the granite, like cracks in an old painting. One merlon came loose and crashed down. A wide crack sprung up from below, cleaving the wall. More chunks fell. Dust rose in clouds. The air itself shook. Men screamed and fled and fell to their deaths. Stonish magic was tearing the city walls as if they were of cloth.

Wilon was organizing a descent, leading his men off the wall and mustering them in the courtyard. Roen gazed down at them numbly, as if seeing them for the first time. Slowly he came to realize what half the Island had learned already: you cannot fight the Stonesons and win. He stood still as the wall-walk creaked, cracked, and finally crumbled.

The wall fell with him. Dust and debris blinded him. Pain exploded in his back, he bent backwards and screamed. Blood filled his mouth. Rocks rained down. For a long time, the rumble of crashing rocks deafened him.

Then, slowly, the noise began to settle. Roen opened his eyes. Between swirls of dust he glimpsed broken limbs protruding from the wreckage. He had fallen atop his comrades, Roen realized. They were buried beneath him.

The din had faded into a grumble of creaking stones and dying groans. Roen could now hear the Stonish drums beating. He heard thousands of feet marching toward the city. The pile of rubble on which he lay was suddenly swept aside, as if by some huge, unseen hand from the heavens. Roen went flying like a rag doll. Through the clearing in the wreckage, the Stonesons came marching into Brownbury in orderly lines.

Healer soldiers who had survived the fall were fleeing madly. Healing himself hurriedly, Roen pushed himself out of the rubble and joined them. The Stonesons thundered behind, marching in steady beat. Roen and his comrades fled through the city's narrow, twisting alleys, kicking up snow. Doors slammed in their faces. Shutters clanked shut. The citizens were locking themselves in their houses. Roen heard screaming behind him, and knew that those who ran too slowly were being butchered. Stone darts whistled around him. Men fell dead. Roen rounded a corner, momentarily saved from the barrage.

Before the Stonesons could catch up, Roen rushed into an alley. Snow piled up over his ankles. He sloshed forward, his armor and helmet wobbling and heavy. He slipped on a patch of ice and fell heavily. When he rose to his feet, he saw two Stonesons standing before him.

Roen's heart leapt. He fumbled for his sword. The Stonesons approached him with drawn steel. Roen knew he was going to die.

While he was saying his prayers, two shadows jumped down from the roofs. Within seconds the Stonesons were dead, their necks slashed open.

"Grom! Nepo!" Roen cried.

Brother and sister stood before him, knives in hands.

"Quick," Grom said, adjusting the patch on his eye. "Come with us. We'll be safe on the rooftops."

Roen shook his head. "I must go see my father."

"Then bring him up to us!" Nepo said. Roen remembered how she had saved him and Smerdin long ago by giving them laceleaf. He wanted to hug the woman for her kindness. But again, he shook his head. If Smerdin saw the rooftops, the outlaws might not let him down. It had been hard enough convincing them to let Roen leave.

Nepo seemed to understand. "Travel the rooftops to your father's house, at least. The streets are dangerous."

Roen nodded. He shrugged off his armor and tossed his helmet aside, keeping only his sword. He followed the two outlaws up the alley wall onto the shingled roof. The snowy domes and spires of Brownbury sprawled around them. Below, squads of Stonesons snaked through the streets, arms outstretched, shooting any Healer soldier they spotted. They moved with grim intent, like hunters, clearing out the city. Roen grimaced and looked away.

Nepo clasped his hand.

"Goodbye, Roen," she whispered. "If the streets ever prove too dangerous, you know where to find us."

Roen opened his mouth to thank her, but before he could speak, Nepo kissed him full on the lips. Her fingers twined in his hair, and it was a long moment before she finally let go.

Guilt filled Roen, and he tried to speak. "Nepo, I—"

She hushed him with a finger to his lips. "I know," she whispered, smiling. "You talk about her in your sleep."

Before Roen could reply, she spun around and leapt away with her brother. Roen watched until they disappeared. Then he turned around. He jumped onto the next roof, moving toward his house.

Finally, sore and sodden, Roen stood on his workshop's roof. He glanced down. Stonesons were scanning the surrounding alleys, but the street outside the shop's door was momentarily clear. Roen climbed down the roof and knocked urgently.

"Father," he whispered, "quick, let me in."

From inside came the sounds of Smerdin rising to his feet and fumbling with the keys. From around the corner, came the sounds of thumping boots and whistling stone darts, coming closer. Roen drew his sword.

Finally, the door opened and Roen rushed in, slammed the door behind him and locked it. Out the window he saw the Stonesons emerge from around the corner. Seeing no one, they marched on.

Roen breathed in relief and leaned against the wall. Smerdin was watching him sadly.

"At least you're safe," the wispy painter said.

Am I? Roen remembered the tales he had heard of the Forest. They said Lale butchered every living thing he encountered there. But then, Lale could not rule tree towns. He *could* rule Brownbury. Roen did not think the prince would destroy what he could enslave.

He laid his sword on the table, wondering if he'd ever use it again. Probably not. Heland was destroyed. All her armies were vanquished. She would not be able to battle Lale. Roen found himself thinking of Aeolia, how determined she had been despite her shyness. The thought gave him comfort. He knew that as long as she was free there was hope, that Sinther had not yet won, that there was still some goodness fighting the dark.

A trumpet blared outside, accompanied by the sounds of marching boots and hoofs. Roen peeked out the window. He saw Lale riding down the street, his troops snaking behind. The prince's silver hair and gray robes sparkled with snow. His one gloved hand rested on the pommel of his sword. The other was coned around his mouth.

"Citizens of Brownbury!" the prince was announcing. "Gather at your palace when its bells toll six to hear your new ruler speak."

Behind the prince, Roen saw something that caught his eye. A woman was walking tethered to Lale's courser, dressed in the manner of Forestfolk. A bucket covered her head, but somehow Roen knew she was beautiful. Stonish soldiers surrounded her, their swords drawn. Who was such a dangerous creature, that she needed to be so heavily guarded? Roen examined her as she walked by his window. From the rim of the bucket on her head, peeked two thick, orange braids.

For a moment Roen could not breathe.

A Forestfellow woman, with two thick orange braids.... No, it couldn't be. There were a million Forestfolk with braids. It couldn't be *her*. And yet... she *felt* the same. The air tingled with the same magic as in his dreams.

Lale kept echoing his call as he rode down the street, but Roen scarcely heard him. He wanted to rush outside, challenge the Stonesons, and snatch the woman free. He could barely keep himself still. Who was she? How could she be real? Lale and the woman disappeared behind the corner, and Roen felt as if his soul were wrenched from his body.

He turned from the window, Lale's words sinking in for the first time. The prince would be addressing the people from the palace. The woman might be there with him. Roen had to see her again.

"I'm going," Roen said.

"You should stay here," Smerdin cautioned. "It will be dangerous for a young man."

"Lale won't suspect me a soldier. I'll wear my cloak and hood. Besides, I must... see the queen."

Smerdin looked sad. "There is no way you can help Elorien. Her fate is in the Spirit's hands now."

"Then I must go learn what that fate is," Roen said.

Smerdin sighed and looked at his feet. Roen thought of the Forestfellow woman, and his heart ached. Who was she? Had she been dreaming of him too? He remembered how they had both been turned to stone, and how he had caught her when she fell. He sat at the table and waited.

Finally, when the snow lay high in the streets, the city bells tolled six. Roen rose to his feet.

"I go," he said and pulled on his cloak, tugging the hood low over his face.

"Are you sure?" Smerdin asked.

Roen nodded. "Lale won't harm me. He wanted to scare us at first, but he's done killing now."

He squeezed his father's shoulder, opened the door, and stepped outside into the cold.

The snow was falling heavily now, flurrying in the wind. Roen shoved his hands under his arms as he walked, and held his head down against the wind. His breath purled white before him. The cold pinched his nose and made his eyes water. He saw drops of blood speckling the houses and knew that more blood hid beneath the snow. Here and there was the white lump of a snow-buried body.

The streets were deathly silent, but not empty. Others were slinking toward the palace to hear Lale speak. At every corner, Stonesons stood with drawn swords, staring from the confines of their helms. Stonemark's flag—a white firefly emblazoned over a gray field—billowed from the roofs of all public buildings.

Finally Roen reached the royal gardens. The fringe of cypresses had been cut down. Roen walked across the snowy lawns, gazing at the palace. One of its towers had been toppled. The Stonish flag billowed from the others. Stonesons stood guard on the walls. The first fireflies of the evening were rising to glow, swirling around the heaps of stones and smashed statues.

When Roen came closer, Stonish soldiers arrived to lead him into the palace courtyard. Several hundred of Brownbury's citizens stood there, mostly women, old men, and children; most of the city's young men had perished in the war. In the balcony above stood Stonish soldiers, but Lale himself had not yet arrived.

Roen remembered that here, several moons ago, Elorien had named Hyan heir. The memory stung his eyes. He had thought those days hard, but now they seemed almost carefree. Everything was so much worse now.

A shadow fell over the crowd as an ogre paced in to join them.

"Grumbolt!" Roen cried.

The gatekeeper gave Roen a sad look and came to stand beside him. He was bleeding from a cut to his head.

"They naughty men," he said to Roen. "They hit Grumbolt's head. They get past gates."

With that the ogre burst into tears. His loud sobs were the only sound in the courtyard. Roen mustered his magic and healed Grumbolt's wound, then stood patting the gatekeeper's arm, trying to comfort him. He himself felt like crying.

A horn blew above, loud and jarring, making Roen start. A Stonish officer on the balcony cupped his mouth and shouted, "Bow before Lale, prince of the Stonish Empire!"

The crowd shifted uneasily.

"Bow before your prince!" shouted the Stoneson.

The people glanced at one another. Several people bowed reluctantly. Most did not.

The Stonish officer gave a quiet command, and the soldiers surrounding him outstretched their arms. Stone darts rained onto the crowd.

Screams filled the air. Several people fell bleeding. Others tried to flee the courtyard, but more Stonesons held them back with strokes of swords. Roen covered his head with his arms. A dart scratched his elbow. Another grazed his shoulder. His heart thudding, Roen bowed, pulling Grumbolt down beside him. The Stonesons continued shooting until everyone made obeisance. The only sounds were the weeping of the wounded and frightened.

"You shall accept your prince in silence," said the officer on the balcony.

Some of the weepers silenced, but others continued sobbing. From the corner of his eye, Roen glimpsed the boots of three Stonesons enter the crowd. He held his breath. The Stonesons slowly paced among the cowering Healers. They stopped by a weeping child and one raised his sword. Roen shut his eyes. He heard the child's weeping cut short. The Stonesons continued strolling among the people, landing their swords on whoever sobbed, moaned, or so much as stirred a hair's length. The bodies were dragged out into the gardens.

Finally silence reigned. The people stood bowing so still they seemed frozen. The only movement was that of a single red firefly swirling over the crowd. The townsfolk stood frozen for what seemed an eternity, the Stonesons gazing with scrutinizing eyes, until finally the horn blared again and the Stonesons bowed as well. With his head lowered, Roen couldn't see Lale enter the balcony, but he heard the prince's voice.

"You must forgive my men. They've been long from home, and their tempers are short." The prince sighed. "Well, all's water under the bridge. You may rise."

Slowly, glancing around nervously, the crowd straightened. Roen saw Lale now. The prince stood on the balcony with his hands on his waist, a small, satisfied smile fluttering across his split lips. No, Roen decided. That was not satisfaction in his smile. It was amusement.

Behind Lale, surrounded by guards, stood the Forestfellow woman. Roen caught his breath. The bucket still covered her head, but the woman stood tall and straight. Pity and desire swirled through Roen, so thick his head spun. Suddenly he realized that, though he had never seen her out of his dreams, he loved her. It was a strange feeling. Lale was speaking again, something about annexing Heland, but Roen had thoughts only for her. He'd have given his life for one chance to lift that bucket and see her face in waking life.

His musing was disrupted when two Stonesons dragged a middle-aged woman onto the balcony. The woman wore rags, and her gray hair lay disheveled over her face. Blood speckled her lips. She looked vaguely familiar. She was probably a beggar he had passed before in a street corner, Roen decided. But why would Lale bring her out onto the balcony?

Lale drew his sword.

"Just to emphasize that Sinther is your only ruler," he said.

The prince grabbed the old woman's hair and pulled her head onto the balcony's balustrade. He raised his sword and brought it down hard. The blade severed the woman's neck and clanged against the railing. Lale lifted the bleeding head and stuck it onto a spike in the balustrade.

"It will stay here until it rots!" he cried.

Finally Roen recognized her. She was no beggar. She was Queen Elorien, the mother he hardly knew.

Grumbolt recognized her too.

"Urmajesty!" the ogre cried and began running toward the balcony, howling.

"Stop, Grumbolt!" Roen shouted, but Grumbolt paid him no heed. Stone darts peppered the ogre, but he seemed not to notice. Caterwauling, he began climbing the balcony's columns. Darts soon bristled from him like a porcupine's quills, but he continued climbing until he grasped the balcony's ledge.

Lale slammed down his sword, cleaving the huge hand, but Grumbolt swung his leg onto the balcony and pulled himself up. He crashed through the balustrade and rushed toward the prince, howling with berserk rage.

Lale's guards whipped around their prince and faced the ogre. Their swords dug deep, but Grumbolt kept standing. He grabbed the guards and tossed them off the balcony like weeds. They thudded against the ground. Grumbolt turned to face Lale.

Suddenly, the ogre froze. He whimpered. Blood blossomed on his back, where peeked the tip of Lale's sword.

Lale drove his sword deeper, pushing Grumbolt toward the balcony's edge. Grumbolt flapped his arms feebly, too weak to harm Lale. The prince put a foot on Grumbolt's stomach and pushed, at the same time pulling his sword with both hands. With a long sucking sound, the blade came free, and Grumbolt tilted backwards.

For a second, Grumbolt teetered on the edge of the balcony. Then he fell. The crowd rushed away, and Grumbolt thudded onto the ground. The earth shook.

Roen cringed and glanced up at the balcony, expecting Lale to shout and order a reprisal butchery. What he actually saw made his breath die.

The Forestfellow woman, now unguarded, had the bucket off her head. She was fighting Lale. She had the same face from Roen's dreams, with the same slanted eyes, deep and green like the woods she came from. Lale slashed with his sword and she hopped away, snarled, and turned into a tiger.

The Forest's Firechild! Roen gasped. He held his breath as he watched the fight.

Lale swung his sword in arcs, not letting the tiger near. The tiger, unable to attack past the slashing blade, turned into a cobra. The snake spat, but Lale blocked the venom with his blade. The cobra raced toward the prince's feet, turned into a woodpecker, flapped onto Lale's crotch, and began pecking madly. Lale screamed and ripped the bird away, but it morphed into a ferret and jumped onto his sword hand. The ferret mauled wildly, biting and clawing. Lale's sword clanged against the floor.

The ferret jumped free and became human again. Slowly, the beautiful woman lifted the fallen sword. She straightened and brought the point to Lale's throat, her eyes cold as snow.

The balcony curtains opened behind her.

"*Watch out!*" Roen shouted at the top of his lungs.

The green eyes caught his own, and Roen saw them fill with fear. The woman spun around and stood frozen before the Stonesons at the entrance. She never even noticed Lale draw his dagger behind her. The prince's blade wiped across her throat in one quick, clean movement, as if it were a handkerchief wiping away her sweat. It was a cut so clean she couldn't have felt it, even noticed it until it began to drip.

Something inside Roen seemed to crumble. He had never known such grief, grief that burned, blinding him. If his mother's death had burdened his heart, this blow shattered it. He wanted to die.

The beautiful woman stood dazed, and Lale caught her as she fell. He lifted her in his arms, like a man holding his new bride, and carried her toward the balustrade. He tossed her over.

Roen rushed forward to catch her.

She landed in his arms, almost weightless. Her neck gaped open like a second, wide mouth.

"What do you think you're doing?" Lale called from above. "Let go of that trollop!"

Horror pounded through him, but Roen shook his head. He wasn't going to let Lale behead this woman, stick her head on a spike and let it rot. She deserved the proper burial his mother had been denied. Holding her in his arms, Roen turned and began to run.

The crowd parted to let him pass. The Stonish guards had left the courtyard to help their prince, and Roen burst unhindered into the snowy gardens. He ran as if on air, his feet flying. Wind billowed his hair and pinched his nose.

He reached the gardens' end and entered the city. He ran alone through the deserted streets, kicking up fresh snow. The sun was low now, and fireflies flitted away from his feet. No one was following him, so great was his head start.

He reached his workshop and rushed inside. Smerdin rose to his feet.

"I'll explain later," Roen said. "Help me clear the table."

Smerdin wiped his arm across the tabletop, pushing off paints, parchment, brushes, and Roen's rusty sword. They clanged against the floor. Roen laid the woman on the table. He took a handkerchief from a drawer and laid it atop her wound. The white cloth turned red immediately. The cut had ripped clear through her throat.

Roen held the girl's wrist. There was no pulse. She was dead, beyond the healing power of magic. A lump swelled in Roen's throat, curving his mouth bitterly. He touched her hair, her cheek, her lips. She was growing cold already. Hot tears streamed down Roen's cheeks. All the grief from the past moons—the grief of the war, the siege, his mother's death—it all came out now. Roen pulled the woman to him and held her, weeping. A feeling of helplessness washed over him, an unbearable sadness that such loveliness could perish, that the only two women he had ever cared for were gone.

"Why did you have to die?" he said, holding the girl tight. "I wish you could live, I wish you could live, I wish you could live, live, *live*."

And with a long, shuddering breath, she did.

Roen leaned back, unable to breathe in amazement. The woman's chest was rising and falling in deep rhythm. Her eyes were still shut. She was sleeping. Her lips were curved into a soft smile. Roen pulled away the handkerchief on her neck. Her skin was smooth and unscathed. She was unwounded. She was alive.

Languid clapping came from behind.

Roen and Smerdin spun around to see Prince Lale standing in the doorway, smiling, surrounded by guards.

The fresh snow, Roen realized with cold dread. In his mad flight he had forgotten the fresh snow.

"What a pleasant surprise," Lale said. "The Healer Firechild."

Roen whispered, "I'm not the Healer Firechild."

"Tell that to my father," Lale said.

"What do you mean?"

"You, like the Forestfellow, are to be given to Sinther as a gift. A pair of pet Firechildren will spruce up that bleak cavern of his."

Roen averted his eyes. There, peeking from the shadows beneath the table, was the hilt of his sword. Roen took a slow, shaky breath. Then he dived down and grabbed the hilt. He drew the sword a second before the prince's guards could draw theirs. He pointed the tip at Lale's throat.

"Drop your swords!" Roen shouted.

For a moment there was silence. Then Lale began to laugh. His head tossed back, and his chest heaved, and he laughed so hard he could not speak. Roen tightened his grip on the hilt, grimacing with fear and anger and humiliation.

"I'll kill you!" he warned.

Lale quelled his laughter with obvious effort, wiping a tear from his eye. He turned his head and spoke to his guards. "Men, if this boy kills me, grab his father and torture him to death. I want it to take at least a week. Then, do the same to the girl. Finally, do the same to the boy." He turned to look Roen in the eyes. "Well, go on. Or have you thought better of the matter?"

Roen slowly lowered his sword.

"Grab him," commanded Lale, his voice now cold and without a trace of amusement.

Two Stonesons stepped forward and grabbed Roen. They bent his arms behind his back.

To the other guards, Lale said, "Grab the father. I want him tortured to death."

"But you said—" Roen cried before the guards slammed their palms over his mouth, stifling his words.

Lale paced toward him slowly, staring with iron eyes. He spoke with a cold voice.

"*No one* threatens me."

He pulled back a gloved fist and drove it forward. Pain exploded, and everything turned black.

Chapter Seventeen
Scorched Earth

Aeolia sat on a bench under a willow, the tree's naked branches weeping icicles like frozen tears. The sky was slowly clearing, revealing a small, twinkling sun. The snow had stopped falling during the night and now lay smooth over the gardens, speckled with thickets of yellow, cloying jasmines. Aeolia wore a cotehardie of the same color, its wool simple and unadorned. She caressed her wedding ring, a thin band of gold. She could see her reflection in it, almond hair collected into a practical bun, honey eyes sad. Her cheeks were flushed pink, but from cold rather than rouge. She wore no makeup today. Today her dream ended. Her stomach knotted at the thought and she shivered.

A mirthless smile found her lips. For so many years as a slave she had dreamed of returning to Stonemark, the land she had once thought her home. Now she feared it. She told herself her fear was unfounded. Her plan was perfect. It could not fail. She went over it one last time in her mind: While Lale marched to Brownbury, she'd lead her army to Heland's coast, catch ships and sail into an unsuspecting Grayrock. There she'd enter Sinther's pit and shackle him. *He won't be able to harm me,* Aeolia told herself. *I need not fear. And Talin is coming with me.*

She smiled again, but this smile was warm. The thought of Talin was so sweet. Since their marriage a fortnight ago, they had made love every night, sometimes till dawn, while linked. Aeolia's days were just as pleasurable, walking in the orchards with her husband, planning their future after the war, what their house would look like, what they'd name their adopted children. *Soon all this bad stuff will be over,* Aeolia told herself. *My plan cannot go wrong. It will not be long, and all my troubles will end. And then Talin and I will have our house, and our five adopted children, and our three dogs and horses, and we will be happy forever.*

Feeling reassured, Aeolia rose to her feet, smoothed her clothes, and followed the cobble path to the palace. She climbed the stairs, running her hand along the gilded railing, and stepped through the wooden doors.

Inside the main hall the air was warm and sweet with incense. Crackling braziers tossed dim light onto the huge, golden firefly embedded into the back wall. Beneath the emblem, between two guards, King Reyn sat slumped in his throne. The king's skeletal hands held his thick samite robe tight around him. His lips were blue as the sapphires round his flabby neck. He looked like a corpse. He stared at Aeolia wearily, his head bent under the weight of his crown.

"Where have you been?" he rasped. "I've been looking for you."

"I was out viewing the army, Your Majesty," Aeolia said. "We have only seven thousand men, a speck beside the Stonish host. But with that Stonish host engaged in Brownbury, and a clear passage through Heland, it'll be enough. We're ready to attack, and I...."

Her voice died as she saw Reyn glumly shake his head.

"What's wrong?" Aeolia asked, a chill flooding her.

The king tugged at his beard. "Best I be straightforward. Brownbury has fallen. Heland has been annexed to Stonemark."

Aeolia's blood froze. From hair to toenails, dread tingled through her. Her mouth fell open, but she couldn't speak. She looked away, grimacing, then looked back up at Reyn, her eyes burning.

"Heland... all of it?" she whispered. "In Sinther's claws? How can this be?"

"The Stonesons found a kingdom at war with itself. Heland's three houses were so busy fighting one another, Lale had to but march in."

"We have no passage through Heland...," Aeolia said, and then a larger horror dawned upon her. "We are engulfed."

Reyn nodded glumly. "Sinther has swallowed us whole. We are enisled in their sea, the last kingdom standing, an enclave in a Stonish empire."

Aeolia lowered her head. She had no plan. The war was far from over. *It's all my fault,* she thought. *I started Heland's civil war, and I could have stopped it by letting Hyan hang, but I didn't. Wherever I go I bring destruction.*

"Is there nothing we can do?" she whispered.

"The Stonesons are marching against us as we speak. They are encroaching from all fronts, tightening around us like a noose. We cannot hope to withstand them, let alone attack their capital!" The king sighed. "What we do is surrender."

Then all is lost, Aeolia thought. There would be no house, no adopted children, no dogs and no horses. All those who had died for her, their deaths had been in vain. She thought of the ogress who had given her her life, and of Taya who had tried to, and of all the strangers who had died in her arms or at her hands.

She spoke quietly. "If I turn myself in, will he spare Esire?"

Reyn shook his head. "If I thought he would, I'd have turned you in myself. No, girl. Lale ravaged the Forest even after he had caught its Firechild. He may want you more than her, but—"

"What did you just say?" Aeolia interrupted, icy fingers gripping her heart.

The king glared at her. "Mind your tongue, girl."

Aeolia wanted to grab the king's shoulders and shake. Instead she forced herself to take a deep breath and speak with a mannerly voice. "Your Majesty, may you please repeat what you said about the Forest's Firechild?"

"I said Lale ravaged the Forest even after he had caught its Firechild, and I said that—"

Aeolia covered her mouth. Tears sprung into her eyes. "He caught her? Spirit, he caught Taya?"

"The news came in yesterday," said the king. "If you'd have spent less time coupling with your husband or giggling with that handmaid of yours you might have heard. Lale had captured this Taya and sent her to Sinther as a gift."

Aeolia shook her head, horror swirling through her. "I have to save her," she whispered. "We must attack Grayrock."

Reyn sagged in his seat. "You're letting your personal emotions interfere with logic. Capitulation is the wisest option."

"I must save Taya!" Aeolia cried. "I must save her—and everyone else. I had promised them as much, and I can't let them down. I have caused so much trouble, and... perhaps I can still mend some of it. Esire must fight."

"I'm sorry, girl, but Esire will officially surrender."

"No!" Aeolia forced back the tears that budded in her eyes. She could not let Esire fall without a fight, not after all these deaths. She took a deep, shaky breath. "Esire is my country now, and it surrenders when I say so."

Reyn laughed; a sickly, empty sound.

"You may be an important figure in my kingdom," he said, "but you do not have authoritative power. You know nothing about ruling a country—you did, after all, grow up a slave."

Aeolia's eyes became unfocused, and she gazed past the king, at the emblem of the golden firefly. She spoke softly, more to herself than to Reyn, and there was uncertainty in her voice. "And perhaps I am like fireflies, and shine only in the dark."

She snapped back to reality and turned her gaze to the guards.

"Draw your daggers," she said, trying to keep her voice steady. She could not believe what she was about to do. It seemed her voice spoke on its own. The day's news had given her this desperate, tragic determination.

The guards shifted uneasily.

"Please draw your daggers," she whispered.

The guards glanced at Reyn. The old man tightened his lips and nodded. The guards drew their blades and stared at Aeolia, perplexed.

"The people will go hungry because of our war," she said. "The golden emblem embedded into the wall behind you, I want you to pry loose. Melt it into coins, and toss them off the palace walls for every beggar to fetch."

Reyn rose to his feet. "That emblem represents the crown of Esire, bound with Esiren magic!"

Aeolia stared at the guards, maintaining a calm facade while her insides quivered. "He says it represents Esiren magic. I am Esiren magic. He says it represents the crown. From hereon I wear that yoke."

"Ignore her!" Reyn screamed. "Ignore her or I'll have you hanged!"

"We can surrender," Aeolia whispered, "or we can win this war. You choose."

The guards glanced at each other, and Aeolia felt her belly roiling like a storm. She could not believe herself; was she truly defying the king—usurping him? It seemed impossible, yet here it was happening around her. Finally the guards sighed, turned, and began working at the emblem. Aeolia breathed out with relief.

Reyn jerked his head toward her so violently, his crown fell and clattered against the floor. As he leaned down to lift it, Aeolia kicked it away.

The old man straightened in rage, his eyes bulging, his hair gone loose. "You're willing to sacrifice thousands of lives!" he screamed. "You're willing to sacrifice Esire for your place in history!"

"The Esiren people have put their trust in me," she said. "I cannot let them down. You are wrong. Esire will not die. I will lead her to victory."

She spun around and paced out of the hall. Once outside, she buckled to the floor, shaking, wanting to cry but unable to.

*****

Queen Aeolia's crown was wrought of silver, and on its crest perched a golden firefly, which she took as her sigil. Word of the new queen spread throughout the Island like wildfire. The Esiren people were quick to hoist their beloved Firechild's banners, driving their erstwhile, hated king into hiding. The Stonish army, marching toward the enclave kingdom, swore to crush it and its new sovereign. The Island watched absorbedly as the stone tyrant and the young queen braced for battle.

Wearing a lilac gown and a necklace of amethysts, her dainty crown atop her head, Aeolia sat on her throne beneath a hole in the wall.

"I'm coming with you," Talin said.

"No, Talin," she said softly. "Stay here, in safety."

Talin crossed his arms. "You don't have enough guards, Your Majesty, to keep me away."

"That is why I must ask you to stay."

"I refuse!"

"Talin, the people cannot see a foreigner... do what we will do. It must be done only by Esirens."

Talin's face became mulish. "They won't know I'm a foreigner. I'll keep my visor down."

"In a tumult," Aeolia said mildly, "Esirens link to one another instead of speaking. Enough a peasant link to you, to plead for mercy, and he will know."

Talin lowered his head. "Then how am I to help?" he demanded.

"Stay here and pray for me. Let me know you are safe and awaiting my return. That thought will comfort me."

"I cannot believe you are riding to war while I stay behind."

"This is not war, Talin." Aeolia sighed. "This is something worse."

She rose to her feet. "Guards, leave us please."

The guards bowed and backed out of the hall, leaving the newlyweds alone. Aeolia approached her consort, her gown fluttering over the floor. She embraced him and laid her head on his shoulder.

"Do you remember when we first met?" she said. "Just as I had freed myself, you tumbled a new heap of stones over me."

"Thank the Spirit I had," Talin said. "Otherwise you might have escaped me forever."

"And I remember when I first realized I love you. In the Forest. I had woken up frightened and you were there beside me."

"I too remember the first time I realized I love you. Just as you had freed yourself, I tumbled a new heap of stones over you."

Aeolia laughed softly. She ran her fingers through his auburn hair. "Dearest Talin. My life might have been unfortunate if not for you. You taught me what joy is."

She kissed him for a long time.

Finally she reluctantly detached from his embrace. "Goodbye, Talin," she said. "I pray to see you again soon."

As she left the hall, she had the feeling that "soon" might be a very long time. Or perhaps an eternity.

* * * * *

Aeolia sat on Acorn, her new armor sparkling in the winter sun. Its engrailed plates fit snugly over silvery chain mail, and her small crown rested in her hair. Firefang, the sword she had found in

Greenhill, hung at her waist, while a quiver of torches dangled from Acorn's saddle. Behind her sat Ketya on her pony, carrying the new queen's banner—a golden firefly emblazoned over a deep blue sky. The two girls faced their army of two thousand handpicked Esiren horsemen, all clad in shining armor and flapping golden mantles.

"We will win this war!" Aeolia cried for them to hear. "But we will win it by losing. Show me your torches."

A sea of hands rose from the Esiren army, holding thousands of torches.

"We will ride to edges of the kingdom," Aeolia said, "and from there retreat back to Woodwall, burning everything in our path."

The army nodded, grimly determined.

"If we are too weak to attack Grayrock," she said, "we are strong enough to defend Woodwall. We've collected enough food for moons of siege. But the Stonesons will find no food in the burned countryside. Hungry and cold, they won't be able to maintain the siege long. We'll outlast them! As long as we'll be at siege, they'll be at siege!"

The army cheered, waving their torches above their heads.

"For Aeolia!" one cried, and his comrades echoed his call. "For Aeolia! For Aeolia!"

Aeolia shook her head. "No. For Esire." She drew Firefang and pointed it skyward. "Split, now!"

The army divided into four groups, five hundred riders in each.

Aeolia passed her blade over the groups, commanding each in turn. "You burn the border with the Forest; you, the border with the Beastlands; and you, the border with Stonemark." She let her blade pause over the last group. "And you will join me northeast, to the border with Heland, where Lale himself rides."

She slammed Firefang back into its scabbard.

"Strengthen your hearts, my friends," she said, "and we will triumph. Now ride."

She dug her heels into Acorn's flanks. The horse neighed, bucked, and burst into a gallop, clopping into the countryside. Ketya galloped behind, her blue-gold banner billowing. Aeolia leaned forward in her saddle, the wind biting her face. The winter fields heaved up and down as she galloped, like a storming sea. Five hundred riders galloped behind her in a thunder.

Aeolia narrowed her eyes and tightened her lips, forbidding horror to overcome her. This task had to be done, she told herself. She who had been slave could not let Sinther enslave her kingdom. True, she thought—Esire would suffer to defeat Sinther, as she had suffered to defeat her old master. Her skin still bore those scars, and no doubt Esire would show its wounds for years to come. But the gold would triumph over the gray, and Aeolia might yet redeem the havoc she had incurred.

Six days they rode, through the snowy fields.

Aeolia led her army at a vicious pace, riding at their lead cold and inspiring as a ship's figurehead. Sores bloomed over her thighs and bottom, her muscles cramped, her entire body ached. Acorn grew weary, her ears drooped, her orbs glazed, her nostrils flared and wheezed. At nights Aeolia's men dropped down exhausted, instantly falling asleep, while Aeolia lay awake, gazing into the cold sky, imagining Lale gazing at the same stars. By dawns they rode again, Aeolia driving her army on ruthlessly, knowing that every hour that passed Lale grew closer.

Finally, on the seventh morning of the grueling journey, they reached the border with Heland.

Aeolia reared Acorn to a stop, and her army halted behind her. A cold wind moaned, rustled the dead grass, roiled the cloudy sky. Aeolia wheeled her horse around so she faced her men. They gazed at her, eyes fatigued but determined.

She said simply, "We begin."

She removed from her belt a flint, and pulled from her saddle a torch. Trying to keep her fingers steady, she lit the flame. The army followed her lead, and in the cold dimness hundreds of torches flickered to life. The army lowered their flames to the ground, and the dead grass reluctantly kindled.

They turned and left, cantering back southwest, back to Woodwall, a wall of fire burning behind them. Carrying their torches, little dots of light, they moved like a swarm of fireflies. They reached their first village an hour later.

Silent and grim as ghosts, they cantered into the village. Icy tears in her eyes, Aeolia led her men to the granaries. Ignoring the peasants, she set flame to the grain. Her tears now hot and flowing, she ordered the livestock slaughtered, the wool set to flame, the barns burned down. The peasants' feeble defenses were soon quelled. Tongues of flame licked the sky. Aeolia and her army cantered out of the village, where they set fire to the surrounding fields and forests, and finally dumped dead animals into the stream to poison the water.

"Spirit," Ketya muttered, her face ashen. "We're doing Lale's work for him."

Aeolia shook her head. "Lale would have used this land. We're simply destroying it."

The flames crackled, painting the sky red, a bloody pall for their first village.

That night Aeolia lay awake, supine, counting the fireflies that swirled like sparks from a flame. When she had reached six score, something rustled beside her, and her hand leapt to the poniard she wore strapped round her thigh. But it was only Ketya, the moonlight limning her form, who had crept up shivering to Aeolia's side, and now stood with her blanket wrapped around her shoulders.

"What is it?" Aeolia asked, tensing. "Stonish outriders? Rebel peasants?"

Ketya did not answer but only stood trembling, and Aeolia glimpsed moonlight flash off a tear on her cheek.

"I miss my mother," the girl whispered.

Aeolia felt a twinge in her heart.

Ketya said, "When I'd have nightmares she'd sit beside me and stroke my hair till I slept, and... I'm frightened now. And I know, I know you're not much older than me, but... do you think... maybe you can...."

Aeolia patted the ground beside her, and Ketya lay down and nestled up in her blanket. Aeolia ran her fingers through Ketya's hair, till at last the girl slept, snoring softly. Aeolia stared at her, the secret of her foster-brother heavy on her soul. She shut her eyes. She wished Talin were with her, stroking her own hair so she too could feel safe. But no; it was her turn to be strong now. She returned her eyes to the fireflies and knew she would not sleep that night.

* * * * *

Many villages followed.

For days Aeolia burned, galloping across the land, ravaging all northeastern Esire. Her soul burned with it, scorching away all pity and emotion. She rode grim and silent, and even Ketya no longer dared approach her. She was a queen of destruction, an agent of ruin. The Firefly Queen, the queen of fire. In years to come, she knew, her name would be uttered with contempt, as the girl who ruined the world. The fire seemed to sear her tears dry, and soon her bravest soldiers quaked when she turned her grim gaze upon them. She feared the monster she was becoming, feared what Talin would find when she returned. But still she burned. Weeks passed, and all Esire rose in flames.

Aeolia was galloping back to Woodwall, but a day away, when Lale caught up with her.

Her army's horns blared their warning in long, mournful wails. Distant enemy drums answered in deep, thundering booms.

Aeolia strained her eyes but saw nothing. Acorn nickered nervously and skittered sideways. Patting the horse's head, Aeolia hunched forward and squinted.

Then she saw them, and her breath died. Rumbling out of the distant smoke, they swarmed like ants. The scorched earth was swallowed beneath them, covered by a gray blanket. Aeolia felt the blood leave her face.

"So many," she whispered.

She wheeled Acorn around. "Come!" she called to her men. "More is left to burn."

They spurred their skittish mounts and galloped through the countryside into the next village. As they set it aflame, the gray swarm swept closer, like a shadow falling. By the fifth village torched, Aeolia could make out individual soldiers in the gray patch. She wondered which was Lale.

Soon Woodwall came into view, a white dot beneath the vermilion sky. Beside a forest of hemlock and pine, Aeolia called her men to a halt.

"I leave you here," she said. "My girl and I return to Woodwall. You stay behind and hide in these trees. When the Stonesons besiege Woodwall, your task will be to prevent their supplies from arriving."

Her men bowed. Aeolia wheeled Acorn around and trotted away without another word.

At first she found the silence unsettling. Used to the thunder of five hundred coursers, she found it odd hearing only the hoofbeats of her filly and Ketya's pony. She could hear wind moan through the trees and the distant crackle of fire. Soon, however, a rumble began to grow, so loud it drowned all other sounds. The Stonish host was close, swarming over the burning land. Their drums pounded loud as thunder, and their horns wailed like wind.

Aeolia and Ketya galloped. Their horses were weary; the beasts' ears lay flat against their heads, their hoofs clumsily kicked rocks and grass and snow. Setting the last few farms aflame, the girls fled toward Woodwall, a tidal wave of darkness rising behind them from the fire.

The city's wooden walls, built with Big Browns and studded with iron, brimmed with grim, pale soldiers. When Aeolia and Ketya rode through the gates, they found an army in the courtyard. The soldiers stared at Aeolia sullenly and did not bow. Aeolia was too weary to care. She reared Acorn to a halt.

"Be brave, my friends!" she called. "Remember they are at siege with us. We will overcome."

The army stared sullenly. *They no longer love me,* Aeolia realized. *Well, I should not be surprised; it is their homeland I have destroyed.* She kneed her horse and trotted through the bleak city. Ketya followed on her pony. They soon reached the palace and dismounted.

"Where is that stable boy?" Aeolia muttered.

"I'll take the horses to the stable," Ketya said quietly. "You go on."

"I thought you were afraid of horses."

Ketya shrugged. "They don't seem so scary anymore."

Feeling unbearably dirty, longing for a scalding bath, Aeolia crossed the courtyard and entered the palace. The main hall was empty. Had Talin not come to greet her? she wondered. Perhaps he had not yet heard of her return. She considered searching for him, but decided against it. She would not bear him seeing her as she was, covered with ash and shame.

She paced down empty corridors to the bathing chamber. It, too, was empty, with not a servant to be seen. *Good,* Aeolia thought; she wanted to be alone. She tossed her blackened armor onto the floor, laid her crown on a stool, and peeled off her dirty, sweaty clothes. She prepared the bath herself and climbed into the hot water. She let out a whimper and closed her eyes.

"Spirit, what have I done...." she whispered.

A reply came from the door. "You've destroyed my kingdom."

Aeolia snapped her eyes open. Reyn stood at the door, two burly guards at his sides. A heavy, jeweled crown sat on his head.

"Get out of here," Aeolia hissed.

Reyn lifted her dainty crown from the stool, his thumb caressing the golden firefly perched atop its silver wires. He dropped the crown to the floor. It clanged.

"No matter how much gold you toss them," Reyn said, "the people will go hungry if you burn their food."

He stepped on her crown, crumpling it beneath his heel.

"We cannot fight each other," Aeolia whispered. "Look what happened to Heland."

Reyn tossed her a towel. It sank into the bath's water.

"Wrap up and come with me," Reyn said. "Your king commands it."

"Get out of here!" Aeolia shouted, tears budding in her eyes. "Leave me, you mean old man!"

The guards took a pace forward. Reyn stopped them with his hand.

"You will come," he said, "or your husband will pay for your insolence."

Aeolia shook her head slowly. Not Talin....

"All right," she said submissively, "I'll come."

Wrapping the soaked towel around her, she stepped out of the bath. The guards grabbed her arms and pulled her out of the room. They dragged her through the palace corridors, letting the servants stare at their bedraggled, dripping queen.

"What will you do to me?" she asked as they pulled her toward her room.

"You will be handed over to Lale as a surrender gift," Reyn said.

Aeolia shut her eyes. "Don't do this. We can't surrender, not now. Not after...."

Reyn glared at her. "I wanted to surrender long ago. It's not my fault you ravaged the countryside in vain."

"We can beat them, Reyn," Aeolia gushed out with sudden passion. "We can win this war."

"At what price?" Reyn snapped. "Enough have died at your hands. Sinther has promised to spare the city, should we let his army in peacefully."

They reached Aeolia's room. The guards opened the door and shoved her inside. She fell to the floor, and the door slammed shut behind her.

Aeolia tried pushing herself up, but her elbows wobbled weakly. Suddenly Ketya's arms were around her, helping her to her feet.

"Lia...," Ketya wept, hugging her and crying. "Isn't it horrible?"

Ketya still wore her ashy clothes, and her tears etched white streaks down her blackened face. Aeolia patted her head silently, staring dry-eyed over the young girl's shoulder. On her canopy bed lay a burgundy gown studded with rubies and garnets.

"They said I should help you put it on," Ketya said. "I wanted the honey-colored dress, but they said Lale sent this one especially, and...." Tears swept her words away.

"Best we do as they say," Aeolia said mildly.

Ketya nodded and blotted her tears. Still sniffing, she lifted the silk gown, careful not to dirty it with ash, and helped Aeolia dress. It was an elaborate gown, and both girls worked for long moments doing its laces and straps. When it was finally on, Aeolia looked into the mirror and blushed. The neckline was embarrassingly revealing, the silk flimsy, and the embroidery florid.

"Well, how do I look?"

"You look...," Ketya said, "you look...."

"Like a courtesan," Aeolia finished for her.

Ketya nodded, laughing and crying.

"I guess this is Lale's taste," Aeolia said quietly.

The door opened behind them, and Aeolia spun around. She froze. Talin stood at the doorway.

"They let me come see you," he said.

Aeolia stared at him numbly, unable to move. As she stood frozen he paced forward and embraced her. She whimpered like a child and clutched him, clinging to him. Tears streamed down her cheeks and she could not breathe for pain.

Chapter Eighteen
Strong as Stone

Taya woke up thinking she was dead. She remembered the knife opening her neck, remembered the spark of life extinguishing. And now she lay in a coffin. She felt its walls push against her. The ceiling was low, and she could not sit up. It was tar black and ice cold.

Someone was breathing beside her. Taya's heart leapt into her mouth.

"Who's there?" she demanded.

The breathing turned into a thankful gasp.

"You're awake at last!" a man's voice said in Northtalk.

"Who are you? What are you doing here?" Taya demanded shakily, in her fright still speaking Woodword.

"It's okay, don't be afraid. I'm a friend. My name is Roen."

Taya switched to Northtalk, straining to pronounce the foreign words. "How you here? This is my coffin."

"This isn't a coffin. It's just a long box."

"I am buried in box? This is shared grave?"

"You're not dead."

"But I remember dying."

"You did die, but now you are alive. I brought you back from the dead."

"Only Healer Firechild can do that!"

"Yes … it seems I'm him."

Taya understood. "So Lale caught us both. He wants give us to his father as gifts."

"Yes, Lale is taking us to Grayrock."

"How long I be asleeping?"

"It's hard to tell. I counted they brought us food fifteen times, so maybe that many days."

Taya winced. "So we almost there."

"Yes."

"I frightened."

"So am I."

"I very cold and hungry," she said. "I sorry, so are you, I know."

"It's easier, being cold and hungry together."

"Yes, yes! At least we have each other. I was frightened more when alone."

"I saw you then," he said. "You didn't look frightened. You walked proud and straight."

"Lale said he pull my toes off if I tilt bucket. That why I walked straight."

"Oh. I'm sorry. It must have been horrible."

Taya thought of those days, when fear and pain were her constant companions. She said, "I never lost hope, though. Even now I have hope. My friend, you see, she will save us. Aeolia will save us!"

Roen gasped. "You know Aeolia? The Esiren Firechild?"

"Yes! You know her too?"

"She freed my father from prison, once. It seems so long ago."

"She will free us too."

"I hope you're right."

"You no sound so sure," she said.

"Well, it's just that... Sinther lives miles underground, in a fortress more heavily guarded than any other on the Island. I don't know how Aeolia can save us there."

"She will. I believe in her."

Before Roen could reply, a rattling sound came from above.

"What that is?" Taya asked.

"They're putting food into an upper compartment of the box. There's another door for us to open. We have to wait until their door closes."

Taya smiled wanly. "They ascared I turn into hoppergrass and escape."

"Yes. Here, their door has closed. I'll get the food."

Taya felt Roen shift, and she heard another hatch open in the low ceiling. After a series of scraping sounds, the hatch rattled shut.

"Here, give me your hand," Roen said.

Taya groped in the darkness and found his hand. He put in her palm a bread roll. Taya ate it in small bites. It was stale and grainy.

"Drink this," Roen said and pushed toward her a small dish. Taya lifted it and drank the brackish water. She drank half and gave the rest to Roen. She was still thirsty.

"That all?" she asked.

"Yes. My magic can ease some of the hunger, though."

"You living like this fifteen days?"

"It wasn't so bad. I thought about you a lot. Sometimes when you slept I would talk to you."

Taya smiled. "And now I can talk back."

The box began to rattle and bounce.

"We're starting to move again," Roen said. "That means it's probably morning."

"Funny. It so dark."

They lay in silence for a while, jostled up and down. Taya shut her eyes. It made no difference, but she found the darkness more bearable when it was confined behind her eyelids alone. She kept twisting her fingers to remind herself she was alive, and eased her fear and loneliness by listening to Roen's breathing.

At length she spoke quietly. "Thank you for bringing me back to life."

"Don't. I doomed you to a worse fate than death."

"Then why you did it?"

"I didn't mean to. I was crying over your body, wishing you lived, and then you did."

"You cry for me?" Taya asked softly. "But why? You not know me. How you find my body?"

"Lale threw you over the balcony. I caught you."

"And Lale sawed you?"

"Yes."

Taya winced. "I sorry, it my fault you here. You no should have brought me back to life; it got you caught."

"No, don't be sorry! I don't regret it."

"You are so kind to me. I not know what to say."

"Just tell me your name."

"Taya."

"Taya...," he repeated slowly, as if tasting the word on his tongue.

"I so sorry. I ruined everything. How can you ever forgive me?"

* * * * *

Time passed slowly. Taya and Roen spent it talking, telling each other stories. Taya told him of her woodland home, how the foliage rustled, how the leaves turned red in autumn, how the air smelled of wood and earth. Roen in turn told her of his workshop, of the smell of pigment and oil, how dust danced in sunrays from the window, how his bristly brushes made scraping sounds as they walked across parchment. Their words painted images in their blindness, and so they talked constantly, not letting the darkness overwhelm them.

As time went by Taya grew to know Roen, as well as she had ever known anyone. She felt he knew her the same way. He let her touch his face once, so she could fashion an image of him. His beard was curly, soft and warm in her fingers, but his skin was always cold. It was the heart of winter. Sometimes Taya turned into a bear to keep warm, and let Roen share her fur. He in turn would heal her when she was hungry, easing the ache in her stomach. Thus they survived together. Taya could not imagine lasting such a journey alone.

And then one day it ended.

Unexpectedly, several hours past food time, the box stopped moving. Taya felt it lifted and carried up a flight of stairs. She clutched Roen's hand. Soon the stairs ended, and from there on, their box was carried only down. Down more stairs, or down slopes, but always down. The descent lasted a long time—hours, maybe. With every minute Taya's fear grew, till she held Roen's hand so hard she probably hurt him.

Finally, the box was dropped. It clanged against the floor, bouncing Taya and Roen against the ceiling. Taya cried out in pain. Fear filled her gut, so thick it ached. She clenched her fists to quell her panic.

"We here now?" she asked Roen, forcing the words past stiff lips.

"Yes, I think so," Roen replied. He sounded frightened too. "Don't be scared. There's nothing he can do that I can't heal."

A rattling sound came from above, and Taya held her breath. The top of the box slid open.

A single torch flickered above them, set in a craggy stone wall. Taya winced and covered her eyes against the light. Cold, musty air flowed into the box. A dark shadow blocked the torchlight, and Taya removed her hands and peeked through wincing lids. She saw a man's silhouette.

"Don't think of escaping," the shadow spoke. "Your magic cannot help you here."

Taya couldn't help but cover her ears. The voice was terrible. It was not even a voice; it was only an echo, a deep rumble like thunder.

"Get out of the box," the echo said.

Wincing with pain, Taya struggled for long moments before she managed climbing out into the dim cavern. Her muscles screamed. Roen climbed out as well, and Taya gazed at him for the first time. He looked vaguely familiar, like a figure from a dream. They held onto each other for support as their cramped legs wobbled.

"Why don't you look at me?" asked the echo.

"I know what you look like," Taya said. "A man of stone."

"Does this frighten you?"

Taya shook her head. "You no more powerful than us. Roen and me are Firechildren too."

Sinther laughed—a terrible rumble that reverberated in the cave.

"Your magic cannot hurt me. I am made of stone. My body cannot be harmed."

Taya turned to look at him. His skin was dark and speckled and rough. She stared up into the cold, stone eyes.

"But the fourth Firechild can hurt you," she said. "Aeolia is more powerful than you!"

Again Sinther laughed, his stone chest heaving. The sound was deafening.

"You may laugh now!" Roen said, gaining some of Taya's defiance. "Aeolia is probably on her way here as we speak."

Sinther grew sober. He stared at Roen with cold eyes. "You speak truth, Healer. The Esiren Firechild is on her way here, but not as you think. She is coming as a prisoner. My son has captured her."

Ice seemed to encase Taya's heart.

"No!" she cried. "You is lying!"

"You will see for yourself soon enough," Sinther replied. "In time, the Esiren's head will grace this room's walls, hanging over your statues."

"What you mean, our statues?" Taya demanded.

"Try to move and you'll see."

Taya tried to take a step. Her foot would not budge, as if it were glued to the floor. She tried her other foot, but it too was frozen. Roen was struggling to move as well, but with no more success.

"What you are doing to us?" Taya cried.

"I'm turning you into stone," Sinther replied.

Taya shook her head wordlessly, unable to speak or breathe.

"The soles of your feet are turned to stone already," Sinther continued. "The magic will gradually rise, turning your feet to stone, then your legs, then your stomachs.... When the stone reaches your faces, you will suffocate and die."

Taya looked down at her feet. Her toes were already turning gray. She took Roen's hand and held it tightly.

"I'm sorry," she whispered to him. "It my fault."

"Don't be sorry," Roen whispered back. "I can think of no better way to die than together."

"Nor can I," Taya said earnestly. "Nor can I."

Sinther only laughed.

Chapter Nineteen
Emperor of Stone

Woodwall's gates creaked slowly open.

Aeolia paced gingerly outside, biting her trembling lip. Her flimsy dress did little for warmth, and she shivered and hugged herself. Blood-red clouds grumbled above, snowing ash.

Outside the city walls, the Stonish army sprawled before her. Rows of cloaked soldiers stood silently, stretching into the horizon. Banners billowed feebly in the wind, listless waves in a vast, gray sea. In the eerie silence, Aeolia heard her shaky breath, the scraping of her shoes as she walked, the rustling of her skirts. She approached the gray mass slowly.

When she reached the stone sea's border, it split in two, opening a path down the middle. Aeolia swallowed and stepped inside, walked down the aisle with human walls on her sides, their cold eyes following her. The sea closed behind her, swallowing her in darkness, trembling, alone. At the end of the path, in front of a carriage, stood a hooded man with a dark sword at his waist.

"Lale," Aeolia said when she reached him.

The man pulled back his hood, revealing the prince's scarred face.

"Aeolia," said he, smiling softly.

Quick as a cane's blow, he grabbed her waist and spun her around. He lifted her into the air, showing her to the city.

"Thank you for this gift, Esire!" he called, this man who had once been her prince. "I will take her to Grayrock, where she'll be beheaded in Town Square!"

He lowered Aeolia to the ground. He crossed his arms over her, pinning her to him. When Aeolia squirmed he only squeezed her tighter.

"Now I'd like you to watch something," he whispered into her ear. "I think you'll enjoy it."

He took a silver horn from his belt and gave a short blow. The Stonish army began marching, tapering into a cone. Like water down a drain, they swept through Woodwall's gates. Lale rested his chin on Aeolia's head and let out a pleased sigh. Aeolia stood still, her eyes moist, watching silently.

"Like two lovers watching the sunset...," Lale said softly. "Is it getting dark enough, Your Majesty?"

In an impossible feat, the vast army finally drained into the small city, leaving behind but a score of guards and the carriage.

"They are searching for your husband," Lale whispered, his split lips touching Aeolia's ear. "I intend to kill him myself. But not yet, not yet.... First, Aeoly, it is time to take you home."

He dragged Aeolia to the carriage, pulled her inside, and shut the door behind them. In stark contrast to his cold, gray army, Lale's carriage was homelike and comfortable. Its cherry walls and glass windows kept the cold outside. A plush couch rested against one wall, topped with pillows.

"Sit down," Lale said and pushed Aeolia onto the couch.

"A cozy seat," she observed. "Have you grown too soft for horses?"

"Some are softer than I," he said quietly, his eyes caressing her exposed flesh. "You will find I can be quite hard."

Aeolia felt herself blush. "So that's what the carriage is for. Privacy."

Lale shook his head. "You must believe me, I had only your comfort in mind."

"Why are you suddenly so concerned about my comfort?"

"Your pain is my pain." Lale smiled sourly. "Literally, in your case."

Aeolia nodded. "You dare not hurt me. I'd simply link the pain back to you."

Lale sat beside her and put his hand on her thigh. "I guess I'll just have to be gentle," he said and licked her cheek.

Aeolia turned her head away. "Do you have any idea how repulsive you are to me?"

"Imagine how much I care."

"Well, then. Try to imagine myself as repulsive as you."

He grabbed her cheeks and forced her face near his. "Don't you wish it."

She smiled crookedly. "I *can* wish it so, you know."

A hint of dread flitted across Lale's eyes. "What do you mean?"

"Rape me, and I'll link to you. My disgust will surmount your lust, and then we'll see exactly who is the soft one."

Lale's face contorted. He lifted his fist.

"Go ahead," Aeolia said. "Hit me. You'll just be hitting yourself."

Lale's face strained as he quelled his anger. Slowly he lowered his fist.

"All right," he said. "You want to play with threats, do you? Well try this one. You have a moon to live before facing execution in your homeland. You can spend this moon pleasantly, with me in this carriage, with fine wine, fine food, and fine entertainment—"

"If entertainment consists of your marvels in bed, I pass."

"Or"—Lale's voice became strained—"you can spend the trip in a cage, frozen and starved. You'll be eating bugs and twigs before we reach Grayrock. Bare your teeth at me, and you'll live your last moon in this misery."

Cold fear flooded Aeolia's belly, but she shook her head. "You want me to serve you out of fear. You want me to have something to lose, so I will consent to be your slave. I will never be that. Once a slave is enough. I won't let you defile me."

He rose to his feet. "Do you think you're doing your wife's duty, Esiren? Do you think this is how your husband would have wanted it? Bah! You are a stubborn fool, playing meaningless games of martyrdom. For ten years I've hunted you. A decade! I deserve you now!" He clenched his fist. "Be mine!"

"Not willingly. No." Aeolia shook her head to strengthen her determination, which was wavering. Her heart pounded, and her knees trembled. She had never been so frightened. "You have stolen me from my husband, but you cannot steal his place. Take me by force if you dare. I bet you dare not."

"And so you will live your last days like an animal! Guards!"

The door swung open and gray-uniformed guards bowed at the entrance.

Lale spoke with a voice strained and shaking with rage. "Take the girl, and bind her arms, and bind her legs, but leave her eyes free. I want her to see the ruin she has wrought upon this land. By the time we reach Grayrock, I want her ruined the same way." He stared at Aeolia, his gray eyes searing. "This is your last chance. Be mine willingly, and I will save you from this torment."

"I don't fear pain," Aeolia whispered. "It has ever been my ally."

The guards grabbed her. Their nails dug into her skin. Their reeking breath assailed her through their yellow teeth.

She knew she had made the right choice.

* * * * *

They began the long journey to Grayrock.

Aeolia's cage was chained to Lale's carriage, dragging behind it over the ground. She was hogtied behind her back, and the bumpy ride jostled her against the bars. By the end of the first day, she had scarce a patch of unbruised skin. But she was too heartbroken to care. They were journeying through Esire's scorched earth, the dismal lands she had created, ruined plains vast as solitude. Bare, blackened soil stretched endlessly, crawling with bands of bedraggled peasants awaiting starvation. She had done this, Aeolia knew. And she had done it in vain.

Lale fulfilled his promise in ruining her the same way. He stayed in his carriage, safe from her link, free to let her suffer. He emerged only rarely to feed her, tossing her petty crumbs to lick from the floor, or sometimes a dry bone. As her cage dragged along, Aeolia reached her bound hands out the bars, catching twigs and eating them, or a bug if she was lucky. She drank melted snow. Hunger was her constant companion, like a child of demons in her belly.

The cold was even worse. Lale gave her only an old, flea-ridden blanket, just thick enough to keep her alive and always shivering. Whenever she cried her tears froze, and icicles hung from her hair. She kept moving her fingers and toes, but she was unable to keep her ears from freezing. At least that was one part of her no longer hurting. Her bound limbs cramped and screamed behind her back, and the rope dug so deep she thought it might touch bone.

Sleep brought no relief. Dreams lurked in its haze, terribly wonderful dreams where she made love to Talin, or laughed with Ketya, and would always end up eating them both, tearing their flesh with her teeth, being warmed by their blood. These dreams were the worst of times, and she would always wake from them sobbing. She did not regret her choice, not for an instant. Better to live like this, hurting herself if it could deny Lale's wish. Better to live in self-chosen pain than luxurious slavery. But, Aeolia slowly discovered as the days went by, the best was not to live at all.

She was praying for death one snowy morning, when Aeolia heard galloping horses. The sound was odd, for they had not encountered any living animal the whole past week, other than bugs and ravens. She looked up, blinking feebly in the winter sunlight, and could not believe her eyes.

Green knights were galloping downhill toward her, armor and swords glistening.

"For the Firefly Queen!" they cried, brandishing their swords.

Aeolia was sure it must be a dream, but still tears budded in her eyes. "Wil!" she cried. "Wil!"

Lale dashed out of his carriage, Bloodtalon in hand, and mounted his horse. He spread his riders out in a wall. As the Greenhill knights came thundering down, the Stonesons outstretched their arms, shooting stone splinters.

Three horses went down, toppling their knights. Wilon led his surviving riders forward, amid the stone darts, more horses falling.

"Aeolia!" he cried, waving his sword, his horse crumbling beneath him. "Lia, I'm here!"

"Swarm!" Lale shouted, and the Stonesons galloped forth to engage the fallen Greenhills. There was a long, terrible battle. Steel rang and blood splashed onto white snow. Stonesons and Healers died. Aeolia watched in anguish as they cut one another down, until only two men were left standing.

Lale and Wilon.

Dead bodies surrounding them, the two men dueled, Lale snarling, Wilon grimly intent. Fearing, perhaps, Aeolia's link, Lale retreated behind the carriage, and the battle moved out of view. Aeolia heard only ringing steel, grunts of anger and pain, and finally a blood-curdling scream, followed by a dull chop and then silence.

Aeolia lay shivering. Who had won?

A dripping ball came flying over the carriage. It crashed against the cage's top bars, spattering blood. It was Wilon's head.

Aeolia screamed, frantically bashed it away, gagged outside and slumped trembling into the corner.

"A taste of what's to come, girl!" Lale cried as he climbed onto his carriage. "Soon your fate will be the same."

Aeolia lay weeping, shutting her eyes tightly only to find the grisly scene dancing behind her lids.

"I'm sorry," she sobbed onto the cage floor. "Sorry, Wil, I'm sorry...."

Lale whipped his horses. Just the two of them, they began to move, the cage dragging over the bloody ground, bumping over dead bodies.

The journey continued.

* * * * *

The days went by, and they left Esire. Aeolia was now dragged over the hinterland of Stonemark, icy plains and frozen forests, rolling hills and craggy mountain passes. Lale did not head straight to the capital. For weeks he traveled in winding routes, passing through towns and villages, displaying the bedraggled queen. The peasants always came to toss rotten fruits and vegetables.

Lale stopped feeding her then. Eat the food they toss you, he said. Aeolia tried, but she always threw it up. If she licked it up again, still it would not stay down. Strange things began happening to her body. All her fat disappeared, and her skin clung to her skeleton like wet cloth. Her breasts melted, and her belly bulged. Her joints bent only halfway, and hair fell from her head. She could not see so well. She could hardly raise her head from the bumping floor.

At least she got to see her home one last time. She could almost smile when she finally saw Grayrock in the distance.

The stone city was a gray heap of turrets and roofs and steeples. A vast city, larger than ten Woodwalls, built with ancient Stonish magic, the ruling center of the Island. Her hometown.

Lale stopped his carriage outside the gates, under the great flint wall. He alighted and stepped toward Aeolia's cage. He held a tray in his hands, full of food. There was a bowl of steaming stew. There were two rolls of bread and butter. There was a jug of milk, and a jug of wine. There was a basket of cherries.

Lale unlocked the cage door and placed the tray before her. Aeolia stared at it.

"It's for you," Lale said. "Aren't you hungry?"

Aeolia blinked at him. Hesitantly, she leaned forward and licked one of the rolls. The fresh, grainy smell tingled her nostrils. Suddenly, the roll was gone from the tray. She had bolted it down and hadn't noticed. Her stomach ached, and she threw up.

"Not so fast," Lale said. "Nibble."

Aeolia nodded, trembling. She leaned over and nibbled the second roll. It stayed down. Then she ate the stew, lapping it slowly. It was thick with beef and carrots and mushrooms, and seasoned with rosemary and pepper. She sipped the fruity wine. She drank the honeyed milk. She ate the plump, sweet cherries.

When she was done, Lale wiped her face clean. "You can come out now," he said.

Aeolia wriggled outside the cage, and Lale untied her feet.

"You may stand up."

Aeolia's arms were still bound behind her back. She struggled on wobbly legs, buckled and fell. Lale was very patient. He stood waiting as she tried again, and again, till she managed standing up. It hurt bad. Her stomach hurt too.

Lale lifted her wispy hair. He closed a collar around her neck. He chained the collar to the back of his carriage.

"You walk from here," he said.

He turned around, climbed back into his carriage, and whipped his horses. The chain tugged at her collar, and Aeolia stumbled behind. She followed the carriage through a gateway in the wall. They passed under fifty feet of flint before emerging into the city. A crowd awaited them there, bowing before its prince.

Lale reined his horses. "Rise and behold the fallen queen!" he cried. "Behold the Esiren Firechild!"

The crowd booed her, and Lale whipped his horses again.

He pulled Aeolia all day through the city of stone. He pulled her through twisting alleys, through market squares, through busy streets and wide, rich boulevards. He would never let her drag. If she fell, he stopped, and gave her milk, and soothed her, till she could walk again. And she walked, her feet bleeding, her muscles torn. Every window held a jeering face, every road a barrage of filth and curses. At one time they passed through her old neighborhood, and Aeolia saw her childhood house. Men she remembered as boys threw snowballs with rocks.

The sun was low when they finally reached the Citadel. The seat of the emperor, the grotesque, massive edifice soared into the gurgling clouds. Bird droppings speckled its dank walls and spires. Gargoyles perched on its crenellations, twisted things of fangs and horns, of snarls and claws. Aeolia was pulled across a wide courtyard toward the fortress, through the jeering throngs and barrages of filth.

The courtyard ended at a stage beneath the looming fortress. The gargoyles glowered down with eyes of jet and frozen leers. Lale stopped the carriage, removed Aeolia's collar, and pulled her onto the stage toward a barrel. He grabbed her hair and pulled her head down onto the wood.

The prince faced the vast crowd. He spoke in a loud voice. "The fallen Firefly Queen is guilty of the following crimes: reading minds, threatening the emperor, sparking war...." The crowd booed with every offense announced, and Lale shouted louder. "...causing stillbirths, spreading disease, withering the crops, flooding villages...."

Aeolia stopped listening. She shut her eyes and thought of Talin, till at last her list of crimes ended.

"Bring forth the executioner!" Lale cried.

The Citadel's great iron doors swung open. The executioner stepped out, wearing a black mask and holding an ax, an ax that could sever a link like a head. He bowed before Lale, received the prince's blessings, then straightened and approached Aeolia.

He stood above her, holding his steel, and Aeolia saw his eyes moisten. His tears tumbled through the air, splashed onto her cheek and ran down to her lips. They were warm and salty, and so Aeolia knew it was not a dream, and that he truly stood above her. For a moment all sound disappeared, and she was no longer aware of the crowd, or the city, or the pain. For a moment the world was only her and him again.

And she whispered, "I never stopped loving you."

Joren's tears splashed down—huge, round drops like the rain that had fallen that night, the night they had said good-bye, and Aeolia smiled because for the first time in weeks she did not feel cold. And Joren grimaced. His eyes winced, and his mouth opened and he wailed, a long, mournful wail of such sadness that Aeolia wanted to cry. His tears fell, and his howl ripped the air, and his ax came down. And with a snap, like the snap of her fetters long ago, Aeolia's bounds tore.

She rose to her feet, her arms free.

The surrounding guards drew their swords and came running toward her.

"Into the Citadel!" Joren cried. "RUN!"

Aeolia could not run, but she limped forward. She heard Joren shout behind her as he clashed steel with the guards. More guards came charging from ahead of her, and she stopped in her tracks. Joren whipped around her, and his ax flew, and blood bespattered her face.

"Take this." Joren slipped a dagger into her palm. "Come, through the doors."

Guards came storming from behind, and Aeolia and Joren hurried into the Citadel. Inside, Joren slammed himself against the doors, grunting and pushing. The doors closed with a deep boom, and Joren dropped a beam into their brackets.

"Watch out!" Aeolia cried as three guards came charging from within the fortress. Joren ran to meet them. He chopped them down in a berserk rage, suffering a gash to his side.

"Joren!" Aeolia said. "You're wounded."

"It's nothing." He embraced her. She felt him crying again. "Spirit, Aeoly, what have they done to you...?"

A boom made them start. The doors creaked, slammed at from outside.

"Let me in, Joren!" Lale's shout came through the wood. "Let me in, or by the Spirit, I'll feed your head to the pigs!"

Again the doors were slammed at. Splinters flew.

Aeolia tightened her grip on her dagger. "They're breaking in!"

"I know where it's safe," Joren said. "Come."

He lifted her. Carrying her in his arms, he moved down the hall, and they plunged into a labyrinth of dank, winding corridors and stairwells. The place was mostly empty. Most people had gone to watch the execution. What few servants remained did not challenge the royal executioner. Probably they thought Aeolia was dead already. She watched Joren's blood leave a trail on the floor behind them.

A crash came from above, and Aeolia started. The fortress rumbled with footsteps and clanking armor.

"I'll drop you into the sewer, girl!" Lale shouted somewhere above. "I'll drown you in my own waste!"

"They've broken the door!" Aeolia said. "They're catching up!"

"We're going to Sinther's antechamber," Joren said grimly. "The guards aren't allowed in there."

Aeolia noticed Joren's face was pale, his breathing shallow. Blood soaked his shirt, trickling incessantly. She knew he could not carry her much longer. Still he continued running, and they descended deeper, down darker tunnels like the burrows of ants, down and down into the belly of the earth. The soldiers grew louder above them, following Joren's trail of blood. Lale's cries echoed through the halls.

After descending what seemed like miles, Aeolia and Joren reached a bare, dark room. In the flickering torchlight, Aeolia saw a stairwell carved into the floor and a tunnel gaping open in one wall. Joren approached the tunnel but paused before it, breathing heavily. His face was pale and his eyes were glazed.

"Put me down, Jor," Aeolia said. "You can't carry me anymore."

Joren looked ready to object, but then he nodded and put Aeolia down. She stood on unsteady feet. Joren took a step into the tunnel.

"This is... his antechamber?" Aeolia asked, not following.

Joren nodded. "This tunnel is what makes the room secret. It's an escape route. Come, quickly."

Lale's shouting echoed above, moving closer.

"Does... Sinther live down there?" Aeolia asked, pointing a shaky finger to the hole in the floor.

"Yes!" There was panic in Joren's voice. "Now come, into the tunnel. Lale's coming closer, Aeoly; I can't fight him!"

Aeolia stood in place, legs quivering. Here the path forks, she knew. One way leads to light, to friends and family. And the other.... Aeolia looked down into the pit. Taya was down there, she knew. Aeolia had to save her, even if it meant her life.

"Tell my husband I love him," she said.

"What?" Joren cried. "Quickly, we must go!"

"Tell him I'm sorry I didn't come back."

"Aeoly, stop this nonsense! Please, I beg you, come."

"Promise me, Joren," she pleaded. "Promise you'll do it."

He paled and she froze. They both remembered.

"I swear it!" Joren cried. "By my life!"

"Then go!"

He whispered, "I love you, Aeolia."

"Go!"

He vanished into the tunnel. Aeolia stayed in place, waiting as Lale's thundering grew louder, until he burst into the room.

"Catch me!" she said and dashed into the stairwell. She limped down the spiraling steps fast as she could. Lale ran but paces behind her. Aeolia saw his shadow in the torchlight, gaining on her. She stopped, grabbed a torch, and spun around. As Lale came crashing down, she tossed the torch at him. He raised his arms to his face, and Aeolia thrust her dagger into his belly.

His old wound opened, shooting blood. He blanched and clutched his stomach. Blood bubbled in his mouth. His sword clanked at his feet. He fell to his knees, staring at the blood flowing between his fingers. Blood dripped around his knees.

Slowly, he looked up at her. His face was white. "I never wanted it to be this way," he whispered. There was pain and fear in his eyes, but also sadness. "We could have run from him together. Oh, Ness, forgive me."

Aeolia stared at him in silence for a moment. Then she grabbed the dagger's hilt, twisted and pulled. It came free with a sucking sound. As Lale folded over, she turned and continued descending the stairwell. She reached the bottom, where stood a stone door, and stopped.

She stared at the door. *Here it all ends,* she knew. *I was born for now.* She shut her eyes and breathed deeply, each breath flowing like a soothing wave. All her pain and sorrows and worries disappeared, melting like sugar in these tranquil waters. She was leaving love behind, but in the cold of now, that love still gave her warmth. *Now is the time,* she knew, *the time to undo all my wrongs, to finally make everything right.* Slowly, Aeolia opened her eyes, opened the door, and stepped in.

In the flickering torchlight she saw him, speckled stone roughly hewn. A man of stone, tyrant of the Island, her childhood king. Shaking with rage and fear, Sinther glared at her, snarling, stone eyes wild.

Aeolia spoke, soft as summer rain. "Let my friend go."

Sinther growled and pointed his fingers. Splinters crashed against Aeolia, jabbing into her flesh, speckling her red. She barely felt a thing. She took a step forward.

"You cannot hurt me," she whispered.

His scream echoed and rang in Aeolia's ears. He waved his hands. Stones slammed into Aeolia, and she heard her ribs snap. She continued pacing forward. She could not see Taya clearly for the darkness, but in the back of the room, she saw a tall dark slab, and she glimpsed a curl of orange hair.

"Don't worry, Taya," she said. "I've come to save you."

Sinther howled and frothed at the mouth. He reached out, his hands shaking, and shot a sharp stone cone. The stone slashed Aeolia's arm, nearly severing it.

"I've come to save everyone...."

She smiled softly and took a deep breath. She linked to Sinther.

Like poison in water, his mind mingled with hers, reeking of blackness and disease, twitching with fear. Aeolia winced. So sad... he was so sad.... He fled to the back of the room and cowered in the corner, howling and drooling like a mad beast.

Aeolia raised her dagger. The blade gleamed in the torchlight, gentle as fireflies' glow. She took a deep breath and placed the sharp point on her breast. All her friends smiled, the people she cared for, flowers from her wedding, white dresses and silky beds, silver and gold. She gasped softly as she pushed. Red blossomed on her white skin like poppies on snow.

Her eyes shut, opened cloudy. She saw Sinther clutch his chest, fall to his knees, fall to the floor beside her. Slowly Aeolia sat down, red spilling from her like wine from a cracked jug. She lay back and gazed up at blue skies. As her heart stilled she clung tightly to his mind, pulling him into slow death with her.

She swallowed weakly. Her eyelids fluttered.

"I'm sorry, Talin," she whispered. "I love you and everyone."

Her honey eyes closed.

Chapter Twenty
Almonds and Honey

Joren stumbled down the tunnel, huffing and moaning, his hand clutched to his wound. Blood soaked his shirt, and his head spun. He had to see a physician soon, he knew, or he'd die. He quickened his step, but slipped and fell in the darkness. For a moment he sat panting, then pushed himself up with a grunt. He resumed limping forward.

After what seemed like hours, he saw light ahead. He plodded toward it. The light slanted in beams from the ceiling, falling through the holes of a sewer's lid. Joren heard muffled chanting above. He pushed the metallic disk aside and heaved himself up. Coughing and shaking, he crawled outside and found himself in an empty alley. He heard the chanting clearly now, coming from around the corner.

"The king is dead," cried thousands of voices, "long live the king!"

Joren shuffled out of the alley. The Citadel loomed ahead, closer than he'd expected; though the tunnel was long, most of its length wound upwards. People clogged the streets, all chanting.

"The king is dead, long live the king!"

Joren stumbled into the crowd. Those around him, seeing his blood, recoiled in shock. Joren gruffly ignored their worried offers of help.

"Tell me," he rasped, grasping one man's arm, "is the king dead?"

The man nodded slowly. "Aye, King Sinther is dead, my friend. And so will you be, if you don't see a doctor soon."

"Never mind me!" Joren snapped, and was overcome by a fit of coughing. The man patted his back hesitantly, and Joren pushed him off.

"And tell me," Joren said when he could talk again, "is Lale now king?"

The man shook his head. "No, Lale is dead too."

Joren shut his eyes. It was a moment before he could speak again. "So who is this new king?"

"Apparently, the prince's will named his heir his best friend, some fellow named Joren. Hey, hey, my friend, where are you going? You're hurt!"

Joren shoved his way through the crowd. They parted to let him through, seeing his blood. Joren ignored the pain, ignored the stares, ignored the offers of succor. Dizzy and shaking, he made it to the courtyard and trudged forward with grim determination.

"The king is dead, long live the king!" chanted the crowd.

Joren fell facedown before the stage. He began crawling up the stairs, smearing blood behind him. The guards recognized him and rushed down to help. They lifted him, half dead, and hurriedly carried him up toward the Citadel's doors.

"Leave me!" Joren said. "Let me stand, let them see me."

The guards reluctantly obeyed, lowering Joren to his feet on the stage. He stood before the vast crowd.

"Behold your new king!" cried one guard and raised Joren's hand. "Bow before King Joren, ruler of the Island!"

The crowd bowed in a great wave.

"Thank you, Aeoly," Joren whispered, tears in his eyes. "I promise I'll be better."

"Hail King Joren!" cried the crowd. "Long live the king!"

* * * * *

Taya sat waiting in the small chamber, fiddling her thumbs in her lap.

It was too quiet. The sounds of battle had mostly faded, Joren's challengers to the throne having been quelled or driven from the city. Only the occasional boom of a catapult now broke the silence. Taya supposed she should be glad. But instead she found herself wishing for... something, some noise, some fanfare. *It cannot end like this,* she thought. *How can everything be so... nonchalant?*

She rose to her feet and began pacing. Her legs were still stiff; they had returned to flesh with the stone king's death, but it would be a while before they were strong again. Taya did not care. Not about herself, not anymore. She stopped by the window and looked outside. Two colors of light danced lazily in the evening, red and orange, hers and Roen's. The other two colors of fireflies were gone. Taya felt a lump in her throat.

The door opened and Roen stepped inside. Taya turned toward him.

"How is she?" she asked.

Roen took a slow breath before speaking. "She is sleeping. She will sleep for a long time. Starvation killed her just as much as her wounds did. She might never wake."

"She will wake," Taya said decidedly. "She tougher than she look."

Roen nodded. "She really did come for us. I wonder if she knew I was a Firechild when she did."

"Her foster-brother tell me she not know. She thought she was giving us her life."

"I only hope I can give it back."

Taya lowered her eyes. "Like you gave it back to me."

"You once told me I shouldn't have; it got us caught."

Taya raised her eyes and looked at him, this man with round eyes, who wore no beard or braids, who had never eaten the heart of a vanquished warrior, and yet who, somehow, in his own way, could still impress her, more then Uaua or Ooor ever could. It felt strange. A year ago she would have scorned a man with no calluses on his hands. Gingerly, she touched the tattoos on her cheeks.

She spoke quietly. "I glad it did, I glad it got us caught. We learn from these hardships, I think. Sometimes awful things can bring the most wonderful ones."

"You know, I loved you from the moment I saw you."

Taya looked away from him. She gazed out the window. The red and orange fireflies danced and swirled in the evening. Taya thought she could discern, floating uncertainly amid them, a single, dim golden fleck, glowing hesitantly. She returned her eyes to Roen.

"You know," she whispered hesitantly, "we terribly mismatched."

"A Healer and a Forestfellow?"

"A painter and a warrior?"

"You're right." Roen nodded. "I think this is an awful idea. But as you know...."

Taya lowered her eyes. Her voice trembled slightly. "...sometimes awful things can bring the most wonderful ones." She raised her eyes and looked at him. "I don't know, Roen Painter. I still learning some things."

He only smiled at her. Hesitantly, Taya returned the smile. It felt good. Outside, the fireflies glowed.

* * * * *

Weeks later, Joren sat uneasily in his new throne.

The seat was comfortable enough, all soft angles shaped to fit his body, the marble carved so smooth it felt silken. But still Joren shifted as he sat. He felt out of place. He hung his hands limply over the armrests and gazed wearily around him.

The Citadel's old main hall had been refurbished into his royal court. Tall windows had been knocked into the walls, to drive out the cold and darkness. Pastel tapestries hung where walls still stood, concealing the dank, rough stone. A thick carpet covered the floor, and baskets of flowers and ivy sat on cherry tables, to drive out the smell of must. Who would have thought this was where, only several weeks ago, he had killed the guards of his old prince?

The front hall was not the only room Joren was changing. At his command, the entire Citadel was being remodeled. He had ordered the gargoyles replaced with marble statues of angels and unicorns. The old paved courtyard was being turned into a garden, which Joren planned to fill with grass and peacocks and fountains. Inside the building, inner walls had been knocked down, turning the old labyrinth of narrow corridors into wide, windowed halls. The lowermost rooms, haunted with unpleasant memories, Joren had ordered filled with mortar. The Citadel was becoming a new place. Joren didn't even call it the Citadel anymore. He simply called it the Palace. The Island's Palace.

He ruled the whole Island, of course—Sinther had conquered it all. But Joren did not rule as king of Stonemark. He did not want to rule conquered lands. He wanted a union, a union of the Island's five countries, whose new palace would be where he sat. He called it a new, brave land where war would never more rage. He had been working hard to promote his vision, appointing ministers of all races, creating a new flag with five stars, one for each of the old realms. He decreed intermarriage legal in all lands. He invited the homeless Esirens and Forestfolk, whose lands had been destroyed, to come till Stonemark's fields. No more separate races, he said. No more Stonish Empire. One land.

His efforts had all failed.

The people hated him. The Esirens still called him Butcher Joren. The Forestfolk blamed him for the destruction of their home. The Healers called him Lale's pet. They all saw him as a despot, and who could blame them? They would always remember his misdeeds. He was Lale's heir. To them, he was another Sinther.

He was a Stoneson, and as long as he reigned, they would see him as conqueror. Joren knew he would have to do more to realize the union he envisioned. He thought he knew how.

A knock at the hall's doors disrupted his thoughts. Joren smiled grimly. The moment he dreaded had come. He rose to his feet and signaled his guards to open the wide doors. As the doors creaked open, Joren found himself clenching his fists.

The man who walked through the doorway looked nothing like the boy Joren once had met. They were the same age, Joren knew, but there the resemblance ended. Joren had always been withdrawn, pensive. This man stood defiantly, fire in his eyes. Auburn stubble covered his cheeks, and his shock of hair was unkempt. *He hates me more than all,* Joren reflected.

The man spoke. "A cruel trick of fortune, that we should meet again."

"Cruel, Talin? I suppose it might be. But then, perhaps it is fate's way of relieving old grievances."

"You know, I often dreamed of this moment. In my dreams I open your throat and laugh as the blood washes my hands, like it washed *his* hands so long ago."

"You can still realize your dream," Joren said. "You wear a sword. I am unarmed."

Talin stepped forward. "You saved her. Why?"

"Because I...." Joren shut his eyes. "Because she taught me something, I think. Something about... love, perhaps? And for that I love her."

"You can never love her like I do."

Joren opened his mouth, then shut it. Finally he spoke. "Perhaps you are right, I...." Again words failed him. How could he possibly say what he felt? How he had wanted her to hate him, wanted her to spit at and curse him, but she only told him she loved him, after all he had done? How at that moment he wanted to die?

"I want to see her," Talin said.

Joren nodded briskly, shaking himself free of his thoughts. "Come."

The two men turned, crossed the carpeted hall, and passed through a doorway. They walked down a corridor, its windows set with colored glass, its walls bedecked with marigolds and hyacinths and bright yellow daffodils. They stopped at the end of the corridor, before a simple door festooned with sheaves of wheat.

"She is still asleep," Joren said. "She has been sleeping for several weeks now. We feed her honeyed milk and crushed fruit, and we heal her with magic, and we think she will wake soon. She often mumbles your name. Perhaps your voice will wake her. Go in. She is inside."

As Talin opened the door, Joren saw that the man's hand shook. This is her true love, Joren realized, and suddenly, strangely, he envied him. He leaned against the wall as Talin closed the door behind him, and waited.

He waited for a long time, smelling the flowers and thinking of Aeolia, so small and weak in her bed, her doll Stuffings in her arms again. Finally Talin emerged from the room. His eyes were moist.

"Let me take her with me," Talin said.

"She needs our Healers."

"I can nurse her back to health. She needs to be home."

"But this is her home."

"This, her home?"

Joren sighed. "You see, I... have done much wrong in my life. I am unfit to rule this island. And so I give the throne to she who has truly earned it, she who had toppled the tyranny. I give it to my sister."

"You are naming her empress...."

"She is suited to rule this fledgling union, more than anyone. She has lived in Stonemark, the Beastlands, and Esire. You have both the blood of Healers and Forestfolk. Your children, with something of every race in them, will unite the Island and her old kingdoms."

"Our children...." Talin echoed, and tears sparkled in his eyes. It was a moment before he spoke again. "And what of you?"

Joren smiled—a wide, peaceful smile. "I have bought a ship, a fast vessel of three masts and a hundred feet of deck, and in her bowels rest a thousand stones of food and sweet summer wine. I am leaving into the green ocean, never to return, to see what I will find." He took a deep, satisfied breath, already smelling the salt air in his nostrils. "But now then, I am keeping you from your wife's side."

Joren turned to leave, but Talin grabbed his arm.

"You're not leaving soon, are you? You will stay till she wakes?"

Joren smiled. "Of course."

He turned and walked down the corridor at a quick pace; his ship was waiting in the harbor, anchor ready to rise and sails ready to unfurl. He knew he would never see her again, but that was okay; they were both too changed to be what once they were. The most important thing he had done. He had kept his promise. He had brought his sister home.

* * * * *

"...you and everyone," she mumbled. "I love... you...."

Her lips stilled, now soft. Everything, soft, silky like swaddling clothes, apple blossoms caressing her skin, babies' breath smoothing her hair. She felt warm, delicate, protected, like a chick in fluffy feathers. Light fell on her eyelids and she moaned. She tried to stir but was too weak, could only wiggle her fingers. She felt other fingers tighten around hers in reaction, and the touch was warm and gentle. Her lids fluttered open. In the feathery light she saw a figure like an angel smiling down upon her, holding her hand. The sunlight formed a halo around his head.

"Talin...," she said, groggy from sleep.

"Lia." He squeezed her hand.

"You are here.... How can this be? I thought I'd never see you again."

He smiled. "You don't have enough guards, Your Majesty, to keep me away."

Aeolia blinked at him. "But I'm no longer queen. Reyn overthrew me."

Talin only smiled. *What a silly thing to say,* Aeolia thought. She wanted to tell him all she had suffered, how she had scorched her soul with her kingdom, how Lale had caged her, how she had relinquished escape. She wanted it so badly she ached, but she could bring none of it to her lips.

"I've been a bad wife," she said instead.

Talin's eyes softened. He slowly shook his head.

"I left you, Talin. I'm sorry."

He stroked her hair. "Don't be."

She looked beside her. Stuffings, her old doll, lay there in bed, tattered as always, but soft and clean. Finally, it had buttons for eyes. Aeolia looked back to Talin.

"Will everything be good now?" she asked him.

"Everything will be good," he whispered, so quiet she barely heard.

"I was so scared, Talin. I was so scared."

"I know," his lips uttered silently. He folded her in his arms and rocked her gently, as if she were a child.

"Hold me forever," Aeolia mumbled into his embrace. "Never let me go again."

About the Author

Daniel Arenson sold his first short story in 1998. Since then, dozens of his stories and poems have appeared in various magazines, among them *Flesh & Blood*, *Chizine*, and Orson Scott Card's *Strong Verse*.

In addition to *Firefly Island*, Daniel wrote the fantasy novels *Flaming Dove* (2010) and *The Gods of Dream* (forthcoming).

Flaming Dove
by
Daniel Arenson

If you enjoyed *Firefly Island*, you'll enjoy Daniel Arenson's dark fantasy novel *Flaming Dove.*

Outcast from Hell. Banished from Heaven. Lost on Earth.

The battle of Armageddon was finally fought... and ended with no clear victor. Upon the mountain, the armies of Hell and Heaven beat each other into a bloody, uneasy standstill, leaving the Earth in ruins. Armageddon should have ended with Heaven winning, ushering in an era of peace. That's what the prophecies said. Instead, the two armies—one of angels, one of demons—hunker down in the scorched planet, lick their wounds, and gear up for a prolonged war with no end in sight.

In this chaos of warring armies and ruined landscapes, Laila doesn't want to take sides. Her mother was an angel, her father a demon; she is outcast from both camps. And yet both armies need her, for with her mixed blood, Laila can become the ultimate spy... or ultimate soldier. As the armies of Heaven and Hell pursue her, Laila's only war is within her heart—a struggle between her demonic and heavenly blood.

Here's an excerpt from *Flaming Dove:*

I am Laila, of the night. I have walked through godlight and through darkness. I have fought demons and I have slain angels. I am Laila, of the shadows. I have hidden and run, and I have stood up and striven. I am Laila, of tears and blood, of sins and of piety. I am Laila, outcast from Hell, banished from Heaven. I am alone, in darkness. I am Laila, of light and of fire. I am fallen. I rise again.

Chapter One

Something is out there, his thoughts whispered. *Something lurking in the night.* Standing on the fort's dank walls, Nathaniel scanned the darkness. He saw only rain and waves, but still the thought lingered. *There is evil beyond these walls.*

It was past midnight, and clouds hid the stars, grumbling and spewing sheets of rain, crackling with lightning. The waves roared, raising showers of foam, pummeling the ancient Crusader fort as if trying to topple it. It was that kind of storm, Nathaniel thought as the winds lashed him. A storm that could tear down the world.

Nathaniel tightened his grip on his spear, the rain pelting his bronze helm. *An unholy storm,* he thought, *and an unholy night.*

A glint caught his good eye, coming from the flurrying sand of the beach below. Nathaniel raised his spear, gazing into the darkness, heart leaping. He shifted his shoulder blades as if he still had angel wings to unfurl. He had lost those wings years ago, along with his left eye, to demon claws. *And you know what happens to wingless angels,* he thought, scanning the beach. *They get stuck with guard duty on stormy nights when even God wouldn't step outdoors.*

Where was the glint? Nathaniel could see nothing, only crashing waves and endless darkness. He must have imagined it.

He cursed himself for his quickened heartbeat, for the whiteness of his knuckles around his spear. He had killed more demons than he could count, had even faced an archdemon once and lived to boast of it; it was damn foolishness that a mere storm should faze him, even if it *was* the worst storm he had seen on this world. And yet... and yet there was something about this night, something of a malice beyond waves and wind, beyond Hell itself, perhaps.

Lightning flashed and there—a glint in the skies. Nathaniel thought he glimpsed great bat wings spread in flight before the light vanished, but... that was impossible. No demon could fly over this beach without triggering all their alarms.

Nathaniel cursed the shiver that ran through his bones, these bones broken too often in battle, now creaky and aching. The waves battered the fort's wall, spraying him with water and foam, and Nathaniel cursed again and spat. He'd had too much rye last night, that was all; he was seeing things.

Something creaked behind him.

Nathaniel spun around, spear lashing.

A cry pierced the night.

His spear banged against metal.

"Sir!" came a voice ahead.

"Who's there?" Nathaniel demanded, gripping his spear.

"Please, sir! It's me." Eyes glowed in the darkness.

"Name and rank," Nathaniel shouted.

"Yaram, sir! Corporal from platoon four, sir."

Nathaniel groped for the lamp at his feet. It lay on its side; he must have kicked it over. He raised the tin lamp, casting its flickering glow against the young, pink-faced angel who stood before him. A dent pushed into Yaram's breastplate where Nathaniel's spear had found it, and the angel's eyes were narrowed with pain and terror.

"God damn it." Nathaniel spat. "Corporal, never creep up on an officer like that; my spear could have hit your face just as easily."

"Sorry, sir, but... I pulled guard duty tonight. I was in the eastern tower, and sir, I saw something."

"And abandoned your post?" Nathaniel clenched his jaw. He should have the angel beaten for this.

"Micah, my partner, guards there now, sir," Yaram said, voice shaking. Thunder boomed. "I came to find you. We saw a shade in the night, like a demon, but...."

Nathaniel cursed under his breath. The rain pounded his helmet and ran down his face. "But it wasn't a demon, was it?" he muttered. So he had not imagined it; there *was* something out there, neither demon nor angel, a creature that had crept past their alarms, that now flew above them as if unfazed by the garrison of angels below.

There was only one creature of such power, of such brazenness, Nathaniel knew. The winds howled and more waves sprayed them, salty against his lips. The lamplight flickered, its shadows dancing.

"Sir?" Yaram said, pale. "You don't suppose it could have been *her*? That *she* has returned?"

Nathaniel raised his spear and pointed it at the younger angel. "Watch your tongue, corporal, or I'll cut it from your mouth. Don't speak of that half-breed here. She fled years ago, you know that."

Yaram swallowed and nodded, rubbing the dent in his armor. No doubt, an ugly bruise was spreading beneath that dent. "Yes, sir."

Lightning flashed again as waves crashed and roared, as the winds howled, and there again—great bat wings under the swirling clouds, and a shriek from above, a shriek that ached in Nathaniel's old bones.

Yaram and Nathaniel stared. They both had seen those wings, those red, burning eyes.

The watch bell clanged in the guard tower behind them, ringing clearly even in the howling storm. *Micah sounding the alarm,* Nathaniel knew.

Clattering footfalls came from the staircase leading up the wall. Nathaniel and Yaram spun, raising their spears. It was Bat El running up toward them, her gilded armor perfectly polished, her blond hair pulled into a prim, proper bun. *Great,* Nathaniel thought with a grunt. If anything could make this night worse, it was the presence of Bat El, the prissy daughter of Archangel Gabriel himself.

"The alarm—" Bat El began, blue eyes wide.

"A winged creature," Nathaniel grumbled. "Neither demon nor angel." He hated that his words made him shudder. *I need a drink.*

"There!" Yaram shouted over the crashing waves, pointing to the beach below. They looked and saw it—a darker shade of black, red eyes burning, a halo of flame wreathing its brow.

"Dear God, don't tell me it's *her*," Bat El whispered, blanching. She unfurled her swan wings and leapt off the wall, gliding toward the creature.

"Damn it!" Nathaniel said. "Yaram, we follow."

He would have to share Yaram's wings; sometimes wingless angels had to give up some pride. He grabbed Yaram and leapt from the wall, pulling the younger angel with him. Yaram spread his swan wings, caught the storming winds, and they hit the rocky beach below the fort. Through the crashing waves, Nathaniel glimpsed Bat El racing toward where they had seen the creature.

Stupid girl, Nathaniel thought. He pushed himself up and began running after her. If that creature was truly her, truly who they thought, none of them could face her. There were few from

Hell or Heaven—not even Gabriel's daughter—who could challenge that *thing* and live.

Yaram screamed beside him. Nathaniel turned to stare with his good eye. Through the crashing foam, Yaram fell, helmet cracked, neck shred open. Nathaniel cursed and raised his spear.

Red eyes burned in the night, two lit coals. Fangs pushed through a chaotic smile. It *was* her, Nathaniel knew.

The demon's daughter. The half-angel.

Laila.

God help us, she's back.

"Bat El!" Nathaniel shouted, when great bat wings slammed against him, sending him flying. He crashed into the waters, salt filling his mouth and nostrils. The waves slammed him against the fort's mossy wall, ringing filled his ears, and he tumbled to the ground. With his last bits of consciousness, he glimpsed the creature gliding through the night, and then the waves slammed Nathaniel against the wall again, and all thought faded.

CPSIA information can be obtained at www.ICGtesting.com
Printed in the USA
BVOW041916020512

289235BV00001BB/1/P

9 780986 602832